DEADLY DECEPTION

Deadly Deception

Ilene Birkwood

Five Star • Waterville, Maine

This novel is a work of fiction. Names, characters, places and incidents are either the product of the author's imagination, or, if real, used fictitiously.

First Edition
First Printing: June 2004

Published in 2004 in conjunction with
Tekno Books and Ed Gorman.

Set in 11 pt. Plantin.

Printed in the United States on permanent paper.

Library of Congress Cataloging-in-Publication Data

Birkwood, Ilene.
Deadly deception / Ilene Birkwood.
p. cm.
Originally published: Waterville, Me. : Five Star, c2004.
ISBN 1-59414-187-8 (hc : alk. paper)
Subjects: 1. Computer software industry—Fiction.
2. Software consultants—Fiction. 3. Women detectives—Fiction. 4. Mountaineering—Fiction. 5. New Zealand—Fiction. 6. Mystery fiction. I. Title.
PR9639.4.B57D43 2004
823′.92—22 2004043303

To Len

Acknowledgments

I wish to thank Jutta Kernke, Jack Hansen, and my niece, Donna Birkwood, for their help in reviewing the manuscript. Thanks are also due to my husband for sharing with me his expertise in the area of computer security, and to LeJeune Whitney for all her help.

CHAPTER 1

One foot twisted inside a tiny crack in the rock face, the other resting on a narrow ledge, he leaned back slightly, letting his fingers take some of his weight, and surveyed his next moves. His blue eyes narrowed as he studied the sheer cliff face, contemplating the route carefully, planning each foothold until he reached a jutting overhang of dark volcanic rock. Rejecting that route, he began planning another. This one started out with a few difficult moves, but looked to be more practical. Spread-eagled on the massive cliff face he was totally relaxed; he might have been sitting in a comfortable armchair playing a game of chess. In his view, it was a chess game; only careful planning of each move resulted in a win. The only difference, of course, was that defeat at the hands of nature would result in a fall to the rocks at the bottom of the cliff.

In a series of swift moves, he continued his ascent. His movements fluid as a gymnast, he moved from hold to hold, centering his weight on the balls of his feet, using his arms only for balance. His shock of blond hair glistened in the strong sunlight; sweat darkened the back of his white T-shirt, and gave a sheen to his suntanned legs. Free of safety harnesses, rope and a companion, he made good progress, estimating he would be back on top of the cliff in another twenty minutes. He found the lack of his sticky-soled climbing shoes a drawback, but it was an easy climb and his running shoes were just fine. The lack of a rope didn't bother him at all; he had long ago conquered his basic fear of falling, and a rope was simply a safety harness. To use a rope as a climbing aid was a definite no-no to David and his climbing companions.

He rested for a moment to catch his breath and plan the next series of moves, then set off again. Left foot firmly planted on a ledge, fingers in crevices, he moved his right foot until it reached the next ledge. Transferring his weight to the right foot, he took his left foot off the ledge and started to search for the next hold. As the volcanic rock beneath his right foot took his weight it started to crumble, slowly at first with small pieces of rock breaking away, tiny fragments of black floating down to the void below, then larger pieces, until chunks began to break away faster and faster until finally the ledge collapsed. Realizing too late what was happening, he frantically tried to move his weight back on to his other foot, but his body lurched towards thin air and a 600-foot drop. As the adrenaline coursed through him, he dug his fingers into the crevices, oblivious to the pain that shot through his broken nails. His numb fingertips took the full weight of his body as it teetered perilously over the sheer drop. Far below, the ocean sucked and hissed, waiting to engulf his body, while gulls, startled by the falling rock, screeched angrily around his head. Finally, the sickening moment passed, his body steadied, and he moved his foot cautiously back to its former foothold. He clung there, motionless, heart pounding, sweat trickling down his back. Pressing his face against the rock, he found comfort in the smooth warm surface. Gradually his breathing slowed, and his heart stopped pounding. He felt the soft, sensual balm of cool soil in the tiny crevices. The sun burned the back of his bare legs, and a soft breeze ruffled his hair. His face broke into a wide grin. He felt wonderful. There was nothing like it.

A few minutes later, relaxed and happy, he was off again moving confidently upwards. As he neared the top of the cliff, a flurry of loose soil and small pebbles brushed past his shoulder causing him to look up, but he could see nothing, only a massive outcrop of rock, dark against the blinding sun.

Two fishermen, lethargic in the afternoon sun, sat watching their lines as they sipped canned beer. The tide had turned, the fish had stopped biting, but still the men lingered, enjoying their beer in companionable silence. The dinghy moved up and down on a slow swell, the waves slapping against the sides, and their catch splashed sporadically in the holding tank. One of them, bored by watching his motionless line, looked up to see if there was any bird activity. "Bloody hell, Bill, there's someone climbing up that cliff over there."

His companion looked in the direction he was pointing and saw a tiny figure, white against the mass of dark rock, moving steadily upwards. "You're right. He's got to be nuts—that's a sheer drop. Some stupid holiday-maker trying to show his girlfriend how macho he is."

"No, I don't think so. Look at the speed he's traveling. That guy knows what he's doing." They watched, fascinated, as the climber moved swiftly across the cliff face, paused for several moments and then started again, moving confidently upwards. "I wonder what makes someone take up climbing? Seems a pretty stupid sort of a hobby."

"Dunno, I can see climbing Everest or Mount Cook or something," Bill answered, draining his can of beer and crushing it in a wide sunburned hand. "Standing on the top must be a real buzz. But I can't understand these rock climbers. I mean, what does he think he's proving? You can walk up a perfectly civilized trail to the same spot. Bev and I took the kids up there for a picnic one time. Makes you puff a bit on the way up, but it's not difficult."

Suddenly, without warning, the climber fell, his body floating down the cliff face like a rag doll. As it hit the ocean, there was a spurt of water, then a wave washed over the spot where he had landed, leaving nothing but the empty sea.

The two fishermen sat frozen in shock, their brains refusing to register what they had just seen. Then in a frenzy of activity Bill hauled up the anchor, his hands shaking and clumsy with shock, while his friend pulled at the starter on the Yamaha motor. After what seemed an eternity, the anchor was up, the engine coughed into life and they were away across the smooth ocean, leaving a widening wake as they gathered speed. When they reached the spot where he landed, they circled frantically, narrowly missing the jagged rocks beneath the cliff, the boat tilting dangerously as Bill leaned over the side scanning the water for a sign of the body.

Straightening up and stripping off his clothes, he yelled, "Cut the engine, Jeff. I'm going over the side. I can't see him anywhere. He must have gone down."

Before the boat had stopped, he flung himself over the side. Again and again he dived beneath the surface while the helmsman tried to hold the boat steady against the waves that sucked hungrily against the rocks. After fifteen minutes, his breath was coming in ragged gasps and his limbs were limp from lack of oxygen. As he surfaced and prepared for yet another dive, his friend shouted, "Give it up, mate. We won't find him now. The current must have got him."

He revved the engine, drew alongside his friend, and

yanked him into the boat. "Let's go out toward the headland; he may have been swept there by the current. Then we'd better get in and get the Coast Guard on the job."

Andrew James stepped through the airport doors and headed straight for the first-class check-in. Impeccably dressed in dark gray suit, crisp white shirt with a light gray stripe and discreet tie, he was every inch the successful businessman. With only one passenger ahead of him, he was soon placing his small bag on the conveyor belt.

"Just one bag is it, sir?"

"Yes, I'll keep my briefcase with me, thanks."

The dark-haired woman on the check-in counter continued to chat as she swiftly processed his paperwork and gave him his seat assignment.

"Successful trip?" Her wide smile made it clear she expected an affirmative answer.

"Very, thanks." His smile was as tight and economic as his movements. As he placed his briefcase on the ticket counter, and put away his ticket and boarding pass, he displayed a gleaming white cuff and a gold Rolex watch. Snapping the briefcase closed, he turned away from the counter and set off for the First Class Lounge. Ignoring the duty-free stores, he went through the door that led to the First and Business Class lounges of the airlines that served Auckland. Entering the Air New Zealand lounge, he showed his boarding card and then selected a comfortable chair well away from the other passengers. After picking up a glass of whisky and a small selection of cheeses, he settled down to enjoy his drink. While he took a few appreciative sips, he glanced around the lounge. It was fairly full, mostly with business people, but with a few affluent older couples. He had selected a seat well away from them, as they tended to covertly study other passengers. Most of the business people had their heads in their briefcases, or were busy congratulating each other on the great deal they had swung.

After a few minutes, he got up and walked over to the magazine rack, taking a somewhat circuitous route looking for a phone well away from the other passengers. He had no intention of using his cell phone, they were notoriously insecure. Although the lounge was less than half full, the passengers were scattered evenly throughout the clusters of armchairs and small coffee tables, and Andrew gauged even a quiet phone conversation could be overheard. He picked up a copy of *The Economist* and returned to his seat. Five minutes later he was on his feet again, this time to exchange the magazine for a copy of the *Wall Street Journal*. Again he walked past the telephones. Finally, when the woman on the reception desk announced that the flight to Melbourne was boarding, the area cleared. Businessmen abandoned the phones, rushed back to their seats, downed the last of their drinks, picked up their briefcases and made for the exit.

Andrew walked unhurriedly over to a phone in the deserted lounge and placed a call to San Francisco.

"Could you put me through to Mr. Schramm, please." His voice was cool, pleasant and English.

"May I tell him who is calling?"

"Gerard Masters."

"I'm sorry, sir, Mr. Schramm is in a meeting at the moment. Is there anything I can help you with? Or perhaps you would prefer to speak to his personal assistant."

"No, thank you, I must speak to him personally. He is expecting my call."

"He is in a meeting, sir. Could I get him to call you back?" the soft Southern accent cooed.

"Please put me through right away. He is waiting to hear

from me." The tone was decisive and fringed with ice.

"Very well, sir, I'll just see if I can get him to come to the phone." The coo turned to strong disapproval.

Andrew waited, not disturbed by the wait or the imminent departure of his flight. If there was one thing you learned in this business, he reflected, it was patience. Do your homework, be prepared for every eventuality and never get flustered. After a short pause, the hapless secretary, who had clearly taken the time to check with her boss, put him through with no more than a brief, "I'm putting you through now, sir."

"Schramm here." The voice was deep and authoritative.

"The deal has been completed. No loose ends." Without waiting for a reply, Andrew replaced the receiver and headed for the exit.

Kelly Brandon put her cell phone down on the garden path and regarded it with deep disgust. "That Graham Bell has a lot to answer for," she said to her young bull mastiff. "I know I've got time to get down to Auckland tonight if I hustle, but damn it, I don't want to rush around." She pulled on her gardening gloves and started piling weeds in a red wheelbarrow. "Look at all the progress I've made on this garden today. I'd have had the lot finished by this evening." She had in fact cleared about twenty percent of an attractive but weed-choked garden. The dog listened, head cocked to one side, big brown eyes watching her every move, but finally satisfied that her angry tone hadn't been directed at him, got up and strolled off with the phone.

Kelly, dressed in old shorts, long-sleeved cotton blouse and faded hat, worked until the wheelbarrow was full. As she tipped the weeds in an empty paddock, she noticed the dog hadn't followed, and turning, saw him seated in a flower bed chewing on the phone.

She trundled the wheelbarrow in his direction. "Come." The dog, his wrinkled face a mass of apology, dropped the phone and moved toward her. He knew he was in trouble, but couldn't tell from the tone of her voice how much, so just in case, he rolled on his back, legs waving in the air and tail wagging slowly across the grass. Kelly, knowing she should discipline him, looked at his ridiculous posture and laughed instead. "You're a hopeless animal. But on the other hand, you were probably doing me a favor trying to get rid of that thing."

Picking up the damp phone, she wiped it on her shorts before punching in the numbers. "Hi, Sally, it's Kelly. Could you baby-sit Riggles for me? I have to dash down to Auckland."

"Sure." Sally's amused voice was warm. "He enjoys wrecking my garden. It's a nice change of diet for him. What's up? What crisis is gripping the software industry today? Are we in for a major recession? If so, you'd better give me a moment to call my broker and sell my two shares."

"Oh, shut up. I'm frosted. Whenever I settle down to get some real work done in the garden, they seem to dream up another situation where my presence is imperative."

"What happened this time?" Sally asked. "You were down there last week. They generally only have a crisis every two or three weeks."

"I don't know. They wouldn't say on the phone. They want to tell me in person, but somehow I don't think this is one of their manufactured crises. Colin sounded far too serious and worried." She reflected a moment. "And sort of sad, really. It was weird. I'm sure I need to get down there."

"Okay, well just drop the dog off on your way. The kids will love it."

"Thanks, Sally, I owe you one." She stuck the phone in her shorts pocket, and stood a moment surveying her handiwork. Then, with a resigned shrug, she stowed her gardening tools away, kicked off her shoes and went inside to take a shower. The dog followed, a model of obedience.

John Celini took a couple of practice swings, teed up his ball and stroked it confidently off the eighteenth tee, then he and his partner strode down the lush fairway. Never having been one of the world's longest hitters, he was away next, but his second shot was perfect, landing in the middle of the fairway within comfortable range of the green. A wedge should see him home and free. His partner went for the green with a powerful shot, but unfortunately it hooked badly, caught a tree, took a bounce left and ended up lying in the rough behind a nasty looking clump of kikuyu grass. As John waited he could hear him muttering, "Left's a hook, right's a slice, straight's a bloody miracle." Tactfully he stayed silent, suppressing laughter, while his partner selected a club and figured out the best way to get out of the mess he was in. As he waited, he totted up his score. It looked like an eighty-four was well within his reach. All he needed was a good wedge and two putts. He grinned to himself. His game was really coming together. This unexpected vacation was turning out better than he had anticipated.

He was furious when he first heard about the assignment in New Zealand. He was working for Zanta at the time, in California's Silicon Valley, and it was proving to be one of his most enjoyable assignments to date. In the first place it was an interesting project, but the real bonus was Jenny. She had swept-back blond hair, big boobs and legs to die for.

When Uncle Tony called and told him he was needed on a project in New Zealand, he argued furiously. The last place he wanted to be was in some backwater in the South Pacific. He loved it in Silicon Valley. California was the only place to be if you were really into software. But there was something in Uncle Tony's voice that told him this was not a debatable issue. And the fact was, accepting Uncle Tony's job offer when he first got out of college was the best thing he had ever done. He was picking up almost twice as much money as IBM had offered him, and working for Uncle Tony's software house meant he moved around quite a bit, which suited him perfectly. Young, single and easygoing, he fitted in smoothly on most projects. About five foot ten inches, slightly built, with a muscular upper body, trim rear end and long legs, he was conventionally handsome with dark, well-groomed hair and warm brown eyes. It was inevitable that whatever the assignment, management welcomed his undoubted talent, and women made the rest of him more than welcome.

Reluctantly, he wound up his job at Zanta and set off for the South Pacific, knowing only that he was to get himself to Auckland, check into a hotel and wait for further instructions. He knew he was going to be working on a major software project, but who for he hadn't a clue. Not that it worried him, all his previous assignments were carefully selected and he had no reason to doubt this one would be any different. However, when he arrived in New Zealand, he got a call from Uncle Tony telling him the project had been delayed and he wouldn't be needed for two or three weeks. Since Uncle Tony didn't think it made any sense returning to California, he suggested John take an all-expenses-paid vacation until they contacted him. Uncle Tony had been really nice. Told him to relax and have a good time. It would be a crash project once it started so he might as well take it easy while he could.

And it hadn't been too tough. He loved golf and hardly got a chance to play more than once every other week when he was in California, and that was always on crowded courses. Here he was in a country of only 3.8 million people where every little town boasted a golf course. He enjoyed the challenge of the spectacular international-type courses, but what he liked best were the ones tucked away in little towns or by the ocean. These were great. He found he could drive up and tee off without waiting. Even when he happened to strike a club day and the course was busy, they all made him welcome, and he had fun playing a new course and meeting new people.

After two more frustrating strokes his partner was on the green. John placed a beautiful soft wedge close to the pin and sunk his putt for a birdie. Hey, what a life! It was only after dinner that night that he stopped to think about the upcoming project. What on earth could be so important that they were willing to let him sit cooling his heels for three weeks without doing a stroke of work?

Chapter 2

Kelly threw some clothes into an overnight bag, flipped the phone on auto and made for the door. She glanced at herself in the hallway mirror and pushed a strand of wet hair out of her eyes. She probably should have taken the time to blow-dry her hair since she was off to the city, but if she did she wouldn't make it before nightfall, and she hated driving on country roads in the dark.

She headed south, making good time on the empty roads. Having spent most of her life living in a city, she still got a kick out of driving for a couple of hours and not passing a single traffic light.

As she neared Auckland, the traffic built, and as she slowed down, she began to wonder what on earth could have happened on the project. The project was a piece of software being developed by a small Auckland company. The software, when completed, would be merged into a major product being developed by Finsat in the States.

Kelly, a first-rate software engineer and an experienced manager, had been asked to consult with the young company. More, Kelly suspected, because she used to work for Finsat, and they trusted her judgment, rather than for her expertise. She was a good analyst, but she wasn't in the same league as the project team that had been pulled together. They had an impressive and diverse set of skills. And that is what baffled her. She had been at a project review only a week ago, and everything had been going swimmingly. They were well on schedule (which in itself was a miracle on a software project), and the work David had done was outstanding. Oh well, she thought ruefully, they probably need me for my mature mind. In her thirties, she felt like an old crone around these software engineers who looked like a bunch of high school kids.

It was at times like this she missed Steve. They could have talked it over, and maybe have figured out what the problem was. Ah well, she thought, grinning to herself and putting her foot down as the traffic picked up speed, at least I didn't talk it over with Riggles.

Kelly had been devastated just over a year ago when her husband, Steve, had been killed. She had a tough time putting her life back together again, but slowly, grindingly, she had done it. First, she had sold off the travel business they built together. Checking out fishing lodges in exotic locations created too many painful reminders of the great times they had together. She spent three weeks trying to figure out what to do next. Should she give up the rural life and move back to the city? The house was way too big for one person, and looking after thirty acres was proving to be too much of a handful. But she hated the thought. Perhaps she should just make a complete break and go back to the States for a couple of years. Neither prospect sat right. She loved living by the beach, and much as she had enjoyed her years in California, she was reluctant to leave New Zealand's relaxed lifestyle. The consulting assignment for Finsat had come totally out of the blue and was an answer to her problem. Anyway, it meant she didn't have to make any decisions in a hurry. The fat consulting fee would keep the property going, and she'd get to travel to and from the States regularly.

Not that she had any money worries. Kelly and Steve had both worked in Silicon Valley, and in fact, had met and married there. Kelly, an Aucklander, was working for Finsat, and Steve, a Californian, was working for a small company engaged in a business partnership with Finsat. When share prices rocketed, they decided to sell up and head down under for the good life. And it had been a great life until Steve's untimely death. They'd found a thirty-acre property in the far north. Set on the cliff top overlooking a perfect semicircle of golden sand, it was the perfect location. Then they'd searched for a lifestyle business. Since neither of them knew anything about farming or horticulture, they decided to give those a miss and instead set up a travel business specializing in fishing and golfing vacations. This they could organize from their clifftop home, working with fishing guides, charter boats and lodges, producing brochures, selling the idea to agents in New Zealand and California. It had all been hectic and fun; particularly checking out exotic locations, and trying their hands at fly fishing. When Steve died, she ran the business on her own for a while, but found it was a painful daily reminder of Steve and no fun anymore, so she sold it.

By the time she drew into a small motel in Newmarket, it was already growing dark, and the parking lot was almost full. As she booked in, the fresh-faced woman on the desk asked, "What are you doing back so soon? Have you decided to do a spot of shopping?"

"No such luck. It's yet another software crisis. Nothing unusual. It'll probably turn out to be a storm in a teacup." Kelly's infectious grin made the other woman smile in return.

"I can't understand how you manage to survive in the software industry. Don't you know you're supposed to be preoccupied and in a hurry all the time? You look far too relaxed and cheerful."

"It's that sea air up north that does it." Kelly picked up

the key and made for the door.

"Just a second, I nearly forgot. I have a message for you."

Kelly picked up the pink message slip. "Call Colin as soon as you arrive. It doesn't matter what time. Must talk to you right away." Damn, what could be so urgent? She smiled a preoccupied smile of thanks and headed for her room. Surely it could wait until the eight-thirty morning meeting. She was hungry and tired, and looking forward to putting her feet up.

As she unpacked, she kept looking at the message sitting on the bedside table. Shall I just ignore it and pretend I haven't arrived yet? Colin will never know. She looked longingly at the bottle of Chardonnay. I've spent the whole day slogging away in the garden and just made a four-hour drive. The thought of kicking off her shoes and enjoying a glass of wine was irresistible. Why, oh why, do I have this guilt complex about not doing everything that has to be done? Wouldn't it be great to be irresponsible just this once? Picking up the phone and punching in Colin's number, she knew the reason. It all went back to third grade when she'd let Gilbert Potts down in the school play. Wonder if I'll grow out of it in old age, she thought.

Colin's friendly voice answered after the third ring. "Hi, Colin, this is Kelly. Just arrived at the motel and they gave me your message."

"Thanks for calling, Kelly. Sorry to get you the minute you arrived," his voice was worried.

"What's up? Hit a real dilly of a problem?"

"Look could you meet me at the Cascade Motel in about fifteen minutes? It's just down the road from your motel. We could meet in the bar for a drink."

Why can't we just talk over the phone, she thought, but

said, "Sure, I'll be right there. I could use a glass of wine after that drive."

As if reading her thoughts, he said, "Sorry, I really don't want to discuss this over the phone. Thanks. I'll see you in fifteen."

What on earth did he want to talk about? She dragged a comb through her hair, and put on a dab of lipstick. Hope like hell there isn't a conference on at the Cascade with a lot of upmarket yuppies running around. She straightened her blouse which was somewhat crumpled after the drive, then looked down at her jeans and running shoes. Making a quick decision, she sat on the floor and took off her running shoes and slipped into a pair of casual Ecco walking shoes. There, all ready for the big city.

Colin was waiting for her in the reception area. He was of medium height with untidy fair hair, a luxuriant, droopy mustache and wore small, wire-rimmed glasses. His smile when he saw her was more a tired apology than his usual beaming grin. "Good to see you, Kelly. Let's go in and get you a drink. You must be whacked after your drive."

She followed him into the bar, noticing the uncharacteristic sag to his shoulders. Finding a corner table, they chatted for a few moments. Colin was quiet and distracted. Placing his glass of beer on the coaster, he traced a line with his finger on the side of the frosty Steinlager glass. He avoided looking her in the eye and seemed to be struggling to find words.

Kelly watched him for a moment, concerned. He was a decisive project leader, able to handle just about every problem that came his way. Seldom raising his voice, he would talk persuasively for hours if necessary to get his way. This was the first time she had seen him at a loss for words. She decided to plunge in and help him out.

"What's the problem, Colin, it can't possibly be that bad?" She kept her voice light, hoping she could jog him out of his obvious depression.

Dragging his eyes from the glass, he turned to face her. The despair in his eyes shocked her. "I'm afraid it couldn't be worse, and I don't know how to tell you. I've never had to do this before."

"Why don't you just say it?" Kelly said gently. "Whatever it is, packaging it won't make any difference."

"David's dead," he blurted out, then slumped back in his chair.

"But he can't be, I only saw him last week." Even as she said it she knew how ridiculous it sounded. She put a hand on Colin's arm. "That's awful. I'm so sorry."

Colin let out a deep sigh. "He was killed when he fell rock climbing. It's ghastly, they haven't even found the body yet."

"Where was he?"

"He fell off the cliff at Waikere Heads. The water's deep there, and rough. His body washed away before anyone could get to him." Now that he was speaking, he seemed glad to be able to get it all off his chest. "It was ridiculous really. We all went up there for a picnic. I had taken them all up to Davidson's Beach for an off-site meeting. I thought a couple of days of sun and sea air would get everyone going again. We'd hit a few nasty snags in the project, and you know what workaholics the team are. They were all working ridiculous hours. I figured a couple of days away from their terminals might get their brains functioning again." He stopped and took another sip of beer. Whenever he thought about the accident his mouth grew dry. "Anyway, we had worked all morning, then we all had a swim, then hiked up to the heads for a picnic. After lunch I felt pretty dozy and lay down on the grass for a snooze." He smiled wryly. "I think maybe I've been working some long hours too, and all that sea air did me in."

"I've been trying to tell you seven-day weeks aren't a good idea." She looked at the dark circles under his eyes. A few people were starting to leave the restaurant and move into the bar for an after-dinner drink. Their cheerful voices made a strange backdrop to Colin's story.

"Anyway, I lay down for a nap, and a few of them wandered off. It's nice up there. It's a steep climb up the trail, but once you're on the top it's pretty flat and there are some spectacular views. There were several other people up there—most of them taking photos. Tourists, I suppose." He looked at the other people in the bar, but it was as though he wasn't really seeing them as his mind replayed the afternoon. "I don't think anyone noticed David had gone off by himself. Well, I suppose if they had, they wouldn't have thought anything of it."

As he spoke, the whole ghastly afternoon seemed to come flooding back to him. The startled realization that David was missing. The frantic calling and searching. Then the mad scramble back down the hill to summon help. The calm police operator answering the call. The police car arriving and telling them a fishing boat had seen him fall. And as the Coast Guard helicopter circled noisily, several pleasure boats dashed out in a flurry of white wakes to join the search.

"But how did he fall? He's an expert climber. Didn't he used to go climbing in the Southern Alps?"

"As far as we can make out, he went for a climb on an impulse. A couple of guys were fishing and saw him fall. They said he was moving up the rock face like a spider. No trouble at all. Then suddenly he slipped." He shrugged his shoulders. "They said it just happened. They were too far away to make out how."

Kelly picked up her glass and took a sip of wine, scarcely tasting it. Her eyes clouded. David was such a nice guy.

"I guess the problem was that he didn't have any of his gear with him. No ropes, or anything, and only running shoes. It was pretty stupid I suppose, but we were all relaxed and having a good time." He pushed his beer away from him and looked around the bar seemingly reluctant to continue.

"That's horrible." She sat for a moment numb with shock. Finally, realizing Colin was looking at her she asked, "Is there anything I can do to help? Do his parents know?"

"Yes, I called them and they flew up from Dunedin. Gruesome for them, waiting for the body to turn up. Anyway," he said, his voice growing decisive, "the reason I asked you to come down is, David being killed is a double disaster. He was absolutely key to the project. We aren't going to be able to continue without him." His shoulders drooped again. "I don't know how to break it to the team."

Kelly looked at him, aghast. In the shock of hearing about David's death, it hadn't occurred to her what an impact it would have on the project. David had a unique set of software skills. An expert in an obscure operating system, developed by a California company, which in itself made him a scarce commodity, he also had a sound networking background. This would make him practically impossible to replace at short notice. The only reason the small, young company gained the contract was because of their unique set of skills. And the key person was David. Without him the project would grind to a halt. They had to find a replacement. The company providing the contract had made it very clear to Kelly, and Colin, that if the project fell behind schedule it would be immediately withdrawn to the States.

Colin looked at her with bleak despair. "I just don't know where we can find someone like David. I had a devil of a time finding all the right people. Carol's from Oz, and she said the number of people in Sydney who know the operating system is about zero. We were lucky to get her. Even if we double up on David and use two people, it will take ages for them to come up to speed."

Kelly tried her hardest to look encouraging. "I'll get on it right away, Colin. Don't worry, I'll find someone." But even as she said it, she didn't believe her own words. She knew she would find someone eventually, but time was of the essence.

"What's worse, I called Joe and he said he'd be over in a few days."

Hell, Kelly thought, why can't he give us some breathing space? The imminent arrival of Joe Brennan from California sounded ominous. Joe was the overall coordinator for the Finsat project. If he was coming over, it sounded as if Finsat was about to withdraw the contract. In less than a year Kelly had come to like Colin's young, talented team. They didn't deserve this. "I'll give him a call and see if I can stall him for a while to give us a chance to find someone."

Colin's worried face lightened, "Would you? With some space we might be able to solve this." Then as if suddenly remembering it, "There's a project meeting tomorrow at eight-thirty, could you be there? I've a feeling it might be a bit sticky."

Chapter 3

Next morning, Kelly scanned the paper while she munched toast and manuka honey. She liked motels where she could make herself a slice of toast and sit in bed and eat. It created a few crumbs in the bed but beat getting dressed and going down to a hotel dining room. Looking through the want ads, she noted very few ads for software types, which was good. It increased her chances of finding someone.

When she walked into the conference room, bang on eight-thirty, the whole team was already there. An ominous sign—normally at least half of them were late. She took a quick glance around the crowded room. Not much larger than a standard office, it had three tables pushed together, surrounded by an ill-assorted bunch of chairs, while a white board and an overhead projector gave it a vaguely official status.

The eight members of the project team sat in atypical silence, eyes fixed on the writing pads in front of them. As Kelly took a seat, they looked up, and a few of them gave her a fleeting smile. Colin, sitting at the head of the table, sprang to his feet as she sat down.

"Good to see you, Kelly. Okay gang, let's get going," he said with forced enthusiasm, "we've a lot of work to get through." He looked around the room searching for some sign of their usual energy. Not a spark was present. "Look," he continued, "I know how you feel. David was a good bloke. But the fact is, we've a deadline to meet." No one looked up. Mike Williams continued to doodle layer on layer of stick men on the desk pad in front of him. "Mike," Colin said, glaring at the top of Mike's untidy brown hair, "how are you doing? Can we expect the A2 module to be complete by the end of the week? It's time we started testing."

Mike lifted his head. "I dunno. There's a lot to do yet, it'll probably take a couple of weeks." His voice displayed a complete indifference.

"A couple of weeks," Colin exploded. "That's what you said three weeks ago."

"Yeah, but I've hit a snag." He shrugged and slumped back in his chair, the line of fat around his middle straining the buttons of his shirt.

With thin white lips and barely contained anger, Colin turned to Carol Andrews, a slender, somewhat neurotic young woman with large, square-rimmed glasses. "How's the user interface coming along, Carol?"

Carol sat up, pulling herself together with a visible effort. "It's moving along well. I have the shell in place. I'd like that ergonomics man you know to take a look at it soon. If this thing's going on the international market, I don't want the Swedes and Germans blocking the sales."

Kelly breathed a silent sigh of relief. At least some of them are making an effort. She thought Colin was exaggerating when he said they were depressed, but that was an understatement; a huge oppressive cloud hung over the entire room. She looked sympathetically in his direction, as he plodded determinedly on. "Greg, how are the security measures coming along? You know the project's dead hush-hush. We need to be very sure no hacker can get into our bit." They all looked up wearily. They had been over this ground a dozen times.

Greg moved over to the projector and rather prissily

began to arrange his slides. "If you could pull down the screen, Col, I'll get going." He placed a slide on the projector, making sure each corner was square. As he spoke in the tones of an elderly school teacher addressing a group of youngsters, the team began to shift in their chairs in irritation. Then they began to look at his slides, find fault and make suggestions. Soon they were all talking at once, and arguing.

Kelly grinned inwardly. Good move, Colin. Greg could always be relied on to stir them up. In his early twenties, he had all the mannerisms of a persnickety middle-aged man and an irritating nasal twang. What had attracted him to software was a cause of constant mystery to the rest of the team. In the middle of the discussion, Mike got to his feet, walked over and switched off the projector. Greg's face reddened and he looked ready to strangle Mike, but in a tight, controlled voice said, "So, what brilliant idea do you have, Mike?"

"None, but do you all realize what a damn, silly discussion this is?"

"Why, what have I done wrong now?"

"Nothing. Don't be so darn sensitive. I just wondered if it had occurred to you bunch of geniuses that we're talking about the security of a product when there is no product anymore."

Carol took off her glasses, revealing unexpectedly beautiful eyes. "What are you talking about?"

"I mean, you bunch of nitwits, that David was developing the kernel. All our pieces rely on the kernel working properly and controlling our modules. Without David's piece, we're dead in the water." He swung round suddenly and looked at Robyn, an overly thin girl with long, dark hair. "At least fifty percent of the kernel was still in his head. Isn't that right, Robyn? How much of the kernel has been documented?"

Color suffused Robyn's long, pale face. "Well, not too much. David said he was doing a lot of built-in documentation." She bit her lip. "It really was difficult to get him to give me the information so that I could write it up. He said it interrupted his thought processes." It was no secret that she was smitten with David, probably because he treated her like a real person, which is more than could be said for some other members of the team. As the technical writer she was considered a second-class citizen.

"So," said Mike with ill-concealed satisfaction, "we've got a half-complete control module and not too much information on how the rest works."

"It isn't that bad," Colin said, "and you know it. David laid the whole thing out on flow charts, and there's no way you could have got this far, Mike, if you didn't know where he was going."

"Surely we can hire someone to take over from David," Robyn said. "I know we'll lose time, but it isn't that bad."

"Hah," Angus snorted. He was a dour Scotsman, with hollow cheeks and a penchant for running marathons. "And where do you suppose we'll find someone with David's expertise? They don't grow on trees."

"We must be able to find someone in time," Robyn persisted.

"Aye, time's the problem though. Don't you realize this is a crash project? Finsat is in a hurry. If they had all the time in the world, they wouldn't be bothering with a little team like us; it would all be done in-house. You can bet your bottom dollar there's a lot of money tied up in this contract, and they're going to lose a bundle if we fall behind schedule. They've probably got some competitor hot on their tail."

"Okay, so we're going to have to find someone as good as David," Robyn persisted, twisting her pen nervously, "or if we can't find one person, why couldn't we replace him with two, one with the operating system experience and the other with networking?"

Colin gave her a sympathetic look. "Unfortunately, it doesn't work that way, Robyn. We have to find someone with his combination or we're dead in the water. It's going to take too long to try to blend two sorts of expertise. As Angus said, if that was the case, Finsat would have found the people."

Kelly noted that he didn't add what he knew only too well. If Finsat could have found someone like David in the States, or if they could have persuaded him to go there, they would not have moved the project off-shore. Fortunately for Colin and the team, David was one of those rare characters who thought lifestyle far more important than money.

Kelly pushed back her chair. She hated gloom and doom meetings; they never got anyone anywhere. "I think we're going to be able to find someone. And if you'll excuse me, I'm going to get on to it right now."

As she walked out the door, Colin said, "Kelly's right. Let's all get back to work."

Once back in her office, Kelly called a couple of employment agencies, then placed large ads in the *New Zealand Herald*, *Auckland Star*, *Christchurch Press* and *Otago Daily Times*. If there were any stray people running around with the right set of skills, that should find them. Knowing full well the chance of finding anyone with David's skills in New Zealand was low, she then turned her attention to Sydney and Melbourne and repeated the process. Next she called an old friend, who worked for a large recruiting company in California.

Looking at her watch she realized it was already three o'clock and she hadn't had a cup of coffee since breakfast. Running a hand through her already rumpled hair, she picked up her purse and headed for the door.

The café was empty except for a few shoppers sipping espressos and attacking some tempting-looking cakes. The lunchtime crowd was long gone. Kelly looked at the selection of salads and wholemeal sandwiches fat with slices of tomato, grated carrot and bean sprouts, and selected an interesting looking Tuscan pie and a cup of coffee. She ate hungrily, then sipped her coffee as she watched the people going by, wishing she had time to linger. But she had placed a call to Joe Brennan first thing in the morning and knew he was likely to call back soon.

Joe was the Division Manager at Finsat with overall responsibility for the software project. Kelly had been surprised when she heard about it. To have a heavyweight like Joe directly responsible for a software project meant it must be something big. She knew the New Zealand part of the project was small, but had no idea of the overall size of the total project. This, in spite of several trips to the States. Joe had been helpful and provided detailed specifications for Colin's project, but whenever she asked for details of the entire project she had been met with a series of evasive answers. Joe explained in his usual smooth way that it was connected to a government project, and the complete picture was confidential. She would be given as much information as she needed to help the team achieve their objectives, but the total picture was on a need-to-know basis.

Sure enough, ten minutes after she had collapsed in her chair following a brisk walk back to the office and a swift run up two flights of stairs, he called.

"Hi, Kelly, what's the problem? I was planning to come

over in a couple of days, can it wait until then?" He never wasted time on trivia.

"Thanks for calling back, Joe, but I don't think you need to come that quickly. I'm in Auckland now working with the team, and I have a whole campaign going to find a David replacement." She kept her voice light and brisk. He liked people who didn't waste his time.

His voice lost its brittle, businesslike tone. "That was a terrible shock hearing about David. Poor guy." He paused a moment, then barreled on. "It sounds as if they have a major problem. There's no way they're going to find someone to fill David's shoes in a hurry. That young guy had real talent. Terrible shame. But fact is we can't allow any slippages, so I think the fast solution is to wrap the project up and bring it in-house. We can fly the core of the team over for the duration of the contract, but it will have to be merged with Sam or someone here."

"But I've got a major search for a replacement under way already. And the project's going well. You've seen the reports they send in each week."

"Sure, but software types are the biggest BS artists in the world. It's always ninety-eight percent finished. The last two percent can take anywhere from three months to two years."

She grinned as she listened to him. He never believed anyone. "They really are progressing well, believe it or not. If you gave me a few days to look for a replacement, it would make more sense. Uprooting the project is going to cause delays no matter how you play it. It makes far more sense to at least let me try to come up with a replacement. If I can manage that, it would minimize the slippage. Whether you find someone there or I find someone here, they are going to have to get up to speed before they can take over David's work." She took a deep breath and continued. "Wouldn't it be a good idea to give them a little time? Then you can come over and make an immediate decision on whether to pull the project. I'd have all the information together for you by then as to who you need to make offers to and who to let go. You won't lose any time by delaying for a few days."

"I don't think there's any way you're going to find someone. We spent months hunting for the right people when the project was launched; that's why they got the deal in the first place. So they can hardly complain if we pull it back in-house." He paused a moment. "Sure we can pick up a few of the team to bring back here, but the contract will have to be canceled—they knew the score when they tendered for it."

Repressing the urge to yell at him, she kept her voice even. "Look, Joe, they've done a great job so far, and I'm sure I can come up with a replacement."

"Kelly," he said with an almost patient voice, "you're way too involved with that bunch, you've lost your objectivity. Face facts, you won't be able to find another guy like David in a hurry. I'm coming over to wrap things up and decide who we should bring in-house. I'll be on UA 841 arriving on the fifteenth."

With a sinking feeling and knowing further argument was pointless, she gave up. "Okay, Joe, I'll organize a hotel for you and pick you up at the airport."

"Good, knew I could count on you, Kelly. Be in touch."

She just had time to say "Bye, Joe" before she heard the click of the receiver at the other end. She leaned back in her chair and stared up at the ceiling. Hell's teeth, what was she going to do now? If Joe wrapped up the project, it was going to kill the team. Ah well, he was coming over, and he was a good guy. Maybe she could talk him out of it when he saw how much progress they were making.

Over the next few days she worked frantically to find a replacement. Calling every contact she could think of in New Zealand and the States, and even trying a recruiting company in the U.K. But by eight o'clock on the evening of the fourteenth she'd made zero progress. Wearily stacking her notes in the drawer of her borrowed desk, she decided to call it a day. She'd have to be up at the crack of dawn to meet Joe's six a.m. flight, and her stomach reminded her that her lunchtime sandwich was long gone. Bending down to take her handbag out of the bottom drawer, she was startled when a quiet voice said, "Could I have a word?"

"Heavens, Robyn, you nearly gave me heart failure; I thought you were all out to dinner."

"Sorry, I didn't mean to startle you."

"That's okay, come on in. What can I do for you?" Kelly said, visions of dinner receding.

"It's about David, I just don't understand why he's so hard to replace." Her face was troubled.

Remembering how it felt to be the most inexperienced member of a team, Kelly tried to explain. "Take a seat. The real issue is the operating system. It's produced by a company that's doing okay—about three billion in sales or so and it's superb software. Way ahead of its time and reliable. It never goes down because it's got a whole series of software backups. However, in the real world companies are scared to leave the fold of big brothers like IBM. If the Information System Manager chooses a new company and things go wrong, his neck is on the line. If they choose IBM or one of the other biggies and something goes wrong, people will be annoyed, but they won't kick him out. It's a straight question of survival. You can't blame them, but it makes it tough for the smaller, leading-edge companies."

"So the company that makes the operating system we're using hasn't sold that many, and there aren't many people experienced on the system running around."

"Right in one. The Davids of the world, the real whizzes on that system, are like gold dust. And they are generally tied up with companies that have no intention of letting them go." Seeing Robyn's serious face dropping, she added, "But I'm sure I'll come up with something. I've got feelers all over."

"They're going to cancel the project, aren't they? I heard Angus telling Carol there's a bigwig arriving tomorrow."

"Not if I can help it," Kelly said, forcing a confident grin. "Have you had anything to eat? I'm starved. How about I buy you some dinner and you tell me how the documentation is coming along."

But as she picked up her car keys and bag and followed Robyn out of the door, she had a sinking feeling in her stomach. She knew her job was well nigh impossible.

CHAPTER 4

Kelly reached the Arrivals area at Auckland International Airport just in time to see Joe's lanky form strolling into view. Even without the boots and before he opened his mouth, he was unquestionably a Texan. Catching sight of Kelly, he stopped in his tracks and beamed at her, causing a minor collision behind him.

She pushed her way through to him and he enveloped her in a bear hug. He stepped back, holding her at arm's length. "You're looking good. Glad to see you have some meat on your bones again." He tactfully didn't mention that the last time he had seen her she'd been overly thin, gaunt and drawn with worry after her husband went missing.

Kelly laughed up at him. "Thanks a bunch. I really needed someone to tell me I'm getting fat! Come on, we had better move, we're holding up the traffic."

As they drove out through the exit, Kelly said, "I'll drop you off at your hotel so you can shower, then pick you up for the project meeting."

"Okay, that sounds good." A troubled look crossed his face. "It was terrible about David. He was a nice guy."

Kelly glanced across at him surprised. "Did you know David?"

"Sure, he was over for about six weeks when he first started, and when I found out he was a rock climber I took him up to the Sierras. He was good. We planned to take a vacation together sometime and hit a few major peaks."

"I didn't know you were a rock climber. That must have been great for David, he was nuts about the sport."

"Yeah, that's what makes it so damn tough."

A few hours later, Joe, in a clean shirt and smelling of Polo aftershave, was seated in the makeshift conference room listening to Colin's briefing. They mostly sat, only half listening to Colin, their eyes downcast. It seemed as if the imminent closure of the project had sapped all their energy.

When Colin finished, he darted a desperate look at his dispirited team, tugged at his straggly mustache, then asked Angus to talk about progress on the links to the operating system. Angus gave a clipped, concise briefing in a voice devoid of all emotion. He was followed by Carol, and in the space of an hour and a half, Joe had been brought up to date.

As Colin wrapped up the presentation, all eyes turned to Joe. "That's fantastic. You've been steaming along. I've been reading your reports, but I discounted quite a bit of it as the usual BS." The lightness of his voice took the censure out of his words. "But I tell you, I'm impressed; at this rate you're going to come in on schedule."

"Does that mean you aren't going to cancel the project," Lindsay blurted out. Angus shot him a look dripping with disgust. These naive kids. Didn't he know Californians always told you that you were wonderful just before they brought down the ax? Joe looked at Lindsay's eager face. "Well, if Kelly can come up with that replacement for David she's promising me, then of course, the project will go ahead."

Kelly's stomach lurched as all eyes swung in her direction. "I've got ads running everywhere. I'm sure we're going to find someone."

Her strong, confident voice masked her misgivings. Then she added, "I don't know about you folks but I can use a cup of coffee. How come you don't have a pot in here?"

Mike said dryly, "Because there isn't any room. It was either Colin or the coffee pot. We all voted for the coffee pot but he outranked us."

Joe stretched his lanky arms above his head and said, "Coffee sounds great. Moving sounds even better. I think my legs have gone to sleep."

Everyone grinned and the mood lightened. Soon they were all talking around the coffee pot, enthusiasm creeping back into their voices as they got down to the technical questions that had been raised during the presentations. While they were all talking, Joe turned to Kelly, "Could you hang around for a while? I need to talk to Colin first, but there's something I'd like to discuss with you."

"Sure, Joe, I have a bunch of calls to make. I'll be in my office when you're done."

She looked up in surprise a couple of hours later to see Joe standing quietly in the doorway. "Hi, Joe, I didn't hear you."

"Any luck?" He didn't need to hear her reply; if she'd found someone she would have been whooping down the hallway.

"Anyway, what do you need? Is there something I missed earlier in my briefing?"

"No," he hesitated. "Would you take me to the place where David fell? I know it's a ways, but I'd like to see where it happened before I take off." He bit his lower lip. "Damned if I know why, but I think maybe it will help me come to terms with it."

Kelly was surprised. Joe was a regular hard nut under his affable exterior. Caring this much about David seemed out of character. But then maybe climbers felt invincible, and when someone fell it gave them a personal jolt.

"Okay, sure no problem. It's rough terrain on the cliff top. Are you going to be okay in those boots? They may get a bit muddy." His boots were soft, tooled leather.

Joe stretched out his foot and admired his boot. "They are kinda pretty, aren't they? How about if we swing by the hotel and pick up my hiking boots."

"Hiking boots! You bring your boots on a three-day trip?"

"Of course, never go anywhere without them. Pack my briefcase, couple of spare shirts, shaver, photo of Sandy and my boots. Ready for anything."

Grinning, Kelly said, "Okay then, while you pick up your boots I'll pick up some lunch. It's a fair old hike to the cliff top and we're going to need some sustenance by the time we get there."

"Good thinking. How about you? Do you need to go back to your motel and change?"

"No, I've got a pair of running shoes in the back of the car. I'll just chuck my jacket on the back seat and I'm all ready for a hike." She was glad she was wearing a cotton pantsuit. The hike to the top of the cliff was a stiff one, and although it wasn't bad going up, coming back down presented some difficulties. The last time she had done it, with Steve, she'd sat on her rear and slid down the worst bits. Not very dignified, but it did the job.

They drove for a couple of hours, talking of trivia from time to time, but mostly in companionable silence. Finally, they turned off the main highway onto a narrow winding road, bordered on each side by paddocks and an occasional farmhouse. At the crest of a hill, Kelly pulled over to let Joe see the view. Two juvenile pheasants, still in their undergraduate brown plumage, scurried across the road and disappeared into the grass on the other side. Down below them a long, straight stretch of white sand was framed by craggy headlands. An unruffled Pacific sent in long, lazy swells which broke on rocks beneath the headlands, and rose into statuesque waves as they neared the shore. The only sound was the far-off shush of the sea.

Kelly, glad to get out of the car, stretched and pointed, "That's the headland over there to the right."

"Yeah, gorgeous spot though. I can see why they all came; just standing here my blood pressure's dropping by the minute. Would you look at that ocean, it looks as if someone polished it."

"Come on, we've got a long hike ahead of us."

The road ended in a small, sand-covered carpark close to the beach. "This is as close as we can get by car—we've got to hike along the beach, then up the trail."

The sand was firm near the water's edge and they strode along at a good pace, Kelly having some trouble keeping up with Joe's long-legged stride. What ticked her off was that he appeared to be strolling while she was walking as fast as she could go. Fortunately, jogging kept her fit so she was spared the embarrassment of puffing and gasping, but she soon began to feel hot and sticky, and wished she was in shorts and T-shirt.

"Oh, this air feels great. If they could figure out how to bottle it, they could sell it for five bucks a time in Silicon Valley."

"Between the recycled air on the plane and that claustrophobic conference room, you're due a bit of fresh air. But aren't you tired? You just got off a twelve-hour flight from L.A. and you've been working all day."

"No, I'm fine. I sleep like a baby on planes. The minute it takes off, I'm away, and I don't wake up until an hour before touchdown when they wave coffee under my nose to revive me."

"Wish I could do that," Kelly said, remembering those long hours wiggling around in her seat, thinking the flight would never end.

Reaching the bottom of the trail, they paused a moment and looked up. The cliff loomed above them, a mixture of grassy slopes, craggy rocks, tea tree and a few pohutukawas clinging tenaciously to the rocks. It was an easy climb initially as the trail wound its way through small gullies filled with vegetation, but as it grew steeper, the vegetation grew more sparse, and Kelly had to grab whatever she could find to pull herself up over the bare, rocky patches. Joe continued ahead of her, the bag of sandwiches over his shoulder, moving upwards with as little effort as if he was walking up a wide staircase. She was damn sure the trail had been made by hunters with long legs, who gave no thought to people who stood only five foot four inches in their socks.

By the time they reached the top, she was dripping with perspiration but feeling great. It was an exhilarating sight. The beach was now way below them, and two people walking a dog, mere specks. The headland stretched out before them, a mix of tea tree, kikuyu grass and big rocky outcrops. On either side a glittering sea was innocent of even a single boat. The only sounds were the wind rustling the tea tree and the far off shushing of the waves. A hawk scouted on lazy wings against a startlingly blue sky.

"I can see why Colin brought them up here, can't you?" Joe said. "As we were coming up the trail there I was wondering what the heck he was doing dragging them all up here. Mike and Robyn must have both had a tough time making it." Mike was way overweight, and Robyn seemed too frail for hiking.

Kelly looked around her, soaking up the spectacular scene. "Up here has a way of putting everything in perspective, doesn't it? Looking at this lot, I can almost understand why you go scaling mountains."

Joe grinned at her without answering, then pointed ahead. "That has to be the place where they stopped for their picnic. Look, it's just perfect, lots of soft grass to sit on and even a tree for shade. I can't believe Colin would have dragged them any farther than this."

"You're right, and it looks damn good to me too," Kelly said, setting off at a brisk pace for the picnic area. "It's okay for you mountain goats, but I've had it. Let's declare a lunch break."

She reached the spot well ahead of Joe, and flung herself down on the cool grass. The kikuyu grass, unhampered by sheep or lawnmowers, formed a thick, comfortable mat. Joe sank down on the grass beside her, and opened up the plastic bag.

"Okay, ma'am, we've got one ham, cheese and salad, and one that looks like lots of salad topped off with bean sprouts. I hope that's the one you chose for yourself. We Texans need lots of meat."

Kelly took a large swig from the can of 7-Up. "Whew, that feels better, that climb worked up a fair old thirst." After they had munched their way through the sandwiches, Kelly threw her crusts to a couple of seagulls that were waiting patiently for some scraps. "Why do these stupid birds hang around waiting for a handout? There's a whole sea full of fish down there, and they've wasted half an hour waiting for one tiny piece of bread."

"Yeah, but fish they can eat anytime, a couple of good old unwholesome crusts are like a box of Godiva chocolates to them."

Kelly dug into the plastic bag and produced a couple of apple turnovers. "This is to compensate for my healthy sandwich; I always believe in a balanced meal."

Joe wolfed down his apple turnover, and sprang to his feet. "Do you mind if I take off for a while, I feel like stretching my legs some more."

"No, be my guest. Me, I'm going to sit here awhile and contemplate nature." After she watched his lanky form disappear along the headland; she lay back on the warm grass. The sun was warm, a gentle breeze ruffled the tips of the tea tree, and the springy kikuyu felt like a comfortable mattress. She'd been working flat out for the past few days trying to find a replacement for David, and spending long hours with Colin trying to figure out ways to complete the project if one couldn't be found. So far nothing worked. They had to do something better. She closed her eyes, and was startled a couple of minutes later when a gull shrieked overhead. She sat up, momentarily disoriented, then glanced at her watch and realized she had dropped off to sleep. Over forty-five minutes had elapsed, and Joe was nowhere in sight. She looked across to where the shrieking gull had gone and saw it dive-bombing something at the cliff's edge.

Curiosity aroused, Kelly got to her feet and picked her way through the rocks to the cliff edge. Peering over the side she was awed by the sheer drop and the carpet of black boulders below. Something caught the corner of her eye and she turned to her right just in time to see Joe climbing down the cliff. Horrified, she yelled at him to stop, but he was off, moving from handhold to handhold, his long legs seeking tiny crevices, as he moved steadily down the cliff. She stood frozen, holding her breath, and watched as he reached the bottom and then started the long climb back. Again, he moved confidently, finding fissures invisible to the human eye from the cliff top, and what seemed like hours later, but was really a matter of minutes, he was yanking himself over the rim of the cliff. Seeing her watching, his face broke into a wide grin. She walked rapidly over to him, pulled herself up to her full height, looked him right in the eye and said in a voice that betrayed her fear, "You stupid damn idiot, that was the most inane thing I've seen you do. That was where David was killed. What were you trying to do? Prove you're better?"

He let the tirade pour over him, then said, "I'm sorry. I didn't mean to scare you." His look was contrite. "But I had to prove something to myself, and I thought I was well out of your line of sight." He turned and pointed to the cliff face. "I studied the cliff face as we came along the beach, then I took a walk and looked some more. This volcanic rock is no challenge at all to a rock climber. It's just littered with footholds and handholds."

"What rubbish." Kelly was still shaky. David's death had upset her more than she realized. "It's sheer rock in some places; it would be easy to fall."

"Look," Joe said, his voice gentle, "come with me and I'll show you what I am talking about." Taking her arm, he guided her towards a rocky outcrop that dominated a portion of the trail.

The outcrop was about one hundred feet high, and well over eighty feet wide. "Now look at it closely. Show me how you would climb it if you had to?"

Still seething, Kelly stepped forward and examined the

rock. “Okay, I can see a few ledges where I could get started, but then there’s a big blank patch with nothing. I’d be stymied after about five feet.”

“Okay, good, you’ve picked out the ledges that would make good footholds, but now look a bit closer. See that tiny crevice that would make a perfect handhold?”

“You’ve got to be kidding, it’s vertical. Even if I could get my hand in there, there’s nothing to hang on to.”

“Once you’ve got your fingers in, you move them around, and ten to one there’s something in there to grip. Or you can spread your hand, twist it and you have a hold. You can even sometimes pinch your fingers around a tiny outcrop and make a hold. In climbing you’re not supposed to drag yourself up by your hands, your feet are supposed to do all the work and your hands are just for balance.” He put his fingers in and demonstrated. “When you get into the sport you learn all manner of holds so you can scale anything. Even what appears to be a sheer overhang. It’s just knowing all the moves and practicing them over and over. David took his climbing seriously. These cliffs wouldn’t have been any sort of challenge.”

As they walked back along the trail, he said, “I’ve known a lot of climbers in my time, and David didn’t take risks. He started climbing when he was sixteen in the Tararuas, then tackled the Southern Alps. And you’re right, there are a lot of macho types in climbing. David said he was one of them at first, but when he saw someone fall on Mount Cook, it shook him up. After that he took lessons with an experienced guide and learnt every safety technique in the book.”

“I’d have thought that fall would make him give up. Why continue climbing? I’m terrified of heights.”

“Yeah, but we’re all afraid of heights. That’s a basic human instinct, and one that saves our lives probably. But learning to conquer that fear is what it's all about. When you can look fear in the face, and carry on, it's a hell of a buzz."

"So that's what it's all about. Just testing yourself to see how far you can push it. Aren't we back to the old machismo thing?"

Joe grinned suddenly, his face lighting up. "Would you believe there are a lot of hot women climbers out there? So, no it's not just machismo. You find more artists and writers up there in the mountains than you would believe. I don't know whether it's because they are arty types that they are drawn to the mountains, or whether the mountains turn them into artists and dreamers. I tell you, Kelly, when you are up there on top of the world with nothing but nature all around you, it has a profound effect. You start to really look at life and wonder what it's all about."

"I'll take your word for it. I don't mind the odd mountain trail for a hike, but climbing peaks I'll leave to you nuts."

"David always said it completely cleared his mind. And he has a point. When you're climbing, the only thing you think of is the next move. It's probably a great stress buster."

"You may be right. For a brilliant programmer he was the most unstressed-out character I've met. How come you spent so much time talking to him? I shouldn't think you stopped for a chat halfway up a mountain."

"Oh, you sometimes spend nights holed up halfway up the mountain. You get to know people pretty well in those circumstances."

Joe looked troubled. "The more I think about it, the more convinced I am that he couldn't have fallen. That climb was ridiculously easy. And he was just too good a climber; he wasn't foolhardy." He swung round and faced her, reaching out to touch her arm again as if to lessen the impact of his next statement. "Was he upset about something? Did something happen recently? I think he deliberately jumped." He paused a moment, letting the words sink in. "It's a good way for a climber to commit suicide. Everyone would figure it was an accident."

Chapter 5

John Celini stared at the phone for several minutes, his dark eyebrows pulled together in a perplexed frown. Turning from the phone, he picked up his coffee cup, but after one sip he pushed it away in an irritated gesture. Uncle Tony's personal assistant called, telling him to go to the top agency in Wellington and give them his résumé. What had happened to this urgent job he had been sent out to do? Why was he being forced to go hat-in-hand to some two-bit agency in Wellington asking for a job, when he could have his pick of Silicon Valley jobs with his credentials? Why was Uncle Tony insisting he stay in this damn silly little country and apply for a job like some left-over from a college recruiting campaign? He'd never had to apply for a job in his life. The companies were fighting with each other to recruit him from college, and once on the circuit he was regularly head-hunted. It was demeaning. Walking over to the window, he looked with unseeing eyes at the flower beds outside.

Maybe this is what his mother had been talking about the day he came home excited having landed the perfect job. Eager to tell her about it. Sure with the certainty of an only child of her delight in his success. He could still remember the shock as if it was yesterday. Her face had turned to stone. Her eyes grew hard, her lips drew down in a long thin line. "What happened to the job with IBM?" her voice was tight with disapproval. "I thought you were going to take that. It's a wonderful opportunity."

She had been proud of him all through his academic

career. All her ambitions tied up in her talented son. His father was a postal worker—good at his job and steady, but with no ambition. His mother wanted to get ahead in life, and when her husband showed no interest in promotion, she turned her attention to her son.

John got a kick of telling her about his studies. He called home regularly, and basked in her admiration for his successes. On the few weekends he visited home, she would sit in rapt attention listening to his stories of college, her face glowing.

That was why it came as such a shock when he told her about the job he had landed. He was excited and expected her to be over the moon. It was a great job with what seemed to him to be an astronomic salary. He was going to be working for Quantum Software, a contract house that enjoyed a high reputation in the industry, only employing top-level software engineers and placing people in all the most exciting projects. It was a perfect setup for a new graduate. Lots of varied experience, and what appealed to John, young, restless and ambitious, the opportunity to move around. See new companies, new places.

Incredulous at her negative reaction, he smiled at her engagingly. "Oh, Mom, but this one I've just landed is incredible. It's almost twice the salary IBM is offering and it's a great company. I couldn't believe it when Uncle Tony gave me a call and told me to interview for it. I thought it was way out of my league. But I tell you, Mom, they made me an offer. It's fantastic."

"Jonathan, didn't I tell you to have nothing to do with Uncle Tony?" He flinched, and his smile faded. He knew he was in trouble when she called him Jonathan.

"Sure, Mom, but that was when I was just a kid. I'm a grown man now, and he seems like a pretty good guy. I'm sure it's because of him I got the job."

"You're making a big mistake. Mark my words, you'll regret it. Give them a call and tell them you've changed your mind. IBM gave you till the end of the week to give them an answer, didn't they?"

For the first time in his life, John refused to obey his mother. She pleaded with him, but he was adamant. He wanted the job. He grew obstinate. Damn it, she didn't know what she was talking about. She'd never been out in the real world dealing with big companies. This was the chance of a lifetime. She'd spent her whole life in the kitchen and talking to neighbors whose sons seldom went beyond high school, and whose main ambition seemed to be to join the Marines. She just didn't understand. He wasn't going to turn down a great opportunity just because of some old family feud she wouldn't tell him about. He accepted the job, and had never regretted it.

But he had to admit that phone call was weird. He'd argued with the assistant and insisted he talk to Uncle Tony, but unfortunately Uncle Tony was in Japan and not expected back until the end of the week. John went over and over all the reasons for returning to the States, but the assistant wouldn't budge. He was to go and see the agency in Wellington the next day. Finally, the assistant mentioned diffidently a $5,000 bonus for him if he followed instructions. John figured they must have read his thoughts. His first instinct when they told him was to hop on the next plane home. He didn't have to put up with a bunch of crap with an employment agency, but when they mentioned an extra $5,000 he changed his mind in a hurry. Sticking around in New Zealand wouldn't be so bad.

As he cooled down, reason crept back. His mother's advice was probably good; there was no question Uncle Tony was an oddball, and maybe he should have avoided him. But hey, after a three-week all-expenses-paid vacation, and a sign-on bonus to boot, he couldn't be all bad. John decided to fly to Wellington on the evening flight; he could go see the agency in the morning.

Sally Whelan sat back in her chair, feeling virtuous. She had written a report that had been bugging her for a couple of weeks, answered all the important email messages and returned most of her phone calls. She had also cleared out all those junk email messages that had been accumulating all week. Why do people keep forwarding inane jokes and long boring reports that nobody wants to read? Hadn't they got anything better to do? On the other hand, she did always have a twinge of conscience when she scanned a report without reading it properly and then deleted it. Maybe that was the way to go—forward it to someone else, then it was on their conscience. At least you had done something about it.

Sally was an expert in the area of domestic violence and worked as a consultant, most often advising groups interested in setting up refuges. She was a striking woman with a laconic, amused attitude that belied her dedicated belief that one person could make a difference. It was while working with a government committee on child abuse that she became so stricken by the plight of young children that she decided to take direct action. Over a period, she adopted three children who had been subjected to years of sexual and physical abuse, all of them well beyond the popular adoption age. With the two youngest it had worked out well. Christopher, adopted as an undernourished two-year-old with frightened eyes, was now a healthy and boisterous child who adored Sally. The two girls were six and nine;

Chantelle, slim and blond and looking remarkably like a young Sally, and Annette, big-boned and sullen. Chantelle had adjusted well, but Annette was a problem. Regular visits to an analyst seemed to have little effect.

Sally stood up, stretched and headed for the garden. It was a beautiful well-cared-for combination of lawn, flower beds, vegetable plot and fruit trees. As she passed the laden lemon tree, she hesitated a moment. It was still heavy with fruit, the bright yellow lemons contrasting dramatically with the dark green foliage. She had used lemons for every conceivable purpose, given bagfuls away, and still it was laden. She shrugged and walked on; she knew when she was beaten.

Getting down on her knees, she started weeding. The sun was warm on her back, and there was a constant buzz from the bees as they worked the flowers. An excited squeaking from the young bull mastiff made her look up just in time to see Kelly trying to get through the gate past an ecstatic dog. Tail going furiously, it was a wiggling mass of delight. She leaned over and patted its silky ears, then pushed by, saying, "Come on Riggles, I want to say hello to Sally. How's he been, Sally, behaving himself?"

"Of course, he only carried off two pot plants this time. Fortunately they were in ceramic containers so he didn't eat them, just turned the plants out."

Kelly grinned. "That's pretty good, he must be slowing down." She looked around. "Where are the kids?"

"They're over at Janice's," and, glancing at her watch, "and how about that? It's cocktail hour. Go on up and make yourself at home while I wash up, and then you can tell me all about your trip."

Kelly was tired from the drive, and the thought of a glass of wine rather than an empty house sounded good. Ten minutes later they were seated on Sally's deck watching the golden light fade over the sea. They chatted amicably about the children, dogs and garden for a while, then Sally said, "So how was the trip? Was it difficult? You have that abstracted look about you."

"I don't know, maybe I'm just tired. It's been a pretty traumatic few days." She ran her fingers distractedly through her short curly hair, and looked with unseeing eyes at the view.

"Well, why don't you tell Auntie Sally all about it? It's got to be more interesting than Christopher whining about having to eat tomatoes—how can a kid not like tomatoes—and Heidi reporting on the latest scandal in the bay." She looked expectantly at Kelly.

"It was awful. David, he's one of the nice young guys on the project that I told you about, was killed."

"What happened? Was it a car accident?"

"No, a climbing accident. Really gruesome. He fell off a cliff and they didn't recover his body for days."

"You mean that was the body washed up at Harris Bay?" Sally shuddered. "I read about it in the *Herald*."

"And as if that wasn't bad enough," Kelly continued, "the whole team was sunk in gloom when I arrived."

"You'd hardly expect them to be full of beans when one of their workmates just died."

"Of course not, everyone liked him. But it wasn't just that. With David gone, the parent company was going to fold the project and move it back to the States. They'd been working like crazy. Felt it was their big chance to make the company roll. Up until this point they'd only been getting small projects that weren't making too much money. To have the thing pulled out from under them would be devastating."

"Why on earth would they fold the project just because

they'd lost one person? Doesn't make sense."

"I know, but David was a whiz kid. Guys like him are hard to come by."

"So couldn't you find a replacement for him? That's your job, isn't it, to help handle the recruiting?"

"Believe you me I have been trying for days. Called everywhere including the U.K. and Oz without any luck. Characters like David are like hens' teeth. As soon as I got down to Auckland I called Joe Brennan and asked for some time to find a replacement. He's a tough nut, that guy. I tried everything but he was adamant it was going to have to be moved back in-house."

"Isn't Joe the guy you used to work with in California. The Texan?"

"That's right. I figured maybe I could persuade him to give me a few more days after I showed him how well the project was going."

"So did it work?"

"Joe was impressed, but no way was he going to go along with a delay. For some reason this project has them all running scared. Software always slips its schedules and people get uptight, but they don't do anything drastic. This one is different somehow." She let out an exasperated sigh. "I finally convinced Joe to give me just two more days. I thought maybe a miracle would happen and someone, somewhere would call and say they had a prospect lined up. Joe's a nice guy, but no fool; he made me pick out the team we would move to the States, and then talked to them all before he left."

"So is it going to be wrapped up?" Sally looked puzzled. "Anyway, why are you so involved? If it goes back to the States, you're off the hook, aren't you? You've done your job, and you'll still pick up a nice fat consulting fee."

"It's stupid I know, but they are all so young and keen, I kind of got involved. I hated to see them let down like that." Kelly fidgeted with her wine glass.

Sally grinned. "I should have known. It'll be the day when you don't get totally involved in whatever project you're on. Anyway, so that's it, it's all over?"

"No, that's what's so strange. When I had totally given up on finding anyone, checked every agency, ran ads everywhere, called every contact I had, all of a sudden out of the blue I get a call from Wellington—they'd found someone. He came up for an interview and he's perfect. He's a man called John Celini who's over here on vacation from the States. Was enjoying himself and really fell in love with the country, so on an off-chance he dropped into an agency and asked what type of opportunities were available. It was incredible."

"Well for crying out loud. Here I am dripping sympathy, and you don't have a problem. You've pulled off a miracle. They'll probably give you a bonus." Sally grinned suddenly, her whole face lighting up. "If you need any help in spending it, I have a bunch of ideas. I think it's time we took off on a trip. You don't mind three kids coming along, do you?"

When Kelly didn't respond, her friend said, "What's up, Kelly? You solved the problem. What's bugging you?"

"I don't know," Kelly replied, chewing on her lower lip. "It was just something Joe said."

"He's giving you a bad time? Kick him in the bollocks—those tall lean types always respond to that type of treatment."

"No, no, nothing like that." She looked across at Sally, mildly annoyed. "I told you Joe was one of the good guys. He's a tough nut, but basically okay. It's strange, I never could understand why they put a high-powered guy like him on this project." She took a gulp of wine and set her glass down on the patio table. "No, it was when we were out at Waikere Heads."

"Waikere Heads? What on earth were you doing there?"

"Sorry, I didn't tell you about that. That was where the project team went for their day out." She told Sally about taking Joe out to Waikere Heads, and how furious she had been when Joe had climbed the cliff where David had fallen.

"What an idiot! Didn't he realize it could happen to him too?"

"Exactly. I really yelled at him. To tell you the truth it shook me up seeing him going down that cliff. When he realized how much he'd upset me, he apologized. Then said he had to prove it to himself." She stopped and took a deep breath. "Then he said something really peculiar. He said it couldn't possibly have been an accident. There is no way David could have fallen, unless he'd had a heart attack or something, and since he was in the peak of physical fitness that wasn't likely."

"So what does he think happened?"

"He asked if David was depressed about anything. He seemed to think it might have been suicide. Thought it would be a clever way to do it without upsetting anyone, since they'd automatically think it was an accident. He was pretty shaken up and so was I. After that, we climbed back down, got in the car, and I drove him back to Auckland. He hardly said a word all the way. Then over dinner he wanted to talk about wrapping up the project and seemed to be evading the whole question." Kelly rubbed her hand across her face in a worried gesture. "Then I put him on the night flight to Los Angeles." Her voice was flat and discouraged.

"Do you think it was suicide? Surely it was just an accident."

Kelly looked troubled. "No, I don't think it was suicide. David was one of the most cheerful characters I've met. He loved his job and was looking forward to a trip to the Himalayas as soon as the project was completed. He wasn't even mildly depressed."

"So you still think it was an accident?"

"No, after what Joe said, I have this horrible feeling it was murder."

CHAPTER 6

"Murder? Are you out of your mind?"

"Joe was convinced it wasn't an accident, and I'm sure David wasn't depressed about anything. There's no way it could have been suicide."

"For goodness sakes, Kelly, if it wasn't suicide, then it was an accident. Accidents happen, even to experts. Just because Joe thinks rock climbers are infallible, I don't. Sure David was supposed to be a great climber, but how about if he had a beer or two with lunch, what about his judgment then?"

"Well, maybe you're right, and I might be convinced," she said, looking anything but convinced, "except . . ." her voice trailed off.

"Except what? Don't tell me there was a large dagger sticking out of his back when they found him."

Kelly grinned in spite of herself, then grew serious again. "No, there's something else that's bothering me. It's the way this John Celini turned up."

"You mean the guy who's the perfect fit for David's job?"

"Yes, that's him. It was weird the way he just appeared. I told you how rare David's skill base is, and I would say it would be at least a five-hundred-to-one shot of finding him in the States where they've got a population of two hundred eighty million. To have him turn up here with our population of four million makes it about a million to one."

"So you got lucky. He just happened to be here on vacation.

He's American too, isn't he? That brings it back to the five-hundred-to-one odds."

"But five hundred to one, and he happens to be on a trip to New Zealand and happens to be available, not tied up on another contract. What odds will you give me on that one?"

Sally threw back her head and laughed, "We're starting to sound like a couple of bookies. Okay, I grant you the odds were long, but face it, you got lucky for once. Everyone gets lucky once in a while. Who knows? I may win Lotto yet, and for sure you are due some luck. Relax. Something good happened."

"I dunno. I still feel uneasy about it. I know I put feelers out all over to find him. But his turning up so quickly was too pat."

"So what are you saying? This John Celini bumped David off to get his job? Haven't you heard it's easy finding a job in software if you're a hotshot? Knocking someone off to get their job sounds a bit extreme."

"No. But someone else might have done it, if they wanted him to be on the project."

"So now you have someone knocking David off in order to sabotage the project? Kelly, I think you've been working too hard; you're going round the twist."

"There's something weird about this project. No one will tell me what it's all about. Every time I ask they get evasive. Even Joe, who I've known for years, sort of ducks the issue by saying it's a government project and he can't talk about it."

"Ho, now this is getting interesting," Sally said, pulling her lips together and looking serious. "It must be a plot to take over the White House. The return of the nerds. I can just see all these young guys with wire-rimmed glasses and old jeans replacing those staid gray-suited senators."

"I'm probably over-reacting as usual, but the whole thing doesn't smell right somehow."

"You're genuinely bothered, aren't you?" She paused a moment, and the silence was punctuated by the loud snores of the puppy happily asleep on Kelly's foot. "If you really think something odd is going on, why don't you go to the police?"

"Are you kidding? Can you imagine the reaction when I tell them David was thrown over a cliff to make way for a new boy on the project? Heck, even you think I'm nuts. They'd probably all roll around the station laughing."

"I guess you're right. You didn't have too much luck convincing them when Steve went missing. They thought you were just another neurotic broad with an over-vivid imagination." When Kelly's husband left without explanation while she was away on a business trip, she had been convinced it was foul play. The police, however, refused to take her seriously, believing that Steve, like dozens of husbands before him, had left without a word and she couldn't accept the situation. It was only later that they had to admit she was right, after his body was discovered and her murder theory proved to be correct.

Kelly winced. She'd totally come to terms with the situation, except when someone talked about it. "They would probably think I'm trying to relive my moment of glory as a super sleuth."

"Okay, so you can't go to the police. So what are you going to do?"

"I haven't figured it out yet. I've just been mulling it over and getting more and more convinced something's wrong." She paused a moment, looking absentmindedly at a tui dressed in its black and blue plumage extracting nectar from the orange blooms of a flame tree. "Why would someone kill off a nice guy like David? It's not right, but you know they are going to get away with it. It was a perfectly faked accident."

"Somehow I don't think they are. I have the distinct impression that Sherlock Holmes is about to ride again."

"Well, why should they get away with it? How do they get off coming to New Zealand and killing a perfectly innocent man, just to get control of a project."

"Okay, okay, hold your horses," Sally laughed. "I see we've moved from a vague uneasiness to a complete conviction that it's murder now." She topped up their glasses. The bottle of Chardonnay was almost empty. "Now with alcohol to clarify our thinking, let's get this problem solved. We have at least another half hour before the kids get back. That should give us plenty of time." She was beginning to enjoy herself. "Let's first establish opportunity. That's in the best tradition of Ruth Rendell isn't it, or was it P. D. James? I never can get those old mystery writers straight. But we have to take a classical approach, so there's no good working out what Sue Grafton would do. How on earth could someone shove him over the cliff when there were a whole bunch of people sitting munching sandwiches a few yards away?"

"Now that's what's interesting." Kelly, well aware Sally was making fun of her, nevertheless continued. "The picnic spot is quite a long way from the cliff edge. It was the only obvious spot to picnic for miles around. They wouldn't have gone searching for miles in the hope of finding another spot. They would have been exhausted."

"So you're saying David wandered away and went cliff climbing?"

"Yes, Joe wandered off, and when I woke up I couldn't see him anywhere, so no one would have seen David from the picnic area. Joe went over on the same spot David did. He had asked Colin exactly where he fell."

"And the bush grows close to the cliff edge?"

"Yes, it would be easy to creep through the bush and toss a rock on top of his head when he was halfway down. The coroner said there was extensive damage to the skull, but of course he felt that was consistent with a fall from a cliff into rocky water. It was a cleverly staged accident."

"Well, there you have it. He would have had to go down head first to get head injuries in the fall. Climbers climb the right way up, don't they? So he'd have gone down feet first. Conclusive proof. It has to be one of the project team. No one else knew he was going to be at that spot at that time. One of them must have followed him. We have it solved. Now all you have to do is work out which one did it. That's going to be difficult since there wasn't a butler. Although," she added reflectively, "if the software projects around here are anything like the pampered creatures you've been telling me about in California, maybe they had a butler along to carry the sandwiches."

Kelly ignored the sarcasm. "I can't imagine why anyone on the team would want to kill him. He was likable, always pleasant even under pressure."

"But wasn't he the one you were telling me about who always had a new girlfriend?"

"Yes, he was a real love 'em and leave 'em type."

"Okay, so that's your motive. A womanizer creates all sorts of motives: a rejected lover, a jealous rival or someone who was ignored by him. You've now got opportunity and motive." She sat back, looking smug.

"I still think it was a total stranger and it's all hung up with this weird project," Kelly said, unimpressed.

Sally's tone changed, "I still think you're nuts. If you

want some advice from your Auntie Sally, it's time you stopped living alone. I bet you talk to the dog, don't you?"

"Of course I talk to the dog," Kelly replied indignantly. "That doesn't prove a thing."

"Okay, okay, if you're determined to pursue this nutty theory, then I think you should explore the obvious before you go after the improbable. Look into the motives of the team first. What about the women on the team—was he having a fling with one of them?" Then, as if she'd been struck by a brilliant idea, "Who knows, maybe someone on the team was in the pay of the evil empire and did it for money. Better check up whether any of them have financial problems. Luckily, I was up here with three alibis at the time, or on the financial motive I'd be the prime suspect."

"I'll start doing some checking on Monday. I have to go back down to Auckland. I'll have a chat with the team then. Find out who was where. If they all stayed together at the picnic site, that gives them all a perfect alibi." Kelly drank the last of her wine and got to her feet. "Well, I think I'll take off before your kids get home." As she started towards the patio doors, she turned and said with a grin, "I know you're just humoring me with my murder theory, but you'll change your tune once I've hunted the killer down."

Sally laughed, but as she rinsed the glasses, her smile faded as it occurred to her that Kelly and her nutty theories had a habit of getting her into deep trouble. She hoped it was just Kelly's overactive imagination this time.

CHAPTER 7

Living alone was addictive, Kelly reflected as she sprawled on the sofa, notepad and pencil in hand. It was Sunday morning and she was still in her robe, unshowered, her hair an unruly mop. On the coffee table, a cooling teapot and a plate of toast crumbs were all that remained of breakfast. Outside, the sparrows were chirping noisily, and occasionally the sound of a tractor followed by the roar of an outboard motor drifted up from the bay. But mostly only the gentle sigh of the sea emphasized the silence.

She should get showered and dressed, but what was the hurry? No one was likely to come calling first thing on a Sunday morning. After the initial aching misery of Steve's death had passed, and she had to admit it took a lot longer than it should have, she found she enjoyed living alone. Being able to sit up in bed and read if she woke up in the middle of the night. Eating meals when she felt like it, slipping goodies to the dog without being reminded that spoiling him now would cause lots of problems in the future. Reading the paper without having to refold it. All stupid little things, but they made being self-centered delicious.

She turned her attention to the blank notebook in front of her. What she needed was an approach to the David problem. Logic told her she was over-reacting, but deep in her gut an uneasy feeling refused to go away. Never one for sitting around and stewing over things, she believed in taking action. She reckoned if she spent a few days following up on whatever leads she could engender, she could then set the matter to rest, or hand it over to the police if her suspicions proved to be correct.

The obvious place to start was with the project team. It wouldn't take long to find out who had the opportunity. She hoped they all stuck together at the picnic site so she would not need to follow up on anyone. The thought of poking around in the lives of people she knew was not an appealing one.

After that she could look around for a sinister stranger. But how? How an earth could she find out who else was up on the headland that afternoon? She chewed the end of the pencil. Inspiration didn't come. She got up and took her breakfast tray over to the sink, and as the tea leaves swirled down the drain, a thought struck her. Joe said something about a shop on the bay at Waikere.

He remarked on what a great place it was to go camping. He rambled on about how wonderful it would be to wake up in the morning to the sound of the surf. She had laughed and pointed out it wouldn't be much fun if the wind got up in the night. With a wind blowing straight in off the ocean, a tent would be a pretty precarious place to be. And, yes, now she remembered. Joe said that was okay, you could sit in that little shop and drink sodas until the wind blew itself out. That was it. There was a shop on the beach. A fair proportion of the people taking a day trip to the beach would go into the shop for an ice cream or a cold drink. And certainly if someone was following Colin and the team, they would probably take a look at the long open beach, then duck into the shop for a while to let Colin get ahead so that following them along the beach would not be obvious. She grinned to herself. She had a place to start. She'd have this thing solved in no time.

By Monday morning she was back in the office, ready to

help Colin brief John Celini. Kelly moved a life jacket and an empty sandwich box off Colin's spare chair and sat down in a corner prepared to watch, take notes and help out whenever she was needed.

John arrived a few moments later, dressed in designer jeans and sports shirt. He was a good-looking man with a sensitive face that looked too mature for his twenty-four years. He was slimly built, his jeans hugging trim hips and slender legs, but his open-necked shirt revealed muscular shoulders, and a powerful, suntanned neck. Observing him covertly, Kelly concluded he must work out with weights and was probably a runner. A question from Colin dragged her mind back from visions of him in running shorts, and as she answered, she realized it was time to start paying attention.

Colin gave a concise description of the project, and John listened with intense concentration. As the morning wore on it became evident that he was very smart, picking up where David was heading with surprising ease. Kelly gave a silent sigh of relief. If he turned out to be as good at creating software as he was at understanding it, it looked as if the project's troubles were over. Then she had that feeling of misgiving again. Wasn't this all too pat? How come a hot-shot like this was just bumming around New Zealand and not wrapped up by one of the major companies? Yet, as she listened to him talking to Colin and saw his guileless, engaging smile, she had a hard time believing he could have any sinister motive.

Back in her office, she realized it was lunchtime and she hadn't even made a start on her investigations. She pushed her chair back, took a sip of cold coffee and tried to think how to get started. Strolling out of the office, approaching a member of the team and asking them if they had murdered

David didn't seem like too cool an idea. She decided to take Carol to lunch. Over lunch it shouldn't be too difficult establishing where everyone was on the day of the picnic. If they had stuck together, they'd all have an alibi, and she would be able to move on to looking for a sinister stranger. She hoped that was the way it was going to turn out.

Ten minutes later she and Carol were seated in a small café with sandwiches and a slice of carrot cake apiece. Kelly started asking Carol questions about her part of the project. Carol answered each question, however trivial, carefully, measuring each of her words, as if they were to be carved in stone. Taking a large bite while she listened to one of Carol's detailed replies, Kelly realized that small talk with Carol was going to be difficult. She had imagined leading her from trivial chitchat to a series of questions about the fateful afternoon picnic. But she could now see that any question about David would be weighed up, and the reasons behind the questions considered before she answered. If indeed, she answered at all.

Trying a change of tack, she started asking Carol questions about Sydney, Carol's hometown. It was an inspired move. Carol had moved to Auckland six months earlier, attracted by the intriguing project more than by the chance of seeing the world, and it was obvious that she was homesick. Soon Kelly had her talking about her family, all of whom lived in the same suburb of Sydney. As she spoke about her older sister's two young children, her pale cheeks pinkened. Kelly told her about her first few months in the States when she had loved the excitement of the job and everything about the California lifestyle, but still found herself comparing everything with New Zealand, and missing all her friends.

Soon they were chatting away like old friends, and as Kelly polished off the last of her carrot cake, she realized she had better get down to business in a hurry or Carol would be on her way back to work. Pouring herself a second cup of tea, she said, "I keep wondering why David took off on his own when you were out on the headland that day? Weren't you all together?"

Carol didn't seem surprised by the question, it was as if that afternoon was very much on her mind. "No, Robyn had wandered off to take some photos, and David said he felt like walking some more. We were all too lazy to join him." She hesitated a moment. "Isn't it stupid, just one moment of idleness and all this happened." Then, more slowly, "Of course, it was hot, and the climb up was tough. I felt tired. But the times I've asked myself, why didn't one of us go with him?"

"It wasn't your fault, Carol. It wasn't anyone's fault, it was just a terrible accident." Then as if she wanted to stop the other woman worrying about what she should have done, she continued, "So it was just Robyn and David who took off?"

"Yes, initially, but then Angus and Mike started arguing about something. Mike got mad, leapt to his feet and took off. Colin started to go after him, but Angus told him to leave Mike alone. He'd soon cool down. And he's right, you know. Mike has a terrible temper, but he gets over it quickly." She stopped and bit her lip, fighting back tears. "We were having such a good time, and then this has to happen."

Kelly realized Carol was lonely. Alone in a strange city. Working with a group of people so focused on what they were doing they had no time for socializing. Then finally time away from the office. Realizing, at last, how friendly everyone was. Then the horror of discovering David was gone. No wonder the poor woman was traumatized.

Sensing that to talk about it any more right now would be a mistake, Kelly said with a lightness she was far from feeling, "Mike and his temper. I still can't get over the time he blew up at you. He went storming out of the office, then was back an hour later with cakes for everyone for afternoon tea."

Carol smiled wanly, "He is a bit on the temperamental side, but you can't get mad at him." She looked at her watch. "We'd better be getting back, hadn't we?"

As they walked back to the office along the crowded street, Carol seemed to withdraw into her shell, and Kelly had time to think about what she had just learned. Robyn and Mike both left the group separately. Neither had an alibi. It looked as if she had two suspects. An unlikely pair as she was ever to find. Robyn, so slight and shy, it was questionable whether she would have the strength to hurl a rock over the cliff large enough to do anyone harm. Maybe David had made a pass at her and then dumped her. Thinking about the plain, thin woman, that seemed unlikely.

Mike, on the other hand, could be temperamental under pressure. Faced with a software problem, he'd walk around for days scarcely speaking to anyone. Then inspiration would strike, and he would work non-stop for twenty-four hours at a stretch, living off candy bars, Cokes and anything else the building vending machine had to offer.

Kelly remembered the time Carol had questioned his design. He had been using the white board to describe his approach so that Carol could work on the interface. Carol, in her serious, considered way pointed out where his design could be improved by a couple of small adjustments. He'd been immediately defensive, screaming at her that she didn't know what she was talking about and finally flung himself out of the office in a deep huff. Carol, Kelly and Colin, who had witnessed the scene, were left standing amazed by the reaction her small constructive criticism created.

Kelly could imagine his reaction if David made a similar comment. He was unquestionably jealous of David. David seemed to design with an intuitive brilliance which, externally at least, appeared to be effortless. Mike, whose creative talent came at a real cost to his body and his family life, must have a hard time designing under David's shadow. But, as she climbed the stairs to the office, she found it difficult to believe professional jealousy could be a motive for murder. And by the time she reached her office and sat down ready to start a round of phone calls, she had discounted both her suspects. Overweight, cuddly Mike, who in his charming moments reminded her of her childhood teddy bear, wouldn't be capable of cold-blooded murder.

CHAPTER 8

The next morning, Kelly set off for Waikere Heads, to see if the owner of the shop could tell her who was on the bay the day David died. Even as she drove along enjoying the sparkling day, she knew she was hunting for new suspects rather than admitting to herself the murderer might be somebody she knew. With fluffy white clouds moving swiftly across the sky, and some high streaks of cloud promising more wind, she suspected rain couldn't be far away. As she crested the hill, she was struck again by the beauty of the spot. The craggy headland looked magnificent, its spring greenery contrasting starkly with the dark volcanic rock.

The shop was festooned with signs for Tip Top ice cream, fresh bread and horse treks. It was difficult to see inside because of the number of notices posted over the glass door. They advertised gardening services—gardening services? There didn't seem to be enough houses with gardens to warrant a business. Someone advertised play school on Tuesdays—there must be some children around someplace, although there wasn't one in sight—kittens, outboard motors, cars and wood for sale. Then Kelly saw the sign she was looking for: "Houses for rent, by the day, week or month, call Bill on 23756."

Completely eclipsed by its surrounding competitors, an oblong sign proclaimed the shop "OPEN."

When she went inside, a man emerged from the back room, brushing cake crumbs from the front of his shirt.

"Good morning. What can I do for you?"

She smiled at him and was answered by a broad, beaming grin. Picking up a bottle of water, she said, "I just remembered how thirsty I got when I took a walk up to the top of the headland last time."

"That's a tough climb."

"I'll take a Kit Kat too, thanks." As he turned to get them, she added, "I was up there the day that man fell off the cliff. God it was awful."

"That was a nasty business, must have been a terrible shock for those poor youngsters who were with him."

"I wonder if it was one of that group that lost the camera."

"What camera was that?"

"My friend and I found a camera on the headland. We ran an ad in the paper and told the police, but no one's claimed it yet. I just don't know what else I can do. I'm a bit of a photographer myself and I'd hate to lose mine."

"Hum," he leaned his big arms on the glass-topped counter. He seemed glad to get into the problem with her. Obviously glad of someone to talk to. "Tell you what. I know how you could contact that group. They rented a house up here for a couple of nights, and I have their address and phone number."

"Do you? You mean you know who does the rentals here?"

"Well, of course, it's me. Gives me a nice little income. Can't make much of a living out of this place. I rent the houses, mow their lawns and do any maintenance required."

Kelly suppressed a grin. So that was the gardening service and rental service accounted for. Wonder if he runs the play school too? Bringing her attention back to the matter in hand she said, "That would be great if you could give me their number." Then as an afterthought, "Were there any other people up here that day—strangers I mean—who might have been taking photos?"

"Let's see. There was an Aussie family. I remember them because the bloke was always giving me stick about the All Blacks. They stayed for a week and bought lots of bits and pieces." Kelly was beginning to wonder why he was telling her about the spending habits of the Australian family, when he finally got to the point. "I remember they bought some film so they could've dropped a camera. I never saw the camera, but why I remember it was that his wife gave him a hard time when he bought three reels."

"So you think it might be them?"

"Yes, that's a bit of a worry. Would have thought they'd have called me though. Although maybe they couldn't remember where they lost it." He rubbed his hand across his head. "Hang on a bit though, I remember now he gave me his card." He opened the till and rummaged through a set of dog-eared business cards. "We got yakking about footie. He was a good bloke. Owned a motel in Brisbane. Gave me a card and said to come and stay there next time I'm over in Oz. Fat chance of a trip to Brisbane on the profits from this place."

Kelly fished a pen and an old receipt out of her bag and made a note of the two numbers. The first one was all too familiar since it belonged to Colin. After she'd made a note of the Australian number, she asked, "Can you think of anyone else?"

"Let's see now, a bunch of different people came in for ice creams, and there was a bloke off fishing. He stocked up on two meat pies and a slab of chocolate. But I don't recall any of them having a camera."

He stood silent for a few moments racking his brain. In no hurry to get back to work now that he had the full attention of a good-looking woman.

"How about people staying up here? Were any of the houses rented? If they were staying up here, they wouldn't necessarily bring their camera into the shop."

"You're right. I'll have a look in my reservation book." He retrieved a hard-backed school exercise book from under the counter. "No problem remembering the date, unfortunately," he said running his finger down the page. "Looks like there were a few people up that week."

Kelly, unable to read his untidy writing upside down, asked, "Could I have their names?"

"Sure," he said unhurriedly, "but I don't think you need the Moores or the Andersons," and as his finger moved down the page, "nor the Wilsons for that matter."

"Why not? Wouldn't it be a good idea to give them a call?"

"No, all those families come up here all the time. Come in for their milk and bread regularly and always hang around for a chat. If they'd lost anything, the first thing they'd do is give me a call. If I hadn't found it, I'd soon find out if anyone else had. Here's a couple that might be useful to you though," he added. "One was a couple up here from Dunedin—the McCulloughs."

"Did they leave a number?"

"Of course, I won't let anyone rent without giving me a contact number. You never know, they might leave something behind, or take the family silver by mistake."

Kelly made a note of the number. "You said there were two names?"

"Yes, the other one was an Andrew James. A pom. Said he was touring and came into the shop on the chance something was available. He said he'd driven up to take a look at the bay and liked the look of it so much he decided to stay over. Paid for two nights in cash right up front without me having to ask for it. Then left after one night."

"Do you have a number for him?"

"Yes, he gave the Sheraton in Auckland as his contact. Said he'd be staying there for a few nights." He gave her the number, then asked, "You said the camera was expensive, didn't you? Very expensive?"

"Yes, one of the most expensive on the market. That's why I'm trying to find the owner."

"Well, I'd say he's your man. He looked like he was worth a few bob. Very expensive-looking watch, and he had this clipped upper-crust type of English accent. Friendly, but sort of cold, you know the way those stuck-up poms are, and had a real tight little smile, like he doesn't give anything away."

Kelly grinned. "You should write a book. I can practically see him standing in front of me. Bet he had black hair and a little mustache, didn't he?"

"No, sandy thin sort of hair, and a long pale face, no mustache," then looking at her closely, "but you're pulling my leg, aren't you?" He smiled, not taking offense. Then he stood a moment thinking about the stranger. "One odd thing about him though, his eyes never smiled." He picked up a cloth from under the counter and gave it a quick wipe as if he wanted to dispel the man's face.

Kelly, taken aback by the bizarre statement, dismissed it. She already had plenty to go on. "Well," she said picking up her purchases, "time I started making tracks. Thanks for your help. I'll give you a call if I find the owner." Stashing away her pen and paper, she asked, "The Australian couple you mentioned. Did they drop by on the off-chance, or did they call and make a reservation?"

"They booked up about a month ahead of time. Not necessary this time of year, but considerate."

Another customer came in, and as Kelly moved towards the door, the owner said, "Hang on a minute. Bill, this lady was just asking me if anyone was up on the headland the day that kid fell. She's trying to find out who dropped a camera."

Accepting the odd explanation, Bill responded, "Sorry, I wasn't up there. We were out fishing."

Kelly realized this was the man from the fishing boat. "But you saw him fall. Could you see anyone else up there?"

"Funny, now you mention it, there was someone. I caught sight of him after the kid fell. Thought at the time he was tossing him a rope, but then he left straight away. I figured he'd gone for help."

Kelly asked him a few more questions, but that was all the information he had. He seemed worried that he hadn't told the police. But as he explained, they hadn't asked.

As Kelly made her way back to her car, she struck the Aussies off her list of suspects. Colin said he'd organized the trip to Waikere Heads on the spur of the moment. There was no way the Aussies could have known the team was going to be there at the same time. If they had followed them up from Auckland it would have been one thing, but since they booked a month in advance, they were off the hook.

Visiting the shop had turned out better than she had expected. Bumping into the man who had been out fishing was marvelous. There had been someone up on the headland, and she bet that was a rock he was throwing, not a rope. She was right. Just as she suspected, someone had murdered David. Unless, of course, the man was feeding the gulls and didn't even see him.

What's more, she had another two suspects to add to her list. Not exactly suspects yet, but they both had the opportunity. Now all she had to do was establish a motive. It was going to be a stretch to come up with a motive for the couple from Dunedin. Why on earth would a couple on vacation decide to push David over the cliff? They were random serial murderers who spent family vacations that way? Not too likely. How about if they knew David? New Zealand was a small country when it came down to it, and coincidences happened. But then even if they knew him, why would they want to kill him? As she overtook a blue Toyota dawdling along at 90 K, a thought struck her. David came from South Island, although she couldn't remember where. Maybe he was from Dunedin, in which case perhaps they did know him. She'd ask Colin as soon as she got back.

The rain that had been threatening earlier started with a few large drops, then turned into a deluge. She switched the windscreen wipers to the limit and they moved frenetically across the windscreen, scarcely keeping pace with the downpour. Within minutes large patches of water were lying on the road. She felt like a submarine whenever a tanker truck passed on the other side. Concentrating fiercely, she had little time to think, and it wasn't until she neared Auckland and the skies cleared that she returned to her deliberations.

As she started to consider the Englishman, Andrew James, even her overactive imagination had a hard time coming up with a motive. An Englishman on holiday, stopping at a beautiful bay by chance, didn't seem a likely suspect. However, if she was going to be thorough she had to eliminate him, however unlikely he might be. She decided to swing by the Sheraton as soon as she got back to Auckland and see if Andrew James was still there.

* * * * *

Taking a deep breath, she walked up to the desk at the Sheraton and asked for Andrew James. The receptionist checked her terminal. "I'm sorry, no Mr. James registered."

"What!" Kelly exclaimed, looking stunned. "We had a business meeting set up. He can't have checked out already! Well to be honest we didn't have a definite time today, but he said if I gave him a call as soon as I arrived we'd set a time." She put her briefcase down and looked dejected. "My boss is going to be furious. I got held up in Tauranga, so I'm a couple of days late. I'm new at this selling business and it takes a lot longer than I thought it would."

The receptionist said sympathetically, scanning the terminal, "We did have a Mr. James staying with us a few days ago, but he checked out."

"Oh, fantastic. Do you have a contact phone number, or an address?"

"I'm sorry, madam," the receptionist said switching to polite professionalism, "we are not allowed to give personal information about our guests."

"That's terrible. I'm going to be in real trouble."

The receptionist continued to smile, but Kelly got the distinct impression her pathetic act was not getting her anywhere. The message was coming across loud and clear that she would not get any more information out of this woman.

"Oh well, I'll just have to write it off to experience. Hope my boss sees it that way." Then on an impulse, "Do you have a single room available tonight?" She had a feeling she might have better luck with one of the other staff; housekeepers, waiters and bellhops were generally a far chattier breed than receptionists.

Having dropped off her bag, she set off for the office

intent on finding out where David had lived. On the way in, she bumped into Mike. "Hey," he said, beaming, "I finished my module."

"That's fantastic, Mike." Last time she had seen him he was convinced it was going to take him another two weeks. But that was Mike all over: total gloom, then a flash of brilliance and he'd solved the problem. "In case I never mentioned it before, you are damn good."

"Aw shucks, ma'am, tweren't nuthin'," he grinned in a fair imitation of Joe's drawl. Kelly was delighted to find Mike in an upbeat mood. This was going to make things much easier. "Can I buy you and Cathy dinner to celebrate?"

"Sounds great, but we'll never get a babysitter at short notice. How about tomorrow?"

"Sorry, I'm probably going to be out of town, but would Friday work?"

"No," he said slowly, "we've got a bunch of people coming over for a barbecue." Then more quickly, "But how would you like to join us? Friend of mine is going diving and promised to bring along crayfish."

"Mmm, barbecued crayfish sounds terrific, but are you sure it's okay?"

"Absolutely, you'll enjoy meeting some of the neighbors. Rowdy bunch, but good fun."

A rowdy barbecue didn't sound the ideal venue for sleuthing, but maybe she could find out more about Mike from the neighbors than from him. "Well that's great. I'll bring a couple of bottles of wine."

"See you around six then."

Popping her head into Colin's office, she asked, "I was just wondering where David lived. Was it Dunedin by any chance?"

Colin looked at her puzzled. "No, why?"

"Oh, nothing important." So much for that brilliant theory. Ah well, there was still the mysterious Englishman. Then, before Colin had time to question her again, she asked, "Has it ever struck you that there is something odd about this project?"

Colin's bushy eyebrows shot up. "How do you mean?" he asked defensively.

"Oh, I don't mean with you, or the team. No, the Finsat project itself. Have you ever worked on a project that was this secretive before?"

"Hell no," Colin grinned, relieved. "But I've never worked on an American project before. I thought maybe they're keeping us in the dark to stop us getting too smart."

"Don't you think it's odd that they aren't giving us more information? From where I'm sitting the piece we're doing is a control module. Surely they should tell us more about what we're controlling."

"Every time I ask questions I'm given exactly the detailed information we need to ensure a smooth interface, but no broad picture. You know, if they'd tell us more, we could make improvements. Working in the dark inhibits Mike's and David's creativity. Well, I guess just Mike's now," he stumbled on, "or I suppose John Celini too. Jeez, it's hard to get used to David's being dead."

"You've told them how you feel? I mean, about being able to improve the design if you had more information."

"Dozens of times, but I always meet a brick wall. I'm told I don't need to know," he sighed. "Sometimes I think we're working for the CIA."

"Colin, why haven't you told me this before?"

"Well, I didn't like to give you a hard time since you're working for them. And anyway, I'm scared of rocking the boat. I thought if I started getting difficult they'd pull the plug on us, and we need this contract. We've been living hand to mouth up until now, but I reckon if we pull this one off, we'll be able to start landing some big contracts."

"I've tried every which way to get more information too, and have drawn a blank every time. Joe's a pretty good friend of mine, but even he wouldn't help. He just insists he doesn't know much more himself, but when I pushed him, he said it's a government project that's been spread out so that no one can put the whole thing together before it's ready."

"Uh?"

"Does sound kind of feeble, doesn't it? I think maybe you're right, it's the CIA or the FBI, or some other bunch of initials. But I still don't see why they'd do a piece of it over here."

Colin looked at her a long moment before he answered, "Maybe I watch too many late-night movies, or something, but I think you'd be smart to stop asking questions, Kelly. People that start getting too interested in the inner workings of the CIA, or whoever, have a tendency to disappear."

Kelly laughed, "And I always used to think I was the one with the overactive imagination."

CHAPTER 9

Back at the Sheraton, Kelly pondered her next move. She didn't have a very good description of Andrew James, so there wasn't much point talking to the bartender. Room service would be a better bet. They checked the name and room number as they made their deliveries. There was a chance they would remember him. She looked at her watch. It was a bit early for dinner, but she reasoned people ate at funny times in international hotels. No one would think it was odd. She looked at the menu and called room service.

Shaun Booker admired his reflection in the elevator's full length mirror. His crisp white jacket and black pants looked great. Having his hair cut short hadn't been his idea, but the management insisted, and the cut suited him. All in all this job wasn't turning out too badly at all.

As the elevator pinged to a stop on the fifth floor, he gave his reflection a sophisticated farewell smile, straightened his jacket and went in search of Room 504.

Tapping quietly on the door, he said, "Room Service," and when she let him in, made a big display of placing the tray on the table and pointing to each dish, "Vegetarian pasta, side salad, glass of Chardonnay and a pot of decaffeinated coffee, is that correct, madam?"

"Great, that should revive me. It's been a tough day."

"Well, I hope you enjoy your evening. Could you sign here?" He passed over the bill and stood ready to make a quick exit.

"I don't suppose you happen to remember a Mr. James who stayed here a few days ago, do you? He was English." The question came with a ten-dollar tip, and since tips were not required, she had his immediate interest.

"Mr. James? No, sorry, I don't recall the name, madam," he said, then noticing she was still looking at him expectantly, he added, "of course, we've been busy the last few days. I don't always remember everyone's name. Could you tell me what he looked like?"

"He has sandy-colored hair, fairly slight build, and a pommy accent."

"We have quite a few English people staying here," he hesitated. "Is there anything else? I don't remember him, but I could ask the others on the shift if you like." He wasn't in a hurry to leave, and the hotel encouraged the staff to be polite and helpful. Not like that job he had at a Shell station. The damn manager fired him just for spending too much time talking to the sheilas. So what if a few blokes were waiting to be served? They could get out and pump their own petrol, couldn't they?

"I know this is going to sound strange," she said, "but I've never met him. He's my sister's boyfriend. She's on her OE in England, and she met Andrew and fell for him in a big way. They've been living together for six months. Then they had this dilly of a quarrel and he took off on a trip. He's an engineer and comes down here a lot on business. She wants me to track him down for her and see if I can persuade him to go back to her. Since she knows he always stays at the Sheraton, she didn't think it would be hard." Then she added, "She's my younger sister, and I've been bailing her out of scrapes for years. She seems to think I can fix anything."

Now that he could relate to; younger sisters were like

that. Janice, two years his junior, was like that with him. "Oh, I see, well maybe someone will remember the name. I'll ask around."

As she continued to stand there smiling at him, it struck Shaun that maybe she was coming on to him. He had heard stories about women on business trips. As he felt himself going pink, he grabbed the trolley and headed for the door. "If I find anything out, I'll leave a message at the front desk."

Once safely outside the door, he took a deep breath and a huge grin spread across his face. Wow, this was great, he'd find out about this Andrew James for her. After all it was only an excuse to see him again, then who knows? She was quite a looker too. Funny how they always fell for younger men.

Chapter 10

Colin sat savoring the conversation with Joe. It had been difficult to start with, as Joe had doubted David's replacement could be any good. He made no bones about the fact that he thought they had come up with a replacement simply as a ruse to give themselves time before the project was canceled. However, as Colin listed John's qualifications and told him how easily he had come up to speed, Joe had finally been convinced and gave the project the go-ahead. It would not be pulled back to California. Colin shook his head in disbelief. It had been so close. They had almost lost the best contract they had ever had. He still remembered Joe's exact words, "You Kiwis are an amazing bunch. You have all this talent stashed away in the most unlikely places. I didn't think you had a hope in hell of finding anyone half as good as David, and now you find another one right under your noses in Auckland." Colin decided this was not the moment to point out that John Celini was an American.

Shaun, barefoot, in T-shirt and shorts, paced up and down his small bedroom. The room was hot and stuffy and the thought of a swim was irresistible, but he daren't leave the phone in case he missed her call. He had left a brief note at reception for Kelly, just saying he had some information and asking her to give him a call. The floor was littered with a multitude of earlier, longer versions, which he had labored over before deciding to be brief. He was afraid if he gave her too much information she might chicken out on meeting him. Not that she wasn't attracted to him, he reassured himself, but she might be a bit nervous.

When the phone finally rang, he nearly jumped out of his skin, but resisted the urge to pick it up immediately. He would not want her to think he was too eager. However, as he answered his voice was breathless. "Thanks for ringing, Mrs. Brandon. You asked me to see if I could find out anything about Andrew James."

"Right, did you find something?" She sounded excited.

He worked hard to suppress the note of triumph in his voice. "I asked around the hotel but no one remembered much about him. He seemed a real anonymous sort of person."

"Did you get an address or somewhere I can contact him?"

"Yes, but do you think we could get together for half an hour? I'd like to tell you what happened."

After a moment's hesitation, she replied, "Sure, that would be fine. Could you do it right away?"

"How would Mecca be? I could be there in thirty minutes."

"Yes, that sounds fine. I'll see you there."

Shaun replaced the phone with a self-satisfied smirk. He knew she would come. All those lonely women were the same. She's good looking too when she smiles. Bit skinny though, and her tits were too small, but apart from that, quite a corker. He hadn't been fooled by that corny story about her sister trying to trace Andrew James. She was just using it as an excuse to keep him talking. Smart enough to work it so that it's outside of the hotel. Probably knows the management would get hot under the collar if they found out he was looking after lonely women during working hours. Ah well, we aim to please on room service.

He inspected himself in the mirror and smiled at the

reflection. Just time for a quick shower before I meet her. Fifteen minutes later, showered, shaved, with Brut aftershave lavished across his smooth jaw, he set off to meet Kelly.

Kelly was sitting at a table outside in the sunshine. Even in the middle of the afternoon several of the tables were full, and a steady trickle of tourists strolled by, enjoying the yachts and stopping to check the restaurant menus as they passed. He walked over to the table with a jaunty swagger and treated her to his most devastating smile. When the waitress came over, he checked with Kelly, then ordered two Perriers. She seemed surprised when he added hummus and pita bread, and bread and dips to the order. Probably wasn't expecting him to be so cool as to add a few hors d'oeuvres. Pity she hadn't wanted wine. He sort of fancied sitting on the waterfront with a bottle of wine and a good-looking woman.

They sat chatting and watching the yachts for about fifteen minutes before Kelly brought up the subject of Andrew James. He tried to hide his surprise, taken aback that she was persisting in the pretense, but then maybe she was a bit shy and needed to keep the pretense going a bit longer. "Yes, I do as a matter of fact," he said smugly, pulling out his wallet and extracting a white index card. Andrew James's name and address were printed on it in the same schoolboy hand that had addressed the envelope.

"That's brilliant," Kelly beamed. "How did you manage it?"

"The receptionist is very young and sweet. It wasn't difficult." She wouldn't know the receptionist was five years older than him. "I chatted to her when we were both on duty the other evening. She couldn't officially give me the address, but after I asked, she conveniently left me in charge of the desk for a few minutes while she went into the office. It was well after midnight and no one was around. I think she fancies me."

The waitress came over with their drinks and Shaun smiled his thanks, sure the girl was impressed by his date with an older woman. Following the train of thought, he added, "She's been after me for a while, but I'm not interested. I prefer older women."

Shaun felt deflated when she ignored his comment, and said, "My sister is going to be delighted, she's been broken up over that man."

However, the moment was saved by the waitress returning and placing two large plates in front of them. Kelly picked up a piece of pita bread and dipped it into the hummus. Shaun attacked his chunks of bread and dips with relish.

"This is really good," she said. "I think after this I am not going to need to eat for a week. Are the dips good?"

"Yes, but I can't work out what they are. One's a bean dip, one's fishy and the other one's hot. Try a bit and see if you can tell."

She sampled each one, then sat back. "You're absolutely right. One's beany, one's fishy and the other one's hot."

He laughed, suddenly at ease with her, and began to talk about the latest movie he had seen. She was good company, and the conversation moved from the movies to the All Blacks last game against the Springboks until finally she looked at her watch. "I must get back to the office," she said, getting up and picking up the check.

"Please let me get that," he said, worried. Wasn't the man always supposed to pick up the check, or now that women were liberated was that a politically incorrect thing to do? He could feel his sophistication slipping.

"Look, I think it's the least I can do after all the trouble you went to."

"It was no trouble at all. To tell you the truth I wanted to see you again." He leaned across the table giving her the full benefit of his aftershave. Then suddenly hesitant, "I thought we might have dinner or something."

"Thanks, that would be nice," she said slowly. "But I have a business dinner tonight."

"Tomorrow then," he persisted.

"Look, I've enjoyed talking to you, but unfortunately, I'm back off up north tomorrow." Her voice was tinged with a suitable amount of regret.

"Couldn't you stay over?"

She hesitated, then leaned forward a little, her smile warm. He eyed her breasts—they weren't any bigger even up close. "Shaun, I appreciate you getting that address. I'm sure you've guessed by now that it isn't for my sister." He sat up a little straighter in his chair. "It's for something much more important than that. I can't tell you about it. Mainly because I don't want to get you involved in something that might cause you a lot of trouble."

He threw out his chest and looked her straight in the eye, "Don't worry about me, I can handle anything."

"I'm sure you can," she said. "But I can't tell you about it. I'm in the middle of an investigation."

"Wow, are you an undercover cop?" His voice rose in surprise, and he looked around in embarrassment, worried that he might have blown her cover.

Evading the question, she continued, "When it's all over I'll tell you all about it. But will you trust me until then?"

With her eyes looking deep into his, he would have agreed to anything. "Of course."

Driving back to the office, Kelly smiled to herself. For all his leering and posturing, he was a nice kid, and what is more he had come up with the information she needed. Andrew James lived in Portsmouth, England. Well that tallied with the English accent. But how was she going to check up on him? And where was Portsmouth? She'd figure it out, because already she was wanting the anonymous Mr. James to be the murderer. But, she thought, tempting though the thought of a dark (well, sandy-haired) stranger being the murderer was, it just wouldn't fly. Happening to be on vacation at the time the murder took place gave him the opportunity, but there was zero motive.

CHAPTER 11

Her ergonomically designed chair creaked in protest as she sat down, determined to clear up some work before she headed over to Mike's for some more super sleuthing, but after a boring two hours working on statistics, she decided she needed a fortifying cup of tea.

As she waited for the jug to boil in the small area that was laughingly known as the cafeteria, John Celini walked in, mug in hand. "Didn't realize you were in today," he said.

"I was late coming in," Kelly said, pouring hot water on her tea bag. "Can I make you some tea?"

"No thanks, I'll go with a coffee. This instant almost tastes like coffee anyway," he grinned, moving over to rinse his cup under the hot water tap.

"Have you discovered any of the coffee shops around here yet? There's a great one about a hundred yards down the road. You don't have to suffer instant all the time."

"Yeah, I've been to a couple that were really good, but I haven't found one near the office."

"Take a right when you leave the building and it's on the left-hand side."

"Great, I'll try it some time. Maybe we could catch a cup together."

"Yes, sure," she agreed politely, then gave the tea bag her full attention. There was scarcely enough room for two people in the cafeteria, and for some reason she found his close proximity disconcerting. She moved aside so that he could make his coffee, but he stood where he was, apparently in no hurry. Giving the tea bag a final squish, she pulled it out by its tail, and flipped it into the waste bin. "So how's the module going?"

"So far, it's going pretty good. David did some tricky things with that code."

Kelly began to find it warm in the confined area. He spooned coffee into his cup and poured on some hot water.

"Would you like some milk, or should I say cream? There's some in the fridge."

"You're putting me on, aren't you? How long were you in the States?" His dark brown eyes were amused.

"Several years, we were in the Bay area. You're from Chicago aren't you?"

"Sure. Not as nice as the Bay area though. Who's 'we'? are you married?"

"I was. My husband was killed about a year ago."

"I'm sorry." His face was concerned as he acknowledged a social blunder, but Kelly couldn't help noticing a quickly suppressed flicker of interest cross his face.

"That's okay," she said, her smile over-bright. "Anyway, I must get on, I have a bunch of work to catch up on." As she headed for her office, she could feel his eyes following her.

Mike lived in a new subdivision on Auckland's North Shore. The street was wide, curving and lined with substantial, wood-framed houses. Kelly pulled in beside a BMW and walked up to the front door. When nobody answered, she followed the newly cemented pathway around to the back of the house. The babble of voices as she rounded the corner explained why no one heard her knocking. The back garden was full of people standing around talking, drinks in hand, several supervising Mike's efforts with a large gas-fired barbecue. Mike, looking flushed and happy, was wearing an incongruous chef's apron over his shorts and T-shirt. As Kelly stood hesitating, Cathy, Mike's wife, a slim, fey woman wearing a multicolored shift dress and pounds of custom jewelry, came over to greet her and lead her to a picnic table laden with a large cooler full of beer, wine and soft drinks, telling her to help herself. Kelly picked up a bottle of Kumeu River Chardonnay, read the label, managed with difficulty to stop her eyebrows rising and poured a glass of wine. Kumeu River for a barbecue?

Cathy introduced her to Liam and Sandra, a suntanned and hyper couple dressed in snowy white T-shirts and skimpy shorts. Liam worked for Merrill Lynch and waved his bottle of Steinlager as he told Kelly about the huge opportunities the market presented in the present financial climate. Sandra sipped her wine and smiled indulgently, then when he stopped talking in order to select a goody from a tray of hors d'oeuvres, Kelly felt a touch on her arm. "I'll introduce you to some more people. I'm sure you didn't come here to find out what to invest in." As they moved away, Kelly saw Liam, totally unperturbed by his wife's defection, move on to the next group.

Kelly continued to circulate among the guests for about an hour, and found herself having a good time. They were an interesting and amusing collection of people: two real estate agents, a broker, the owner of a small string of hardware stores, a yacht designer, a beauty consultant and a salesman for sports equipment. Interestingly, not a single software engineer or anyone else involved in the computer industry.

The barbecue was great. Kelly settled on crayfish, green salad, cold vegetables and a large chunk of olive bread, found herself a shady spot on one of the two kwila tables and sat down, ready to do justice to the meal. Sitting beside her were the two realtors, and another couple whose names she had already forgotten. One of the realtors, Josh, was digging into a plate piled high with food. After every third mouthful, he took a large gulp of red wine. His heightened color and overloud voice made it clear he had drunk a fair amount before the meal.

When Josh finished eating, he polished off the last of the red wine and set off to find another bottle. Returning a few minutes later, he topped up everyone's glass, then sat back and beamed, "Boy, that feels better. I was starved. It's been a shocker of a week; I don't think I got as much as a cup of coffee all day."

The unidentified red-headed man at the end of the table joined in, "You're selling a bunch then, Josh?"

"Got to keep at it. The sales are there, but they take a lot of chasing. I worked it out that I need to average two sales a week just to keep up with my mortgage and car payments. That doesn't even take into account the IRD and our credit cards."

His wife grinned. "Isn't that the truth? You know we're always telling our clients what a great investment property is, and how it makes sense to overextend yourself on the mortgage because it'll pay off as values rise. But it wasn't until we did it ourselves that I realized it's okay when you say it quickly. On a month-to-month basis it's pretty crippling."

"These houses must be pricey," Kelly said, knowing realtors would be happy to talk about house prices.

"Six-hundred-fifty thousand on an average I'd say when they first went up. Now the swimming pools are in and the landscaping's done, they're going to be worth quite a bit more." Josh beamed with satisfaction and poured himself more wine.

"It's reasonable for this area, and they're going to appreciate well," his wife added. "But it still doesn't help right now. That mortgage repayment coming round every month puts a lot of pressure on you. That's if you like enjoying life at the same time." Kelly had caught a whiff of Estee Lauder perfume and noted the copious amounts of jewelry.

Josh put his overweight arm round her slim shoulders, "Yes, my love, but we can pull in the sales can't we? So it's okay. I tell you," he said looking across to where Mike was sitting on the patio steps eating his dinner, "I wouldn't want to be on a fixed income. I don't know how Mike manages. What with a kid and Cathy not working. I talked to him about it last week after Cathy had gone to give that young monster his tea. There's no way they can afford this lifestyle on one salary. I said he should encourage her to get back to work, but he seems to think it will ruin the child's life if she does. She read some damn silly book about how important the early years are, and how a child needs its mother. No," he added planting a wet kiss on his wife's cheek, "these days you both have to pull your weight, and fortunately Cherie here punches well above her weight."

Kelly shot a look at Cherie who was not looking so convinced. After a tough week, perhaps the thought of whipping a vacuum around in the morning and then lounging by the pool all afternoon didn't seem such a bad idea. As Josh continued to regale them all with stories of his latest sales, her mind drifted. She knew how much Mike was earning, and she had a hard time figuring out how he could afford his current lifestyle if Cathy didn't work too. He drove a year-old BMW, and at department lunches he often talked about his boat, a Reflex cabin cruiser—not cheap. She started making mental calculations and it didn't add up; he'd be well short. Still, maybe if he'd paid cash for his car and only had a small mortgage it would work. But then where did the money come from for a new BMW—all cash—and a large down payment? She was brought back to the present when everyone started laughing at what Josh had said, so she hastily joined in. Refusing his offer of another glass of wine, on the strength of having to drive back to her hotel, she got up and started to mingle with the other guests.

As she circulated, she found it easy to gather information. Nothing like a few hours of free-flowing alcohol in the hot sun to get everyone in talkative mode. She learned from a slim, dark-haired woman called Helen that Cathy had stopped work as soon as the child was born. Taking an elegant sip from a well-filled glass she added, "Her excuse is that she must concentrate all her efforts on young Gavin," her voice dripped disgust, "but look at him." Kelly followed her eyes to where Gavin was happily pouring red wine on the picnic table and watching fascinated as it poured down between the cracks in the wood. "He's spoiled rotten. I don't think she spends anywhere near enough time raising him properly. He's just an excuse to be lazy, or mess about making jewelry, or painting."

"Perhaps she's not used to working hard. Handling a child and a job can be pretty tough," Kelly said in a conciliatory tone. "Are her parents well-heeled? Could be she didn't have to do anything around the house at home."

"You've got to be joking," Helen snorted. "She comes from South Auckland and was working her tail off waiting on tables before Mike came along."

So much for the theory of Cathy bringing cash to the table. She continued to chat uneasily to the waspish, silk-shirted Helen, hoping someone would come by and rescue her. Gossips were a great source of information, but not the nicest people she'd met. Fortunately, Danon, a quiet, good-natured man who had the misfortune to be Helen's husband, came by and apologized for whisking her away. They disappeared towards their car with Helen complaining bitterly about leaving.

Seeing Kelly temporarily stranded, Mike's next door neighbor, Chris, ambled over to chat. He was a towering giant of a guy who had known Mike since grammar school. It wasn't at all difficult getting him to talk about Mike, particularly the young Mike, since the pair of them had been inseparable.

As Chris talked about their childhood with lots of reminiscent chuckles, she learned that Mike had grown up in a middle-class neighborhood. His father worked for the government, and his mother worked part-time at an electronics company. It was unlikely they had enough money to give him a lump sum to put down on the house.

Driving back to the hotel that night, Kelly was troubled. Where was Mike getting the money to support his lifestyle? His salary wouldn't cover it, his wife didn't work and it was difficult to see who else was helping him out. So who was paying him, and for what? There was no way, with the intensity of the current job, that he could be moonlighting. The money had to be coming from somewhere. She was reluctant to follow the thought any further.

Chapter 12

The early morning quiet was broken by the steady click of keys from Carol's cubicle. On an impulse, Kelly walked in. Maybe she could eliminate Mike and Robyn as suspects if she checked how long they were away from the group. It was a fair distance from the picnic area to the spot where David had fallen. She estimated that it would take a minimum of thirty minutes round trip and obviously quite a bit longer than that if the murderer had to wait for the right moment to hurl a rock down the cliff. Even the thought gave her the shudders. There was no way either Mike or Robyn could do something like that.

Kelly, remembering that social chit-chat was not on Carol's agenda, knew she'd better come up with some reason for dropping by before she asked the crucial question. "I just popped in to pick up some files, then I'm off up north for a while. I was wondering if you would like to come up for the weekend."

Carol's pale face went a light shade of pink. It struck Kelly that if she would get rid of those old-fashioned glasses and visit a good hairstylist she would be an attractive woman. "I'd love to, but I've still got so much to do."

"You're right, it probably isn't the right time, but you have to see our beaches up north. You Aussies don't have all the good ones, you know."

"No, you're right. I've heard about those beaches." Carol was far too serious to rise to the usual Kiwi baiting.

"Well, okay, maybe when the project's wrapped up

you'd like to come up for a few days. I've tons of room. I sort of rattle around in an overlarge house which somehow I can't bring myself to sell. If you come up, you'll see why."

"That would be great." Her eyes were already starting to wander back to the terminal. Kelly realized she had better get to the point of her visit in a hurry.

"Carol, that day you were up on the headland you said Mike got into a tizzy and wandered off. Was he gone for long?" With Mike's mercurial nature he might well have cooled off in a matter of minutes and come right back.

"Yes, he was. I didn't like the way he got into a fight with Angus. Seemed such a shame on a lovely day out." She hesitated, apparently appalled by what she had just said. "I mean, at least it was until it turned into a complete disaster. It was almost an hour before he came back, but," she added, "he was all full of apologies when he returned."

So much for clearing Mike, Kelly thought. Still, since she was on the subject she said, "How about Robyn, was she gone long? Did they meet up maybe and take a walk?"

"No, Robyn was only gone about ten minutes. She came back spitting tacks. It turned out she had forgotten to bring an extra roll of film." Great, Kelly thought, at least that lets Robyn off the hook.

As Kelly drove north, the clear morning light turned the hills to a startling green and created miniature amphitheaters as it sharply defined each sheep track winding around the hillocks. Vast panoramas of rolling hills backed by blue mountains spread out before her, spectacular displays of tree ferns lined the gorges and then the drama of Whangarei Heads and the Hen and Chicken Islands. The islands floated suspended between a peerless blue sky and glassy sea—the Heads a crouching dragon guarding the harbor.

Finally, she was off the highway and onto the little country road leading to Dolphin Bay where she passed grazing herds of Santa Gertrudis, huge, black and beautiful. Miniature calves followed their mothers, or lay sleeping on the grass, and massive bulls stood peacefully enjoying the sunshine like a bunch of latter-day Ferdinands. Nearing the bay, the rolling paddocks gave way to bush-covered slopes. A mixture of tea tree, giant ferns, a scattering of rimu and some shriveled toi toi trying to recover from a blistering easterly that had swept in from the sea and stripped them of their glory.

For once, Kelly was oblivious to the scenery. All the way home her mind continued to race. With Robyn out of the loop, only Mike and Andrew James remained as suspects, and as much as she wanted it to be Andrew James, there was no possible link. The only explanation was the obvious one—he was a tourist.

Richard Peterson stood on the hillside deep in thought. Hands thrust in pockets, dressed in an old work shirt and jeans, he was a striking figure. Over six foot four with a lean, muscular frame and chiseled features, his hair was dark and his gray-green eyes were fringed by sweeping lashes. He was saved from being classically handsome by a jaw that was not quite square enough and a nose bent slightly by some childhood accident.

He had a problem. He'd just received an offer for his property. When a persuasive agent had talked him into letting a prospective South Island client look over the place, he'd had no intention of selling, but as the agent had said, what harm is there in letting someone take a look. Wouldn't it make sense to find out how much the place was worth? The problem was, when the offer came, it turned out to be twice what he expected. Ten years ago, when he bought the run-down property, it was a steal. Paddocks starved of fertilizer, broken fences, patches of yellow clay showing through where sheep had eaten each last blade of grass, acres of gorse, a ramshackle farmhouse and neglected outbuildings. With his wife Jane, they'd scraped together every penny they could muster, took out a large loan and bought it. They thought it was marvelous.

After three years of unrelenting hard work, never taking a holiday, they'd turned the corner. The paddocks were lush with new growth, fences were mended and their small herd of Angus steers thriving. Then disaster struck. The government changed, and the new Labour government withdrew all farm subsidies. To make matters worse, interest rates rocketed. They were in real trouble.

Around them any number of farms had gone into receivership. Trying to compete on the overseas market with farmers in other countries flush with government subsidies was too much. Somehow Richard and Jane survived. She took a part-time job to help service the loan, and they redoubled their efforts. Now here he was, ten years later, with a beautiful 2,000-acre property stocked with a pedigree herd of cattle and a mob of sheep. As he contemplated the shining rumps of the Angus bulls moving slowly across the paddock tearing clumps of grass as they went, his smile was bitter. All this, and no one to share it with. A couple of years ago, Jane, exhausted by the unrelenting toil, tired of living in a ramshackle house had left him. Ran off with a bloke from Auckland. He couldn't blame her. He hadn't had time to pay her much attention, and he supposed the bare house in need of a coat of paint and full of threadbare furniture didn't help either. But they couldn't spare any money for the house; everything had to go into building up the property.

Maybe he should sell up and start all over someplace new, but looking over the rolling paddocks, and the hills with their scars healing as the thousands of pines he had planted grew, he felt a sentimental attachment to the land he had nurtured. He walked back to his three-wheeler. He'd give Kelly a ring and see if she was on for dinner tonight, then talk it over with her. She had plenty of commonsense, probably be able to help him decide. Even as the thought occurred to him, he rejected it. She might encourage him to move away.

He had met Steve, Kelly's husband, when they had first moved in. Steve had stopped by to introduce himself and ask for some advice. Steve, proud of his thirty acres, wanted to run a few steers on his property, and had heard that Richard was the most knowledgeable farmer around. Richard, bitter and lonely after his divorce, had immediately taken to the easy-going Californian. He'd got a big kick out of helping Steve and soon he was a regular visitor at Steve's house. He loved Steve and Kelly's quirky sense of humor, and slowly his bitter loneliness faded. When Steve was killed, he was shattered. Since then he'd spent a lot of time helping Kelly out with her property, taking over a lot of Steve's chores until she got herself together. And over the months he had found himself growing increasingly attracted, hoping she'd eventually look on him as more than a friend. That's why he was reluctant to talk about selling up. Selling up was decision time, and he didn't want to scare her off.

When he got back to the house he tried her number again, and this time she picked up after the second ring. She readily agreed to dinner that night, and he picked her up and they drove to the Harbourview Hotel. The hotel, built around the turn of the century, was a two-storied building, the decks on each level shaded by a curving iron overhang. The terrace sported wooden tables shaded by large, green umbrellas and an out-of-control wisteria rambled along the little fence encircling the property. They selected a table on the terrace with a good view of the sport fishing boats, yachts and small commercial trawlers lying at anchor in the harbor.

After Richard had ordered drinks, Kelly looked out across the placid harbor water. "You'd never know there was a wind blowing. It's gorgeous."

"Yes, it is nice," Richard said, frowning slightly as if he were trying to think of something to say.

Kelly, well aware of his conversational difficulties with women, asked, "Have you bought any steers lately?" Farming was always a good safe topic with him. At least until he'd finished his first drink and relaxed a little.

"No, but I went down to Kaipara to pick up a couple of bulls. A mate gave me a call and told me they looked good and the price was right." Then, surprisingly, he added, "While I was down there I decided to drop in on Murray."

"Who's he?"

"A mate from school days. Hadn't seen him in ages. He talked me into staying overnight so that we could go out fishing next day. When you're around him it's hard to keep the work ethic. He reckons I'm crazy working so hard."

The waitress brought their drinks, scarcely looking at Kelly but smiling at Richard. Once she was out of earshot, Kelly grinned and said, "I think you just made another conquest."

Richard looked startled, shot a worried glance after the waitress, then took a sip of his gin and tonic to hide his embarrassment.

Amused, she decided not to pull his leg anymore. "So did you go fishing?"

"Yep, we had a good day out, but the best bit was when we got back. We had a fantastic barbecue, and as usual when Murray's around I drank too much. He just gets going on all these stories and you sit there sipping and listening, and all of a sudden you're nearly blotto." He grinned, his eyes crinkling. "One of them was incredible. He said they were out fishing a couple of weeks back when a pod of dolphins came by."

"That's not too incredible, is it? A lot of dolphins come in there at this time of year."

"No, what was odd was that one of the dolphins was traveling along slowly, swimming on the surface. They thought it had some kind of problem, caught on a piece of stray net or something, so they started up and went over to see if they could help, but when they got close they saw it was a female carrying a baby across her back. The ghastly thing was that the baby dolphin had been dead for a long time, and all the rest of the pod were escorting her just like it was a funeral procession."

"Is that right? I knew they held up sick dolphins so they didn't drown, but I never heard of them carrying their dead."

"Murray reckoned it's to stop other fish eating it."

Then to break the melancholy caused by the thought of the dead baby dolphin, she asked, "So did he have any good jokes? If I remember he was full of them when he was up here."

"Not that I can tell you; they were all pretty raunchy." Then he leaned back his head and laughed. As he laughed his reserved, uptight expression dissolved and was replaced by the relaxed happy face he must have had before he was hit by major financial problems, capped by his wife's desertion. "But he did tell me a bunch of funny stories. He was telling me about the speed trap the cops set up on a long straight stretch on the road that leads to Whitney Bay. He was saying everyone belts along there at one-forty kilometers; well, it's the only straight stretch on that road. What baffled the cops was that everyone dropped their speed to ninety kilometers just before they reached the camera. They thought they had it all sussed out too. Their camera car was positioned behind a grove of trees so you couldn't see it until you were right on top of it. But they were there for days and didn't catch a soul. Finally gave up and moved on to more lucrative grounds."

"So what was remarkable about that?" Kelly asked, perplexed as to why a speed camera not catching a bunch of road hogs was a funny story.

"Well, the reason everyone knew they were there was that as you came over the rise, you couldn't see the cops' car hidden in the trees, but you could see the paddocks on either side of the road, and there was a great mob of young steers standing staring at their car. When steers are standing staring you can bet your bottom dollar something's going on. They get bored out there in the paddocks all day. It was a dead tip-off to the locals."

Kelly smiled dutifully, not really amused. Richard was a strange guy. He hardly said a word for hours on end and then suddenly he'd get going and would talk non-stop. She guessed it was living alone that did it, and she began to wonder if she was as bad. However, she decided to keep him talking about Murray. The nervous looks he shot in her direction from time to time made her worry that he wanted to talk about something serious. She was acutely aware of the fact that he wanted to be more than friends, but she just wasn't ready for it. Maybe she never would be. The idea of anyone taking Steve's place didn't bear thinking about.

"Did he have any more funny stories?" she asked, prepared to listen with half an ear.

"Yeah, he had a good one, and it's true. It turns out that Murray and his mate Trev have a happy baccy patch up on the Waikere Heads. He lives on the other side of that head where that young fella from your outfit fell over. You've been round there in a boat, haven't you?"

When Kelly looked puzzled, he started to explain, dipping his finger in the gin and tonic and drawing a diagram on the table top. "You remember there's the beach where your group went up onto the headland. You can get to the beach by road, but on the other side of the headland where Murray lives there's no road. So you've got a headland jutting out. On one side there's a beach and a trail up to the top of the headland. On the other there's no beach, only some pretty serious rocks. The only way you can get to the headland from Murray's side is by boat, which of course is perfect for Murray and Trev. They take their boat across and cultivate their crop without anyone knowing."

"You mean people see them taking off in their boat with bags of fertilizer, spades and shovels and don't notice something odd is going on?"

"I think the few people that live around there just ignore it. Probably a lot of them are doing the same in their back garden. Anyway," he continued, polishing off the last of his gin and tonic, "they were just on their way over to do a little gardening when they saw this guy go puttering across in a dingy with an outboard. There's an old guy that lives down there that rents out dinghies and canoes as a side line. Can't imagine he does much business. They thought it was kind of odd so they hung around a bit, pretending they were fishing instead of going to their spot. He kept right on going, then beached the dinghy on the headland and started off inland. About now they were completely panicked."

"Why?"

"Because they thought he must be from the drug squad. Why would anyone else be going out to the headland unless they were a hunter, and they reckon he didn't look dressed for that and he didn't have a gun. So they went like the clappers, beached as quickly as they could and started up the slope after him. They reckoned he must be after their cannabis patch. Mark you, I don't know what they intended to do to stop him finding it."

"They're a bit paranoid, aren't they? The drug squad uses spotter planes these days, don't they? Anyway, I can't imagine someone from the drug squad going up there alone. Couldn't he have just been someone out for a hike? It's a long way round to the headland by road from that side. Going by sea seems like a smart idea."

"Yes, but hikers have back packs and generally wear shorts and boots. What freaked them out was this guy was in expensive slacks and shirt, and he didn't look like a hiker. Wasn't even sunburned, looked much more like an inside type."

"So what happened?"

"They caught up and started tracking him. They know that terrain like the back of their hand so it wouldn't be difficult. They said he was really fit and clipping along, which made them even more convinced he was from the drug squad. Indoor types aren't generally that fit." He swirled the melted ice and lemon around in his empty glass and took a sip. "Now we get to the funny part."

"Funny ha ha, or funny peculiar? It sounds peculiar to me."

"It was a real laugh. The joker just kept on going, right by their patch without even seeing it. When he reached the top, he looked all around, then made off in the direction of the trail that goes out to the headland. He must have been a tourist or something. And here was Murray thinking jail was looming. They'd wasted most of the afternoon tracking him, and all he was was a sightseer probably going up there to take photos."

"Did Murray say what the man looked like?"

"Just that he was slightly built, fit, but pale, and yeah, they said he had fairish hair. He wasn't even wearing a hat."

Kelly was stunned.

"What's up? Don't you feel well?" Richard said, his face a picture of concern.

"No, no, it's not that," she said. "What day was it that they went up there? Did they happen to say how long ago it was?"

"Yes, they said it was the day that bloke fell off the cliff. They remembered it well, because they felt such fools for following the joker. Then they wished they had continued on up over the top because maybe they could have helped in the search."

"My God, Richard, I think that was my mysterious stranger, Andrew James." He fit the description the man in the shop had given her, and surely there couldn't have been two slightly built, fair-haired strangers on the headland on the same day. It was too much of a coincidence.

"Who on earth is Andrew James?"

Abashed, Kelly realized she hadn't told him about her theory that David's accident was really murder. Get real, Kelly, she chided herself. Of course, you haven't told him because you know he'll tell you you're being a complete idiot. "Oh, it's just some man the project team thought they saw up on the cliff the day that David fell. For some reason they were all curious about him." As Richard waited for an explanation, she finished her drink and added, “It wasn’t anything important. Hey, how about we eat? I don’t know about you, but I’m starving.”

Looking unconvinced, but as ever too polite to ask questions, Richard got to his feet and said with a marked lack of enthusiasm, “Yes, let’s go try out this new chef.”

Feeling guilty, she resolved to tell him all about it in a couple of days when she had had time to think it through.

CHAPTER 13

Kelly was sitting on her deck, listening to Sally's account of Christopher's school project. It was a long story, and Kelly listened with one ear as she watched the huge swells, stirred up by some far-off storm in the Pacific, rolling into the beach. The overcast sky had turned the sea to a comfortless gray, but from time to time the sun broke through, turning a searchlight on a group of distant islands. The waves rolled up the beach, gathered sand and retreated, creating a moving pattern of beige among the elegant green and white curl of the breakers.

"Kelly," Sally said with marked emphasis, "you are not listening with rapt attention to my fascinating tale." Then looking at her added, "You've got something on your mind, haven't you? Now why is it that my brilliant intuition tells me it has something to do with your latest Sherlock Holmes endeavors?"

Kelly gave an apologetic smile. "Sorry, you're right as usual."

"Okay, so what's up? You haven't done any more sleuthing, well, not if you skip lightly by finding out Mike is up to his ears in debt, and as likely a suspect as you're going to find."

Ignoring the comment about Mike, who she refused to put on her list of serious suspects, she said, "I had dinner with Richard on Saturday night."

"So, what happened? Did Richard pluck up courage and propose?"

"No, don't be ridiculous. He did tell me something interesting though."

She related the tale of the two men following a stranger on the day David fell. When she finished, Sally looked at her with ill-concealed amusement. "What a fascinating story. A fit, well-dressed stranger with sandy-colored hair climbed up on the headland on a nice day. Kelly, my girl, you have been hanging out with Richard too long. Your idea of interesting is a little on the dull side."

"Can't you see? He fits the description of the guy I tracked down to the Sheraton. I tell you, Sally, that was Andrew James. I think he followed David from Auckland, watched them all set off, then dashed round to the other side of the headland."

"You mean he crept across the top and gave David a shove?"

"Sure," Kelly said, oblivious to Sally's amusement. "He's a hit man—David's wandering off by himself was a gift. He was probably reckoning on shooting him from a distance. If David had been shot, everyone would have been looking for hunters on the same trail the group took. It wouldn't have occurred to anyone to look in the other direction. Well, anyway, not until it was way too late and Andrew James was long gone."

"You know, my girl, you're wasting your time in the computer industry. You put Linda LaPlante's plots to shame. You really think they would bring in a hit man from England just to bump off a software engineer?"

"Yes. There's something odd about this project. There's a lot of money tied up in it if the tiny piece we're involved in is anything to go by. It's important for some reason that no one is talking about. And the answer lies in the States with the mother project."

"So, it's an important project. What's that got to do with David's death?"

"Think about it. If someone wanted to sabotage the project, what better way than by getting rid of one of the key engineers, and putting in your own guy. It's the perfect way to install a mole. And doing it in New Zealand is perfect. Who is going to find anything strange about one of the project members dropping out and being replaced?"

"An unfortunate choice of words if you don't mind me saying so."

Kelly grinned in spite of herself. "That's carrying dropping out to extremes, isn't it?"

"Okay, so now they have a mole on the project. What's he got to do? Send secret messages back to the States?"

"I doubt it. It must be something more important than that."

"Kelly, old dear, this plot of yours needs work. It's ludicrously far-fetched even for you." Getting to her feet and moving to the rail looking out to sea, she added over her shoulder, "Yes, but hang on a minute. Where's the connection with England? Didn't you say this Andrew James was English?"

"That's simple. Andrew James was working under contract to whoever wanted David out of the way. Think about it, all the companies in the States use contract employees from all over the world. So why not a hit man? After all, the English are far less noticeable here than Americans. You get all these new poms coming over, and then there are the other ones who sound as if they just got off the boat, although they've been here for thirty years."

"Okay, I'll agree with that part of the plot. Americans tend to be more noticeable than Brits, so an English hit man could blend into the scenery better. Although you might tell him next time you bump into him to buy a bush hat and some shorts if he's going to go clambering around up here."

"You see why I can't go to the police with this, don't you? Even you think I'm being stupid."

"Hah, I bet you didn't try it out on Richard did you?"

Kelly looked glum, "No, you're right. I need to gather up a whole lot more facts before I try it out on anyone who doesn't know I'm round the bend already."

Sally laid an arm on Kelly's shoulder. "Thanks for that vote of confidence. Your secret is safe with me." Then after a slight pause she added, "It's a wacky theory, but you might be right. Perhaps there is something going on. Although are you sure you aren't dreaming up this hit man connection to avoid having to face the fact that Mike is the obvious suspect? You said he was jealous of David, and he needs money." She hesitated, picking her words carefully, "I'm sure he didn't set out to kill David, but he could have promised to engineer an accident."

"You're right. He's a possibility, but Andrew James is the most likely suspect, and I intend to track him down."

"Are you kidding? You mean you'd go over to England?"

"Sure, why not?"

"Well, for one thing it's a mite expensive, or haven't you noticed?"

"Not, old dear, when you are working for Finsat. It just so happens the big boss wants me to go and report on progress. I think they suspect Colin of faking the replacement to keep the project down here. Can't blame them really. Anyroad, I have to go and give them a progress report. So that means my airfare is paid to L.A.; all I need to do is make up the difference, and I'm in England."

"But England's the same distance again. It's twelve

hours to San Francisco, then another twelve to London, isn't it?"

"Yes, give or take an hour here and there. However, old dear, with the wonder of airline economics, it's only an extra thousand dollars."

"Sounds like a thinly veiled excuse to go gallivanting in London to me. Good on you, gal. You haven't had a vacation for a while."

"No, and I figure I can stay with Mark and Ginny."

"Then you'll definitely have a good time unless three years in England has turned them into staid British types. Although somehow I can't imagine it." Kelly picked up the coffee cups and headed for the door. "Wait a minute. Assuming you go ahead with your English boondoggle, what are you going to do when you get there?"

"I'm going to see Andrew James, of course, that's the whole purpose of the trip," Kelly said, disappearing through the door.

Sally followed her in and leaned on the black granite kitchen counter. "You're going to go knocking on some man's door, and ask him if he shoved a Kiwi over the cliff?" She started to laugh. "Bet he'll think it's a nice change from the Jehovah's Witnesses."

Kelly looked embarrassed. "Well, I haven't quite worked out the details yet, but I've got a long plane ride ahead of me. First priority is to dig up some more information on this Finsat project. I'm sure if I start chatting to some of the software guys over there I'll find out something."

"I don't suppose there's any point in my telling you what you're planning to do is nuts. If your crazy theory is wrong, you're going to make Finsat management furious if they find out you've been snooping around. That's a jammy consulting job you have there, and my bet is it will come to an abrupt end. They'll also put the word out that you can't be trusted, so you'll find yourself scratching for jobs." Sally paused, giving time for her words to sink in. "Then there's Andrew James. People can get pretty annoyed if they are falsely accused of murder. You could end up facing a lawsuit."

"For goodness sakes, Sally, what a gloomy view you've got of life. Living on the bay is starting to get to you. It's sapping your spirit of adventure."

Sally ran her hand over her immaculate blond hair. "You're right. This life of domesticity is starting to get to me. But I'm serious about this trip. Maybe I'm overstating the situation if it turns out you're wrong. But what if you're right? If Andrew James is a hit man, doesn't it occur to you that when you start asking questions about him, he'll eliminate you without a second thought? After all that's his day job."

"You're turning into an old hen. There's zilch to worry about. I'm just going to do some digging around and if I find anything at all I'll go straight to the police."

"Sure you will."

CHAPTER 14

Kelly stepped out of the terminal and crossed the road to the car rental pick-up point. The dry California air felt good after the confines of the plane, but the clear, bright sunlight hurt her eyes and she fumbled in her bag for sunglasses. A river of buses, cabs, limousines and cars swept by, and behind her, aircraft engines roared as they prepared for lift-off. She clung to her briefcase as the courtesy bus hurtled through the huge construction site known as San Francisco International Airport heading for the pick-up point. The bus was full, the luggage rack crammed with bags. Japanese businessmen in neat, dark suits looked around anxiously, tired California salesmen sunk back gratefully into their seats and the computer engineers stared straight in front of them, careful to avoid catching anyone's eye. The few returning vacationers clutched duty-free bags and looked glad to be home.

Installed in a Toyota Camry, she manipulated her way to the 280 freeway and headed south. The lanes were wide and the traffic light so she tuned into the classic station and sat back to enjoy the drive. The scenery was as attractive as ever; rolling hills of grass burned to a light brown hue contrasted with the dark green of the scattered oaks.

When she reached San Jose, she checked into her hotel, made a series of phone calls, then, too restless to take a nap in spite of the lost night's sleep, wandered around the shops until it was time for dinner with Joe.

He was already waiting at the bar sipping a Miller's

when she arrived. Catching sight of her, he grinned, waved, then turned to the bartender and ordered a Chardonnay. She slipped onto the stool beside him and gratefully accepted the glass. Without any preliminaries, he asked, "So, how's it going down there? Is John working out?"

"He's doing great. Came up to speed in no time." Sitting down she realized how tired she was. Maybe she should have taken that nap when she first got to the hotel. "Fortunately, he's a team player, and seems to have a way with the other guys. They're all helping him out."

"Phew, that's a relief," Joe said, draining his glass and leaning over to catch the bartender's eye.

"Are you all set for the report tomorrow? We're on at ten o'clock. There'll be just Craig Bennett and his assistant there, so you don't need to make a bunch of copies of your slides."

Kelly raised her eyebrows. "Just the CEO? This is pretty hush-hush, isn't it?"

"Yep, we like to keep tight security on this one—it's pretty much state-of-the-art and there's a lot of poachers out there. Craig is becoming a bit impatient. You're here to reassure him it's back on track."

Kelly looked curiously at Joe. "Why didn't you have Colin come over and give the report? He's the project manager; I'm only a consultant."

"Look, Kelly, you know that, and I know that, but do you really think they'd let a key project like this go down under if you weren't around? The man likes to have people he can trust on the project." During her years with Finsat, Kelly had acquired a reputation as a manager who could handle temperamental people and difficult situations, invaluable skills in the software industry.

"Okay," Kelly agreed wearily, "I'll tell the man what he

wants to hear, but I tell you, that team's one of the best I've worked with and they deserve some recognition."

Joe's eyes drifted away from Kelly as a leggy blond in a clinging dress walked briskly across the restaurant to some friends at a table. "I always like the scenery in this restaurant," he said appreciatively. Then turning back to Kelly, added, "They'll get the recognition when the project's finished. Right now they're behind schedule. We can't have them boondoggling to California."

"Well, it's hardly their fault they're behind schedule," Kelly responded hotly, then swallowing her annoyance, "how many other modules are being developed outside the facility here?"

"Quite a few," Joe answered noncommittally. "Are you ready to eat? I'm kinda hungry."

"Okay," Kelly said slipping off the stool, her half-filled glass in her hand. "Pretty unusual to have it dispersed this much, isn't it?"

As Joe got to his feet he gave her a long look, which Kelly found vaguely disquieting. When he spoke though, it was with his usual pleasant drawl. "Yeah, but it's just an experiment to see if we can handle it. There's no real reason for software to be developed in one place."

"It's a strange time to be experimenting, if the project is as key as you say it is."

"You know me, Kelly, no risk, no gain," he said closing the subject. "Let's eat." He strode over to the desk, leaned towards the hostess and smiled. "Evening, honey. Joe Brennan, table for two. I made a reservation."

The woman looked down the list in front of her, peering a little in the dim light, her dark hair falling over her face as she perused the list. "Ah, yes," she said with great relief as if she had just discovered the key to a treasure map, "table for two. Brennan." Kelly felt like leaning over and whispering in her ear, "If you put your glasses on, you'd be able to read it a whole lot better," but smiling politely, she stood back as the woman picked up two oversized menus, and with a dazzling smile, asked them to "Follow me, please." Joe, following the swaying rear end, seemed more than happy to comply.

"Here we are," she said brightly, indicating a table in the middle of the room and waited while they sat down. Placing the menus in front of them, she added, "A waiter will be along in just a moment to take your order." With another flash of her perfect teeth, she departed.

While they waited for their meal, Joe said, "Hey, did you know they started support groups for millionaires here in the Valley? All ready to help people deal with the trauma of newfound wealth."

"You're kidding."

"No, I'm serious. It's all these people who became millionaires overnight because of the incredible run the stock market had. Think about it. All these young guys were founding members of those Internet companies that went ballistic. The shares went leaping up—some companies moved as much as seventeen points in a day. Even the people who joined the company after it was rolling were given stock options—and sometimes a whole bunch to lure them away from other companies. So here they all were, having worked for a company for a few short years sitting on a pile of stock that's worth a fortune. A lot of them have cashed in rather than continue on the treadmill."

"So what's the problem? All of a sudden they've got all the money they need and can do whatever they want. Doesn't sound like too much of a hardship to me."

"The problem is they may be very smart engineers, but

that doesn't make them particularly clever about mundane matters like how to manage their money and organize their lives."

"You're right there. I've never met so many incredibly brilliant people with so few smarts."

"You know there was one case of a couple who got approximately three million dollars from stock options. Flush with all the money, they bought a new house for one point five million, two new cars, a beach house, and took off on a vacation to Europe. When they got back they were zapped with capital gains tax which, of course, they hadn't budgeted for. They ended up having to sell the house to pay the taxes."

"Why didn't they just get a mortgage on the house to pay the taxes?"

"Because the dummies had given up their jobs so no one would give them a mortgage. I think people figure once they have a million or two they are invincible. Unfortunately, it doesn't work that way. Running expenses can be pretty high if you don't plan."

Bemused, Kelly said, "Okay, maybe you're right, they do need support groups. Only in Silicon Valley would you have to form support groups for millionaires!"

"It was worse than that. You couldn't get anything done anymore. If you called up an electrician or a plumber, you'd get an answer phone and no one would call back. Sandy couldn't even get hold of a chimney sweep in midsummer for a week. Then a friend of ours wanted to build an extension on their house, and they couldn't get a quote for three months, let alone a start date."

"Hey, it's the Gold Rush all over again. It's the tradespeople who will be rich while all those poor young millionaires will be destitute!"

"Don't you mock. You Kiwis living the good life have no idea how we suffer. Anyway, enough of this talk about money, it's making me hungry. What are you going to have?"

Kelly perused the menu for a while. "I think I'll go with the roasted vegetable starter and the chicken dish. That looks pretty good." Around them the restaurant had filled up and a steady hubbub of voices formed a backdrop to their conversation.

"Did you hear the joke about the engineer playing golf?" Joe asked.

"No, but I'm sure you're going to tell me," Kelly grinned, pleasantly surprised. Joe had a never-ending supply of engineer jokes generally reserved for late-night drinking sessions. Dinner was usually ninety percent shop talk.

"There was an engineer, a doctor and a priest playing golf. They were moving along quite well, when they came up behind a really slow foursome. And when I say slow, I mean slow. It took this foursome ages to putt, they doodled around for hours on the tee and could never find their ball on the fairway." He paused and took a sip of wine. "The trio behind them were patient to start with, but gradually got more and more annoyed. After all, if they were going to play that slowly, why didn't they let them play through? Finally, the greens keeper came by, so the trio stopped him and complained about the slow group in front.

" 'Those guys are blind. We had a terrible fire in the clubhouse a while back, and these were the fireman that rushed in and saved everyone,' the greens keeper said. 'Unfortunately, the heat and smoke caused them all to go blind. But the club is so grateful we said they could play whenever they wanted to.'

" 'That's so sad,' said the priest. 'I'll get the congregation to pray for them on Sunday.'

" 'That's terrible,' said the doctor. 'I've got a friend who's an ophthalmologist. I'll set up an appointment and see if he can do something for them.'

"The engineer looked troubled and said, 'Why don't they play at night?' "

Kelly sat back and laughed, "You know, having been married to an engineer for years, I can believe it!"

The waiter arrived with their meal and for a few moments they ate in silence, both hungry, and the food was good. When they finished their starter, and before Joe could launch into another joke, or bring up another topic, Kelly decided to tackle Joe about the project. She hadn't liked the way he had terminated the conversation when she had brought up the subject earlier, and he seemed determined to talk about anything except work ever since.

She searched around for an approach that would goad him into some sort of response. Bringing up Colin's idea that it might be a CIA or FBI project didn't seem like too good an idea. Joe was a good friend, but a suggestion like that might make him hit the roof. She looked across the table at him and said, "What is this project all about, Joe? Is it some sort of lottery?" A lottery seemed like a nice neutral topic.

"A lottery?" he drawled. "Could be. All I know is I was told to put in a bid on a contract for a system capable of handling two hundred thousand terminals, all feeding into a central data base."

"But you must know more than that. How can you spec out a system when you don't know what it's for?"

"I do know what it's for," Joe replied with an irritated edge. "It has to send out information to terminals, receive information and process it, then send it out again."

"But why such heavy security?"

"I've told you several times now," he said, his eyes stony, "it's a government project. Security has to be tight. If it isn't, then it will be the last government contract we see."

Realizing she'd overstepped the mark, she backed down gracefully. "Sorry, Joe, didn't mean to talk shop," she said lightly. "Comes of living in the boonies. It's a real change being able to talk to high-powered folks like you." But even as she spoke, she felt the doubts creeping in. Joe talked shop incessantly. She'd never known him to want to change the subject before, or for that matter not be totally open. Maybe he's getting burned out, she thought, but looking at Joe's keen, intelligent face, it seemed unlikely.

Chapter 15

Next morning, Kelly, dressed in a light gray Armani suit, black blouse and black shoes, swung through the doors of Finsat Corporation. Her softly curled hair was swept to one side, giving her what she fondly hoped was the corporate look. Having signed in and been given a badge stating she was a visitor and Kelly Brandon, she sat down to wait. She only had time to read one article in *Business Week* before a trim, well-dressed woman appeared. "Hi, Kelly? I'm Annette. Joe asked me to come down and get you as he's tied up at the moment." She put out her hand and beamed at Kelly. "I only joined Joe a couple of months ago so we haven't met."

Kelly noted the cool, blond good looks and slim figure, and thought Joe was running true to form. As they reached Craig Bennett's office, the woman asked, "How was your trip? You're just in from Australia, aren't you?"

"Close. New Zealand."

"Oh!" She looked puzzled. Weren't they the same place? Aloud, moving to safer ground, she asked, "Was it a pleasant flight?"

"Yes, thank you." Kelly felt relieved when she asked her to take a seat, saying Joe would be along in a few minutes. She wasn't quite sure she could relate to Joe's latest bubble-brain.

Joe arrived a few minutes later, dressed in an elegant dark blue suit. His pointed boots shone. "Morning, Kelly, we're on in five minutes. Are you all set?" He stood poised for action, weight on his front toes, ready to go.

"Ready as I'll ever be."

Joe led the way to the CEO's conference room. A long mahogany table dominating the dimly lit room was set up with projector, yellow writing pads, ballpoint pens and a large dish of jelly beans.

Kelly began to arrange her slides while Joe fidgeted. First he poured a cup of coffee, then put it down untouched, strode up and down the length of the room several times, sat down, took a pen out of his inside pocket, then picked it up and put it away again. Fifteen minutes later Craig Bennett and his personal assistant arrived.

Kelly shook the outstretched hand; his handshake was warm and firm. He was a handsome man in his fifties, every inch the captain of industry. He settled down in a chair, his personal assistant a few seats away, pen at the ready. Joe moved to a seat opposite Craig, looking cool and calm, all his previous hyperactivity gone.

"We thought you'd like a report on the New Zealand module. Since Kelly happened to be in town, it seemed like a good time," Joe said by way of introduction. Kelly managed to keep her eyebrows under control. "Just happened to be in town" be damned. She'd flown over 6,000 miles specifically for one ten-minute meeting.

Craig Bennett switched his gaze to Kelly, and smiled in her direction. The smile didn't reach his eyes, but it made his fine square jaw look a little squarer. "Okay, Kelly, why don't you go ahead?" He had a warm, strong voice, guaranteed to instill confidence in shareholders.

Kelly took a sip of water, pushed back a stray piece of hair with a sunburned hand that contrasted sharply with the light gray of her suit and began her report. She gave a quick rundown on the state of the project, keeping an eye on

Craig Bennett, gauging his reactions.

Kelly was not impressed by the man she was addressing. She had known his predecessor, an untidy giant of a man with a dynamic personality. Giving a presentation to him was an exhilarating experience. She had been alternately questioned, bullied and charmed, and was forever grateful that she had done her homework. When his health collapsed, he selected Craig Bennett as his replacement. Craig, a Harvard MBA with an undergraduate engineering degree, was everything his predecessor was not. Beautifully dressed, smooth, urbane, always saying the right thing, being seen in the right places. The press loved him.

Kelly had been a bit overwhelmed the first time she met him. His aura of confidence and urbanity made her feel awkward and inferior. However, at their second meeting, she began to feel she was dealing with a cardboard caricature; the man lacked substance. He was also gutless. Never making a decision. Always managing to adroitly maneuver the situation so that someone else made it. Someone who could be blamed if things went wrong, but where he could pick up the glory if it went right.

As she finished the last of her slides, she looked questioningly in Craig Bennett's direction. "So you feel the project is under control now? It will come in on time?"

"As I explained, there will be a month's slippage because of the personnel change, but apart from that it's going well. I can't see any other problems." She moved away from the projector and took a seat next to Joe. "The only thing that worries me is the geographic dispersal. As each piece comes in, I think there will be problems here as they work on the interface."

"Yours is the only piece being developed outside this facility. So there's no problem." Kelly raised her eyebrows, but said nothing. Doesn't he know that Joe has it spread all over the compass?

The personal assistant, a slight young man in a snowy white shirt and dark suit, who Kelly felt sure had some very impressive degrees, said, "If the New Zealand team has followed the specifications exactly, then there should be no problem at all." He seemed rather pleased with himself for having made this profound observation.

Get real, Kelly thought, where do they find these naive creatures? Aloud she said, "Of course, they are following everything closely, but don't forget the number of modules they have to interface with. If one developer here makes a change, we could be facing delays. It won't be a major problem, but all those little wrinkles take time to iron out."

Craig Bennett frowned, a deep furrow spoiling his perfect brow. "We can't afford a slippage. This project must come in on time." His voice was heavy with emphasis.

Joe sat forward in his chair. "Of course it will," he said smoothly. "Kelly just likes to worry. I think it's called covering your ass." Seething, Kelly smiled graciously in Joe's direction.

The CEO faced Joe. "Look, Joe, you're responsible for the overall project. There can be no slippage."

"I understand that," Kelly interjected. "We're doing everything possible to speed things up. They're a first-class team." She paused a moment, then fully aware of Joe bristling beside her, added, "The one thing that could help would be more information. If we knew what we were dealing with, we could cut some corners. We've some whizzes on the team who could come up with some ideas to move things along."

"Joe tells me he has given you all the information you need to do the job." His tone was icy. "I'm tired of all these feeble excuses you software types come up with. I know you all think the completion date is up for arbitration, but in this case, it's a solid date. I expect you to meet it." He got to his feet. The meeting was over.

Kelly felt her tense shoulders relax as he moved towards the door, but as he reached it, he turned towards her and said, "You're sure nothing else can go wrong?"

"No, someone being killed is something we couldn't have anticipated, but we've found a first-class replacement. I'm confident we'll come in on time." Kelly had her fingers crossed under the table. She knew if they made it right on time it would be a miracle, but she hadn't spent all those years in the corporate world for nothing. Tell them what they want to hear.

As she spoke, she was startled to see a strange look flicker through Craig Bennett's expressionless eyes. Could it have been fear, or was she imagining things?

"Well done, Kelly," Joe said, resting his hand on her shoulder. "I think you calmed him down for a while. Sam said he'd like to see you as soon as this was over." Sam Schroeder's project interfaced with the Auckland software.

Sam's office was on the other side of a door marked "Authorized Personnel Only." Behind the official door, the usual software chaos reigned. Untidy offices, boxes everywhere, flip charts and whiteboards crammed with diagrams. The offices were glass-fronted, but wherever a wall existed, it was covered with calendars, cartoons, pictures of sailing boats, whales and the Sierras. Ten-speed bicycles with crash helmets and leather gloves sat in the corner of several offices, and all but three offices had empty Coke cans sitting on the desk.

Sam was glued to his terminal when Kelly walked in.

When she spoke, he swung round in his chair and a delighted smile lit up his homely face. He had a small ink mark at the bottom of his shirt pocket, which contained an ill-matched line of four pens.

"Good to see you, Kelly. Want a cup of coffee?"

"Sure, I deserve one after a session with Craig Bennett."

"So tell me, what fictitious tale did you weave for Craig?"

Kelly brought him up to date. By the time they were through, Kelly was left with a pile of notes to take back with her and a mild headache. Glancing up, she noticed Sam's frown had been replaced by a wide grin.

"You're enjoying this, aren't you? I didn't think old cynics like you got carried away. Thought you left that to the teenagers down the hall."

His brown eyes shone. "I tell you, Kelly, this is going to be a terrific system when it's done. Do you have any idea of the size?"

"It's two hundred thousand terminals and a central data base, most of it floating around out there on the net, isn't it? That's not such a big deal for you, is it?"

"That's where you're wrong. We've built in extensibility. We can keep on adding more terminals and more storage while the system's on-line. We could go to ten times that size with no trouble at all."

Kelly stared at him. "That's not what the spec says."

Sam shrugged. "I know. It was Joe's idea." He was unconcerned about building something outside the original specification. "He sort of put it to me as a challenge. I don't think he believed we could do it. But with the whizzy team he let me hire, it was a pushover. Expense no object. I've got some of the best brains in the business on this one."

"You're telling me those two scrawny kids at the coffee

pot were MIT whiz kids, aren't you?"

"Right on. All I had to do was offer them twenty percent of the State of California and they came like lambs." Expecting Kelly to laugh, he noticed her worried expression. "Geez, Kelly, don't get upset. Nothing we've done affects the interface." He looked sheepish. "I would've liked to tell you about it before, but everything is so hush-hush on this system, I'm scared to tell my wife what I'm working on."

"You mean you haven't told Colin this?"

"No, I was told to keep the whole thing under wraps. As long as I kept the interface intact, it wouldn't affect your bunch." He ran his hands through his wiry hair. "The fact is, I shouldn't have told you, and I'll be in trouble if Joe finds out. You're not going to go off the deep end with him over this, are you? My head will be on the block if you do."

"No, of course not."

"Look, I shouldn't have said anything, and I don't know why I did. I guess I got a bit carried away." He continued to look worried, regretting what he had told her.

Kelly wondered for a moment too. But then, she reflected, people did have a habit of telling her things. Must be that I'm a sympathetic sponge, I guess. "Don't worry, your secret's safe with me. I'm dying to tell Colin, but you're right, if Joe wants this under wraps we'd better keep it between ourselves."

As she packed up her stuff and made her way out of the building, her expression was troubled. What was this system and why all the conflicting information? There they were in Auckland building a control module for a system that could be ten times the size of the spec, and here was Joe scattering pieces of the project all over the place and not telling the CEO. Something weird was going on.

CHAPTER 16

Two days later, Kelly scanned the throng at London's Heathrow Airport for Mark and Ginny. Finally she caught sight of the comforting bulk of Mark, waving and beaming in her direction. Beside him, initially obscured by the crowd, Ginny emerged, small, dark-haired and earnest. The two of them elbowed their way to Kelly, hugged her, then whisked her out of the melee to the quiet of the garage. The drive to their flat in central London went quickly as they all caught up on the latest news.

Their flat was on the third floor of a newly converted building with an unimpressive facade. Coming into the mundane front hall, rising up in a small elevator made smaller by Mark's bulk, and then being whisked through a narrow front door and an even narrower hallway, left Kelly unprepared for the living room. It was all white: carpets, furniture and ceiling. Nothing to detract the eye from a stunning panoramic view of the city provided by a floor-to-ceiling window. The only color in the room was a splash of yellow and red cushions on the sofa and two modernistic paintings.

"Wow," Kelly exclaimed, "this is fantastic. What a view."

Ginny and Mark beamed as if they had created it. "Cost an arm and a leg when we bought it, but it's already worth twice what we paid for it. So we can't complain," Mark said. "Anyway, take a seat. What can I get you? Cup of coffee? Or would you like to take a shower first?"

"A shower sounds great."

Ginny showed her to her bedroom, and as usual the shower made her feel like a human being again. Dressed in casual wool pants and a light sweater she went in search of her hosts. Ginny and Mark were sitting on the sofa sipping wine, not speaking, just happy to be together. Kelly swallowed the lump that rose unbidden to her throat and wished yet again that Steve was still around. As they both turned to greet her, their faces shining with friendliness, the moment passed. Mark leaped to his feet and said, "Come and join us. We're having a nice drop of Cloudy Bay Sauvignon Blanc just to make you feel at home."

And as he bustled off to the kitchen to get her a glass, Ginny said, "Lunch is all ready. Just something light to tide you over, then we'll eat tonight."

"So how are you two enjoying life in London? Must be a bit of change from Los Altos." Mark and Ginny had owned a tree-filled acre in one of Silicon Valley's better neighborhoods.

"We love it, don't we, Mark? London's great fun. Always something going on. I love the theatre. Mark isn't so keen, although I am gradually converting him."

"Yea, well I enjoy the ones with the nice bods like *Chicago*, but some of those plays you drag me to are a bit of a pain. At least when it's on TV you can turn it off if you don't like it." Anxious to get off the subject of the theatre, he asked, "How come the trip to London? Are you here on business?"

"Yes," Ginny added, "we've been trying to get you to come over ever since Steve died. Then all of a sudden you call up and are here within a couple of weeks."

"We figured we could all hop on the Eurostar and have a weekend in Paris. Could go hunting for paintings. Are you on for this weekend?" Mark asked.

"I still can't get used to the idea of just being able to hop on a train and be in Paris for dinner." She hesitated a moment, wondering how much to tell them. "Actually though, I have something I want to get done before I start gallivanting."

"Has Finsat got a subsidiary over here?"

"No, it's not work. Well, not official work, but there's something I need to do."

"Okay, get that out of the way, then we can all have a ball. I assume you've got time for lunch before you take off?" Mark said, grinning.

"I'm not in that much of a hurry, but I would like to get down to Portsmouth as soon as possible. That isn't too far, is it?"

"No, about ninety minutes by train, but why on earth are you going there?"

"It's sort of a long story," Kelly said.

"In that case, how about we all go and get some lunch, and you can entertain us with your tale while we munch," Mark said. "I don't know about you two but I'm starved."

It wasn't until the plates were cleared and they were sipping coffee that Kelly started to explain. She told them about the call from Finsat asking her to keep an eye on a project in Auckland, and had them in fits of laughter as she told them stories of the young project team. Then they grew serious as she told them about David's fall. But when she started to talk about Joe's visit, and her growing suspicions about the whole Finsat project, they both began to look uncomfortable.

When she finished, there was a long silence. Kelly looked at them both in consternation, and could feel her color rise as she realized how bizarre her accusations must sound.

Suddenly Mark banged his hand on the table, causing the glasses to clink ominously, threw back his head and laughed, "Kelly, that's wonderful. What a plot. You're really putting us on, aren't you? We always said you'd write a book one day with that imagination of yours."

Ginny frowned, her brown eyes worried, "Mark, hon, I don't think she's trying out a story line on us. She's serious."

Kelly blushed, something she hadn't done for years, sat stunned for a moment, then said, "Ginny's right. I'm dead serious. There's something weird going on. If you want to put a virus in a major project, New Zealand is a perfect spot. You have got all the time in the world to work on it without anyone suspecting a thing. By the time the module is shipped, it will be totally self-contained and only the interfaces will be tested."

"So if you really believe that, why haven't you told the powers that be at Finsat?" Mark asked.

"In the first place it's only just suspicions at the moment, and secondly I just don't know who is involved. I don't even think I trust Joe anymore."

"But, what you're talking about is murder," Ginny said. "Go to the police. If that Darren or David you were talking about was pushed off a cliff, that's a matter for the New Zealand police."

"I just don't have enough information. So far all I've got is a theory and a set of strange coincidences. All they are interested in is facts. I can't blame them; I suppose they have their hands full as it is without listening to half-baked theories." She straightened the knife and fork on her plate. "That's why I'm here. If I can just find out something about the elusive Mr. James, I'll have enough facts to at least get them interested."

"Kelly," Ginny said, picking her words carefully, "aren't

you getting a little too much involved in this thing? Are you sure you aren't doing it just to get some kicks? I don't mean consciously. Perhaps you're just trying to fill the void Steve left."

Kelly, acutely aware of Ginny's undergraduate degree in psychology, replied, "No, Ginny, I thought about that myself, but I can't shake this thing. Something's wrong. If it isn't, then I have to prove it to myself, or I'm not going to be able to sleep nights."

"I wonder if that guy getting killed hasn't brought back all the bad memories of Steve's death," Ginny said. Then added, out of the blue, "What happened to that nice Richard who was so helpful after Steve died? Aren't you seeing him?"

Before Kelly had time to answer, Mark jumped in, "Hold your horses, you two; before you start getting into Kelly's love life, let's talk a little more about this murder. You're saying you're going down to Portsmouth to knock on the door of the hit man and ask him if he happened to shove someone off a cliff in New Zealand. Give me a break, Kelly, you've got to be crazy."

Ginny rose to her feet agitated. "Kelly, you can't do this. If he is a murderer, it's dangerous. If he's not, he's going to be furious. You could be in real trouble."

"Oh come on, you two, I'm not that stupid. I'm just going to root around and get some facts on him. Find out what sort of a man he is. I've no intention of going anywhere near him." She grinned, her face lightening, "He'll probably turn out to be some inoffensive little accountant who used up his savings to take a trip to New Zealand."

Mark got up and put his arm around his wife. "Ginny, my love, don't waste your breath trying to talk her out of it. She's got her Crusader Rabbit shirt on. I can see the look in her eye. Remember how she used to be at work? Once she decided on something, no one could stop her."

"But this is different Mark, it could be dangerous."

"I tell you what. How about you leave it till the weekend Kelly, and I'll come along as a bodyguard? Could be a lot of fun. I've always fancied myself as a minder."

"Okay, Mark, you're on, that would be fabulous. But I tell you what I'll do. I'll go down to Portsmouth tomorrow, stay at a hotel and pretend I'm a tourist." And as inspiration struck, she brightened. "I know, I'll tell them I am tracing my family tree. Kiwis are always doing that. Good old great-grandpapa James hailed from Portsmouth. A seafaring lad he was. I can ask all sorts of questions about the James family that way without raising anyone's curiosity. Fortunately, it's a common name too. Even if Andrew James got wind of it, which to put it mildly is totally unlikely, he'd think it was some other family called James."

Ginny looked unconvinced. "Okay, I suppose that's all right, just as long as you promise to wait until Mark arrives before you go looking for Andrew James."

Kelly had no intention of waiting for Mark. Trying to ask inconspicuous questions with Mark around would be impossible. His booming voice and huge bulk made him stand out everywhere he went. "Okay, I'll give you a call when I'm down there. Meanwhile, how about we clear the dishes and take a walk."

CHAPTER 17

Once clear of London, she made good time, traveling south in the middle lane, enjoying the English countryside. As soon as she pulled off the motorway and started looking for her hotel, all that changed. When she had booked the room the night before, she had asked for directions, and over the phone they seemed straightforward. No one bothered to explain about the one-way streets and roundabouts. Having gone round one roundabout three times, she began to wish she had come by train and taken a taxi to the hotel. Wouldn't she ever learn that old cities were designed for pedestrians and carriages, not cars? Worse than that, the older houses had no garages, so everyone parked on the street, making negotiating the small streets a nightmare.

Arriving at the hotel sticky and exhausted, she was pleasantly surprised to find an attractive Victorian hotel, beautifully restored, situated on the sea front. Between the hotel and the sea was a large green open space and a wide promenade. The recommendation of the Tourist Office had been a good one. Southsea was a great deal pleasanter than what she had seen so far of the rest of the city.

The man on reception was full of sympathy when he heard about her troubles finding the hotel. "Why don't you put your bag in your room, miss, then come down and have a pot of coffee in the lounge, you'll feel right in no time." He handed her a large key to a room on the first floor. "I'd offer to give you a hand with your bags, but that would be overkill," he added, indicating her small overnight bag.

"Planning to stay a fortnight are you?"

Smiling, feeling better already, she headed for the wide Victorian staircase with its walnut banister and thick carpet. Her room, facing the sea, was spacious, with high ceilings and lots of light. If the Victorians were stingy with the size of their roads, they certainly knew how to build houses. She hung up her clothes, then went downstairs in search of a cup of coffee and some information.

She selected a large, wing-backed chair in the lounge, with a good view of the sea front. Within a few minutes of sitting down, a middle-aged woman dressed in a dark dress and a white pinafore came through bearing a silver tray with a pot of coffee and plate of cookies. Plodding along on huge legs clad in beige stockings and sensible shoes, she set the tray down carefully on the table in front of Kelly.

"Nice day for the time of year," she said in a broad Portsmouth accent.

"Yes, it is. It was very pleasant driving down."

"Come far, have you?"

"Just from London."

The woman looked puzzled, as if it wasn't the answer she was expecting. "Australian are you?"

"No, you're close, I'm a New Zealander."

"Oh, I'm sorry, miss." Kelly loved the way the Brits always apologized for getting your nationality wrong.

"On holiday, are you then? Not a very nice time of year for it. Plenty of room on the beach though."

Kelly looked out at the sparsely populated sea front and the mound of pebbles leading to the sea. "No, I'm here to do some sightseeing, and also want to see if I can trace my family tree. My great-grandfather came from Portsmouth originally."

"Did he now?" the waitress said with renewed interest.

"Fancy that. Small old world, isn't it?"

"I think he was in the Navy." Her new-found role as undercover agent had made her very inventive.

"Well then, you'd enjoy going down to the dockyard and seeing the *Victory* and the Naval Museum. That makes a nice day out, that does. My Harold and I, we've done it two or three times."

"Is it far from here?" she asked, thinking about another horrendous drive trying to find her way around. But if she was going to build her cover as a tourist, she needed to act like one. She had no intention of waiting for Mark before she saw Andrew James, but on the other hand, she saw no harm in using a little caution.

"Oh no, it's easy from here. Just drive straight along the sea front, and you can park right there."

Kelly glanced gratefully out of the window at the wide sea front streets. "Don't forget to visit the *Mary Rose* while you're there. They're doing a good job of restoring it."

"The *Mary Rose*, what's that?"

The hotel was empty and the waitress seemed glad to stand around and chat. "Oh," she said, delighted to meet someone who didn't know the story. "The *Mary Rose* was Henry VIII's flagship. Pride of his fleet, it was. She put out to sea along with the fleet to fight off a French invasion. They were always trying to invade us those days." Her ruddy, weather worn face broke into a smile. "No point anymore is there, we're all one big happy family these days, squabble like one too, most of the time. Myself, I think we should have stayed clear of Europe. Hasn't done us much good joining up with them." Kelly poured herself a cup of coffee. This was obviously going to be a long story.

"Well, to get back to the story n'that, Henry was down to review the fleet before they went into battle. Just as the

Mary Rose went out past Southsea Castle where Henry was standing, all the sailors rushed to the side to give him a cheer. The weight capsized the ship and down she went. All hands with her." She finished her story with a self-satisfied grin. "Bit like that Millennium Bridge, small technical problem."

"You're kidding!"

"No, it's as true as I stand here. You go down to the dockyard and see. Mark you, the French claim they sank it—they would, wouldn't they—and other history books say it went down in battle. But not one shot was fired. Must have given poor old Henry a nasty turn."

"That's terrible. There would've been about a couple of hundred men on board, wouldn't there? Did they all swim ashore okay?"

"No, ones on top all had their armor on, n'that, ready for the fight, and I doubt the poor devils down below had any chance at all. Only saved about thirty-five sailors out of four hundred they say." As a gray-haired lady, leaning heavily on a stick, and her elderly husband entered the lounge, she looked up and prepared to leave. "Mark you, it led to a lot of reforms in shipbuilding, so maybe it was a blessing in disguise."

As the waitress left, Kelly decided to go and take a look at the *Mary Rose* and the *Victory*, which, if she remembered from history lessons correctly, was Nelson's flagship. And as it turned out she had a thoroughly enjoyable day.

Next morning, after a run on the sea front followed by a substantial English breakfast, she felt ready to go in quest of the mysterious Andrew James. As she walked past reception, dressed in slacks, jacket, and comfortable shoes with a street map under her arm, the man behind the desk greeted her like an old friend. "Morning, miss. Did you enjoy the *Mary Rose*?" He was obviously ready for a chat.

"Yes, thanks, it was great," she said, moving towards the door.

He leaned on the counter. "You know nobody appreciates poor old Henry VIII. All they remember is him and his wives. Did you know he founded the British Navy?" Kelly stopped and turned back. This was interesting. "And it was the Navy that created the British Empire, yet all kids learn about is how he chopped off Anne Boleyn's head."

"It was probably the Tudor Sunday papers. All they reported was the scandal—ignored everything else." Kelly could never quite get over the lurid British Sunday tabloids.

His blue eyes twinkled with amusement. "Never thought of that one. I always thought it was Tudor women's lib playing down Henry's part in Elizabeth's success. She'd have had a hard time conquering the Spanish Armada in a couple of canoes." He looked across at the map under her arm. "So where are you off to today?"

"I thought I'd take a walk around the city and get a feel for the place. I'd like to know what kind of town my great-grandfather lived in. I think I'll try the main library too. They'll probably have records of the family, or can point me in the right direction."

Once inside her car, she checked the map to find Gordon Street. Andrew James was bound to be at work during the day, so she could do a little reconnoitering without raising any suspicion. She was still not sure what she was going to do, but she felt sure as she neared his lair, inspiration would strike.

Twenty minutes later, Kelly was driving slowly down Gordon Street looking for number 37. Gordon Street appeared to be identical to all the other streets she had passed, but on closer inspection she found that wasn't true. Several houses had made brave attempts at individuality, even to the extent of completely replacing the old Victorian front with a modern brick or stone facing, with bay windows and studded oak doors.

Finding it impossible to stop in front of Andrew James's house, she decided to find somewhere to park and then walk by for a closer inspection. Number 37 proved to be unremarkable. It had the standard Victorian facade with net curtains obscuring the front room from the gaze of passersby, a tiny front garden devoid of flowers, a wooden gate that needed a lick of paint and a low cement wall which had once been topped by a wrought iron railing. Looking along the street, she noticed all the railings were gone thanks to World War II when all the iron was harvested for the war effort. It was interesting that in all the poorer areas, the railings that helped to decorate dreary streets were gone, but in front of Buckingham Palace, and in fact, in all the affluent English suburbs, the rails still stood in all their glory. She remembered reading somewhere that gathering the iron railings had been a huge publicity effort backed by Beaverbrook to convince the population that Britain was totally committed to the fight. Most of the railings rusted on scrap heaps, never used.

As Kelly continued walking along Gordon Street, she was hit by a fit of depression. It was hard to believe number 37's dreary facade concealed a psychotic killer. She didn't know what she had expected, but it certainly wasn't this. She began to think the whole trip to England was a major waste of time. Doggedly she plodded along the street towards the corner shop. Having come this far, she felt she should do some checking, so, catching sight of a shop, she decided to try there. The shop was literally on the corner, with windows facing two different streets, and the entryway diagonally across the corner. Kelly smiled vaguely in the direction of the shopkeeper, who was leaning disinterestedly on the counter, and started looking round the shelves for something to buy. She decided on a small bottle of shampoo since she had discovered small seaside hotels did not run to complimentary shampoo, picked up some apples and a bar of Cadbury's fruit and nut chocolate and took them over to the counter. While the shopkeeper rang up the purchases, she asked, "Do you happen to know an Andrew James? I believe he lives somewhere near here."

The shopkeeper, a middle-aged man with a sour face, said, "No, dunno anyone of that name. Sure you've got the right street?"

"Yes, I know it's Gordon Street, but unfortunately I don't have the number." The man eyed her dubiously with watery eyes. "He's a distant cousin of mine. I'm over on a visit from New Zealand, and an aunt of mine who lives in London said he lived here. So I thought I'd look him up. Unfortunately, she couldn't remember the number. She's a little scatty."

"Yes," he said wearily, "they do get a bit that way, don't they?" He bent over to pick up his newspaper, and seemed surprised to see her still standing there when he straightened up.

"Have you any idea how I might find him?"

"Try the telephone book. Bound to be there," he said, starting to turn the pages of the *Daily Mirror.*

"Unfortunately, he's not in the book," Kelly persisted.

"Don't see how anyone could manage without a phone these days. Maybe he's unlisted," he said, not bothering to look up.

Swallowing her annoyance, Kelly said, "Thank you

anyway," and headed for the door. Corner shops were supposed to be mines of information—heck, didn't these people watch *Coronation Street*? Thinking of *Coronation Street* gave her an idea; she set off in search of the nearest pub. The King's Head turned out to be several streets away, and surprisingly, three streets away from Gordon Road the neighborhood took a distinct turn for the better. The straight, narrow streets widened, and large trees spilled over the pavement from the gardens of large, imposing houses. She retraced her steps and walked away from Gordon Street in three other directions, but finally, footsore and thirsty, she decided the King's Head would have to be Andrew James's local.

It was a pleasant old pub, with tables outside for warm days, and a cozy lounge bar inside. Realizing it was already noon and she hadn't stopped for morning coffee, she ordered a lemon and lime to slake her thirst. Several people were sitting around having a drink before their pub lunch. Hopping up on a bar stool, she waited while the barman opened up a bottle and carefully poured her drink. Then as he rang up her money, she said, "It's warm out there today when you're walking around."

The barman wiped the counter with a soft white cloth, smiled at her and asked, "Here on holiday are you?"

"Yes, but I'm in Portsmouth trying to track down some of my family. We're trying to compile a family tree."

The barman smiled indulgently; all these Aussies were interested in where they came from. "Where you from then?"

"New Zealand."

"Honest? I've always wanted to go there. Looks a great place. Wouldn't want to mix it up with those All Blacks of yours though. Look like a tough bunch."

Kelly grinned, "I think they're quite tame off the field. Do you happen to know an Andrew James? He's a distant cousin of mine, and an aunt up in London said he lived somewhere near here. Gordon Street, I think she said."

"No, can't say as I do, but then I haven't been here that long." He leaned across the counter and shouted in the direction of a gray-haired man with an elderly spaniel at his feet, sitting in the corner nursing a pint. "Hey, Fred, know someone called Andrew James? Lives in Gordon Street?"

Fred looked up, pleased to have someone to talk to. "No, don't know an Andrew," he replied slowly, reflectively chewing his lower lip. "There was a James lived on Sudan Street but his name was Joe. Joined the Navy ten year back. Should straighten him out. Pity they did away with National Service. You wouldn't get all these lager louts at the football if they had some discipline in their lives. Didn't happen in my time, I can tell you." He took a drink of his pint, the level dropping dramatically. "D'you know I can't even go and watch Pompey play n'that anymore. It's a bloody disgrace, that's what it is." He put his beer glass down with an outraged gesture.

The barman, having heard it all before, turned to Kelly, "Sorry, love, doesn't look as if he can help. If anyone else comes in from around here before you leave I'll ask them for you."

She took her drink over to a corner table and sat down. It felt good to be off her feet. She must have walked a lot farther than she realized. As she sipped her drink, she thought she might as well have some lunch. That way she could hang around the pub for a while on the off-chance someone came in who knew Andrew James. Drink half finished, she went over to the bar and ordered a slice of cheese and onion pie. Ten minutes later it arrived, served by a friendly, plump woman. "There you are, love, would you like some ketchup?"

Looking at the crisp brown pastry and delicious bubbling cheese and onion concoction, Kelly shook her head, "No thanks, this looks great."

"They are good," the woman grinned, patting her ample hips. "Love them meself, but they don't do my hips much good. Doesn't look like you've got a problem there though, so enjoy." She bustled off in the direction of the kitchen.

The pub was filling up fast, and people were attacking plates piled high with chips topped off with two large fish fillets, large plates filled with cheese, pickles, salad and crusty rolls, and in the far corner two women were polishing off portions of bread and butter pudding, and apple pie and ice cream. This is the life, Kelly thought, digging into the cheese pie which was as sinfully good as it looked. A short cholesterol-filled life and a happy one.

After an hour, Kelly decided she had hung around long enough. Looking around the packed bar, it was obvious that all the regulars had arrived for their lunchtime drink or meal, and no one had come forward with information on Andrew James. She stopped just short of the heavy door with the large brass handle and called, "Thanks for your help," to the barkeeper.

He grinned in her direction as he pulled a pint, "Good hunting, love."

Feeling full and tired, the thought of more sightseeing was unappealing. She decided to go back to the hotel, take a nap, and then call on Andrew James in the evening when she was sure he would be home. Trailing around, talking to miscellaneous strangers in the hope they could tell her something, was getting her nowhere. The obvious answer was to knock on the door and talk to him directly. After all, what could he do to her on a well-lit busy street?

CHAPTER 18

A light drizzle was falling as Kelly drove towards Gordon Street. The windshield wiper, set to the lowest level, intermittently swept the clinging dampness from the windshield. The street lights created deep shadows on the houses, giving the dreary Victorian frontages a sinister air. The few pedestrians on the sidewalk hurried along under umbrellas, heading for the welcoming glow of the pub, or their own homes.

Finding a parking space at seven o'clock turned out to be a lot easier than during the day. Under her feet the sidewalks were wet, with a sticky, grubby feel to them. As she walked down the street, she noticed that numbers 33 and 35 were dark, but there was a light on in number 37. She gave a sigh of relief; Mr. James was home. Much as she enjoyed sightseeing, she wanted to get this whole thing over and done with. As she walked along the dreary street, the rain saturating her jacket, she thought longingly of home and sunshine.

Opening the tiny gate to number 37, she walked up the path and rang the bell. There was no reply. She looked idly at number 39 where a reflected light showed through to the front room. They were probably all in the back watching TV. She rang the bell again. Still no reply. From somewhere down towards the end of the street a dog barked.

Andrew James must be at home, unless he had gone out leaving a light on. She moved over to the bay window, leaned on the dirt-streaked white windowsill and tried to see through the lace curtain. She could just make out a room furnished with an uncomfortable looking sofa and one chair, devoid of family clutter, obviously seldom used. He must be in the back of the house, she thought, and can't hear the bell. Frustrated she moved across the small garden looking for the back gate, hoping fervently he didn't have a large dog. She was surprised to find no back gate, only the fence to the next property. If you wanted to go out into the back garden, assuming there was one, you had to walk through the house.

Kelly went back to the front door and knocked. She heard footsteps. At last someone was going to answer the door. The door opened, yellow light spilling onto the door-step. Kelly took a step backwards so that whoever was inside could see her. The door stopped moving. "Yes, who is it?" The man's voice was older than she had anticipated.

"Good evening. Mr. James? Can I speak to you for a few minutes?"

Evidently her New Zealand accent piqued the curiosity of the man behind the door. He opened it a little wider and peered out. She could feel the drips from the narrow porch starting to run down the back of her neck. Why hadn't she thought to bring an umbrella? The man at the door was dressed in baggy gray trousers and a long, woolen beige cardigan, and was about seventy. This couldn't be Andrew James, but perhaps it was his father.

"I'm looking for Mr. James," she repeated.

"No Mr. James here," he said, preparing to close the door.

"Oh dear, I've come an awfully long way to find him. I was sure he would be at this address." The old man, taken by her pathetic tone, stopped closing the door and poked his head out to peer again, narrowing his eyes so that he could focus after the bright light inside.

There was a noise behind him in the passageway. "Who's that then? What are you doing out there? Come on in, you silly old devil, you'll catch your death of cold."

A woman, not much younger than he, but with a wiry physique and bright alert eyes, came up behind him and flung the door wide open. She looked surprised when she saw Kelly. "Who are you then, and what do you want? You trying to sell Avon products or something?"

"No, no," Kelly replied, giving the woman what she hoped was a reassuring smile. "I'm not trying to sell anything. I'm looking for someone who I thought lived at this address."

"Who you looking for then? Think we've got someone tucked away in here, do you?" She leaned over and pulled her husband out of the way, preparing to close the door.

"Please don't go. I've come a long way looking for Mr. James and I was told he lived here."

"Mr. James. We don't know a Mr. James, do we, Father?" The woman continued, not expecting an answer from her husband, who Kelly suspected seldom got a chance to say anything. "You from Australia, are you then? You sound a bit like Freda's cousin, he was from there. Didn't look much like those lifeguards though. Scrawny little chap."

"Is there a Mr. James that lives anywhere on this street?" Kelly asked desperately.

The woman looked at her, her little eyes beady. "You'd better step inside a minute. We'll all catch pneumonia standing here answering questions." Grumbling to herself, she headed off down the passageway. Her husband followed, shuffling in his woolen slippers. Kelly walked in after him, closing the door behind her. The narrow passageway was made narrower by a large umbrella stand containing one large black umbrella that had seen better days.

Following them into the back room where a talk show was chattering on the TV, Kelly was hit by a wave of heat given off by a gas fire turned on full blast.

The woman sat down in her armchair, placed her slippered feet on a low footstool and said, "Close the door after you, we don't want to sit here in a screaming gale."

Her husband settled into his chair, a more elaborate wing-backed version with a crocheted rug draped over the back and crocheted armrests. With great deliberation, he lifted one slippered foot and placed it on the footstool in front of his chair, then followed it carefully with the other. Meanwhile, Kelly looked around for somewhere to sit since it was evident no one was going to offer her a chair. She found an uncomfortable leather chair in a corner facing the center of the room. The other two chairs faced the TV which dominated everything else both in size and volume. No wonder they didn't hear the doorbell, she thought, with the TV blaring away and the door closed.

The couple, who seemed to have forgotten Kelly, settled down to watch TV. The man peered at the screen, while the woman picked up her knitting, glanced at a pattern book, then sat back comfortably to watch the show. Kelly cleared her throat and said tentatively, or as tentative as she could make it and still be audible over the blaring TV, "Um, I was wondering if you bought the house from a Mr. James."

The woman looked at her as if amazed that she was still there. "No, we bought it from an estate agent. It was empty when we looked at it. Right old mess too, wasn't it? People must have moved out sometime before we saw it. It was damp." She sniffed disapprovingly.

"Are you sure there's no one else called James on the street? Maybe someone who moved away recently," Kelly prompted.

"No, no James that we know of. Mark you, there's some new folks have moved in at number 27. Pakis they are though, so I doubt they're called James."

The old man began to wheeze. Kelly looked at him in consternation, then realized he was laughing. A glance at the TV which was showing a very unfunny refrigerator commercial couldn't be the reason. " 'Spect their name's Rumjumfulman," he said delightedly. "You heard that story about the Indian bus conductor? Man was waiting at a bus stop in the rain, and when it came by the conductor wouldn't let him on. Said, 'It's rum, jum full, man.' Man said, 'I don't care what your name is, mate, I just want to get on the bus.' " He wheezed loudly.

His wife frowned in disapproval. "That's a racist joke, Father. We'll have none of that here. Them Indians are good Christians same as us." She put down her knitting and faced Kelly. "Sorry, miss, we can't help you," she said in obvious dismissal. If this young woman was going to get Bert started on his jokes, it was time she left.

Kelly got to her feet.

The old man looked sorry to see her go. "Why don't you try the police station, it's just over on the next street. They'll be able to help you."

"Not a bad idea. Although they weren't much use when Gerald lost his bicycle." With this profound statement, she ushered Kelly to the door.

After the stifling heat of the TV room, the cold air outside felt good. However, the light drizzle had turned to a downpour. Kelly turned up the collar of her jacket and ran for the car, but by the time she was inside she was soaked.

A smartly dressed constable looked up as she walked into the empty police station. "Evening, miss. Lovely weather for ducks," he observed as she stood dripping in front of his desk. He was a pleasant-faced youngster with straw-colored hair and large ears. "Can I help you?"

"I'm looking for a Mr. James who I thought lived at 37 Gordon Street, but when I got there the people didn't know him. Is there any way you can tell me where he lives? I'm sure it's Gordon Street."

"Thought perhaps you'd come in to report a stolen umbrella," he grinned. "Relative of yours is he, madam?" He noted the wedding ring. Pity, she was a nice looking bird.

"No, I live in New Zealand, and Mr. James left a valuable camera behind. Since I was coming to England on business, I thought I'd return it to him."

"So you're a Kiwi. Don't get many of those dropping into the station. My pal moved there a couple of years ago, and came back this summer to show off his new wife. Regular corker she was from Hamilton. James," he continued, diving under the desk and coming up with a telephone directory. "No, he's not listed." He looked apologetic. "I always go for the obvious first. It's amazing how many people don't check the directory." He rummaged around on the desk and started to look through a well-thumbed street directory.

Sergeant Doyle heard the exchange through his open door. Picking up on her accent, he wandered out to see who she was. The fact was, he was bored. It had been a quiet day at the station, and he'd spent a numbing day typing reports and clearing up correspondence. He'd be off duty in another hour, and all he had to look forward to was an empty house and a dinner sitting in the fridge, on a plate covered with Glad Wrap. It hadn't been like that a year ago. Then he used to come home to golden brown meat pies and three veg steaming hot on the table for him, lamb stew and dumplings, apple pie. His stomach growled just remembering. And Beryl sitting there waiting for him, watching him eat with beaming face, pleased that he enjoyed her cooking. After that it was a cozy evening in front of the tele. Beryl watching Morse while he snoozed.

"Evening, madam." He glanced in her direction as he walked over to the constable's desk. Well dressed, confident, about five foot four. Not upset about anything, so she hadn't come in to report a lost cat or husband.

"Say, Sarge, this lady's looking for an Andrew James, supposed to live in Gordon Street. You live just round the corner from there, don't you?"

"Relative of yours, madam?" He was a small man, but his serious face and eyes that looked as if they had seen it all, gave him an authority that belied his stature.

"No, I just explained to the constable that he was in New Zealand on holiday and left a camera behind. Since I was over here, I decided to return it."

She reddened under his unwavering gaze.

"I don't somehow think you have the right Mr. James, madam."

"Oh, but I'm sure I have," she said hauling a notebook out of her soggy handbag and showing it to him. "This was the address I was given."

"So, he isn't a relative of yours then? Close friend of the family?"

"No, I didn't even know him, the owner of the house he rented knew I was coming to England and asked if I'd return it. She didn't want to mail it because she was afraid it might get damaged. It's very valuable."

"You Kiwis are a considerate lot," he said with only the slightest trace of sarcasm. Then added, "Ah, then if he isn't a friend of yours, or anyone you knew . . ." he paused a moment, "the Andrew James that lived at number 37

Gordon Street died a couple of years ago. Killed in a nasty accident on the M23, sideswiped a lorry and went right off the motorway. He was traveling so fast I doubt he knew too much about it. Car was a shocking mess."

Kelly stared at him. "But he was in New Zealand two weeks ago."

"No, dear, not this Mr. James. He's lying peacefully in the crematorium. That is, if ashes lie peacefully."

"But he can't be," she insisted, her voice rising.

"Look, madam, I'm sure you got the address wrong. Your Mr. James will be lively as a cricket someplace anxiously waiting for you to turn up with his camera. Wish people were as honest round here. Save us a lot of trouble." The young constable grinned, showing eye teeth that made him look like a chummy wolf.

"I know I didn't get the address wrong," she said stubbornly.

"Did he personally give you the address?" She shook her head in response, scattering drops of water on the desk.

"Well, perhaps whoever gave it to you got it wrong. Why don't you give them a call and check?" The sergeant's voice dropped to a steady monotone. Dealing with intractable people was an everyday occurrence.

"I saw the address written down and made a note of it. I'm sure I didn't make a mistake."

"I'm sure you're sure, but it's surprising the things people do. Had a man call us the other day reporting a stolen car. Parked his car every night in front of the house, and when he woke up that morning it was gone. We had the traffic police look out for it. They found the car all right. Parked outside the off-license, right where he'd left it. He drove there, came out with a couple of bottles and walked home. He was pretty sheepish when we told him about it."

"I know I've done some pretty stupid things in my time, but in this case I know I haven't made a mistake about the address. It was too important. I've come a long way to see Mr. James."

The sergeant's heavy eyebrows went up, "I thought I heard you say you were over on a business trip, and were asked to drop off his camera."

Her shoulders sagged, and all her former confidence seemed to have left her. "Sergeant, can I tell you a long story? You aren't going to believe it, but I'll give it a whirl anyway." She looked him right in the eye. "I believe Andrew James committed a murder."

The sergeant remained impassive. Another cuckoo on his hands, but at least this one wasn't confessing to the murder herself, and it was a quiet night. "Why don't you come through and tell me about it, madam." He turned to the young constable, with a half grin hidden from Kelly. "Go and get us a couple of teas will you, Sandy?"

He ushered her into his office, not much larger than a cubicle, and sat down ready to hear the whole story. A few minutes later, Sandy came in and placed a steaming mug of tea in front of her, and she took a grateful sip of the scalding liquid. The sergeant listened intently, not interrupting, but when she was finished said, "I don't see how his giving a false address makes him a murderer. I'm sure you mean well, but it's all a bit farfetched." His kind expression took the sting out of the words. "You say the verdict was death by misadventure. A coroner was satisfied there'd been no foul play and you couldn't get the New Zealand police interested?"

"To tell you the truth, I haven't even tried talking to them. I knew I had to line up a few facts or they would think I was some nut. So I decided to do a little digging and see if I could find something solid to get them interested."

"And you think the British police would be more tolerant of circumstantial accusations, do you? You're making some pretty nasty accusations." His impassive face grew sterner. "Taking the law into your own hands is an offense, madam, even in this country."

"No, I didn't think you would believe me, but you didn't believe the camera story either, so I didn't think I had anything to lose."

His stern face relented. She was beginning to sound like his Katie when she'd been caught out telling lies. "Has it ever occurred to you how dangerous it is, what you're doing? If your theory had been true, you'd have been knocking on the door of a murderer. You should thank your lucky stars there was no one home." He leaned back in his chair and crossed his hands together on the desk. "Does your husband know what you're up to?"

"Am I supposed to get a note from him?" she retorted.

He ignored her remark. "Why don't you leave it with us? We'll see if we can find the elusive Mr. James. You go on home to that beautiful country of yours."

As she got to her feet, her shoes squelched. "Thank you for listening, Sergeant. I knew you'd have a hard time believing it. But tell me, why would someone travel to New Zealand using someone else's identity? They'd only do it if they were trying to cover their tracks."

"Yes, but that's assuming he left the correct address. Maybe he's married and gave a false address so that no one contacted him after the holiday. He might have been up to a bit of hanky-panky. Bit far to go, but you never know with all these frequent flyer points they give you these days. Or he might work for an airline. Whichever, he had a free ticket so he took his secretary along instead of the wife." He looked in the direction of the constable at the desk. "I don't have those temptations with young Sandy out there."

Seeing her look at him with renewed interest, he smiled, his whole face softening. "You see, if you start using your imagination, you can dream up all sorts of things people might do without anyone knowing they were doing it. All perfectly innocent. Fortunately going on holiday with someone other than your wife isn't an offense, or we'd be run off our feet."

As she thanked him and moved towards the door, he looked at her sodden clothes which were starting to steam in the station's warm atmosphere. "And if I were you madam, I'd go right back to your hotel and take a steaming hot bath. I know you came here to catch a murderer, but in my experience it's a whole lot easier to catch a cold in this weather."

At knocking-off time, Sergeant Doyle turned off his terminal and started towards the door, but stopped in mid-stride. Picking up his phone, he punched in some numbers and waited. "Bill, Harry here, fancy a pint? I'm buying." He listened a moment. "Okay, great, see you at the King's Head in twenty minutes."

CHAPTER 19

Bill and Harry had been friends since they were twelve, when Bill's parents moved to Portsmouth. Starting a new school, awkward and quiet, Bill had a hard time making friends. He was tall for his age, and already stooping his broad shoulders to disguise his height. A couple of bullies, threatened by Bill's gangling bulk, decided to plow in and sort him out before he got any ideas. Harry, seeing the rumpus at the end of the school yard, elbowed his way through the ring of boys who were cheering the antagonists on and leaped into the fray. With Harry harassing the bullies like a little terrier, Bill was able to get in a few good shots, and the bullies with bloody noses decided it was time to go and change their library books. Bill, with skinned knuckles and grazed knees, looked down at his scrawny little rescuer and grinned from ear to ear. They'd been firm friends ever since.

They joined the police force together, enjoying the training, and finally had pounded the beat side by side. However, as the years went by they drifted apart. Harry was perfectly happy in the uniform ranks while Bill, big and restless, moved on to CID. They still got together from time to time, but day to day their respectively busy lives left very little opportunity for the close relationship they had enjoyed as youngsters. Faced with the prospect of another evening at home alone, however, Harry had, on an impulse, decided to ask Bill out for a drink. It turned out to be a good idea. Just what he needed after his long boring day.

Their local was comfortably full, not too crowded, but just enough people to provide a steady babble of conversation, a good white noise that meant they could gossip happily about cases without anyone listening in. Harry went over to the bar and picked up another couple of pints of bitter, and watched fascinated as Bill sank half his in one enormous swallow.

"I don't know where you put all that stuff, Bill. If I drank at the rate you do I'd have a gut the size of a whale."

Bill tapped his flat stomach. "It's chasing all those tea leaves, Harry. You should get out from behind your desk more often. Get a bit more exercise."

"Don't you start, mate. It's bad enough with Beryl on my case all the time. All she gives me to eat these days are bean sprouts and yogurt."

"Still on the health kick, is she?" Bill asked.

"Yeah. When she signed up for the French classes I thought the end was in sight. We had some brilliant meals when we took that trip down to Provence a couple of years ago. I could just see the coq au vin, followed by crème brûlée, all topped off by a nice bottle of Chablis." He took a gloomy sip of beer. "Fat chance. Hardly cooks a thing. She's too busy rushing out of the kitchen to hit the books."

"Never mind, mate. Think how healthy you're getting. They'll have to beat you to death when you're ninety." He took a look at the next table where three young men were downing lagers from the bottle and discussing the new girl at the office. Satisfied they wouldn't be eavesdropping, he launched into a long story about an aggravated assault case he was working on. Bill had the knack of turning all his stories into comedies, no matter how gruesome the details. Soon Harry was wiping the tears of laughter from his eyes, the problems of his home life forgotten.

"Tell you what, Bill, you're not the only one who gets some weird cases. Had a woman come in today who reckoned she was on the trail of a murderer from down under."

"Those Aussies been knocking off backpackers again, have they?"

"No, you berk, she was from New Zealand, not Australia. Reckoned this guy had pulled off the perfect crime—totally convinced he's a hit man."

"Where do all these cuckoos come from? I thought we had enough running around the streets in Pompey without starting to import them."

"Funny thing was, she didn't look like one of the regular cuckoos at all. Well-dressed woman in her thirties who works as a software consultant for some big American outfit."

"There you are then, mate, that's it. If she's in the software business she's bound to be nuts. Most of those nerds don't live on this planet."

Annoyed by Bill's arbitrary dismissal of his story, Harry persisted, "It was a way-out story, but she was very convincing. Didn't have a shred of proof other than the fact that the perp was traveling on a false passport, but the story certainly hung together. When she told me about it, she said I wouldn't believe it."

Bill looked speculatively at his friend, "Good-looking bird, was she?"

"Yes, not bad at all. Bit skinny for my taste, but attractive enough."

"There you are then. You're all ticked off with Beryl and then some damsel in distress comes in and spins you a yarn. You'd better watch it, Harry, you'll be getting a dolly bird next."

"I don't fancy her," Harry said a little too emphatically,

"I just thought the story was totally far-fetched. But she was so damned sure, and she'd come all the way to England looking for proof, maybe there is something in it. There's no question she had the name and address of a man who traveled to New Zealand using the identity of a poor sod who was killed in a road accident two years ago."

"Been watching too many of those TV mysteries, if you ask me. The BBC is causing us a lot of grief in CID, everyone reckons they're better at the job than us."

Harry took a deep sup of bitter, and decided to drop the subject.

Bill, perhaps realizing that he might have upset his friend, launched into one of his anecdotes. "Say, Harry, I was talking to an old codger the other day who fought in World War II. He was in the paras, same as your dad. I was buying him a pint trying to get some information out of him so I had to listen to him rattle on for hours about what it was like with the Yanks over here. Well dressed, well paid and stealing all the girls—he said it was all pretty hard to take. But he came up with a good one about an American who had returned from the front and was traveling north on a train. Seems the poor devil got on feeling totally shattered and couldn't find a seat anywhere. Pushed his way through the crowded corridor twice, and finally found a carriage with an upper-crust type woman sitting on one of the seats with her poodle on the next seat. As politely as you like, he asked if she would mind moving the dog.

" 'Certainly not, young man; you Americans have no manners, how dare you suggest you take Mitzi's seat.'

"Disgruntled, he tried one more time pushing his way up the corridor, but still the dog had the only available free seat. So finally he came back to the same carriage, asked one more time politely for the woman to move her dog, and when she wouldn't, he tossed it out of the window and sat down. A very elegantly dressed gentleman sitting opposite, having watched the whole episode, said, 'Really, you Americans are the limit. You can't get anything right. Drive on the wrong side of the road, eat with your fork in your right hand and now you've thrown the wrong bitch out of the window!' "

Harry threw back his head and laughed, causing the young men at the next table to look around. "I knew it was a good idea having a pint with you, Bill. Even your hopeless jokes beat the empty house and tele."

When Bill set off for home, the rain had stopped and the still-wet streets shone beneath the street lights. The air was light and balmy and he was in that contented afterglow left by a few good pints with pleasant company. I really must make the time to see more of Harry, he thought. Did seem a bit steamed up about that Kiwi and her story. Not a bit like him, he's too much of a cynic. After twenty years on the force, you've heard and seen it all. Wonder why? He stepped out in the road to pass an elderly couple walking slowly along, towing an overweight spaniel. Sounded like she was quite an attractive bird. Maybe he's starting to get a wandering eye now that Beryl's so wound up with her classes and stuff. Perhaps old Harry could do with a little more attention from his wife. Somehow, though, he couldn't imagine his friend being interested in another woman; he hadn't shown the mildest interest over the years. Perhaps he really believed the woman. He did seem convinced she was level headed, and she had come all the way to England just to prove a point. Think I'll get the name and address from Harry then give Liam at the Met a bell in the morning. The drug squad might be interested in someone traveling on a phony passport.

CHAPTER 20

Kelly returned to London the next day, glad to leave Portsmouth after her frustrating experience. Arriving in the middle of the afternoon, she decided to call Ginny. "How does tea at Fortnum & Masons sound? I need cheering up, and cream cakes and decadence seems like the right combination."

Ginny gave a deep throaty chuckle. "If you're talking sinful cream cakes, I'm out of here. Meet you there in about half an hour."

Twenty minutes later she pushed her way through the heavy doors of Fortnum & Mason and was engulfed by the wonderful aromas of the food hall. Having a few minutes to spare before she met Ginny, she wandered around admiring the fascinating array of food: wild boar and hare pâté in stone containers, whole smoked salmon, cheeses, cherries in brandy, marmalade with whisky, Scottish shortbreads, mouth-watering pastries, tea in fancy canisters, wine, champagne, caviar, handmade chocolates, glacé fruits. It just went on and on. Reluctantly, she tore herself away and headed for the elevator.

The restaurant on the fourth floor was in a different world. Downstairs the food hall had bustled with people, smelling, tasting, buying, jostling each other as they headed for the restaurants, or the clothes, accessories and antiques floors. Up here, peace reigned. Impeccably dressed waiters and waitresses moved silently among the sparsely populated tables. In the corner an elderly man played show tunes softly on a grand piano. Conversations were subdued and only the chink of china disturbed the peace.

When she explained she was meeting a friend, the head waiter ushered her to a table with a good view of the elevator, although Kelly had a hard time believing Ginny would not be able to find her in the largely deserted restaurant. Ginny swept in a few minutes later clutching her briefcase, her face warm from hurrying along the crowded streets. She sank gratefully down into the comfortable chair. "Phew, what a zoo getting here." Then looking around appreciatively said, "Hey, this was a good idea, even without the cakes."

"How was Portsmouth? Did you run your quarry to ground?"

"Let's order tea first, and then I'll tell you all about it. You look worn out."

"It has been a mite hectic today, and you're right, I could murder a cup of tea. Don't know what it is about England, but tea always seems the right idea."

"It's just the notion of having a china tea pot and a tea strainer that appeals to you," Kelly said, looking around and laughing.

"What's so funny?"

"I bet there isn't a single English person in the restaurant. The next table are Americans for sure because I can hear them talking. The other couple over there are German because the head waiter brought them by here and I could hear their accents, and those three have got to be Spanish."

Ginny looked around. "I think you're right. Although that white-haired lady in the tweedy suit with the younger woman is probably English. 'Course she might be from Boston. So anyway, what shall we have?"

"I'm going to have the afternoon tea. Why don't you have the high tea—it sounds great, and I just saw one of the Welsh rarebits go by. It was incredible. A huge puffy thing."

"I'll go with the afternoon tea too. It sounds good. Sandwiches and decadent cakes, can't beat it. We have to make a decision about what tea to have. Why don't you pick? I've learned to like tea, but I haven't graduated to the more elite brands yet."

"Okay then, Assam it is."

Ginny settled back comfortably in her chair. "So let's have it. How did the master sleuth do?"

"Not too hot, to tell you the truth. Andrew James doesn't live at the address I had so I went along to the local cop shop and told them all about it. It turns out Andrew James who lived at 37 Gordon Street was killed in a road accident about two years ago. So the man that shoved David over the cliff was traveling on a phony passport."

"Not too hot! You're a hard one to please. How on earth did you find out that Andrew James was dead?"

Carefully omitting to talk about her visit to Gordon Street, Kelly recounted the whole tale, throwing in some of her sightseeing as well. "So," she concluded, "I've come to a dead end, if you'll forgive the pun. I feel like an idiot. I've come all this way for nothing. It was a complete waste of time and money."

"No it wasn't. You've got the police interested by the sound of it. If there's anything to it, they'll follow up. And that was your purpose, wasn't it?"

"I think they were just humoring me," Kelly said disconsolately. "It was a dreadful night, I was dripping all over their police station so they gave me a hot cup of tea and let me talk about my troubles. I think it was because I'm a Kiwi. The Brits seem to have a soft spot for us for some reason."

The waitress came by with a laden tray and placed a china tea pot, jug of milk and cups and saucers in front of them. This was followed by an elaborate three-tier contraption displaying sandwiches, scones, jam and cream and an assortment of cakes.

"This is the life," Ginny said. "There's a bunch of things in the U.K. that drive me up the wall. But I tell you what we have a lot to thank them for—afternoon tea. Marvelous."

"Cream or lemon, madam?" Kelly asked, pouring the tea carefully through the strainer. "Note, you ignorant colonial, that when in English polite society you always pour the tea first and add milk or lemon afterwards. Only the lower classes—that's us, mate—put their milk in first."

"Less of the 'ignorant colonial' bit. You Kiwis haven't progressed as far as we have. We at least drink our tea without milk." Grinning, she helped herself to a smoked salmon sandwich and munched contentedly. After a few silent happy moments, she continued, "So you don't think they'll follow up?"

"No, I'll be written off as another crackpot. Think about all the people that go along to the nick and confess to a crime they didn't commit." There was a tinge of despair in her voice.

Ginny said, "Aren't you taking all this a bit too seriously? David wasn't a personal friend, was he?" She took a quick look at Kelly. "You weren't involved with him, were you?"

"No," Kelly said, irritated, "for goodness sakes, he was only in his twenties."

"What's wrong with that. You're a liberated woman, aren't you? If Tina Turner at sixty can live with a younger man, I don't see why you shouldn't. It's about time you started living a bit. I haven't even heard about Richard in a while."

"You're impossible. David was just a thoroughly pleasant person, and no, I wasn't even remotely interested in him in that way. I know the big four-oh is starting to loom on the horizon, but I haven't reached the point of yearning after younger men." As she said it, for some reason John Celini popped into her mind. Pushing that thought firmly away, she continued, "No, it's just that I talked to David's mother, and I saw what hell this is for her. Why should someone get away with cold-blooded murder?" She picked up another sandwich and bit into it with unnecessary force, biting her tongue in the bargain.

Ginny laid a conciliatory hand on Kelly's arm. "Kelly, you're not even one hundred percent sure it is murder. You've got no real facts to go on. You've done everything you can to check on it. Traveling halfway round the world is pretty extreme. You've done your bit. Relax. If there is anything to it, the police will follow up."

"They won't," Kelly said bitterly. "No one will do anything, and whoever it is behind all this will have got away with the perfect crime. It makes me furious."

Ginny, about to tackle an éclair, put down her fork. "This is ridiculous, and you know it. You got into this investigation for no good reason at all. I think you're just trying to fill the void left by Steve. Forget it. Get on with your life."

Kelly straightened in her chair, lifted her chin, ready to lash out at her friend for the cutting remark. Then she grinned, her whole face lighting up. "I am getting to be a pain, aren't I? I think it's the approach of senility, all this getting het up about things. I'll be writing letters to *The Times* next." She paused a moment. "It's your own fault, you know. You have this nasty sympathetic personality. I feel I have to come up with problems."

Ginny smiled back at her. "You're right. I always wanted to be a psychologist, but some idiot told me there was more money in education."

"Were they ever wrong!" Kelly said.

The sunlight filtering through the blinds woke Kelly up, and she opened her eyes slowly, stretched and gave a contented sigh. It was good to be home again. The room was already warm from the morning sun, and when she pulled the blinds she looked out on a sparkling day. Only a few fluffy clouds against an azure backdrop, and the sea a sheet of glass. Over towards the headland a solitary crayfish boat checking its pots was the only hint of energy on the seascape. Seagulls dozed happily on the rocks, and gannets sailed in the thermals, ignoring the rich bounty beneath them. With zero swell, it looked like a perfect fishing day. On an impulse, she picked up the phone, and when Richard answered, said, "Are you game for a spot of fishing today? It looks perfect out there."

"Kelly! You're back. How was the trip?"

"Okay, thanks, but I'm glad to be home."

Richard's voice sounded inordinately pleased, but instead of voicing his pleasure, he said, "Can't manage fishing this morning, I'm afraid. I've got a delivery arriving at eleven. But how about this afternoon? Do you know what the tide is doing?"

"Hang on a minute," Kelly said, walking through to the living room and with phone cradled between ear and shoulder, then rummaged through the *Herald* until she found the tide table. "That would work. It's low tide at three, so we'd have plenty of beach for launching and we'd catch the turn."

"Great, I'll be over about one-thirty. Have you got any bait? I've got a bunch in the freezer so you don't need to worry."

"Thanks, I'd have to go out and buy some. Okay, if you

bring the bait, I'll cook dinner when we get back."

"That's the best offer I've had in weeks. See you this afternoon. You can fill me in on your trip then."

"Oh ye of little faith. We'll be so busy catching fish there won't be any time for conversation."

Putting down the phone, Kelly went outside to find the dog snoring on the deck. "Come on, you lazy mutt. You're supposed to be dashing around ecstatic at your mistress's return. Let's go for a run on the beach."

Ten minutes later she was jogging along the beach, the dog at her side. The early morning beach was deserted, and she ran along the water's edge avoiding the tendrils of the incoming tide. A scattering of shells decorated the firm, golden sand, and her running shoes slapped wetly on patches of wet sand. Oyster catchers had left a trail of empty tua tua shells, and she followed a set of size eleven shoe imprints accompanied by the paws of an overlarge dog. Above the high water mark, a grandiose sandcastle had survived the night. Laughter floated down from one of the holiday homes where a group of four scantily-clad vacationers were enjoying breakfast on the deck. The rest of the holiday homes with curtains drawn stared blind-eyed out to sea, oblivious of the splendid panorama of sand, sea and off-shore islands.

At one-thirty on the dot, Richard's car drew up outside the front door, and looking bronzed and handsome in shorts and T-shirt, he jumped out and came over to give Kelly a welcome home hug. Standing back slightly from her, he said, "You're looking tired. Was it a tough trip?"

"No, no, it was good. It's just long plane trips, they always do me in. I thought a bit of fishing therapy was called for."

"Okay, well let's see if that old tractor of yours will start up and we'll be on our way."

They spent several hours fishing contentedly, chatting occasionally, but mostly concentrating on their lines. By the time they headed back to the bay, cleaned up the boat and filleted the fish, it was early evening. Feeling sun-drenched and happy, Kelly took a shower and, with her hair still clinging damply to her head, set about preparing dinner. Hearing Richard come inside after parking the tractor, she called, "Help yourself to a shower. There's a stack of dry towels in the closet next to the bathroom."

By the time he emerged in clean T-shirt and jeans, she had prepared the fish and rice and was busy chopping onions and peppers.

"Can I do anything useful?" he asked.

"You can open up a bottle of wine. There's one in the fridge. As the sage said, 'I always cook with wine, and sometimes I even add it to the food.' "

Grinning, Richard opened up a bottle of Chardonnay and poured them both a glass. After the meal, they both collapsed in the living room, Kelly sprawled on the sofa, and Richard in one of the leather armchairs. "I've never figured out what it is about fishing that is so exhausting. All I do is sit all afternoon looking at my line, and I'm completely worn out."

"It's got to be the sea air or something, but since you live right on the beach, that's hardly an excuse. Anyway, tell me how you got on on your trip. Did you find out anything about the mysterious Mr. James?"

"No, that turned out to be a dead end. Literally." She told him about her investigations in England, and her discussion with the police sergeant.

"So at least you're growing sensible in your old age," Richard said, relieved. "If you are as bothered as you say you are about the whole thing, let the police handle it."

"I doubt anything will come of it. I'm sure they'll just write me off as another crackpot. So, if I can't get anywhere with Andrew James, I'd better do something about the other two suspects." She sighed. "I really hoped it was going to be him. I hate the idea of having to investigate Mike—he's a sweetie."

Richard looked amused. "You know, I don't think detectives are supposed to care about the suspects. You can't go taking sides. Trying to find evidence against some poor unwitting pom just because you like the other one."

"I'm being totally objective," Kelly said hotly. "Andrew James was acting far more suspiciously than Mike. In fact, Mike hasn't acted suspiciously at all, other than being up on the headland at the same time as David."

"Okay, so your prime suspect turns out to have died two years ago, and you've zero leads to the phony who used his passport. You don't genuinely suspect Mike at all. How about you call the whole thing off, and we have a cup of coffee?"

"The coffee I'll go along with," she said getting to her feet, "but I can't give up yet. The trip to the States convinced me even more: something weird is going on."

"Come on now, Kelly, if Andrew James had been a hit man, he would have followed you up to London and pushed you under one of those big red buses."

"Don't you start making fun of me too."

"Now would I do that? How about I make the coffee as a peace offering?"

Kelly turned on the CD and they sipped contentedly on their coffee and listened to Domingo doing his thing. The light had faded over the ocean and to the west the clouds displayed a brief glorious moment of pinks and reds, then faded away to a grayish dusk. Finishing his coffee, Richard moved over to sit beside her on the sofa and tentatively put an arm around her. Relaxed, she nestled into his shoulder. After a while, he gently bent over and kissed the top of her head. She knew this was the cue for her to turn up her face for a steamy encounter. Sitting there, relaxed and happy, comfortable in his company, it seemed like a pretty good idea. It had been a long time since Steve had died, and there'd been no one. But as he bent over to kiss her, she stiffened, and he immediately released her. "Sorry, Richard, somehow I'm just not ready." Seeing his hurt look, she added, "I know I'm being a pain, and I love your company, but I've a feeling something died along with Steve."

He moved away from her, and took her hand. "Okay, maybe it is too soon. I'm prepared to wait."

Looking at him, handsome, rich and single, she thought, Kelly, my girl, you've got to be nuts.

CHAPTER 21

Looking around the restaurant, Kelly felt glad she had accepted the invitation to Lindsay's birthday party. Everyone was in high spirits, and there was a constant babble of conversation, while the wooden floors of the spacious restaurant gleamed and the open flaming ovens provided a warm and comfortable ambiance. After working under pressure for weeks, none of the team was taking the opportunity to relax lightly. While Lindsay, looking pink and pleased, presided at the head of the table, Kelly found herself sitting between Carol and John Celini, with Colin and Angus opposite.

As the evening wore on, and more wine and beer were consumed, the level of voices grew higher. In contrast, John's soft Midwestern accent was soothing, and Kelly found herself talking to him more and more. He was obviously enjoying himself in Auckland, but she could tell by the eagerness with which he asked her about her trip to California he was suffering from a mild bout of homesickness. They were soon talking about all things Californian: San Francisco restaurants, golf at Pebble Beach, the Monterey Aquarium, skiing at Tahoe, the Napa Valley wine district, Bear Valley, the religious hush of the giant redwoods and the freezing Santa Cruz ocean. The discussion of Napa Valley naturally led to New Zealand wines, and Kelly became animated as she sang the praises of several outstanding wines she had drunk recently. Having spent time in the States enjoying the Californian wines, and French wine on her U.K. trip, she felt strongly that New Zealand wines ranked among the world's best.

"Is that right?" John asked, his brown eyes on her. "I've tried a few, but I really don't know what I'm drinking. They all taste pretty good, but I just pick up whatever's on special at the supermarket, and when I'm in restaurants I go for whatever is the mid-range price."

"That's probably as good a way as any to go, but believe you me if you just do a little research, you can drink some fantastic wines for mighty reasonable prices."

"So how do you go about doing research on wines other than drink yourself silly trying them all? Not that that sounds such a terrible way to go," he added with his slow smile.

"You can buy a wine guide—that will cost you under ten bucks U.S.—and you make up the cost in no time. Those guys know what they're talking about. And, of course, you can go tasting in the wine districts. That's great fun."

"You mean there's more than one district? The only one I have ever heard of is Marlborough. That's Cloudy Bay and Sauvignon Blanc," he said, looking pleased with his knowledge.

"Believe it or not there are a lot of districts. Hawkes Bay—that's on the East Coast, Martinborough—down near Wellington, and of course Auckland—which is just twenty minutes down the road. Then there are oodles of smaller ones like Canterbury, and the ones near Queenstown. It's really good fun going sampling. Steve and I used to do it quite a bit. The wineries are all fairly small, and they are prepared to spend a lot of time with you, explaining the winemaking process and their vintages."

"That sounds great. How about taking me on a tour this Saturday? You're going to be down all week, aren't you?"

"Okay," Kelly answered impulsively, "you're on. I'll drive and you can sample."

When it came time to leave, they all moved outside where a cold wind blowing in off the harbor made them hunch against the cold, wishing they had brought jackets. As they walked across to the parked cars, John said to Carol, "I'll give Kelly a lift back, Carol, she's right on my way home." And in response to her dubious look, "And I only had one glass of wine, so don't look like my mother."

Kelly, not used to being bundled around like merchandise, grinned at Carol, and followed John to his car and got in. Outside her motel, he pulled over and switched off the engine. As she prepared to get out, he put a hand on her arm. "I've enjoyed this evening, Kelly. It was good talking to you. You're such a comfortable person to be with."

Oh God, Kelly thought, why does being comfortable make me seem dumpy and middle-aged? I suppose ten years difference in his eyes does make me an old woman. She suppressed a sigh, then looking across at him as she prepared to say goodnight, she noticed the way he was looking at her. If he looked at his mother that way, that would be incest.

The next morning, intent on finding out some more about Mike's financial situation, she dropped by his office and asked him if he and Cathy would like to go out to dinner. He looked at her blankly for a moment, his mind a million miles away, and she added, "Remember when you invited me to the barbecue, I promised to take you both out."

His face broke into an engaging grin. "That would be great. Let me check with Cathy and see if we can get a babysitter. Wednesday would be good for me if that works for you."

* * * * *

On Wednesday night they met at a Thai restaurant in Newmarket. Cathy kissed Kelly lightly on the cheek, her lips soft and gentle, and then settled into her seat like a fairy princess ready to preside at a feast. As Mike sat down, his shirt bulged just above the waist, exposing a small sliver of freckled belly.

Kelly looked around. "This was a nice idea, Cathy. I've never been here before."

"It's one of our favorites," Cathy said. "Not that we get out often. While Gavin is this young, it's difficult to get out much."

"Is it a problem finding sitters?"

"There are plenty around, but most of them are hopeless. They've no idea how to entertain a two-year-old. They just want to plunk him in bed and get on with their homework, or watch TV."

Kelly tried to stop her eyebrows rising. Entertaining young Gavin would be a problem if his behavior at the barbecue was anything to go by, but by the way the pair of them glowed at just the mention of his name, she could see they regarded him as perfect. "He's a gorgeous looking little boy," she commented. "Are there many children for him to play with in the area?"

"No," Cathy replied, "that's a problem; very few people with young families seem to be able to afford our area. Most of the other children are at school."

"How long have you lived there?" Kelly asked casually, making a big display of unfolding her napkin and placing it on her lap.

"We moved in about nine months ago, didn't we, Mike? Hard to imagine where the time has gone. Getting the garden fixed up has taken quite a while. It's amazing how expensive it gets once you start buying plants and trees."

"You must have some pretty hefty repayments to cope with too. It's a great-looking house."

"Oh no," Cathy replied ingenuously, "we bought the house with cash so we don't have to worry about monthly payments."

"Fat chance we'd have of managing those on my salary," Mike grinned.

Kelly was momentarily stopped in her tracks. She intended to dig into their financial situation to see how he was supporting his high standard of living, but it had never occurred to her that they might have bought their house all cash. But if they had, where had the cash come from? Around them the restaurant was filling quickly and there were two couples waiting to be seated. From the kitchen she could hear the clatter of dishes. "Whew, I'm impressed. It took Steve and me years to save up for our first house. You must have won lotto, or are you regulars at the casino?" She kept her tone flippant.

Mike spoke quickly, before Cathy could say anything, his tone echoing Kelly's, "Something like that. Actually," he added confidentially, "Cathy found a pot of gold at the end of a rainbow."

Looking at the fey woman, Kelly could almost believe it. "I hope that food's going to arrive soon. If it tastes anywhere near as good as it smells, I'm going to eat myself silly," she said, diplomatically changing the subject. "Of course, that means I'll have to go running tomorrow, but what the heck."

"Do you go running?" Cathy asked as if that was an extraordinary pastime.

"Yes, about ten kilometers three times a week. Sometimes more if I start putting on weight. How do you manage to stay so slim if you don't run? Do you go to the gym?"

"No, I'm into yoga." She launched into a long, earnest discourse on the peace of mind you can achieve by practicing yoga. Kelly listened with half an ear, smiling in all the appropriate places. Mike had acquired, or been given, a large sum of money relatively recently. Her mind shied away from the implications. Someone could have paid him to get rid of David.

"Are you okay, Kelly?" Mike asked. "You look a little pale."

She smiled weakly, "No, I'm fine. Just hungry I think. I haven't had anything since breakfast and that seems a long time ago." At that moment the waitress arrived with the first of the dishes and she was spared further comment.

They passed a pleasant evening, Mike and Cathy talking about a trip to Great Barrier Island on their boat. Then the conversation turned to the house once more, and the time it was taking to get the garden in shape. Finally, Kelly managed to steer the conversation back to work by telling Cathy what a wonderful job Mike was doing. Cathy, vaguely bemused, clearly having no real idea how Mike spent his days, smiled fondly at him, "Oh, I'm sure he does a brilliant job. He works such long hours. I hope it's going to let up soon. You've no idea how difficult it is coping with Gavin in the evenings after I've had him all day. I need Mike at home more."

"It won't be too long now, Cathy," Kelly said reassuringly. "If it hadn't been for losing David, we'd be a lot further on." A loud clatter of dishes, and some hastily muffled exclamations from the kitchen, caused everyone's head to turn, but since no irate chef with a knife or a crestfallen waitress came dashing out, everyone relaxed, and the level of dinner conversation filled the restaurant once more.

Cathy looked upset at the mention of David's name. "That was awful. He was so nice."

Mike scowled irritably, "It hasn't made that much difference losing him off the project. He wasn't anywhere near as marvelous as everyone seemed to think. John Celini seems to be picking up right where he left off without any trouble, so he wasn't any kind of genius."

"It was awful though, Mike," Kelly said smiling sympathetically at Cathy, "everyone misses him." She looked directly at Mike. "Do you really think John is as good?"

"Absolutely. I think he's going to bring us home right on time."

"That's encouraging news. I really thought for a while there that David was irreplaceable. If you think he's good, I'm relieved." But as she intentionally flattered Mike, she was troubled. Unexplained money landing in his lap, and still with a chip on his shoulder where David was concerned. It didn't look good.

Bill Robson picked up the phone and called a friend of his in the Met. Harry's story from the night before, about some nutty woman who had traveled all the way from New Zealand to try and track down a murderer, had refused to go away in the night. He was a great believer in sleeping on it. Over the years he'd made a lot of progress in murder investigations by letting his subconscious do the work in the night. Just line up a lot of silly bits and pieces and instead of worrying them to death, or chasing one piece or another, he'd turn in early and in nine times out of ten he had an answer in the morning. Not, he admitted to himself, that the answers were necessarily major breakthroughs, but they had often led to some good clear thinking and some nice lines of inquiry.

Harry had been uncertain about it, and Harry was the world's biggest cynic when it came to con artists and nutters. He could pick them at a thousand yards, but here he was half convinced the woman was telling the truth. As he brushed his teeth he came to a decision; he'd call up his friend Liam in the Drug Squad. The one solid fact Harry had to go on was that someone had traveled to New Zealand and had used the name and address of a person who died two years ago. That smacked of phony passports, and in his experience the biggest customers for phony passports were the drug transporters. Liam just might be interested, and if he wasn't, so what, it would only take five minutes.

Liam Murphy's answer machine told him in a broad West of England accent that he was, "Out right now but if you leave a message after the beep, I'll get back to you as soon as I return."

Bill left his name and a short message saying that it was non-urgent, then set about his day's work.

It was five-thirty when Liam returned his call. "Bill," he exclaimed genially, "long time no see. You should come up to the city once in a while, and I could show you how real detectives work."

"Thanks, old son, but last time I read your statistics, I recommended all the crims from Pompey move up to London. It would be safer for them."

"So how have you been? They keeping you busy? See Pompey still hasn't a clue how to play football," he chuckled, enjoying rattling Bill's chain. Then to rub it in, "The gunners are doing great this season. I've got season tickets and actually managed to get to two matches this year. It was fun. I'm thinking of becoming a postman so that I can get away more often."

"You'd die of boredom in a month if you had to leave all

that undercover stuff behind. I've often thought the reason you guys do it is that you're frustrated actors. You all like dressing up and pretending you're someone else."

"Anyway, Bill, old son, I'm sure you didn't call just for a chat. What's up?"

"I learned something yesterday that I thought you might be interested in. Probably nothing, but you never know. Some woman from New Zealand dropped in the cop shop here looking for a man who was killed in an accident two years ago."

"Blimey, those Kiwis are a bit slow, aren't they? Didn't she miss him before?"

Ignoring the facetious comment, Bill continued, "Some English guy visiting Auckland gave his home address as 37 Gordon Street—and it turns out the man of the same name who lived at that address was killed two years ago in an accident. Sounds to me as if someone is picking up news clippings about people killed in accidents then using their name and address on counterfeit passports. And if the stuff that happens down here is anything to go by, the drug runners would be the biggest customers. It was a Portsmouth address, but I very much doubt he has any Portsmouth connections. Much more likely to be your lot."

Liam's voice quickened, "Okay, give me that name and address again, and I'll run a check. Did she give any other information that would be useful?"

"No, just said he was slim and fit, medium height, sandy-colored hair, spoke with a clipped English accent. The thing that made him stick in the Kiwis' minds was that he was a pale face."

"Not too helpful, but never mind. I'll see if anyone's interested, and give you a bell if I find anything out. Cheers." Without further ado, Liam hung up.

* * * * *

Liam pushed his chair back and started off down the corridor and swung easily through the door of an office on the left. Without bothering to knock, he walked in, pushed some papers off the corner of an empty desk and sat down, totally ignoring the fact that the owner of the office was deep in what sounded like a very personal conversation. He waited, listening unabashedly, while the other man swung round in his chair, presenting his back to him, and tried to talk without being overheard. When he had finished his conversation, he replaced the receiver with a frown and then turned his attention to the intruder. “What the hell do you want?”

“And I’m delighted to see you too, Brian, me lad. I take it the little bit on the side is not working out too well.”

“Mind your own damn business,” Brian retorted. “What do you want anyway? Somehow I doubt this is a social call.”

“And here I am trying to be helpful. You’ve got some deal going with a bunch of international drug runners, haven’t you?”

Brian’s irritation dropped visibly, and his gray eyes were all attention. “Yeah, it’s an interesting one, this. Have a couple of locals who were squeezed out by the big boys, but instead of curling up their toes and retiring to the country on their ill-gotten gains, they decided to make one more play for the big time. Got quite an operation going. So what do you have?”

“Some bird from New Zealand was trying to trace a bloke who had been there on vacation, and she dropped into the local cop shop down in Pompey to ask about him when he wasn’t at the address she was given. Friend of mine down in Pompey gave me a bell, he figured someone was producing phony passports using the name of people pushing up daisies. He's a pretty smart bloke—figured it had to be a drug runner."

"You mean to say she came all the way from New Zealand to follow some man who had a fling with her on vacation?" Brian's eyebrows went up. "Either he's some sort of Romeo, or he left her up the duff."

"No, that was the weird bit. She's convinced he did a murder down there. Had a real cock-and-bull story to back it up. That's probably a bunch of cobblers, but fact is, he was traveling on a phony passport."

Brian rubbed his chin with a bony hand. "Could be something in it, you know. The couple of entrepreneurs we're watching do include New Zealand in their empire." He grinned suddenly, "You've got to hand it to them. Talk about thinking big. They're moving stuff between London, Singapore, Auckland, Sydney, L.A. and back to London. In case you haven't noticed, that's an airline route. You can get some great deals on round-the-world tickets these days. Just as long as you keep heading east, or west as the case may be."

"So?" Liam shifted his weight. The corner of the desk was poking him in the rear.

"Well, they've set all these people up who take off on great vacations all expenses paid. Only have to do one small thing, and that's carry a little something from country to country. Specialty drugs come from all different places these days now that everyone's got a chemical lab in their back porch. The beauty of the whole scheme is that the airline baggage handlers are in on it. They make sure the bags containing the stash never go through customs."

Liam whistled, "Impressive. So they could be setting up their runners with different passports so that Immigration doesn't catch on that these women carrying babies and men in Hawaiian shirts are taking several vacations a year."

"You're not so thick for a country lad, are you? That's exactly it. Problem we've got is proving it. We can pick up the runners, but we haven't been able to get anything on our two entrepreneurs yet. We've got several of the runners under surveillance, but no joy yet."

Liam dug in his shirt pocket and came up with a crumpled scrap of paper. "Here's the name and address of the Portsmouth corpse. Well, not that he's living there now, but that was his home till he had an argument with a lorry on the M3."

"Thanks, Liam. I think I'll give that woman a bell. You never know. Probably won't get us anywhere but we're due a break."

CHAPTER 22

Saturday turned out to be one of those wonderful Auckland days: sparkling sunshine, a light breeze, and fluffy white clouds floating across a flawless blue sky. Getting into her car, Kelly realized she was looking forward to a day's wine tasting. It had been almost two years since she and Steve had toured the South Island wineries. Steve loved it. It was his idea of the perfect vacation: friendly wineries and magnificent scenery, and of course they played some golf along the way just to kid themselves they weren't only interested in the wine. It had been a marvelous three weeks. They'd started off in the Canterbury region taking a leisurely drive out of Christchurch to Giesens, where they had been dismayed to find they had run into a group of buyers from across the Tasman. They decided to sample quickly and be on their way, but the friendly woman behind the counter insisted they move out into the sun-dappled garden, and she followed them with a tray of bottles. Their wine sampling turned into a delightful conversation in the shade of a giant tree.

And that was the way it went throughout their vacation. Friendly wineries where they were invited by the winemaker to come back to where the huge barrels lay fermenting to see how the wine was made, picnics under the trees, long dusty roads flanked by row upon row of vines stretching across the pebbly soil of the Wairau Plains. Following the sign post to a winery beside the spectacular Kawerau Gorge, resulting in a nail-biting drive perilously close to a sheer drop to the gorge below, but being rewarded at the end by a magnificently situated vineyard set on a ledge seventy meters above the gorge, with an uninterrupted view to Coronet Peak. Climbing Mount Aspiring Road to stand spellbound in the Rippon Vineyard, glass of Pinot Noir in hand, looking at the rows of vines stretching down to the shores of Lake Wanaka below, and beyond the blue water view of the lake, the majestic snow- and cloud-capped peaks of the Buchanan Range in the Southern Alps. The memories were all of outstanding wines, convivial company and magnificent views. Oh, and of course, she reflected as she pulled up outside John's apartment, the golf was pretty good too.

He was already on the sidewalk waiting for her. Slipping quickly into the passenger seat, he said, "Good morning, great day," then looking at her closely, added, "you look happy. It suits you."

She smiled back at him, "I was just remembering our wine-tasting tour of South Island. It was great."

"Well, if it makes you look that good, let's get at these wineries." He settled in and clipped his seat belt. "Is it far? Can we stop off for a coffee or something along the way?"

She laughed, "It's a whole twenty minutes to Kumeu. This is New Zealand, fella. We've got everything here right on the doorstep."

"So where are you going to hide vine-clad slopes so close to the city?"

"We take a fifteen-minute drive along the motorway, and then believe it or not you're in the country. Why don't you flip the radio on and we'll listen to music while we drive, or there are a bunch of CDs if you prefer." She was interested to see what type of music he would go for; she picked him for a country-western fan for driving, with rock for the rest.

When he tuned into the classics station, her eyebrows went up, but she said nothing. Somehow she had the feeling this was going to be a good day.

They were soon driving along State Highway 16, a narrow two-way road that wound through pretty rural countryside. She decided to visit just a few vineyards to give him a feel for the fun of wine tasting. He could then bring his girlfriend, or whoever, out here later. For no reason at all, she felt a vague disquiet at the thought of him with another woman.

As they drew up outside Kumeu River, she said, "You're going to love the wines here. This was originally set up by the early Dalmatian settlers. Way back the Dalmatians worked the gum fields up in the north, then when the gum fields were stripped, they moved down to Auckland and set up wineries and market gardens. We owe a lot to those guys."

He seemed to enjoy the charming atmosphere of Coopers Creek, tucked unobtrusively away beside the main highway, and stocked up with a few more bottles of wine. As he explained to Kelly, it was the least he could do since they were all so helpful answering his questions and pouring generous samples. She agreed that it made far more sense than going home and buying it from the supermarket.

After that, they went back to the small village of Huapai and bought fresh bread, cheese, sausage, fruit, flaky apple turnovers and some bottled water. "We're going on a picnic?" John asked, puzzled. "I thought we were wine tasting. Not that I've any objection," he added hastily. "Drinking wine makes me hungry. I'm more than ready to eat."

They drove up to the handsome Matua Valley winery, set on a knoll overlooking vine-clad slopes, and spread their food out on a table under the shade of a large tree. Lunch turned out to be a lot of fun. They were both hungry and the food turned into a feast. Quiet and sensitive most of the time, today John was in hyper mood, and his quick wit and sense of the absurd appealed to Kelly's warped sense of humor. She found she was laughing more than she had for a long time. While she was still laughing, he grew very still, leaned across the table and laid his hand lightly over hers. "You look fantastic when you laugh. I think you should do it more often."

Laughter dying immediately, she drew her hand away and began to pack up the remains of the picnic. She was a private person and wasn't sure she was ready to be analyzed by this young American. "Thank you," she accepted what she assumed was a compliment gracefully, "but then you only see me at work where I'm trying to impress everyone as to what an important consultant I am."

He grinned, understanding only too well consulting with a small software company was minor league compared with her previous job with Finsat. "You were quite a big wheel with Finsat, weren't you? How come you left?"

How did he know what she used to do, Kelly wondered? Had he been checking up on her? "We decided we'd had enough of the rat race and decided to escape down here. It was great while it lasted." Getting up quickly to curtail any more questions, she gathered up the empty packets and walked over to the waste bin. By the time she returned to the table, he had picked up the remains of the cheese and fruit, and was ready to head for the car. He didn't ask for an explanation of her last statement, apparently picking up on the strong indication that further prying into her private life was unwelcome.

They drove back into the city chatting occasionally, but

mostly listening to the classic station. Kelly pulled up outside his apartment and said, "Okay, sir, end of the line, this is where you disembark."

He unclipped his seat belt and swung round in the seat to face her. "Thanks, Kelly, that was a blast. Would you like to come up for a coffee?"

"No, no thanks. I'd like to do a spot of shopping this afternoon. Living up in the boonies I don't do too much shopping other than for groceries so when I have a spare few hours I like to catch up."

He made no move to get out of the car, but instead said, "Well, how about dinner tonight? It's the least I can do for you after driving me all around. You didn't even get to sample much."

She tried to think of a plausible reason for turning him down, but he already knew she was staying overnight, and after all, she needed to eat dinner. "I had in mind an evening with my feet up in front of TV, to tell you the truth."

"Come on now, that's what little old ladies do. Let's have dinner together, and this time I'll drive so that you can enjoy a glass of wine. Lindsay was telling me about a new place that's just opened up—I think we should try it."

Dinner with a bottle of wine and pleasant company was appealing. "Okay, it sounds good. Want to pick me up about seven? You know where I'm staying." She had a feeling for some odd reason that she was going to regret the decision.

He beamed at her, got out of the car, leaned back through the open window and said, "See you at seven."

The new restaurant turned out to be good, although service was on the slow side, but with John there were no awkward silences, and Kelly found that she was enjoying herself more than she had in a long time. While they waited for the main course to arrive, she asked him about his parents. Once she was comfortable with a person, she tended to do this. Having her parents die in a car crash when she was in her teens made her intensely curious about what life would have been like living with parents once you were an adult.

John smiled, his brown eyes growing warm as he told her about his father. "He's great. He was wonderful when I was growing up, taking me to ball games, going camping, and we still get along now. Not that he says much. Talking's not his strong suit. All I can ever get him to talk about is sports." He laughed affectionately.

He stopped talking as he pulled his chair in closer to the table to let an amply built couple squeeze by, then continued, "But my mother is something else. Never stops. Always doing something. She's on God knows how many committees, and the only TV she watches is Peter Jennings reading the news, and the occasional PBS drama. Reads constantly, and I swear she knew more about my masters thesis than I did."

"They sound quite a combination."

"He drives her nuts with his lack of ambition, but they've been married forever. They're great parents."

Kelly raised her voice slightly to be heard over the noise of a foursome at the next table, "Do you have any brothers and sisters?"

"No, I'm an only child, but I've a bunch of cousins so I was never lonely. We're a Catholic family so all the cousins came from full households."

"Sounds chaotic. Do you all get along?"

"All the younger family do, but my mother seems to have some problem with my Uncle Tony, which she won't talk about." He took a sip of iced water. "I can't understand it. He's a real neat guy. In fact, he was the one that helped me get started with a software contract house. I was all set to go to IBM right out of college and he opened up the possibilities for me. I ended up making about twice what I'd have made with IBM. It was a great suggestion. My mother nearly went bananas. She'd always told me not to have anything to do with Uncle Tony."

"Why? Was he the black sheep of the family, or something?"

"I've no idea. She never would say," he answered, his relaxed tone changing.

"Sounds like he was a bad 'un," Kelly pressed, trying hard to appear disinterested. Uncle Tony sounded like he could be mixed up in something dicey.

"No, I don't think so; he's been really good to me. Probably some old family feud," he said dismissively.

After dinner he drove her back to her motel, and insisted on escorting her to the door. "Come on, John, it's only a few yards to the door."

"Where I grew up, young woman, gentleman were always compelled to escort their dates right to the door. That's what my mother always used to say anyway," he said, getting out of the car and curtailing the discussion.

As they walked across the road together, Kelly said, "I've enjoyed today John. It was fun."

"Great," he said enthusiastically. "How about tomorrow? Want to take me over to Waiheke Island to check the vineyards there? We could take a picnic along."

Mildly taken aback, Kelly answered, "No, sorry, I really must be getting back. I've a lot to do at home."

"Oh come on, one more day won't make a difference. You should take pity on a poor lonely tourist," his tone was bantering, but there was no question he was serious.

Kelly led the way up the steps to the motel door and took out her key. "No, really, John, I can't stay down another day, and anyway you should be going out with some of the gang from work, they're far more your age." She stopped, key in hand, and added, "Mike would probably take you out on his boat if you asked. The Hauraki Gulf's beautiful, and chances are he'd take you over to Rangitoto so you could go climbing up a volcano. Think how impressed the folks back home would be." Without waiting for his reply, she leaned over and kissed him lightly on the cheek. "Good night, and thanks again."

As she turned to put her key in the door, he grasped her wrist lightly and swung her round. "Kelly, I don't want to go out with anyone other than you." He looked deep into her eyes, and pulled her to him, kissing her lightly at first, then with increasing urgency. Taken totally by surprise, Kelly stood immobile for a long moment, then in spite of herself found she was responding to his kisses. For several minutes they stood locked in an increasingly heavy embrace until Kelly pulled away, and said in a shaky voice, "No, John, this is ridiculous. I'm old enough to be your mother." She opened the door, stepped decisively inside and closed it gently in his face. Once the door was closed, she stood, face pressed to the painted wood for a long time.

When Kelly returned home, the answer phone was blinking. Tossing her bag on the desk, she hit the playback button. A message from the vet reminding her that Riggles was due his booster shots, a message from Sally asking her to call as soon as she got back, a call from the local pharmacy saying a courier package had arrived for her, one from Richard and one from London asking her to call Brian Davis collect when she returned, the caller politely reminding her there was a twelve-hour time difference. She checked her watch. No point calling England in the middle of the afternoon; whoever Brian Davis was, he wouldn't appreciate being awakened at three-thirty a.m. She'd no idea who he was, but assumed he must be a friend of Mark and Ginny coming on a trip and needing some advice on things to do and places to go.

After dinner, she decided it was late enough to call Brian Davis. She was surprised when she dialed to find she was talking to the Metropolitan Police in London. She immediately felt guilty. She couldn't imagine what she'd done though, unless a speed camera had caught her somewhere, although an international phone call seemed a bit over the top. There was a moment's delay while they checked, and then she was talking to Brian Davis. "This is Kelly Brandon, you left a message asking me to give you a call."

"Yes, madam, I understand you were in England recently making some inquiries about an Andrew James who lived at 37 Gordon Street, Portsmouth."

"Yes," Kelly replied guardedly.

"Is he a relative of yours?"

"No."

"A friend perhaps?"

"No."

"Why did you make inquiries about him at a Portsmouth police station?"

"I'm sure you know why, or you wouldn't be calling me." Kelly was getting steadily ticked off by this interrogation.

"You're perfectly correct. It was an interesting story. Would you mind repeating it for me please, madam?"

"I'll be glad to for what it's worth, but I wish you would stop calling me madam. I'm beginning to feel like I run a bordello."

There was a deep, throaty, most un-CID like chuckle at the other end of the line. As she repeated her story, he listened silently without interrupting, then when she was finished asked, "And you came all the way to England to check up on him?"

"That's right."

"Why didn't you go to the New Zealand police?"

"As I explained to the sergeant in Portsmouth, I didn't have enough facts. I didn't think they would believe me."

"And you think we are more gullible?"

"No," she said emphatically, voicing her irritation, "I didn't expect anyone to believe me without some facts to back up what I'm saying. That's why I made the trip."

"Bit expensive, wasn't it? Or are you a private investigator or something?"

"Good heavens no. To tell you the truth it wasn't particularly expensive. Finsat, the company I consult for in the States, paid my fare to San Francisco, and it was less than a thousand dollars to add on the London trip."

"Well, you managed to convince the police sergeant, and he passed the information on to me. Tell me a bit more about that software company you work for."

Relaxing slightly, Kelly told him about the project and the events leading up to David's death. After asking her several more questions, he appeared satisfied that she was on the level, and told her he was investigating the illegal passport trade. He had been watching a group for several months who used the names of people killed in car accidents. Since the press conveniently provided names, age, location and frequently photos as well, it was a perfect setup. Forged passports were produced using the victim's name, general description and place of birth. Since the victim would not be traveling, it was a safe method.

"When you turned up asking questions about someone who no longer exists, it was a stroke of luck from our point of view. We're trying to get to the source of these passports, and just maybe this character can give us a lead. You said in your original statement that he was of medium height, slightly built and with sandy-colored hair, is that correct?"

"Yes."

"You also mentioned he was very fit. How did you know that? Was he well built? Looked like a weightlifter maybe?"

"No, nothing like that. It was just that the men who followed him up on to the headland, which is about fifteen hundred feet and a very tough climb, were pig hunters. I doubt you have too many pig hunters running around in London so I should explain they go hunting on foot in very rugged terrain. The dogs get the scent of a pig, and the hunters follow the dog. Since the pig is being chased it doesn't care about where it runs, so these men end up practically running in incredibly steep terrain. They literally haul themselves up in some spots by grabbing on to the roots of trees or any sort of bush that will take their weight. So if you're a pig hunter, you're generally fit."

"So, how did that lead you to believe this Andrew James was fit?"

"Simply because the pig hunters had a hard time keeping up with him when he climbed the headland. They were shattered. They thought they were following some pale-faced wimp and all of a sudden they were being left behind. They figured he belonged to the drug squad. The pig hunters were pot growers, by the way."

Pulling in his stomach, Brian just managed to stop himself making some slick comment about how fit they all were in the drug squad. He hadn't enlightened her as to his role as yet. Illegal passport trade was enough for now. "Okay, that makes sense. Can you tell me anything else about him?"

"Not really. The only other thing that struck me when I was asking about him at the Sheraton was that nobody remembered anything about him. He seemed to have been a very anonymous sort of character."

"So you made inquiries at the Sheraton about him, did you? You've been a busy lady."

"That's how I got his address," Kelly retorted angrily.

"Smart thinking," he said. "I'll see if we can sign you up after all this. Tell me, anything else?"

"There's just one other thing," Kelly hesitated a moment, feeling foolish mentioning it. "Two people I talked to mentioned his eyes. The shopkeeper said he remembered him having gray eyes, and he said his eyes didn't smile, which I thought was a pretty strange comment coming from the most unpoetic-looking man you can imagine. Then the bellhop at the hotel said his eyes were dead, gave him the creeps."

"You've been very helpful. I wish our other witnesses were as observant as you are. What I'm going to do now is put together an identikit and shoot it out to some of the other offices, see if it rings a bell. Thank you, we'll be in touch."

Chapter 23

Brian Davis sat back in his chair with a self-satisfied sigh and tapped his empty shirt pocket before remembering he'd given up smoking. Right now a celebratory cigarette would go down well. Against all the odds, the identikit and fax he put together from Kelly's information had done the trick. Working on the assumption that Andrew James had a record, he distributed his description to all the police stations in Greater London and Surrey. Three possibilities had surfaced, all fitting the general description. Of the three, one was currently locked up behind bars in the Scrubs. Another was a petty criminal called Todd Miller who had been in and out of the nick for years. Brian looked up the data on him, but somehow he couldn't see him fitting the bill. All his crimes had been minor and seemed to be marked by a complete lack of imagination. No self-respecting drug runner would put him on the international circuit. The third, Georgie Small, was a more likely candidate. So he started there.

Between the central database and a lot of phone calls, he knew a great deal about Georgie Small by the end of the day. Georgie had started out young, and by the time he was seventeen had been picked up several times for joy riding in cars, stealing from small retail shops, and was finally sent to Borstal after an innovative but unsuccessful attempt to grab the takings from a small clothing factory. The attempt would have succeeded if his partner in crime hadn't panicked when a security guard turned up, stood rooted to the spot until he was caught, then blurted out everything. Georgie, who had taken off at the first sign of trouble, reasoning they could always do it the next week, was picked up the next day. His spell in Borstal simply served as a training ground for more sophisticated crime, and six months after he was released, he was jailed for a year. After his release, his file had been clean for fifteen years.

From all the evidence it would appear that Georgie Small had learned his lesson and was now a God-fearing citizen. However, a call from a uniformed desk sergeant late in the day made him change his mind.

"Have you found the man you're looking for yet? I saw the description you put out a few days ago."

"No, not so far, although I've got a couple of possibilities," Brian said warily. The sergeant sounded like one of the old school, and he wasn't sure where this conversation was going.

The sergeant gave a satisfied grunt. "Sounds like Georgie Small to me. Haven't heard that young tow rag's name in years. What happened to him? He was an interesting little character—much brighter than the usual dimwits. I always knew he'd end up big time. So I'm curious, what have CID got on him?"

Brian put a finger to his left ear to block out the noise from the adjoining office. "Why do you think it's Georgie Small?"

The sergeant hesitated a moment, then measuring his words carefully said, "General description fits. Though it could fit half the population, but it's the eyes that did it. Never seen anything like that little character. Even when he was sixteen he would look at me and give me the chills."

Trying to hide the excitement in his voice, Brian asked, "So what else can you tell me about him?"

The sergeant's voice smiled, "He was a charmer when he wanted to be, and he got a lot of attention in Borstal. He was so intelligent they thought they could turn him into a model citizen. You know how those psychologists are, everyone can be reformed, it was because their mother didn't love them or some such cobblers they turned to crime. Most of the young crims I know are all set for a life of crime whatever you do." He paused, as though remembering. "I have to admit though Georgie was different, and there was a big push on at the time to find ways of preventing young offenders from becoming habitual criminals."

"So what happened?" Brian prompted. "Did it work? Apart from one lapse he seems to have been clean for a long time."

"The psychologists gave him a glowing report. Congratulated themselves no end on the fine job they'd done. They must have looked pretty silly when he was tossed in the slammer six months later."

"Why don't you think he went straight after that? Maybe a year in real prison made him realize being a crim wasn't such a hot idea. You said he was a smart one. Wouldn't it occur to a young man that it would be more fun on the outside than cooped up with a lot of old lags?"

"Yes," the sergeant answered dubiously, "but it doesn't work that way too often. The smart ones spend their time inside learning their trade, and they come out pretty proficient criminals. It's sort of a graduation course. You go in an amateur and come out a pro."

Brian doodled on his desk pad as he spoke, "God, you're a cynic, mate. I thought I was bad enough."

"My money's on the sure bet. Call around and see if you can track him down. If he's turned into an honest citizen that should be easy. He'll be a registered voter and a taxpayer. Course if you can't track him down, he's changed his name and is still busy at it, but far too smart to get caught. Let me know will you? I had a sneaking admiration for young Georgie—figured he'd either straighten out and do very well, or if he stayed a crim, he'd be in the big time. I'm interested to know what he did."

It was several days before Brian could get back to locating Georgie Small. He had a pile of work to do, and no solid reason for working on Kelly's theory. Sitting in the cafeteria tackling a huge plate of sausage, egg and chips liberally laced with ketchup, he was joined by two other members of the drug squad. After a brief greeting, all three men applied themselves enthusiastically to their laden plates. Brian pushed back his plate, stirred his tea and looked at the other two properly for the first time, "Blimey, what have you two been up to?"

Both men were lean, muscular men in their thirties, one with dark, close-cropped hair and an earring, the other with reddish gold hair and a cherubic face. They wore blue work shirts with rolled up sleeves, jeans and trainers. Their clothes and their hair were covered in a fine layer of dust, making the dark-haired one look prematurely gray.

The cherubic face broke into a beaming smile. "We're in the building trade this week, old son. Have been up on this block of flats under construction keeping an eye on some dodgy dealings. You'd be amazed what moves around a building site, but Christ it was cold up there. Glad I don't have to do that for a living." He stopped talking, put down his knife and fork and took a gigantic gulp of tea. "Whew, I can feel that going down to my toes. Hey, I've been meaning to talk to you. Didn't you put out a description of a guy recently? Odd sort of a description, talked about 'dead eyes.' "

"Yeah," his friend broke in, "I noticed that too. What's with you? You getting poetic, or are you about to start writing *Tales from the Crypt*?"

Brian attempted to shrug off his embarrassment. "Well, that's how some bird from New Zealand described him. And believe it or not a desk sergeant gave me a call and says he remembers someone like that."

The man with the red-gold hair, Ed Williams, pushed his plate away from him and said, "I could go a big lump of apple pie, but somehow I don't think I'd better; we've got to go out on surveillance tonight, and I'll probably fall asleep if I eat anymore. I noticed it, Bri, because it sounds sort of like someone we've been keeping an eye on. New Zealand you say?" He straightened the salt and pepper shakers with a long, freckled hand. "We've got a character that keeps hip-hopping out of the country, and we're sure he's a drug runner but we can't get anything on him. He's got weird eyes too. Doesn't give you the warm fuzzies if you look at him."

"His name isn't Georgie Small by any chance, is it?" Brian laughed, swirling the last of his tea in his cup.

The dark-haired cop gave him a strange look. "Blimey mate, are you psychic or something? Talking about dead eyes and coming up with the name of the crim we're watching. I'm going to start wearing a bunch of garlic round my neck in case I bump into you in the locker room."

"You're kidding," Brian said disbelievingly, "you're not really watching Georgie are you?"

"Straight up, we are," Ed replied. "Of course, he's called Alistair Jamieson these days and lives in a fancy pad down in Surrey. Passport Control noticed how often he was traveling and tipped off Customs who picked him up on a couple of trips, but they couldn't find a thing. Squeaky clean. Even used the sniffer dogs around his baggage when they weren't apparently checking him, but still nothing. They passed his name on to us because for some reason they weren't convinced he was a legitimate businessman. All the papers in his briefcase were too neat and tidy, and he certainly wasn't a tourist. No labels, no suntan."

"That's a bit of a stretch, isn't it? Maybe he's just a meticulous businessman. They're a nosy bunch of sods." Brian had little time for HM Customs ever since they'd caught him with an extra bottle of booze when he was coming back from a fortnight's holiday in Spain. Delayed him for over an hour, and made him feel like a right idiot before they let him go.

"I dunno, these Customs blokes are damn good, and they get a feel for people. Anyroad, we thought it was worth running a check on him, and sure enough he had a record, and he was traveling on a fake passport. So he's up to something."

"That's for sure," the dark-haired cop added. "Has a beautiful home, drives a beamer, eats in all the best restaurants and he's got no visible means of support. I know they dish out a lot of money on the dole these days, but a four-bedroom house on half an acre in Surrey seems a bit over the top." He fidgeted restlessly in his chair. "The frustrating bit is that we can't find out what he's up to. We're sure it's drugs, but we've had our eye on him for over three months now and we haven't managed to catch him contacting any of the players in the drug game. He's obviously not small time, but however he's doing business beats me."

"My sons," Brian said, "let me buy you another cup of tea, and then I'll tell you a story. But there's one condition. You can't interrupt until I get to the end, because I didn't believe a word of it when I first heard it either."

The other two exchanged amused looks. "If he's going to spring for another cup of tea, what have we got to lose," and as Brian got up and went over to the counter, Ed called after him, "and a couple of lumps of fruit cake would go down well with it."

Brian returned with a tray bearing three cups of tea, and three pieces of carrot cake. "Sorry they were all out of fruit cake, so you'll have to make do with this." He handed around the tea and cake, then put the empty tray on a table behind him. "Now if you're sitting comfortably, children, we will begin. Once upon a time, a woman from New Zealand walked into a police station in Portsmouth and told the desk sergeant an interesting story about a man called Andrew James. Who by the way bears a striking resemblance to young Georgie Small."

The other two listened with half an ear while they piled sugar into their tea, stirred vigorously, then applied themselves to the carrot cake, but when Brian reached the part where Kelly had come up with the theory that Andrew James was a hit man, they both stopped eating and listened. When Brian finished, he waited for the wave of cynicism to hit, but instead Ed said, "A hit man. You don't get too many people dropping into their local cop shop and accusing Mr. Sanders down the road of being a hit man. Hang on a bit though, you said she said he knocked someone off in New Zealand. What was she doing in Portsmouth?"

"She was doing a Miss Marple. Came over to check up on this Andrew James, but drew a blank because he didn't live at the address she'd been given. That's how she ended up in the police station. The old couple at the house suggested she try there."

"You mean she came all the way from New Zealand just to check up on this bloke?"

"That's what made me listen to the story in the first place," Brian said. "You'd have to either be a complete nutter with more money than sense, or totally convinced you were right. The Portsmouth desk sergeant believed her, and he's been listening to crackpots for over twenty years. So I gave her a call and talked to her for a long time. She sounds level-headed. Lives in New Zealand but spent a lot of time in the States, and is consulting for a software company there now."

"What did she reckon she was going to do when she found Andrew James?" Ed asked.

"I don't know. Rattle his cage, I suppose, and hope she could come up with some evidence."

"Gutsy lady. Not too smart though."

"Well, I wouldn't say that," his partner added, apparently fascinated by the strange story. "What do you reckon we ought to do now?"

Ed's face broke into a wide smile, displaying large even teeth. "Go down and rattle Georgie Small's cage?"

They all laughed, and then pulling on his earring, the dark-haired cop said, "You know for sure he's using a phony passport right, and he has been to New Zealand recently. What are the New Zealand police doing about it?"

"They aren't," Brian said. "She didn't have enough evidence to get them interested." He paused and thought for a moment. "But you know if you've had him under surveillance, you'd have a record of when he was out of the country. If that was when she says the murder happened, we could be on to something."

"That'll just take two minutes to check. Let's go along to my office."

They all got up and followed the dark-haired cop as he dodged nimbly round the tables and rushed off down the corridor. In fact, it took about half an hour to get the information they needed, but they discovered Georgie Small, aka Andrew James, aka Alistair Jamieson, had been out of the country, apparently on a trip to Australia.

"That sounds likely," Brian said. "He travels to Australia as Alistair Jamieson, switches passports and travels to New Zealand as Andrew James. He's hardly likely to go directly to his destination if he's a hit man, or a drug runner for that matter."

A look of delighted triumph crossed Ed's face. "You know Brian, old son, they may make a detective of you yet. I think you've just broken our deadlock."

"What are you going to do?" Brian asked, relieved that they were taking him seriously. Throughout the whole story he had the nasty suspicion they were going to laugh their heads off, then spread the story around CID.

"What we're going to do," he said decisively, "is go down and have a word with Alistair Jamieson. We're going to tell him we know he was traveling on a phony passport, and we want to talk to him about a suspected murder in New Zealand. That should get him going."

"That won't do any good," his partner said. "We've tried questioning him before. He's a cool customer. He'll have answers and just tell us to get lost."

"Not," the other one added, "if we tell him we have a witness. There's a woman from New Zealand who can identify him. That should shake him up a bit."

His partner still looked dubious. "We can try it, but we need some more on him. Let's put the word out to a couple of snouts, and see if they can come up with anything. When we tried it looking for drug connections it didn't work, but if we change the tune to murder it could be different. If he works for the Mob, and it's got to be someone big like that, they've got lots of minions running around, and they like to boast about their connections. Someone in a pub will have heard something."

"Okay, you're on," Ed said, the freckles on his face standing out as his color rose. "Thanks, Bri, I think you may have put us on the right track." He got to his feet and slapped Brian on the back. "We'll be in touch if anything breaks. But right now," he said turning to his partner, "we've got work to do."

Brian walked towards the door, but just before he left, turned and said, "This business of telling him there's a witness could be a bit risky. Mrs. Brandon asked a lot of questions in Pompey. It wouldn't be difficult for a lad like Georgie to work out who the witness is."

Chapter 24

Alistair Jamieson, aka Andrew James, aka Georgie Small of Brixton sat in the high-backed leather chair in his book-lined study and sipped his glass of Bruichladdich slowly, savoring the smoky flavor. A Saville Row suit and hand-made shirt gave his unremarkable looks a pallid distinction, and the hand that caressed the glowing glass of Islay malt was slim and well-manicured. Taking Penelope out to dinner in the new French restaurant had made for a pleasant evening. She was good company, but the best bit was the envious looks from the men at other tables; with her swept-back blond hair, classic oval face and long shapely legs she was a knockout. She seemed to enjoy his company too, particularly his anecdotes about his recent trip to the Caribbean. Obviously, it made no sense to talk about New Zealand, and it was easy to come up with stories about the Caribbean—he had been there once on a job—and it was always safer to stay close to the truth. The meal had been first class, not one of those designer jobs where your plate looked pretty, but you went home ready for a hamburger. After dinner he drove her home in his BMW 700 series and dropped her off at the door, declining the invitation to go in and meet her parents, and was gratified to see the look of disappointment, quickly suppressed, that crossed her face.

Playing it cool was the way to go with this one, he had long-term plans in mind. As much as he wanted to invite her back to his house and see how long it took to ruffle that sophisticated calm once he got her going, he suppressed the urge. The time had come to get out of his current profession and settle down, and she was exactly what he needed—a class act with a father who was loaded. Daddy was a financier, and Georgie had it all worked out that daddy could help him invest his considerable nest egg, all carefully stashed away in off-shore accounts under a variety of names. Then perhaps he would turn his hand to finance; it looked like a doddle compared with his present profession. He had come a long way over the past few years. Not a trace of the Brixton accent remained, his clothes and taste were impeccable and he knew how to act in all the best places. Learning that was all part of the trade. You never knew where you were going to have to go and when, and the more you could blend into the scenery, the easier it was. Voice coaches and social coaches were easy to find. All those poor buggers from public school who couldn't get jobs were itching to take his money.

It had been a good life. To start with he did jobs for small timers in the U.K., but as his reputation grew so did his clientele. One day he received a call from a man with an old Etonian accent who said he would like to get together and discuss a business proposition. The business proposition, taking out the head of a new gang trying to muscle in on the lucrative East London rackets, for a very fat fee, went well. After that, Georgie received all his instructions over the phone from the same voice. It was a good arrangement. As the importance of the assignments escalated, so did the fees. He had no idea who his new employers were, but they were very generous, and as he started to receive assignments in Europe and later the States, he felt sure it must be the Mob. But Georgie was far too smart to ask any questions. This assignment had been his first time down under. He had found it quite exhilarating.

However, his contact made a peculiar comment when he called about the check. Said something about the boss being bothered about a loose end. When he had pressed him, he said it was some woman from New Zealand asking questions in California, but he assured him there was nothing to worry about. Georgie was sure he had done his usual impeccable job, a clean job with no witnesses, but if they were getting nervous, it was time to get out of the business.

He got up, moved over to the cabinet, and poured another measure of malt whisky into his crystal glass. A slight noise outside caused him to stop pouring and listen. Hearing nothing else, he topped up the glass and went back to his chair. There was no point in going out to look, if there was anyone there his two Dobermans would let him know. Sleek and well fed, trained by the best guard dog school, they didn't miss a thing. The electronic security system was turned on as additional backup; you couldn't be too careful these days with all these petty criminals trying to steal from the affluent. He sat down and sank back into the soft leather contentedly. Yes, the evening had gone well and the trip down under had been a piece of cake.

Georgie remembered with a wry smile how worried he was by the assignment initially. It was exciting to visit a new country, but it was difficult to see how he was going to pull it off. Carrying out an assignment and melting into the background in a big city was one thing, in a sparsely populated country like New Zealand it was something else again. The police there had a nasty habit of solving crimes quickly. Thoroughly researching a job was one of the major reasons for his success, and before taking off for New Zealand he read extensively about the country and its population. New Zealand House in London was very cooperative, providing newspapers, magazines and books.

After arriving in Auckland, he spent three weeks studying David and his work habits. Georgie grew increasingly worried as the days went by. People were friendly, and they noticed strangers. Staging an accident was going to be difficult. None of his normal plans would work. Then he had a stroke of luck. His quarry headed north with a group of his workmates for a weekend of rest and relaxation. Georgie followed and rented a house on the same bay. Holiday makers spending the weekend were unremarkable, and the locals simply smiled and went about their business. Then the shopkeeper at the little shop in the camp had been a gift. Delighted with an interested audience, he was only too happy to talk about the group staying at the O'Donnell's house on the sea front. Secure in the knowledge that his quarry was going to be in one place for the next two days, George set about reconnoitering the territory and preparing a succession of opportunities. Then all he had to do was wait. Luck was when an opportunity happened and you were ready for it.

When the group set off for the headland with several large knapsacks, it had to be for a picnic, so he had time. And he was well prepared. On a beach with no entertainment other than swimming and fishing, a hike up to the headland seemed an obvious way to spend an afternoon. So he had checked the other side of the headland the previous day and discovered the only access was by sea. It was an easy matter to find an old man more than willing to rent him a boat for two days. Cash in advance. So once they were on their way, it was a simple matter to drive around to the other side of the headland, hop in the boat, and reach the headland from the other side. A quick hike up the steep, bush-covered slope and he was in time to see David and his group enjoying a picnic. He chuckled to himself as he remembered how David had played into his hands. While he sat, concealed behind a clump of tea tree, trying to think how he could get close to David without the rest of the party seeing him, David took off by himself and went climbing on the cliff face. A couple of well-aimed rocks and it was all over. He didn't even have to use his gun. Yes, every once in a while things just fell into your lap.

And now he was on a roll. It looked as if things were working out with Penelope. It had been pretty obvious this evening that she wanted to come home with him. Patience was paying off. She was hooked. But then why shouldn't she be? Secret Service agents were not too thick on the ground in Surrey. Well, leastways, not ones who were willing to tell her in confidence what they did because they intended to leave Her Majesty's Service shortly and live off the fortune the parents had left. She was not at all surprised to learn that he had simply joined the Service for the excitement. Raised by parents who had more inherited wealth than they knew what to do with, she craved excitement too. The great thing about telling her he was an agent was that she could not check up on him, or his background. It was great cover. He started to think about his next date with her and how far he would take it that time. Stringing a woman along slowly like this was enjoyable. His patience had been one of the reasons that made him so good at his trade, and after all, where Penelope was concerned, he had all the time in the world.

The logs in the fire had settled to a low glow, almost time for another log, but he decided to have a cigarette first. It always gave him pleasure selecting a cigarette from the ornate silver box that he had picked up on his last trip to Spain. The lid had a satisfactory heavy feel. He surveyed the neat rows of cigarettes and selected one carefully, tapping the end lightly on the table before placing it in his mouth. Then he sat admiring the hunting motif around the edge of the ornate lighter before flicking it alight.

The explosion killed him instantly. The dogs, drugged in their kennel, never heard it.

Ed and his partner, Andy Brownlow, sat shivering in the cold night air. Even with the windows closed, the damp air seeped into the car and down into their bones. This was their third night sitting in a pull off close to a high hedge watching Alistair Jamieson's house.

"Any coffee left?" Andy asked.

Ed picked up the stainless steel thermos and gave it a shake. "Not a drop," he said gloomily.

Andy made a fist with a tattooed hand, and blew on it in a vain attempt to warm it up. His eyes fixed on the curl of smoke rising from Jamieson's chimney. "Look at that. First he goes out with a gorgeous-looking bird, and now he's sitting in front of a roaring fire. Did it ever occur to you, Ed, that we're on the wrong side of this business?"

"Frequently, old son, but no one's offered me any bribes or even a decent job. I think I'll send my resume into the Mafia and see what happens. Sitting around waiting to be recruited doesn't seem to work."

"Not a bad idea. Mark you, our resumes for the last few months are going to look pretty ropey. Builders' mates and professional car bum sitters. And to think I joined the CID for a life of excitement. There was more excitement patrolling Kensington High Street."

"Yes, but think . . ." Ed's reply was cut short as an explosion ripped through the night air. Smoke and flames billowed out of Georgie Small's house as the two detectives tore open the car doors and almost fell out on the road in their haste to reach the house. Ed, hair glinting in the muted light, ran flat out, while his partner, still running, pulled out his phone and called in for backup. Ed ran across the road, leaped at the high garden hedge and rolled over the top, then pounded up the drive to the house. Finding it impossible to kick in the front door, he took out his nightstick and smashed a window, only to be driven back by the intense heat. Andy, meanwhile, circled to the back of the house, and managed to break in through the kitchen door. He charged through the house, making for the study where they had seen a light shining. But it was far too late to do anything for Georgie Small.

Later that night, driving back to London drained and exhausted, Ed said, "Jeez that was horrible. What a terrible way to go. They're a ruthless bunch of bastards."

"I hope they don't figure out it was that Kiwi woman that put us on to him," his partner replied, "or she could be in real trouble."

CHAPTER 25

Kelly, hauling clothes from the dryer to the bedroom for sorting and folding, heard the phone ringing and cursed softly. Who on earth was calling this early in the day? Dumping the clothes unceremoniously on the bed, she grabbed the bedside phone.

"It's beautiful down here sitting watching the waves. Would you care to join me for coffee?"

"John," Kelly said astonished, "where are you?"

"Right here in Dolphin Bay sitting on the deck of a little cabin. Spartan, but I can dash straight out of the door and into the surf, so who's complaining. It does at least boast two coffee cups so I can entertain you in style."

"What on earth are you doing here?" Kelly said, with a mixture of irritation and pleasure.

"That's not the sort of reception I was expecting. Aren't you Kiwis renowned for your hospitality to foreigners?" He hesitated and continued in an uncertain voice that reminded Kelly of Sally's kids when they were expecting to be scolded. "Since you wouldn't stay down in Auckland, I thought Mohammed might as well come to the mountain."

"You're impossible. Why didn't you tell me you were coming?" And who the hell invited you to my neck of the woods anyway, she thought, but aloud said, "When did you arrive?"

"I drove up last night. Made it most of the way in the light, but it was a bit hairy finding my way once it got dark. Nice guy that rents the houses out, though. When he knew I was arriving late, he'd turned on the lights and left the key under the mat."

Kelly sat down on the edge of the bed and twirled the phone cord in her hand. "Well, since you are here, you'd better come up and have a coffee. I can make a decent cup with a coffee maker. I bet the best you can offer in that bach is a cup of instant."

"You're right there," John answered, sounding pleased, "I had some last night and it was pretty grim. A decent cup would be great. How do I find your house?"

Kelly, remembering the untidy lounge with the breakfast dishes unwashed, yesterday's paper scattered around, and a mangled chew bone discarded by Riggles, said hastily, "Give me twenty minutes, will you? I'm right in the middle of the washing and want to get it put away. Just walk back along the road the way you came into the bay last night and you'll see our driveway." It had been almost a year now and still she could not get used to the idea of saying "my driveway."

"I'm impressed by the domesticity. By the way, I can see why you are always in such a hurry to nip off home, it's gorgeous up here. What a spectacular beach. And no one on it. It's marvelous."

"See you in about half an hour then." She spent the next twenty minutes running around like a demented hen trying to make the house look vaguely presentable, then as she whisked a cloth around the washbasin in the guest bathroom she caught sight of herself. Her short curly hair was an unruly mop as a result of leaving it to drip dry after the shower. She'd meant to whip a brush through it before it dried properly, but somehow between the newspaper and chores, she hadn't got that far. She dashed into her en-suite bathroom and a quick brush tamed it slightly but left it a long way from styled. Then she put on a small amount of lipstick and decided it would have to do.

She hurried through to the study and was just about to tidy up the piles of papers and correspondence that always seemed to accumulate, when she saw him walking up the driveway. He was strolling along looking around as he approached the house. Wearing a white T-shirt and tight jeans that emphasized his slim hips, he walked with the easy stride of an athlete. His dark hair, tousled by the wind, fell over his forehead, and only his deep brown eyes with their sweeping lashes, which gave him an air of little-boy vulnerability, saved his even-featured face from being too good looking. When he caught sight of Kelly he smiled broadly. Kelly swallowed quickly, but the moment was saved by Riggles who rushed over to John, his tail wagging so enthusiastically that his whole rear end moved with it.

"Sorry, I should have warned you about the killer dog. He'll lick you to death if you don't watch it." Remembering Saturday evening and feeling awkward and not a little foolish, she was glad of the dog and his persistent intrusion.

John crouched down to greet the dog who was busily inspecting his shoes. Once down on his level Riggles wasted no time in licking John's ears, but repelled by John's clever moves finally threw himself on his back to have his tummy rubbed, his tail still wagging as he lay on the drive. "He's great," John laughed, "what a beautiful soft coat. He must cost a fortune to feed."

"No, believe it or not, once they've stopped growing they eat very little. I used to have a Corgi that ate more than my last bull mastiff."

John stood looking around. "This is a nice property. How much land have you got?"

"About thirty acres total. Most of it bush, but I've a

couple of paddocks that I let a local farmer use. Steve had great plans of raising a few steers, but I sold them off after he died." She turned back towards the house. "Come on through and I'll make you that cup of coffee. You'll enjoy the view from the deck."

She opened the door and they went into the lobby with its black slate floor and rimu-trimmed walls. It was still and quiet after the breezy garden, and their soft shoes made no sound as they walked through to the tiled kitchen. "Go outside and take a look at the view. You'll get a whole different perspective on the bay from up here. I'll put the jug on and get some coffee going."

Instead of going outside he stood leaning on the black marble counter and watched as she filled the jug and put it on to boil, then hauled the coffee beans out of the freezer and put them through the grinder. Raising his voice over the noise of the grinder, he said, "You keep your coffee beans in the freezer? Don't you drink coffee?"

"Old trick a Brazilian friend told me one time. Keeps the coffee fresh." She spooned the ground coffee into a coffee pot, and while the jug boiled, put mugs, milk and cookies on a tray. "So have you come up to do some sightseeing? You're too late for the Cape Reinga tour today, but you should definitely do that tomorrow. You could drive in to Kerikeri and see the orange and kiwi growing region. That's pretty, and the town has some good cafés for lunch. Mangonui would be a nice drive too—they have the world's best fish-and-chip shop there. You can eat fish and chips out of the paper, or have scallops, crayfish, mussels—you name it—even a glass of wine. It's the most civilized fish-and-chip shop I've been to." She was talking too fast, intent on filling the silence. He just stood there watching her, saying nothing.

"Kelly," he said softly, "I came up here to see you. Not to go sightseeing." He moved across the kitchen towards her, but she turned deftly and poured boiling water on the coffee grounds, placed the plunger in the jug and then set it on a tray beside the mugs. Safely barricaded behind the tray, she ignored his remark and set off purposely for the deck. Taking the hint, he stood back and then followed her out on to the deck. Once outside he said, "Man, this is spectacular. What a view!"

Below them the bush-clad slopes swayed in the morning breeze, the pink and white tea tree dominating, but tree ferns and the occasional pohutukawa giving them dramatic emphasis. Below the bush, small waves broke on the rocky outcrop at the northern end of the bay, and to the south, a perfect oval of yellow sand stretched away to a towering headland. The holiday homes fringing the bay looked like toy houses carefully set out by some wayward child trying to decorate the edge of the beach. The gentle shush of the waves provided a background to the angry screech of gulls and the sound of a tractor hauling the first of the fishermen's boats down to the water's edge. John leaned on the rail, fascinated by the view, while Kelly depressed the plunger and poured coffee.

"Take a seat. You can still see the view from the deckchairs although I must admit the rail does get in the way sometimes."

He wandered back to where she was sitting, sank down in the comfortable padded Italian deckchair and stretched across to pick up his mug. His slender brown hand was terminated by bluntly shaped but cared-for nails, and he wore a Rolex watch. "It would be nice to do some sightseeing. Could you make the time to be tour guide? I've never enjoyed touring on my own much, and I've heard there's a lot I should be seeing up here." His voice had a pleading note, defying her to reject him.

"Well, okay," Kelly said reluctantly, wondering what she was getting herself into. She knew she should just tell him to get lost, but how could she? She had to work with him, he was key to the project, and he was a stranger to the north. And Kelly, my girl, she said to herself, you know damn well you want to be with him. "Let's start working on an itinerary, since I assume you have to get back to work pretty quickly."

"Yea, I worked sixteen hours on Sunday so that I could legitimately get away, and I've brought my laptop along, so I'm not really playing hooky. I really need some of the stuff Mike is working on before I can go too much further, and he still has a couple of days' work to get it ready for me."

"Okay," Kelly laughed, "I'm not going to report you to Colin."

As they sat laughing together, the door leading to the deck opened from the inside, and Sally breezed out, saying as she turned to close the door, "I knocked at the front, but you couldn't hear me. Since your car's in the garage I guessed you must be out here slurping coffee." Turning, she stopped, momentarily taken aback by the sight of John lounging in a deckchair laughing with Kelly. Then in her inimitable way, she walked over to his chair and said, "Hi, I'm Sally Whelan, a friend from down on the bay and unpaid dog sitter." She extended a long, elegant hand as he struggled to his feet.

Kelly, watching John get up and shake her hand, could almost see the wheels in Sally's head turning. Early morning coffee on the deck with an attractive man, no car outside. Oh boy.

"Hi, I'm John Celini, stranger in town, and a workmate of Kelly's."

"Since you two have taken care of the introductions, why don't I go and get a cup for Sally?" She went through to the kitchen, glad to be able to hide for a moment from Sally's knowing look. As she closed the door, she could hear the scrape of the deckchair on the wooden deck as it was maneuvered into place. By the time she returned, the chairs were in a friendly semi-circle and Sally and John were chatting away like old friends.

"John says he's rented the Anderton's place for a couple of days. He must be a glutton for punishment, that's one of your truly basic baches. I don't think they've spent a penny on that place since they bought it, and all the furniture looks like it came from the Salvation Army."

"Are building lots cheap on the sea front?" John asked, puzzled. "It's great that people with no money can afford a sea front home. You need real money to own anything on the ocean in California."

"No," Sally laughed, "any section on the beach is pricey. The section probably cost the Andertons about one hundred fifty thousand; the bach was included, of course, but if that's worth thirty thousand I'd be amazed. It ought to be pulled down."

"You mean people buy a piece of beach front property in a sensational spot like this and then just put up a cabin," he said incredulously.

"Yes, it's a good old Kiwi tradition. All you need is a building with a kitchen and a bathroom; any old shed seems to suffice. Then Christmas time all the rellies come piling up and stick tents all over it. They have a ball. You should see this place at Christmas; it looks like an Arab convention."

"So you're saying the owners aren't poor?"

"No, they've got a huge house in Kohimarama; that's one of the ritzier Auckland neighborhoods."

"Wow, you live and learn every day. Don't think I'd be too thrilled if I was one of the permanent residents up here, and I suppose there must be quite a few, having these cabins around."

"Oh, it doesn't bother us natives. Give the property owners their due, they all pay the local lawn-cutting service to keep the places neat and tidy and they don't leave any old cars around. Actually, since most of their cars are late model 4x4s, they're not likely to."

"I guess you're right. I was looking at the houses as I walked up here and it's nice. The residents do a fantastic job with their gardens. I stopped to admire one of them, and could hardly get away from this nice old lady. Seems her son is living in the States. Hey, she even offered me a bag of lemons. Talk about friendly folk."

Kelly grinned; until you lived in the North you didn't realize what a liability a lemon tree was. She decided not to disillusion him.

John swallowed the last of his coffee and got to his feet. "I'm really looking forward to some sightseeing."

"You're in good hands with Kelly," Sally said, "she used to run a travel business when she first moved up here."

"Did you?" he asked, his eyes alive with interest.

"Yes," she said shortly, not wanting to get into it. It brought back too many painful memories of Steve. "But I think the first item on the agenda when we've finished our coffee is a walk down through the bush to the beach. It's a whole other world in there. Then a walk along the beach to headland. Did you bring your swimsuit with you? We could take a swim if you have."

"Yes, I did but it's in the cabin."

"We'll be walking right by there so that's no problem," she said briskly. "I'll take a couple of towels. Then after the swim, you'll be getting hungry and we can take a drive out and get some lunch in Mangonui. Then we can go sight-seeing."

"Sounds like you're going to have a busy day, John," Sally said dryly, and Kelly was uncomfortably aware that she had been making far too big a deal of how full the day was going to be. She wondered whether she was trying to convince John, herself or Sally. Drinking the last of her coffee, Sally got to her feet. "Time I was on my way too. I just came up to see if I could borrow that Isabel Allende book you were talking about, Kelly. I haven't got time to get to the library, and I suffer withdrawal symptoms if I don't have something to read in bed."

"Sure, I'll get it for you. It wasn't at all what I expected when I started reading it, but I thoroughly enjoyed it." She too got to her feet and gathered up the coffee mugs. John rushed across and opened the door for her, and after dropping off the mugs in the kitchen, she went through to the living room in search of *Daughter of Fortune*. Meanwhile she could hear Sally saying goodbye to John and hoping he enjoyed his stay in the North. When Sally came in from the deck, she held out the book to her and then walked her to the door. As Sally left she squeezed her arm gently, "Gorgeous. Go for it, girl."

Kelly found herself perilously close to blushing, "He's just a friend. Way too young for me, but he's nice company. Turned up totally unexpectedly."

"Of course," Sally said, smiling infuriatingly.

Kelly rinsed the mugs and put them in the dishwasher, picked up the dog's lead and went out on to the deck. "Okay, are you set for a hike through the bush?"

A flight of shallow steps led from the back of the house to a gate in the chain link fence. Once through the gate, they walked along a path that zigzagged its way down to the beach. The canopy of tea tree and carpet of fern deadened the sound of the surf, and they walked along in a hushed silence. Kelly, who was leading the way, brushed aside the huge cobwebs that had been strung across the path. Halfway down they reached the summer house that sat concealed within a grove of pohutukawa and puriri trees. Behind the summer house, a sloping tangle of giant ferns provided a spectacular backdrop.

John stopped in his tracks, and looked around, "This is great. It's a whole different world in here. Feels sort of like the redwoods."

Kelly smiled to herself. The bush was silent except for the birds, but it was a totally different feel from the hush of the giant Californian redwoods. Theirs was a cathedral stillness, made awesome by the majesty of the huge trees, while in the clearing where they were standing with the canopy of pohutukawa and puriri, it was a comfortable, friendly quiet. She recognized the symptoms, he was homesick and looking for the familiar. "You've no idea how great it is until you've been swimming and have to trek up this track back to the house. It doesn't seem too steep on the way down, but it's downright exhausting coming back. You're going to be very glad of somewhere to sit and take a breather."

"What a neat idea. Lead on, a swim is starting to sound like a good idea."

They walked down the long winding trail, then stepped onto the soft warm sand and made their way out to the rocks where they spent half an hour looking for small crabs in the rock pools. Then they made their way along the beach to the bach John had rented, and Kelly waited outside while he got into his swim trunks. Kelly, trying hard not to look too appreciatively at his lean, tanned body set off to perfection by a skimpy Speedo swimsuit, peeled off her T-shirt and shorts and together they ran down into the sea, gasping initially at the shock of cold water. Once their bodies adjusted to the temperature, it felt great and they spent a long time swimming and body surfing. Finally, exhausted, they ran back up the beach and flopped on their towels to dry off in the sun.

After a while, they got up and walked along the beach to the headland, feeling the sun hot on their backs. Finally, as they turned for home, Kelly said, "I don't know about you, but I'm starting to feel peckish. How about we take a drive to Mangonui and I'll introduce you to the best fish and chips you've ever tasted?"

"Growing up in Chicago, you don't exactly become a connoisseur of fish and chips, but I'll take your word for it. Actually, I'm starving, so anything sounds good. I didn't think to stock up on too much food for my cabin, and I don't imagine there's a supermarket for miles around," he said hopefully, angling for an invitation to stay over.

"There are some shops in Mangonui and Coopers Beach so we can stock you up after lunch," Kelly said, knowing as she said it she was beginning to sound like a fussy maiden aunt. John gave her a long look, but said nothing.

Gathering up their towels and shoes, they made their way back along the beach and up the long trail to the house. It was a fairly stiff climb and they were both glad to flop down on the seat in the summer house to get their breath. They sat there for a long while enjoying the peace, and when John took her hand in his long, slim hand she let it lie there.

Once back in the house, she showed him to the spare bedroom with its en-suite bathroom, and then showered in her room. Twenty minutes later, feeling fresh and clean, they set off for a drive along the East Coast bays until they reached the little town of Mangonui. Houses were scattered attractively on the hill above the harbor along with a charming old church and schoolhouse while on the waterfront there was an accumulation of small shops, cafés, several real estate offices, a minute courthouse dating back to the 1800s and a Four Square store that doubled as the local post office. A working wharf jutted out into the harbor, and commercial fishing boats shared the space with yachts, motor cruisers and tiny dinghies.

The fish-and-chip shop was built over the water, and the fish was always ultra fresh. Kelly ordered fish and chips and told John to select his pieces of fish. While they waited for it to cook, they sat outside on the deck and drank a glass of wine. Then they sat eating fish and chips out of the paper with their fingers, which as Kelly pointed out, was the only way to eat them.

After lunch, she took him for a drive past the small bays making up Doubtless Bay, ending up at Kauri Kingdom so he could see the giant logs retrieved from the kauri swamps, and the furniture and ornaments made from 30,000-year-old swamp kauri.

He was a gratifying tourist, fascinated by the beautiful kauri furniture, and entranced by the proliferation of bays, but at five p.m., he turned to her and said, "I'm completely worn out. Do you think we can go home now?"

"Of course," Kelly said, making her way back to the car. "You'd never make it on one of those packaged tours, you know. They have you out and on the road by eight-thirty, and you don't get back to your hotel until about seven." She said it flippantly, trying to make light of the fact that she was working very hard to keep him occupied. He kept looking at her sideways, saying nothing, but speaking volumes.

Finally, they drove home, and after dinner they sat outside with their coffee. They watched the light fade over the ocean and a huge moon rise up from behind the headland and climb slowly up the sky. Above them a morepork called, and the puppy snored loudly at their feet. After a while, Kelly stood up and walked over to the rail and stood looking down into the darkness of the bush. She realized that for the first time in a very long time she felt totally relaxed. John came up behind her and wrapped his arms around her, his skin warm against her arms that had grown chilly as the light faded. They stood a while looking at the dark swaying bush, then he gently turned her round to face him and when he kissed her this time, she did not resist.

CHAPTER 26

Kelly was working in her Auckland office when Mike appeared in the doorway. It seemed to Kelly he had put on even more weight since she saw him last, his pale blue shirt stretched tightly across his stomach and his baggy pants did little to hide the expanding hips. "Hi, Kelly, how are you doing?"

"Up to my ears in it as usual. Keeping Finsat off your backs is turning into a major job these days. Talk about a bunch of nervous Nellies." Her bantering tone covered her surprise. Mike never came visiting.

"I was wondering if I could have a word," he said quietly, moving towards her desk.

"Sure, pull up a chair. Want a cup of coffee?" she whisked a stack of reports off her one visitor chair and waved invitingly in its direction.

He looked over his shoulder to see if anyone else was within earshot. "No, I'd like to talk to you privately. Do you think we could get together after work for a drink? Somewhere the rest of the gang doesn't usually go."

"Okay, that will be fine. How about Finz? We can sit outside there. What time?" All the time she was speaking she was wondering what he wanted to talk about. More than likely he was going to be complaining about Colin or someone else on the project. Criticizing other people's work, and finding the cloud behind every silver lining, were Mike's trademarks. However, Colin dealt with it all the time with never-ending patience, knowing that managing prima donnas was all part of the job if you wanted truly creative software. I bet he misses David, she thought, equally talented and never a tantrum.

"See you there about six then," Mike said, his face troubled. Without saying another word, he left the office, glancing in both directions before stepping out into the corridor.

The rest of the afternoon passed quickly as she worked on the report for Finsat. Joe had called earlier in the day wanting more information, even though she had sent in a report only a few days before. Reading it, he had immediately emailed with a dozen questions, clearly doubting that they would come in on time. As Kelly meticulously replied to all his concerns she realized even she was surprised at the progress they were making. John had slipped right into the project with no problem, and as far as she could tell, he was rapidly making up the time lost after David's death. It wasn't until the terminal screen blacked out that she realized she had stopped typing and was daydreaming about the two days she had spent with John.

She parked her car in the downtown parking building and walked across the road to the viaduct basin, past several restaurants already busy with people having a before-dinner drink or an early meal. Mike was already waiting for her. She noticed he had selected a table well to one side of the outside dining area, even though few people were sitting outside. As she felt the chilly wind blow through her light suit, she realized why. Mike was sitting in his short-sleeved shirt looking warm and comfortable. Being overweight has its advantages, she thought, that nice lining of blubber keeps you warm; perhaps she'd have pie and ice cream for dessert tonight.

Catching sight of her, Mike got to his feet and beckoned

her over to the table, and once she was seated asked what he could get her. When the waitress came by he ordered a glass of Chardonnay and a Steinlager. "How are you doing, Mike? I haven't had a chance to talk to you since we had dinner together with Cathy. I really enjoyed that, by the way, she's good fun."

He looked across the wharf to where half a dozen people were climbing aboard a water taxi. "Can't understand why people pay ten bucks for a ride around the basin."

"I've been on one of them and it's fun. You get a commentary on the yachts and a worm's eye view of the luxury ones. Anyway," she added grinning, "not everyone has a fancy boat like you to tootle around in."

The waitress arrived with their drinks. Mike poured his Steinlager carefully and took a sip, "Cheers."

Kelly, wondering when he was going to tell her what this getting together was all about, waited impatiently while he took another sip and looked around at the people sauntering by. Finally, visibly making up his mind, he said, "I should be talking to Colin about this, but somehow I don't think he would listen. He'd just think I was bitching again." He stopped. Kelly sipped her wine and said nothing until at last he blurted out, "There's something not right about John Celini."

Stunned, Kelly asked, "What do you mean?"

"Well, look," he shifted restlessly in his seat. "I know I find fault with other people on the project. Well, I can't help it, they do such dumb things, what does Colin expect me to do, sit back and let the whole project get screwed up?" His tone was defiant.

Kelly, studying his worried face, said carefully, "So what's the problem? Do you want to tell me about it?"

"I know I was always picking on David because I didn't

like his approach," he said defensively, "but this isn't the same."

Come on, come on, Kelly thought, get it out. "Why isn't it the same?" Even to herself she was beginning to sound like a psychologist, echoing the patient's last few words to keep them talking.

"There's nothing wrong with what John is doing. He's doing a brilliant job. I don't know where you found him, but it was a bloody miracle when you did. We'd be up the proverbial creek without him." He hesitated again. "That's why I feel so bad mentioning this to you, but Cathy said I should talk to you. I haven't been able to sleep for nights. She seems to think you're really level-headed—didn't know you made such an impression the other night, did you?" he said with the glimmer of a smile.

"So what is it Mike? It can't be that bad."

"It's the way John works that is weird. He won't talk about what he's doing, just sort of gets it done, keeps to the schedule and stays quiet. I've met plenty of inarticulate types before—software crawls with them—jokers that can't talk, can only communicate with their mother by email, but he's not one of them. He comes out for a beer with us after work sometimes, and has us in stitches telling us about some of the projects he's been on back in the States." He stopped again, uncomfortably, and ran his finger down the side of the frosted bottle, leaving a small, even trail. "Saying this out loud while we're sitting out here in the sunshine seems stupid, but although there's no problem working with him—in fact, he couldn't be more helpful where the interface is concerned—he isn't normal; he never talks about the module he's responsible for."

Kelly, feeling inordinately relieved, pushed her glass away from her and looked squarely at Mike. "That's mildly odd, but not any weirder than a whole bunch of working practices I've seen. Maybe he's just superstitious or something, feels that if he talks about it before it's done it won't work."

Mike let out a heavy sigh and looked even more uncomfortable. "I suppose I'd better come clean. I feel as guilty as hell ever since I did it."

Kelly managed to keep silent, sure she was going to get a confession from Mike about taking money to sabotage the project. She knew she'd been right. There was no way he could live the way he did on his salary. However, once he started talking she was glad she had.

"One night I came in to work at about eleven-thirty. I like working at night. It's quiet then, you don't get all the phones ringing and people dropping by asking dumb questions. I saw a light on in John's office, so I thought I'd tell him I was there so he didn't get a fright if he heard someone moving around. But he wasn't there. He must have popped out to get a sandwich or something. He was obviously coming right back because he'd left his terminal on. So I went over to see what he was doing. It was just natural curiosity," he said defensively. "He never would talk about his work, but he seemed to be ripping along so I wanted to take a look and see how he was doing it." He looked around as two men in business suits sat down at the next table. Lowering his voice slightly, he continued, "I couldn't get into his files, of course, he had all those locked away behind a password I didn't know, but I did take a look at his working file. I guess he thought it was safe to leave it there since it was the middle of the night and no one else was around."

Sitting back, he took a long swallow of beer. "Anyway, I took a look at what he was doing and it was something different."

"How do you mean different? Different from what?" Kelly was beginning to get irritated. Mike had no business snooping around other offices at night. She had the uncomfortable feeling he might have looked through her desk drawers. She decided to put a mousetrap in one next time she left for home.

"Different from the specs. What he was developing wasn't what the specification set out for that module. I know what it was supposed to be because David and I had a hell of an argument about it. I knew I could improve the performance if he made some changes to go along with the ones I was making. He didn't agree," he said belligerently. "Such a damn whiz kid, he always had to do it his way."

"So what's so unusual about that?" Kelly asked. "I've yet to meet the software type who did things exactly the way they were specified. You all reckon specifications are some vague guideline."

Ignoring the jibe, Mike said emphatically, "But that's just the point. John is Mr. Holier Than Thou where specs are concerned. He does everything by the book. I think it must be something to do with working for a contract house all these years, having to slot in with other people's work at short notice. Anyway, he is great to work with; it's a breeze interfacing my software to his because it's all exactly as specified."

"So what's the problem? What are you saying?" Kelly asked, scarcely suppressing her irritation.

Mike looked her right in the eye, all his former hesitation gone. "What I'm saying is that when I looked at what he was doing it wasn't the same as the specification. Externally it was exactly right—couldn't have been more identical to the spec—but internally it was something very different. It didn't match the spec at all."

"So what was it?"

"I don't know. That's the problem. I heard him coming in the door and decided I had better get the hell away from his terminal. I would be frosted if I caught someone snooping around in my office." He looked uncomfortably aware of what he was saying.

Puzzled, Kelly said slowly, "So you're saying that on the external workings of his module, the ones he has to report on, and you have to link up with, he's meticulous about being one hundred percent correct, but internally you think he's doing something different from what Colin wants." She absently took a sip of wine. "And he isn't talking about it. You think it isn't just the normal wandering away from the original design?"

"No, it's far more than that. It's different functionally." Even now Mike had a hard time believing it. He told her when he first started looking at the software, it appeared to have normal minor changes, but the more he looked, the more he realized something was being developed that had nothing to do with the original software Colin's team had been asked to develop.

"You think he's up to something?" Kelly asked slowly, feeling faintly sick.

"Yes," he said emphatically, slapping his hand on the table and looking relieved to have got it off his chest. "I've been worrying about it for days, but I didn't know how to tell Colin. I don't think he'd believe me." He watched Kelly carefully, waiting for her reaction.

Kelly, her thoughts in a whirl, said nothing for a long time. Finally, she looked at Mike, her face bleak. "You know I wish I didn't, but I have a horrible feeling you may be on to something, Mike. It would explain a lot of things. Leave it with me for a couple of days, will you? I've some serious thinking to do."

Mike's chubby face was still troubled. "I think the worst thing about all this is that he's such a nice bloke. I hope it's nothing. Maybe I should have just gone ahead and asked him about it; there's probably a simple explanation."

"No, Mike, I think you did the right thing. We need to think about this very carefully before talking to John, or to Colin for that matter."

He looked at her sympathetically. "You like him a whole lot too, don't you?"

"Yes," she said miserably.

Feeling too sick to eat dinner, she went straight back to her motel, planning on flopping on the bed and trying to sort out where she went from here. She unlocked the door and went inside, shutting out the sound of grinding gears and blaring horns. Inside it was quiet and cool, and the room was spotless with freshly Hoovered carpets and a bed to make a hospital matron proud. Leaving the blinds drawn, she flung her bag on the spare bed with unnecessary force, kicked off her shoes and lay on the bed.

What an idiot she had been believing a young, handsome guy like John could be swept off his feet by her charm. He must have been sent over on an assignment to scuttle the project. What, or who, wanted to sabotage the project she couldn't imagine, but right this minute it didn't matter. The fact that John was mixed up in it was the gut-wrenching part. Her bruised ego took another pounding as she recollected how clever everyone thought she was when she pulled off the miracle of finding exactly the person with all the right skills to replace David. Clever, my eye, she thought; it was all a setup. First they get rid of David, and then they have their man sitting waiting to take over. Those gullible little New Zealanders won't think it a bit strange that the perfect candidate just happens to be on vacation at the precise moment the vacancy occurs, and of course, they are so enchanted by their country, why wouldn't an American taking a three-week vacation decide to look for a job and stay permanently?

Even now she could not believe John was involved in David's death. That had to be someone else. Her skin crawled at the thought of a murderer touching her. No, she clung to the thought, it was much more likely to be the elusive hit man Andrew James. John must have been sent over because of his skills. He worked for a contract house, and hadn't he said something about a dodgy Uncle Tony setting it up so that he was offered a job with the contract house in the first place. Celini, Italian, and she knew he was Catholic. Her fertile mind went sweeping off to scenes from *The Godfather*.

Clearly, John had been sent over because of his unique skill set. He was the mole set up to insert a virus in the control module which the unsuspecting Auckland team would ship to California to be incorporated in the overall project. The virus would lie dormant, completely undetected by final system testing, until the first customers received the product. Then all the bad guys, whoever they were, had to do was activate it. Then disaster. A major system, developed at the cost of millions, shipped to a valued customer fails completely. Finsat stock would drop like a stone.

She realized that someone, somehow had noticed she was asking a lot of questions. Discretion never had been her strong suit, and anyway, when she started asking questions and looking around she was only working on a hunch. There was no basis for her suspicions, and even to herself she had to admit it was all probably nothing. Maybe the trip to England had triggered it. She'd made no secret of the fact she was going there on vacation, talking to John about it before she left for California, and to Joe when she was at Finsat. How about that? Maybe Andrew James really was the key. Pleased with her brilliant deductions, her flagging spirits started to revive.

They took a nosedive the next moment as she thought about what happened after someone noticed she was asking too many questions. John started taking an inordinate interest in her, and she, stupid, naive woman that she was, fell for it hook, line and sinker.

Springing off the bed, no longer content to deal with where that line of thinking was going, she stripped off her shirt and slacks and got into her running gear. A good workout was what was needed right now. As she tied double knots in her Reebok laces and tucked the motel key into her back pocket, her face set into determined lines. She padded softly down the steps from the motel and set off running toward Cornwall Park. Dodging pedestrians, almost tripping over a dog leash, she was soon on quieter streets, where she enjoyed jogging along the wide pavements until she reached the park. Here she was able to step up her pace and she strode out along the tree-lined paths, the smell of freshly cut grass and flowering bushes soothing her battered spirits. Dogs of all shapes and sizes were being exercised. Some small and fat plodding along behind their ancient owners, others young and feisty, straining at the leash, wanting to reach a spot where they could chase a ball. By the time she turned and started back toward the motel, the perspiration was soaking through her T-shirt and her suntanned legs glistened with a thin sheen, but she was starting to feel good.

Arriving panting at the motel, she collapsed on the lower step and sat waiting for her heart to slow down and her body to cool. Finally, she made her way up the steps and let herself back into her room. By now it was growing dark and she flipped on the bedside lights before going to take a shower. Showered and refreshed she was suddenly hungry, but far too exhausted to start cooking or even to go out to dinner. Considering a takeaway, she rejected the idea and instead rummaged in the refrigerator to see what she could find. Soon, wearing pajamas, she was comfortably ensconced in front of the TV with a large tomato sandwich. After a massive bite of sandwich, she sat back contentedly. Nothing like a run to clear your head. She knew exactly what she was going to do. Not even the Mob should underestimate a Kiwi when she was mad.

Chapter 27

Next morning, looking tired but totally in control, Kelly was once more in the conference room with the project team, all crowded around the inadequate table. Lindsay yawning widely, Carol, her long hair veiling her face, doodling a series of flowers and butterflies across the top of her notepad. When Kelly came in, Mike said hello but looked away quickly, his smile embarrassed. It was the same with John. Mike said hello, but his eyes slid away, avoiding contact. Watching him covertly she noticed he never looked in John's direction throughout the entire meeting. She too found she was having trouble treating John normally. He had smiled at her, his face lighting up, and throughout the meeting she could feel his eyes on her. She smiled abstractedly in his direction as she took her seat, shuffled some papers in front of her and tried to pretend she was absorbed in some small point near the bottom of the page. She also found herself paying very close attention to Angus and Carol when they gave their progress reports. Anything rather than look in his direction.

After the meeting, John followed her to her office. "You're looking tired, Kelly. Are you feeling okay?" He sounded genuinely concerned. She slid in behind her desk, anxious to put some space between them, because she found in spite of what she suspected, she still found him overwhelmingly attractive.

"No, I'm fine," she said, smiling reassuringly, "I just didn't sleep too well last night. I keep forgetting to close the window, and then about two a.m. those damn trucks' gears start grinding and wake me up. I ended up sitting and reading for quite a time before I could get off again."

"You're just spoiled being lulled to sleep by the sound of the sea every night. That's fantastic up there; I can see why you bought that property." He moved closer to her desk and glancing quickly over his shoulder to make sure no one was in earshot, asked, "How about dinner tonight? I'm a great cook, you know. I thought we could have it at my apartment. Seven o'clock be okay?"

"Sorry, John. Not tonight. I've got a business meeting. We'll make it another night if that's okay with you. I'm planning on staying down a few more nights."

"Great. Better get going. Don't want the gang to start gossiping." He turned and made for the door, and she watched his slim figure disappear.

After answering a couple of phone calls, sheaf of papers in hand, she strolled over to Mike's office. Quietly, she said, "Would it be okay if I came over to your house tonight, Mike? I think it would be safer meeting there. Do you think Cathy would mind?"

"No, that's fine," he said, his eyes alive with interest. "Have you come up with an idea?"

Anxious not to be seen spending too long with him, she dropped off a piece of blank paper, making it seem she had just dropped by to give him some information. "You betcha. See you about six-thirty if that's okay."

He grinned conspiratorially. "See you then," and turned back to his terminal.

When Kelly arrived at Mike's house, Cathy greeted her at the door. "Sorry, Mike isn't home yet. He shouldn't be long though. He called to let me know you were coming.

Come on through to the kitchen. Gavin's playing in there and I was just getting dinner ready. Mike said you wouldn't have had time to eat."

Kelly followed her through to the kitchen, where Cathy was setting the table, putting each item in place with light, delicate movements. Kelly, apparently forgotten while all this went on, wandered over to the corner of the room where Gavin was making huge red slashes with a crayon on a large sheet of poster paper. Leaning over, she said, "Hi, Gavin. That looks exciting. What are you drawing?" He turned round, put down his crayon, punched her on the leg and then continued drawing. Kelly, suppressing the urge to swat him, moved over to the table and sat down. Mike appeared a few minutes later with a Chinese takeaway.

When they were all finished eating and Mike had cleared away the plates, Cathy made a pot of tea and produced a packet of rather sad-looking cookies.

Politely declining a cookie on the grounds that she was already way too full, which was true—a few more meals like this and she would be about ten pounds overweight—Kelly asked Cathy how her day had been. Cathy described in great detail all the clever things Gavin had done during the day, and then said, "I'd better get him in the bathtub. It's almost his bedtime and I'm sure you two want to talk shop."

"Yes," Mike said, "I think Kelly's come up with an idea."

"You mean you told her what was bothering you," Cathy exclaimed delightedly.

Mike walked over and put his arms round her, "You were right as usual, Cath. I feel much better now I've got it off my chest."

Kelly, eavesdropping, was glad she hadn't heard this

conversation last night before she had figured out what was going on. Cathy's apparent belief in her ability to sort it all out for Mike was a trifle overwhelming. She turned back to the couple who had now disengaged; Cathy gathered up Gavin for his bath, and Mike started clearing off the table. "Can I give you a hand, Mike? I'm a dab hand with dishes. Steve was a great cook so I was always the kitchen helper."

With soy sauce bottle in one hand and salt-and-pepper shaker in the other, he stopped what he was doing and looked at her sympathetically. "You must miss him," he said simply.

"Yes, all the time, but I've learned to live with it." Even as she said it, she felt a pang of guilt. Steve certainly hadn't been on her mind last weekend.

"Must be tough. I can't imagine life without Cath," he said, stashing the condiments away in a cupboard over the sink. "We'll leave the dishes until later. I'm dead keen to hear what you think we should do. Let's move into my office, we can close the door. Gavin can get stroppy sometimes at bedtime." Irate screams from upstairs underlined his statement.

The office turned out to be a minute third bedroom equipped with a desk, beaten-up typist's chair, Mac computer, an upright light pine kitchen chair that had seen better days, a bookcase overflowing with computer manuals, text books and a whole shelf of science fiction paperbacks. Every inch of wall, which as far as Kelly could tell was painted an attractive off-white, was covered with cartoons cut out from various publications. A cycle helmet and a cap with a Line 7 logo had been flung in the corner. The wastebin and the wool-carpeted floor immediately around it was full of crumpled paper. Mike sat down on the typist's chair and swung it round to face Kelly who was already sitting in what she assumed was the visitor's chair. It was hard and she strongly suspected a splinter was making its way through her cotton pants.

While he looked at her expectantly, she ran her fingers through her short curls, wondering where to start. Finally she said, "I thought a lot about what you said last night and unfortunately, it makes sense. Look, I'd like to tell you what I've been thinking for a long time now—well, ever since David died—but before I do, there's just one thing bothering me." She hesitated and straightened a pile of papers that were teetering on the edge of his desk. "Mike, I hate to be personal, but there's something I must ask you. When I tell you why I'm asking, you'll understand, but the problem is I can't explain until I know your answer."

Mike, totally perplexed said, "What the hell are you talking about, Kelly? That's the most convoluted way of asking a question I've ever heard. You aren't popping pills or anything these days, are you?"

"No," she said, outraged.

"Well then, for Christ's sake just ask whatever it is you want to ask."

Taking a deep breath, she said in a rush, "Mike, you live in a large house in an upmarket suburb, you drive a fancy car and have a big boat. Are you moonlighting or something? You can't possibly be living this high off the hog on the salary Colin's paying you," and as he looked up startled, she added, "I have to know all your salaries so I can work out how much to offer new hires."

Mollified slightly by that explanation, he looked at her for a long moment, and then started to laugh. First his face broke into a wide smile, then his shoulders started to shake, and then his overweight belly wobbled in time with his shoulders. Kelly, mystified, watched him until she could feel the laughter bubbling up inside. With his soft hair falling over his face, his face red from laughing, and his whole cuddly frame shaking, he was an infectious sight. Taking two deep breaths and exhaling slowly, he finally managed to get his laughter under control. "What on earth did you think I was up to, Kelly? Moonlighting with the opposition, or pushing drugs on the side?"

"Neither actually," she said miserably, laughter evaporating instantly, "but, unless you have a very rich auntie or something, you must admit it's all a bit odd."

"It couldn't be more simple. You're looking at a financial genius. Well, maybe a slight exaggeration, but I've made an incredible amount of money over the last few years. Particularly in the bonanza times." He rummaged around in a desk drawer and came up with an old exercise book. "Financial records," he said smugly, sitting back like a business tycoon. He flitted through the pages and said, "A lot of my mates have moved to Silicon Valley. Can't blame them. They're earning twice what they could here and they haven't got a government that rips them off the minute they make money."

"So how has that made you rich? You their agent or something?"

"No," he laughed, "we stay in touch over the net. They always want to know the footie scores, I don't think the *San Jose Mercury* is too big on Kiwi sport. Anyway, several of them have moved to start-up companies, and they've told me all about what they're developing and how they think the company will do. They all have these illusions that with the stock options they are offered to jump ship and join the start-ups, they'll be filthy rich when the company goes public. I reckon they all want to make it big time and then come back here and live it up. Can't see the point myself,

I'm living the good life already."

Kelly fidgeted slightly on the uncomfortable chair, wishing he would get to the punch line. "Anyway, they tipped me off about IPOs coming out, Initial Public Offerings," he added by way of explanation. "I scraped up every penny I could, and even borrowed from my parents. They're good. Never questioned what I was up to when I said I could make a lot of money, even though it would have been pretty grim for them if I lost it." He swung irritatingly to and fro in the office chair. "I jumped in with everything I could on the IPOs. Invested in five of them. Two went south—and they were the first two—I nearly died, but fortunately the other three came up: doubled my money on one, quadrupled it on another and came out on top with the last one. I tell you, Kelly, those Internet stocks went up like rockets. When the feeding frenzy was on, people bought anything even remotely connected with the Internet. Fortunately, I was getting some good information so I was betting on sound products. You could lose your shirt pretty badly if you backed the wrong ones."

"That's for sure. For every ten start-ups in Silicon Valley, eight go belly-up. But whew, if you back the other two you're an overnight millionaire. Leastways, the venture capitalists are, and sometimes the founders too." She remembered what happened to several of Steve's friends.

"And the people who got in on the IPOs too," Mike added. "I'm not exactly a millionaire or anywhere close, but I did make a pretty penny. Enough to buy this house mortgage free," he added smugly. He sat glowing with self satisfaction for several minutes, glancing proudly round his tiny office and through the window to the neatly laid out garden and the BMW sitting on the driveway. Suddenly remembering what they were talking about originally, he said sharply, "So why did you need to know? I didn't mind you asking, but I can't see why you couldn't tell me why straight up."

Kelly tried to make herself comfortable on the wooden chair, and then began to tell Mike about her suspicions. The things that led her to believe David's death was not an accident. When she reached the bit about the too-pat arrival of a perfect replacement, he grinned widely, "And here we all thought we had some recruiting genius on our hands. I always wondered why those head hunters got such big bucks, but when you magically produced the perfect candidate, I could see why. Ah well," he sighed, "another illusion down the tubes."

"I must confess I was pretty pleased with myself at first. Downright ecstatic if I'm honest, because I knew Joe was going to cancel the project if I didn't find someone."

"The bastard," Mike said bitterly, "after all our work they were just going to haul it back to the States at the first problem."

"Come on now, Mike, be fair. You know as well as I do the chances of replacing David were about a million to one, and without him the project would have ended up being months behind schedule. And for some weird reason, the CEO of Finsat seems downright fanatical about no slippages. I don't blame Joe for being jumpy."

A motor mower started up in the next door neighbor's garden, followed by excited yapping from a young dog. "So anyway, you thought things didn't seem right, but that's all, and I still can't for the life of me see what this has to do with me and my financial situation."

"You're right. I had nothing but vague suspicions but it was bugging me. John's arrival was just too pat. I kept having the feeling something fishy was going on, so in the end I decided to do something about it rather than sit around and worry."

He started his irritating rocking to and fro again. "You're right, it's the only way to go. Cathy always gets on my case when I'm worrying about something. She believes if something is bothering you, you should do whatever you can about it, and after that if you can't resolve it, forget it." Kelly had a hard time equating this sound commonsense approach to the fey Cathy. "So what did you do? I can't imagine how you would approach it."

"I went on the assumption that someone killed David. If they had, then they had to have both the motive and the opportunity." She grinned shamefacedly. "Well, according to all those TV mysteries anyway. Since I didn't have a clue at that stage as to motive, I decided to work on the opportunity angle. That," she said emphatically, "is where you came into the picture. You wandered away from the rest of the group the day you were up on the headland, so according to my fine logical rules I had to count you as a suspect. Problem was I couldn't for the life of me see you doing anything wildly like that, and I couldn't see a motive. So you dropped to the bottom of my list."

"Hah," he said his eyes shining with intelligence, "but you worked out that I might have a financial motive. Hence the question." He sat up a little straighter in his chair looking like Winnie the Pooh playing at being a corporate executive. "I sort of fancy that. Mike Williams, gun for hire."

Kelly heaved an inward sigh of relief. Knowing she had to be sure of him before she took him into her confidence, she dreaded the moment when she had to confess he was a suspect. Mike, for all his cuddly charm, had an explosive temper, and calmly telling someone face to face that you suspected him of murder was not conducive to a pleasant relationship. And here he was in his usual completely unpredictable style being rather flattered by the whole idea.

She went on to tell him about finding out about the mysterious English tourist, and his eyebrows went up as she described her abortive attempt to track him down in England and her conclusion that he was a hit man hired by whomever it was that was trying to sabotage the project.

"But, when you told me about John changing the code in his module, it all fell into place. I'm convinced that some rival company is planting a virus in our module that will be shipped back to the States. Then it will be incorporated into the whole system without anyone suspecting a thing. If it's as big a deal as Joe has been making it out to be, it could be disastrous for Finsat."

Mike looked faintly sick. "That's horrible. Do you realize that means John is working for them too?" He sat stunned for a moment as if the fact had finally sunk in. "Why would a nice bloke like that be involved in industrial espionage?"

"I don't know," Kelly said wearily. "I couldn't sleep all last night just thinking about it, but I can't see any other explanation."

There was a light tap on the door, and Cathy poked her head in the room. "Can you go up and kiss Gavin good night, Mike? I've read him two stories but he refuses to go to sleep until you tuck him in."

"Sure," Mike said. "My rear end is going numb on this seat anyway. How about making Kelly comfortable in the living room while I go up and give Gavin a hug?"

Kelly, more than pleased to move from the uncomfortable chair, followed Cathy through to the living room and sank gratefully onto an overstuffed sofa while Cathy went out to the kitchen saying she would be right there. Kelly looked around the comfortably furnished room with a large TV in one corner and a big box of children's toys in another. A beautiful floral arrangement stood on top of a high bookcase, and there were some good watercolors around the room. Moving over to admire the largest one which held center stage, a blue vase full of irises, she was surprised to see Cathy's signature in the corner. She turned just as Cathy came into the room carrying a pot of coffee. "This is beautiful, Cathy, you're very talented."

"Oh, I've a long way to go yet, but I'm learning gradually," she glowed under the praise. "I've been taking classes whenever I can get a sitter for Gavin."

"Good idea," Mike said as he burst into the room and spotted coffee. "We've some planning to do." He settled down in an oversized armchair. "You can help us, Cath—it's going to take some pretty heavy thinking to outwit those bastards. Kelly thinks some outfit knocked poor old David off, and we intend to get to the bottom of it."

Cathy's eyes widened in shock. "You think David's death wasn't an accident?" She shuddered and folded her arms around her body.

" 'Fraid I agree with Kelly, but I've no intention of letting them get away with it. They're not going to pick on poor old Dave and then calmly make millions out of it." Cathy's face lightened. She was obviously used to Mike taking care of things.

"What do you think we can do about it? I can't see confronting John is going to do any good, he'll just swear blind we are mistaken and we've no way of proving anything. The police would just laugh at us." For the life of her, Kelly couldn't see how to tackle the problem.

"I don't think we need the police." Mike said. "These guys did this to make a lot of money. John's not going to benefit, he's just a minion, probably not really aware of what they are doing."

Kelly looked at him gratefully, wanting to believe that John was only peripherally involved. "So what do you think we should do?"

"I'm going to get inside that module and insert an antibiotic. If John's capable of dreaming up a virus that no one can detect, then I'm sure as hell I can figure out how to stop it without them knowing until they try to activate it."

"How on earth are you going to get into his code? You don't even know his password." She was fascinated by Mike's colossal confidence in his own abilities.

"I haven't met a password I couldn't crack yet. I could make a fortune if I decided to take to a life of crime. But I'm going to need your help. You're going to have to keep John occupied while I work at his terminal—given enough time I might find some clues lurking around in his desk drawer. He's got to be working from something. It can't be all in his head."

"You want me to lure John away for a while?" A few days ago the thought would have been appealing; right now it made her skin crawl.

"Yeah, it's going to take me several hours, or maybe two or three goes. Can you take him out to dinner or something? He's obviously smitten with you, it shouldn't be too difficult."

Kelly winced, convinced up until now that no one had noticed the attention John had been paying her. "Okay, I guess," she said dubiously. "When do you want to get started?"

"How about tomorrow night? See if he's free. If he is, just give me the nod and I'll get to work. See if you can talk him into a movie and then dinner, and perhaps you could invite him back to the motel for coffee; I'm going to need plenty of time."

Catching sight of Kelly's face, Cathy turned to Mike and said, "Can't you do it some time when he won't be in the office? I don't envy Kelly having to entertain someone you think is mixed up in some funny business. He could turn nasty, you know."

"No, unfortunately, he works all sorts of odd hours so there's no guarantee he wouldn't just pop in and catch me. Don't worry, Cath, Kelly can take care of herself, and he's really smitten with her; I think he'll love it. Won't suspect a thing."

Two nights later Kelly was sitting in a darkened movie house with John beside her. When she had asked him if he would like to go to the movies, he broke into a slow smile and looked at her in a way that made it hard for her to believe he was the devious manipulator they suspected. "That would be great. I haven't been out to the movies for months. What a cool idea. I'll only come if you'll let me buy you dinner afterwards though." Perfect. She would be able to keep him occupied for several hours. Within minutes she was strolling by Mike's office and giving him a surreptitious thumbs-up.

"What time?" Mike mouthed.

"Movies six-thirty, dinner afterwards," she mouthed back, feeling as if she was in the middle of a kindergarten game. Mike's eyes lit up, but he kept silent.

Halfway through the movie John took her hand in his, his hand warm, slim and comforting. This was going to be a whole lot more difficult than she had imagined. Away from John she could convince herself that she had simply been manipulated by a skilled crook. With him, she fell under the spell of his naive charm, and felt an overwhelming compulsion to tell him what was going on, and have him reassure her that he had nothing to do with it.

Surprisingly, he took her to the Sheraton for dinner. As they drew up outside the door, and the Oriental doorman summoned a valet to park John's car, she looked faintly puzzled. "Somehow I wasn't expecting to come here. With all the great restaurants around town these days, this seems a very American touristy thing to do."

"Just you wait until you see the buffet. A buddy of mine from Chicago stayed here a couple of weeks ago and I joined him for dinner. I thought it was great. Let's see what you think."

He led the way across the lobby to the bar, and said, "Let's start off with a drink here, shall we? What would you like?"

He placed the order with the waiter and when the drinks arrived took one sip of his drink, and said, "You know, I just remembered I need to pick something up from the office. I totally forgot when we headed off for the movies. Would you excuse me a minute? I'll only be fifteen minutes or so." He looked slightly abashed. "I know it's rude of me deserting you in the bar, but I think you're good and safe in the Sheraton." The only other people in the bar were a group of four white-haired tourists looking absolutely exhausted after a day's sightseeing.

Panicked, Kelly said as calmly as possible, "Oh, John, must you? Surely it can wait until tomorrow." She put her hand on his arm, trying to look madly disappointed to lose him for a few moments. Somehow she didn't think she was pulling off the wilting Southern belle act very well.

Getting up, he said, "Sorry, I know it's rude but I

absolutely have to pick up some stuff to mail first thing in the morning. I won't be long, honestly," and with an apologetic smile he was gone.

Kelly watched his back disappear through the glass doors, and then hauled her cell phone out of her handbag, spilling a lipstick and packet of tissues on the floor in her haste. She dialed Mike's office number, praying that he wasn't in one of his creative trances. When he was, he totally ignored phone calls and everyone who came by to talk to him. The phone rang, and rang, and rang. She could feel the perspiration forming on her upper lip. Come on, Mike, answer the bloody phone, will you? Still it rang, and no one answered. She glanced at her watch. John would be well on his way by now and it was only ten minutes to the office. Still the phone rang. Perhaps he would be held up with the valet parking, they could be slow sometimes. She found she was clutching at straws. Her watch was ticking relentlessly on. He would be nearly there by now. She could imagine poor Mike working away at John's terminal totally confident that she had John occupied for the evening. Knowing Mike, he would be having the time of his life. Nothing gave him a bigger kick than outsmarting another software engineer.

The phone continued to ring, and she grew desperate. She couldn't think of anything else to do to warn him. Then, like a thunderclap it hit her. Of course, you idiot Kelly, he would be working in John's office, he would never hear his own phone ringing from there. With fumbling fingers she dialed John's number, almost forgetting to hit the Call button in her panic.

Mike had waited five minutes after John and Kelly disappeared into the movie house in case they couldn't get a seat, then, satisfied, ran across the road to his car and drove to the office. Parking sloppily, he leaped out of the car, locked it, dashed into the building and impatiently punched the elevator button. Fretting, he waited what seemed like an age for the doors to slide open. He stepped quickly inside and hit the button for the fourth floor. As usual, nothing happened. Impatiently he stabbed the close door button and the doors slid to. Hurrying out of the elevator and into the empty office he dashed around from cubicle to cubicle making sure he was alone. The unnatural quiet should have told him: no phones ringing, no raised voices, no hum of terminals, click of keys, or hum of the copying machine. He stood a moment, savoring the silence. He loved empty offices. It was wonderful to walk around completely free, no one to bother him. Being alone was something he relished.

Once in John's office, he methodically went through the desk drawers. A stack of manuals stashed in one; a lunch box, box of tissues, comb, several 2B pencils, a stack of index cards, an eraser and an address book in another; a small pile of manila folders in the other. He rifled quickly through the manila folders and the address book looking for a password, file names, anything that would give him the key to unlock John's computer files. Frustrated, he turned on the terminal and started cruising around trying a variety of approaches. He raised his eyes to the ceiling for inspiration then tried John's first name, then his last, his hometown. Nothing worked. He must have a list somewhere, Mike fumed. He can't possibly keep them all in his head. He got up and moved around the tiny office looking for a clue, but it was one of the neatest offices in the complex with none of the untidy piles of books, manuals, files and sports equipment that characterized the rest. Looking at his watch he realized he had already wasted almost an hour; the movie would be well underway now. Unable to think of what to do next, he fumbled in his pocket for a dollar and went along to the Coke machine. The dollar sliding down inside the machine, and the Coke hitting the metal holder at the bottom, sounded like a rocket going off in the unnatural stillness. He grabbed the Coke, popped the top and, sipping as he went, walked back to John's office and sat down at the desk. Pulling out the small panel at the top of the desk for his Coke, he looked once more at the terminal which had been humming vacantly while he searched for clues. The screen sprang in to life as he moved the mouse, and as he waited, he turned to sip his Coke. Replacing the can carefully on the slide-out panel, anxious not to spill Coke on John's desk, a thought struck him, and he ran his hand underneath the panel. There was something there. Excited, he got down on his knees and discovered a piece of yellow paper carefully cello taped to the underside of the panel. With a sigh of relief, he saw it contained a list of file names and what had to be a password. His chubby face beamed. He was in like Flynn.

Totally absorbed in what he was doing, he heard a phone ringing somewhere. In his state of total concentration it seemed to come from a long way off, almost as if it was underwater. Its insistence began to bother him. Why didn't they hang up, obviously no one was here? When the phone on John's desk rang, he almost jumped out of his skin. Who was calling John? Should he answer? If he did, the person at the other end would wonder what he was doing in John's office. He decided to let it ring for a while. Hopefully, it would go away. If not, he'd pick it up and say he was working in another office and heard it ringing. The sound of the elevator moving downwards surprised him. Someone in the insurance office upstairs must be working late.

Gingerly he picked up the phone and said, "Hello."

Kelly's frantic voice said, "Mike, why the hell didn't you answer the phone? Get out of there NOW. He's on his way to the office—I couldn't stop him. He should be there any minute. He left here about twenty minutes ago."

Horror stricken, Mike closed down the file he had been working on, and shut down the terminal. The shutting down routine seemed to take forever, and while it was flashing messages at him he heard the elevator move again. Coming up this time. The minute the terminal sighed to a stop, he switched it off, hastily stuffed the scrap of paper he had written the file names on in his top pocket, grabbed his Coke, pushed the panel back into place and looked around distractedly to make sure nothing was out of place. Now the elevator was stopping and any moment the doors would open and John would walk in. Adrenaline pumping, he flew across the office in his soft running shoes, and as he heard the elevator doors open and the click of John's leather shoes in the hallway, he rushed into his office, fell into his chair and switched on his terminal. He heard John walk into his office, then a few minutes silence and then the sound of a desk drawer opening. When John came across to his office, he turned round, a look of total surprise on his face.

"Hi, John," he said, "I didn't expect to see you in tonight. Going to be working late?" He hoped John wouldn't notice his red face and damp hair.

"No, just popped in to pick something up." He looked hard at Mike. "You look hot. You want to turn the air conditioning up. It gets stuffy in here late in the evening."

"You're right," Mike said weakly, aware of the damp patches under his arms. "I'll do that in a minute."

"Don't worry, I'll flip it down for you as I go out. I've got to get right back. I left my date sitting in a bar, and she's a good-looking chick; someone else might pick her up if I'm too long."

"Okay, night then, thanks." Mike turned back to his terminal and heard John's footsteps recede along the passageway. He sat for a long while paralyzed. Sure he'd made it out of the office in time, but the way John was looking at him and the silence when he first went into his own office worried him. Did he suspect something? The terminal would have been warm, but then why would John touch it? Shrugging his shoulders, he waited another ten minutes, then went back to John's office and got to work.

Chapter 28

Waking out of a deep sleep, Kelly groggily snaked an arm out of the bed and picked up the phone without opening her eyes. She managed a croaky "Hello."

Mike's cheerful voice said, "Come on, Kelly, wake up, it's a lovely day."

"What on earth time is it?" She rolled over and picked up her watch off the bedside table—six a.m. "Why are you calling this early—is something wrong?"

"No, well, hopefully not. I just want to talk to you about last night, and I can't do it in the office, and if we are both out at the same time during the day John may get suspicious. So I thought we could meet for breakfast," he said brightly.

She groaned, it had been a late night and she'd promised herself a lie-in until seven-thirty a.m. "Okay, want to meet at the motel restaurant just along the road from me? By the time you get there, I can be up and dressed."

"See you then," Mike said, and she was left listening to the dial tone.

Hastily falling out of bed, she took a quick shower, brushed her teeth and put on a blouse and slacks. Half an hour later she was sitting in the motel restaurant nursing a cup of tea and waiting for Mike. The restaurant was surprisingly full for the early hour. When Mike arrived, wearing a freshly pressed shirt and creaseless trousers, his soft hair carefully combed, she realized that first thing in the morning he was a different person from the crumpled teddy bear she normally saw. Spotting her, he walked quickly over, said good morning, then picked up the menu. "Have you ordered yet?"

"No, I was waiting for you. I'm going with the continental."

He quickly perused the menu. "Well, since I'm out for breakfast I might as well live it up."

"So how did you get on last night? Did you get anywhere?"

Mike's face broke into a wide smile. "You betcha. Told you there was no system I couldn't crack. Mark you, finding his list of files helped a whole lot!"

"Are you saying he left a list of his files and a password lying around? That means he can't possibly have anything to hide." She felt an overwhelming sense of relief.

"No, they weren't exactly lying around, I found them taped to the underside of his desk panel. And, what's more, he definitely is up to something. The code he's written is nothing like what it's supposed to be. It's very clever, because externally you can't see a thing, and although the linkage points are kosher, the inside of the module isn't doing what they are calling for in the specifications."

Her face fell. Another evening with John had convinced her he was way too nice to be mixed up in anything underhanded. "So was I right? Is it a virus that's going to lurk until after the system is shipped?"

"No, that's the weird thing, as far as I can tell it's nothing that sinister. It's just a whole bunch of straightforward transactions. If it matched the specs, it would be fine. Problem is I can't for the life of me imagine what it is."

"You mean you can't tell?"

"No, I was there until about two-thirty this morning working on it, and it baffles me completely."

"Two-thirty! You're looking remarkably chipper for someone who was up that late."

"I just went home and took a shower, and then waited till it was a decent enough hour to call you. I'm completely psyched on this thing, it's intriguing. You did a brilliant job of keeping him occupied."

"Except when he decided to nip back to the office. That must have given you heart failure."

"It did. I've never moved so fast in my life." His eyes were bright with excitement. "Only problem is I think he may suspect something. That's why I don't think we should be seen together. He spent a while in his office—longer than it would have taken to pick up the package he had in his hand, and then when he came over and talked to me I was sweating like a bull. He looked at me sort of oddly." He stopped talking as the waitress placed a pot of coffee on the table and two large toast racks, one white and the other brown. "I hope I'm imagining things."

"He didn't say anything when he came back to the Sheraton. Just apologized for leaving me so long, and then we went to dinner."

The waitress placed a large plate filled with two fried eggs, sausage, bacon, tomatoes and mushrooms in front of Mike. "Just help yourself to the buffet, madam. Can I get you some more tea?"

"No, this is fine, thanks." Mike waited politely, eyeing his sizzling plate hungrily. "Go ahead, Mike, before it gets cold. I'll go and get my breakfast."

When she returned, she asked, "So where do we go from here? If you can't work out what he's doing we're kind of stuck, aren't we?"

Mike swallowed a large mouthful of sausage and said eagerly, "No, I worked that out. That's what I was doing this morning while I was waiting for you to surface." He munched a piece of toast complacently.

"So what have you worked out?" Kelly asked, resisting the urge to scream at him.

"To find out what he's up to, we have to know what the overall system is doing. My bet is that he's doing something that affects the data gathering part of the system. Once we know what the system does in some detail, then it will be a doddle to figure out what's going on."

Kelly ate a spoonful of cereal slowly, then said wearily, "Mike, I've been trying to find out what the system does for months. I've asked Joe. I've asked one of the project managers, but they're all like clams. I just don't think I can get the information you need. I'm sorry, I think we're stuck." She felt an overwhelming sense of disappointment. Mike had been so sure that if he looked at John's code he would be able to find out what was going on.

Mike polished off the last of his bacon before putting down his knife and fork and looking at her, his eyes dancing. "I'm not asking you to find out. All I need from you is for you to swing a trip to the States for me. I'll put it to Colin that I must work with the project over there for a couple of weeks to finish my piece. If you back me up, he'll let me do it. You've got him eating out of your hand. He's always been mildly in awe of you, and when you pulled off the finding-John coup, he reckoned he'd got a genius on his hands. If you say it's essential, he'll buy it."

Kelly put down the piece of toast she had been buttering, and said, "Yes, but how is that going to help? Nobody will talk over there. They've all been told it's top secret. I couldn't get anywhere."

"Of course you couldn't. You've been talking to all the up-front guys—they never know what's going on. The people who know everything are the invisible ones."

"The invisible ones? What are you talking about?"

Several businessmen had already left, and the tourists were picking up guidebooks and fussily making their way to the door.

"The office cleaners, the guards, and the neophytes on a project. I read an article about it one time, and it's very true. You've no idea how much information they have. Managers sit talking on the phone late in the day, and take no notice of the cleaners coming in to empty wastepaper baskets. Guards overhear snippets of conversation as people walk across the lobby together, then they ask a secretary about it. And they love to show off their knowledge. I always have a chat with the guard when I leave late at night. They're lonely and bored. You'd be amazed what I know about that insurance company upstairs. To say nothing of who's sleeping with whom."

"You're just an old snoop. I'm going to check who's around before I talk on the phone now," she laughed, and then getting serious again, "but how's that going to help? They'll just have snippets, nothing solid." Mike was beginning to worry her, first looking round the offices late at night, now gossiping with the guards to find out the latest scandal. Still, she reflected, where would we private eyes be without sticky beaks to help us out?

"Now that's where the neophytes come in. Those sweet little wet-behind-the-ears whiz kids from MIT or Berkeley or wherever. They love to talk about their work. Can't talk about anything else, most of them. I just take a couple of them out for a beer, and start telling them they don't know what they're talking about. That's too much for them."

"How do you mean?" She could just imagine Mike in his sarcastic mode pulling apart some young kid with big ears and half a dozen pens in his pocket.

"They have to prove to me that what they're working on

is a key piece of the project. They think I'm some kind of dinosaur who is working on a mundane piece of software because that's all I'm capable of. So very patiently they explain to me what it is they're doing, and what state-of-the-art design is required to do it. I listen in wide-eyed awe, and they're happy. I tell you for the price of a pizza and a few jugs of beer, I can take out half a dozen of them, and build up a real picture of the system." He paused reflectively, "I must hand it to them, they're damn good. These kids make me think I'd better make my fortune quick and get out of this business." From his smug face, Kelly knew he didn't mean a word of it. Mike still believed he was God's greatest gift to the software world. "What I can glean from them, plus the management stuff I'll find out from the guards, cleaners and cafeteria staff, will give me a pretty good idea of what's going on. Then there's our stuff to go on too."

Kelly was impressed. Mike was really getting into this amateur sleuth business. Although if he was going to go round asking lots of questions, someone might get the wrong idea. "Mike, you will be careful, won't you? If this is as big as we think it is, asking questions could be dangerous."

"Don't be ridiculous Kelly. You, they might suspect. Who's going to suspect an overweight nerd of anything that smart?"

Looking at his round cuddly face and his chubby body, she had to agree. It was a bit like suspecting Winnie the Pooh of being Mata Hari.

"Okay, well, you talk to Colin this morning as soon as you get in, and when he talks to me about it, I'll back up your story. Now," she said, downing the last of her tea, "we'd better get going. I'll pay on the way out and go straight to the office. You sit and finish off your toast. We'd better not both arrive at the same time."

His round face beamed. "This is great. It's like being dropped into the middle of a James Bond movie."

Knowing how persuasive Mike could be when he wanted something, Kelly felt confident talking Colin into it would be easy. "Is that right, Colin? If he thinks it's important, I'm sure he's right. He's got such a big ego, it must have been hard for him to say he needed help from the Finsat guys, and you know how he hates being away from Cathy and Gavin. I think we should spring for it. It's probably going to save money in the long haul, because if Mike bogs down we'll be in trouble."

Colin pulled on his straggly mustache. "I suppose you're right." He hesitated a moment and then let out a large sigh. "Oh well, we'd better keep Mike happy. He's so damn temperamental, he's liable to walk out on us if he doesn't get his way."

Kelly left Auckland early in the afternoon aiming to beat the commute, but as she crossed the harbor bridge the traffic was already beginning to build even though the afternoon configuration of extra lanes going north were in place. Once over the bridge she made good time, but as she drove, her thoughts were troubled. Mike was now caught up in the thrill of the chase and seemed to have totally adjusted to the idea of John being an industrial saboteur, but she, with the memory of another delightful evening in his company, was having a hard time believing it. She turned on the CD player and let Bryn Terfyl's voice fill the car until thinking became impossible.

Two days later when the phone rang at seven a.m. Kelly

was about to enjoy her first cup of tea of the day. She had got up, put the jug on to boil, let the dog in, opened up the kitchen windows, hunted in the living room for yesterday's crossword, then returned to bed to enjoy a leisurely cup of tea over the *Herald's* crossword. Annoyed, she picked up the phone and managed a semi-gracious, "Hello, this is Kelly."

"Mrs. Brandon?" a very English male voice asked. She tried hard to place him. As best she could tell it was a sort of middle-of-the-road, London-type accent, or was it South of England? The only two English accents she could place with any confidence were Yorkshire and the East End of London, the latter as a result of watching *East Enders* for several seasons while she was in the States.

As she hesitated, he added, "This is Brian Davis from the CID, we talked a few weeks ago."

"Oh, of course, I just wasn't expecting to hear from you."

He chuckled, "No faith in the great investigative powers of the Metropolitan Police, madam?"

"It's not that. I thought you had all written me off as some kind of crackpot from down under. You were awfully nice in humoring me in my hunt for Andrew James, but I didn't give you anything solid to go on, so I just assumed you asked a bunch of questions for PR reasons and tucked it away in the miscellaneous nuts drawer."

"I must confess it was a pretty bizarre tale, but you had me convinced. Remind me never to buy a used car from you." Then his voice deepened as it grew serious. "We followed up on the information you gave us and discovered that Andrew James was an ex-petty crook called George Small, who somehow or another was mixed up with some very nasty people on the international scene. We put him under observation to see who his associates were, but while we were watching, his house was bombed."

"What?" Kelly exclaimed, almost knocking her mug of tea off the bedside table.

"Look, I shouldn't be telling you this, and if you ever say anything about it, my head will be on the chopping block." He paused. "But, I think you were right. He was a hit man. We did a total trace on him through the drug squad and immigration. He was in and out of the country like a yo-yo on several fake passports, lived like a king on no visible means of support, but was not a drug runner. We're pretty sure though, that he had a connection to a heavyweight gang. It dated right back to his spell in prison several years ago. One of his cellmates was a member of the gang, and I think young Georgie must have impressed him. I know it sounds bizarre, but we suspect he started off doing small jobs for them and then worked his way up to international hit man. He was the coolest customer any of the prison guards and probation officers had ever met. Turned from a cocky little East Ender to an upmarket, stockbroker-belt resident."

"You're kidding," Kelly said, causing the dog to look worried at her tone of voice. "You really believe he was a hit man? I can't believe how much you found out about him."

"Yes," he answered, his voice warm. "Thanks to you we got a lead on him and were well on our way to a scoop until someone eliminated him. If that 'accident' you talked about happened while he was in the country—and that checks with our dates—he probably did knock off your friend, although there's no way anyone can prove it now."

"No," she said reflectively, "it's a genuine dead end. Anyway, it sounded as if he got his just desserts, so it's all square."

Through the window Kelly could hear a tractor moving

along the beach. "So why are you telling me all this? It's nice of you to put me in the picture, but since I can't do anything with what you're telling me, why call? Why not just let me believe it was all my wild imagination."

"The reason I've been trying to get hold of you is to tell you to stop asking any more questions. I'm sure by now you're back home, and hopefully have dropped the whole thing. But on the off-chance that you haven't, I just wanted to warn you."

"Warn me?" she looked out at the clouds moving slowly across the sky, not really seeing them.

"Yes, anyone who employs a hit man is big time. I know you hear these stories about disgruntled wives offering money to undercover cops in pubs to knock off their husbands, but believe you me that hardly ever happens. Hit men are used by organized crime, politicians—not in New Zealand of course," he added hastily, "and large companies. In fact, anywhere that someone has to be removed who's in the way of progress as they see it. So if you've been running around asking questions about Andrew James, you could be in real trouble. They went to the trouble of eliminating him so there were no leads, and he was on their side."

Kelly looked at the bedroom door and was suddenly aware of the unlocked front door and open windows. Did she remember to lock up last night before she went to bed? That used to be Steve's job and she was pretty sloppy about it. "But they wouldn't know who I was, and anyway I'm no threat to them, whoever they are."

"But yes, they would. You ran around Portsmouth asking lots of questions. You weren't even remotely discreet. You used your own name, you have a New Zealand accent, and they don't get too many Kiwis in Pompey. It wouldn't be difficult to track you down."

Kelly's mouth felt suddenly dry, and she took a quick gulp of tea, almost scalding her throat. "But if he's dead, and I'm back home, I'm no problem to them anymore." She said it confidently, trying hard to convince herself.

"Well, no, I suppose you're okay, but I want you to be on your guard. Don't go asking any more questions or stirring anything up. These are ruthless people you are dealing with."

Kelly, horribly aware of Mike asking questions in California, and John probably assigned to keep an eye on her, said, "Hang on a minute. Why did they suddenly decide to get rid of Andrew James or George whatshisname? He was working for them, wasn't he? How could they have possibly got wind of my looking for him in Portsmouth? It doesn't make sense."

There was a deep sigh at the other end of the phone. "Unfortunately I think we probably caused the problem. We had a hunch it might be Georgie so we asked a couple of our snouts to dig around for us and see what they could come up with. One of them came up trumps, but the other one might have decided it was more profitable to tell the crims CID were on to Georgie."

"But there's no connection to me. You're the Metropolitan police, aren't you? You've no real connection with Portsmouth, and that's the only place I asked questions."

"I wouldn't be too sure about that. If they thought we were on to Georgie, they would do some backtracking to find out where he slipped up." He paused a moment and then continued, "They'd realize he must have made someone in New Zealand suspicious. After all, that was his last job, and it was a place he hadn't been to before. Never mind though, you've probably nothing to worry about as long as you didn't do much poking around in Auckland before you headed for Portsmouth."

"No," she said weakly while her constricting throat could still function. "It was fantastic of you to call. I'll certainly be careful, but I'm sure they'll have lost interest in me by now." As he said goodbye and told her to take care of herself, she looked across at Riggles and said, "I hope I'm right, or you're going to have to live up to your reputation as a guard dog." The puppy wagged his tail and tried to look intelligent.

Chapter 29

Kelly shrugged off the warning from the CID and plunged into several days of frenetic gardening. First she tackled the lawn, which was threatening to turn into a meadow, then trimmed around the trees with the Flomow. Then it was time to turn her attention to the flower beds, and by the time she had deadheaded the roses, getting scratched several times for her pains, and weeded the flower beds, it began to look as if someone lived in the house. Even after a long, hot soak in the tub with a generous helping of Radox and lavender essential oil, her bones still ached when she went to bed. Finally, after reading a Michael Connolly, she fell into an exhausted sleep, only to wake up at the slightest noise. It would only take a bird on the roof, or the screech of a kiwi to have her sitting bolt upright in bed, all senses alert. Telling herself she was being ridiculous, she still got up and walked around the house checking the locks and making sure the windows were closed. Then she got herself a glass of milk and a couple of cookies and sat reading in bed for an hour.

Sally, arriving at the door one morning at nine a.m., was amazed when Kelly greeted her in a robe. "What are you doing loafing around in bed at this hour? Aren't you the freak who's normally out running on the beach at six-thirty?"

Kelly, looking rumpled and sleepy said, "I guess I must have overslept. I woke up in the night and couldn't get back to sleep. Come on in, I'll make some tea." She gave a huge yawn. "Might wake me up. You know I even tried the milk and cookies trick to get off to sleep. Hasn't worked for three nights, but I'm enjoying myself and putting on pounds."

Sally followed her through the door and into the kitchen where Kelly filled the jug and put it on to boil. "You haven't slept properly for three nights? What's up?" She leaned on the counter, cool and elegant in cream slacks and a yellow shirt.

"The other morning, a detective from CID in London called."

"What for? Did they find Andrew James?"

"Yes, they did actually," Kelly said without looking up as she squished the tea bags and extracted them from the mugs. "He called to tell me Andrew James is dead."

"Well you knew that for goodness sakes, Kelly; you found it out for yourself in Portsmouth. Someone else was using his passport."

Kelly added milk to the mugs, put the milk away in the refrigerator and then carried them through to the living room. Sally followed and made herself comfortable on the sofa. "But it's the someone else who is dead. They found out it was a crook called George Small who was traveling on Andrew James's passport. They suspected him of being a drug runner so they put a surveillance team on him. Two detectives were outside his house when he was blown up."

"Blown up! Blimey, what was he, an IRA terrorist, or something, bungling a homemade bomb?" Sally grinned as she picked up the mug, apparently amused by the idea of a mad bomber going up through the roof instead of his hapless victims.

"No, they think he was killed by the people he was working for because he had been careless and aroused the suspicions of the CID. They wanted to make sure he wasn't around to talk when the CID came calling."

"For goodness sakes, they sound like some pretty ruthless characters." She took a delicate sip of tea, her long fingers with the perfectly shaped nails caressing the mug, "You sure we haven't wandered into a rerun of *The Godfather*? But that's terrific. Isn't it? If he was the character that knocked off poor old David, he got his just desserts. Congratulations, Sherlock, you solved another crime."

Kelly smiled weakly. "Not really, because the real criminals are still getting away with it. Andrew James was just one of their peons."

"Oh come on now. You hunted down a murderer and CID watched him go up in smoke. Enough already." She stopped and Kelly could almost see the thoughts going through her mind. "But if you're still worried after the CID called, what did he tell you? Surely hearing from him would have been reassuring."

"What he told me," Kelly answered quietly, "was to be careful. If this organization, whoever they are, got wind of me asking questions in Portsmouth, and he seemed to think they might, they could decide to get rid of me too."

Sally looked shocked. "No wonder you're having trouble sleeping at night. Have you been to the police and asked for protection?" She took an exaggerated theatrical look out of the window. "I don't see our local constable sitting at the gate."

Kelly sighed, got up and, wandering over to the window, idly watched some surfers paddling out to wait for a good wave. "I don't suppose there's anything to worry about really. It's just once he'd put the idea in my mind, I find I'm jumping out of my skin at the slightest noise in the night."

"I can relate to that. I only have to watch a creepy movie and I'm scared to turn the light off when I go to bed. But I think he's right, you know, you should be careful for a while. Why don't you come down and stay with us for a few days? You can have Christopher's room, and he can sleep on the camp bed in my room. He'll love that." Her eyes twinkled. "It'll put a crimp in my love life for a while, but hey, what are friends for?"

"No, I'll be fine," Kelly said, more robustly than she felt.

"No, you won't. You're way too isolated here. There's no neighbor you can yell out to, and anyone that wants to creep up on you has all this bush for cover."

"Thanks a bunch, I feel much better now." She looked with new eyes at the swaying bush that spread from the beach up the long hill to the edge of the deck. The tea tree with its tiny white flowers, the pohutukawas showing their new growth and the luxuriant fronds of the tree ferns bursting out from their tea tree cover to dominate the scene. She loved the bush, loved walking down the cool, shady path to the beach, enjoying the tiny ferns and creepers that seemed to pop up everywhere, and the wood pigeons that lived happily in the big old puriri tree. Suddenly it took on a sinister note. It was impossible to see anyone climbing up from the beach, the tea tree provided perfect cover. Then turning back to Sally, she said, "Thanks, I really appreciate the offer, but I'll be okay. I'm off to Auckland again in a few days anyway."

Looking unconvinced, Sally said, "You won't be okay. You're being stupid."

"I will be," Kelly answered, temper rising, "but anyway, if there really is a risk, do you think I'm going to lead the crooks to your house and hide behind Christopher? No way am I going to put the kids in danger. You too, for that matter," she added, grudgingly.

Totally unmoved by Kelly's outburst, Sally calmly

finished her tea and sat considering it for a moment. "You're probably right. I hadn't thought about the danger to the kids. I tell you what though. Why don't you go and stay with Richard?" She paused. "Can't imagine why didn't I think of that before; it's perfect. He's a big guy, he's got a gun and about half a dozen dogs that make an incredible racket whenever anyone gets near the house; you'd be safe there."

"I am not going to stay with Richard. You know how he feels about me. That would be a disaster."

Sally started to laugh helplessly. "I just don't believe you, Mrs. Brandon. You'd rather wind up on a slab in the morgue than suffer a fate worse than death at the hands of the wicked laird. I suppose someone with a few thousand acres qualifies as a laird, doesn't he? Your whole life recently has been a cross between a Ludlum plot and *The Godfather*. It's refreshing that we've now moved to *True Romances*."

The following Tuesday, Kelly set off for Auckland once more, eager to hear what Mike had found out. He wouldn't arrive until the next day, but she thought it wise to arrive the day before so it wasn't too obvious that she wanted to see him. Before she left, she locked the house securely, checking to make sure that all the windows were firmly closed. As she tossed her bag into the back of the car, she stopped a moment to admire her handiwork. The garden looked great. Scarcely a weed in sight, and although the grass was growing at the rate of knots, it still looked respectable.

Rather than book in at her favorite motel, she had made reservations at the Sebel Apartments on the waterfront. Located in the America's Cup Village, an area that always had people around during the day and fairly late into the night, she should be safe. Although she told herself there was no real danger, she saw no reason to be stupid.

Later that afternoon, she was dealing with her stack of mail in the office when John dropped by. "Hi, Kelly. It's good to see you. I didn't know you were coming down today." His brown eyes regarded her seriously. "I don't suppose you're free tonight, are you?" His voice quiet and strangely humble.

"No, sorry, John, but maybe we could get together tomorrow." It was hard meeting his gaze, but she had to keep him believing she knew nothing. Hopefully Mike would have found out enough so they could finally resolve this thing, but until that time, the cat and mouse game had to continue.

He picked up a pen off her desk and rolled it around in his long, tapered hand. "I've missed you," he said softly. "I wanted to follow you up North, but Colin has been on my case to get this module completed. Shall we meet for a drink about six-thirty tomorrow?" He continued to look at her and she grew uncomfortable under his penetrating gaze.

"Yes, that would be great," she said, trying hard to sound sincere. She knew this would all be a whole lot easier if he wasn't so damn charming. He turned and walked quietly out of the office.

Next morning when she had just settled down at her desk, the phone rang, and Mike's excited voice was on the other end of the line. "Kelly, we need to talk. We can't do it in the office, so how about you meet me somewhere for a coffee."

"Welcome back. What time did you get in?"

"Couple of hours or so ago."

"Don't you want to get some sleep?"

"No, I'm way too hyped up. If I come into the office,

I'm not going to be able to talk to you. Well, not without rousing John's suspicions, and I've heaps to tell you. How about meeting me at that café in Mt. Eden you like? You know, the one where several of us went to lunch the other week. Can't remember its name."

"Yes, I know the one you mean. I'll be there in about forty minutes. I don't want to rush out with unseemly haste. I'll just bring my briefcase and pretend I am off to some important meeting somewhere."

"This IS an important meeting," Mike said, putting down the phone.

By the time she had driven to Mt. Eden, found a parking space and reached the café, Mike was already there. It was mid-morning and the cafe was half-full, coffee drinkers scattered around enjoying lattes and some great-looking muffins. Mike got to his feet when he saw her, his round face beaming, and she went right over and hugged him, his large cuddly frame somehow very reassuring. "It's good to see you. You know it wasn't until I saw you just then that I realized how worried I'd been about you."

"You don't need to worry about the great detective," he said, "wait till I tell you what I found out. But first, what would you like?"

"An espresso would be good, thanks," Kelly said, taking a seat and putting her briefcase on the spare chair while Mike went over to the counter and ordered the coffee.

"So tell me what happened," she said the minute he sat down. Around them there was a pleasant buzz of conversation, the coffee machine whirred and hissed and outside the traffic rumbled by.

He leaned his elbows on the table and said, "It was brilliant. It worked just the way I thought it would. I got all sorts of gen from a cleaner and this cute little secretary that I bumped into at the coffee station. She was really tickled by my accent. Said she'd always wanted to visit Australia. I think *Crocodile Dundee* did more to educate the Americans about the South Pacific than anything that's happened in the last fifty years or so."

"So what did you find out?"

Mike was not to be hurried, he was enjoying himself too much. "After I got the tidbits from the cleaner, I started on the MIT whiz kids. I tell you it's tough being treated like an old man when you haven't even hit thirty. But they fell for my backward country boy using archaic software routine, and couldn't help themselves. They had to explain exactly what they were doing." He stopped talking as the waitress came over and gave Kelly her coffee. "It was still very difficult to figure out what it was all about though."

Kelly sighed. "You're saying you still don't know?" She felt bitterly disappointed. She'd been convinced Mike would come through.

"No, I didn't say that. I just said it was tough, but just as I was thinking I was getting nowhere other than putting on about five pounds with all the beer and pizza I was guzzling while I was interrogating the youngsters, I bumped into the *Crocodile Dundee* fan. She wanted to know all about New Zealand, when I gently pointed out that was where I'm from, so I offered to take her to lunch." His grin was self-satisfied, sure he'd made a hit with the impressionable young woman. "It turned out she was personal assistant—she sorted me out in short order when I called her a secretary—to the Product Manager. She told me a lot about the product without realizing what she was doing. It's interesting, something I've never noticed before," he added reflectively, "if you don't understand what it is you're talking about, you repeat things you've heard without having any idea whether they are important or not."

Kelly sipped her espresso and waited impatiently, knowing he had to get to the bottom line sooner or later. Mike took a gulp of coffee and continued, "Well, as we'd thought, it's a very large system. Huge actually, and the security is very tight, but that's probably because it's handling a lottery of some sort. Whenever gambling's involved they're paranoid about keeping the system secure. It could be a lottery, but if it is, it's very large—do you think maybe they're going to legalize gambling on football?"

"Could be. It has to happen sometime, and if it is then it would be a gigantic project. But you're not sure."

"No, I couldn't find out. It could also be another state lottery where they're expecting gigantic participation." He took a large bite out of a Danish and chewed silently for a few moments. "What I do know is that the system is set up to handle millions of financial transactions. Now think about that for a minute."

Kelly stared at him for a long moment. "You mean you've got a huge system, handling oodles of money, with a module tucked away inside one of the control modules, that's set up to do something dicey."

"Exactly," he said excitedly, banging his hand on the table and causing the two gray-haired women at the next table to look up startled. "A module that could filter off money and stash it away in some Swiss bank account."

"But come on, Mike, they would suss that out in no time. Disappearing chunks of money have a tendency to make people nervous."

"Ah, but the size of the system says there are going to be millions of transactions, and each transaction could be anything from a couple of dollars to a hundred, depending on the size of the bet. If you simply take some minute amount like one-tenth of a percent off each one it would add up in a hurry, but wouldn't be detected."

Kelly looked impressed. "You could be right, and with that sort of money involved, and with the amount of muscle they've used so far, it must be some very well organized bunch." She sipped her espresso and sat looking out of the window at the shoppers walking by, some peering in the window, then moving on, others liking the look of the place and coming in for their morning coffee. While she was watching, her mind raced, trying to remember something. A man in his sixties and his wife sat down close by and began to talk in a broad North Country English accent. "That's it," she said excitedly to Mike, "I knew there was something I'd seen about lotteries. It was a while back when Britain's National Lottery was up for grabs. Camelot, the company that had been running the company for years, was competing against Richard Branson's company for the contract. He'd formed a not-for-profit People's Lottery, or some such weird thing. Both bids were turned down initially because their proposals were weak."

Mike, finishing his Danish and rubbing his mouth with a paper napkin, looked puzzled. "So what has that got to do with our outfit?"

"Patience, my man, I haven't got to the interesting bit yet. The new lottery was due to start in 2001 and most people assumed that since it had been running very successfully for several years, Camelot, the incumbent, would have its contract renewed for another seven years. Now, this is where we get to the interesting part. The commission said that they rejected the proposals because they were too optimistic, but they also said they had concerns about the honesty and reliability of Camelot's software supplier and partner."

"Why, what did they do?" Mike was all attention now.

"It turned out the software company admitted covering up a software glitch sometime early in 1998 which had caused over one hundred thousand small prize winners to receive the wrong amount over the first three and a half years. Think about that for a minute. Three and a half years a software glitch can go undetected as long as you're not hitting the big time winners. Just think how much you could filter off if you only take small amounts. I think it must have given our crooked bunch the idea."

"That's incredible, Kelly. How come you knew about it?"

"I think I read about it in *The Herald* initially, but then I talked to my friends in London. They thought it was hilarious. Another software bungle on the grand scale."

Mike stopped and thought for a moment, then said, almost to himself, "If you heard about the Camelot software problem, then Finsat must have heard about it too. They'd have looked at the Brits' system to see how well it worked before they designed their own. And on the strength of that, they would have put it through extensive tests. Not just in-house, but actual field tests where real terminals take in money from customers and pay out winnings. They'd have run a check to make sure every red cent was accounted for before they released the system to the general public."

"You're right, Mike, I hadn't thought of that. Of course, they would have." Kelly sipped her coffee and pondered, "I can't see how they did it. There's no way it would have got through field tests."

"I can. Don't forget I've looked at the way that thing works. What they'd do is have a trigger in there somewhere which could be flipped at the last minute before release and after all the testing was over."

"And, of course, John would go straight back to California after the module is released from here, wouldn't he? He would have instructions to get back to Quantum and to be on hand if Finsat called him in to put in fixes. And, of course, they knew there would be," she said excitedly. "He must have set it up so there would be some minor problem during field testing that they'd need him to fix. While he's fixing it, he flips the switch and the system is in siphon-off mode."

"Brilliant, isn't it?" Mike said, his eyes shining. "I'd love to meet these guys, they're fantastic." Then he went very still, sitting back in his chair, thinking, saying nothing. Kelly waited, wondering what he was about to say. "All of a sudden I can see why John did it. I've had a hard time seeing a nice guy like him as part of a crooked organization. It's been bugging me how he could be so shabby, and I just couldn't work it out. But you know what," his voice quickened, "he did it because it was such a fantastic challenge. He had to produce something that fooled all of us—and I'd be hard pressed to come up with something that would get by Colin and Angus." Kelly's eyes widened. That was the first time she'd heard him acknowledge how good Colin and Angus were. "Then, it had to get by all the Finsat tests. I'd have loved to have a crack at it. You wouldn't even have to pay me."

Kelly's thoughts were in a turmoil. Why hadn't she thought of that? All these software types loved a challenge. Look at all those hackers that break into high security databases. Then there was the money angle too. She didn't want to say anything to Mike, but the fact was the salary Colin was paying John was way below what he would get working for Quantum in the States. As if reading her thoughts, Mike continued, "One time I answered the phone and it was

Quantum wanting to talk to John. I asked him why they were calling, and he said when he'd decided to stay in New Zealand, they had given him a leave of absence. I guess they didn't want to lose him."

"No, they'd want to keep tabs on him in case he got tired of New Zealand and decided to go back to California." She thought for a moment, "And, of course, that's how he got his instructions." And probably a nice hefty top-up to his salary, she added silently.

"Want a Danish? I'm going to have another one. This detective stuff makes me hungry, and I think we've got some serious thinking to do now we sort of know what they're up to." Mike pushed back his chair, making a loud scraping noise on the hardwood floor, and got to his feet.

"Well, if you insist, but I'd like a blueberry muffin and another cup of coffee. Long black this time." Mike walked over to the counter and placed the order. The English couple watched him with interest. Both very slim, they regarded his overweight frame with amused complacency.

When he returned, Kelly said, "You know, I think we know what's going on at last, or sort of, but I don't know where it leads us." She quickly filled him in on the call from CID and the demise of Andrew James, adding that they both needed to be very careful from here on in. "But I can't see how we can do anything about it. At least the man who killed David got what was coming to him, but the people who put him up to it are still going to end up making millions."

"Yes, imagine if the federal government in the States came up with a National Lottery on the same line as the Brits. When you think how much money is taken on state lotteries, that would run into billions. Probably be enough to support all those baby boomers when they hit pensionable age."

"And whoever was milking off each transaction would make millions too," Kelly said bitterly. "I wish there was some way to put a spoke in their wheels."

Mike tapped his fingers on the table and looked blankly at Kelly for several minutes. Even when the coffee and Danish arrived, he still sat motionless. Finally, as Kelly tackled the blueberry muffin, he said, "I think I've got an idea."

Chapter 30

Ed Miller joined the FBI when he graduated from the University of Southern California with a Master's Degree in Economics. Of Greek origin, although it was many generations since his forbears landed at Ellis Island, he was a straight A student, a member of the chess team, a keen tennis player, with a black belt in karate. He was fluent in Spanish, German and Russian, all spoken with an accent that belied his modest San Franciscan heritage. Tall and lean, with dark curly hair and a fresh complexion, women, particularly older women, found him attractive, but if anyone had told him, he would have thought they were being kind.

As he logged onto his computer on a foggy November morning, he thought ruefully about the illusions he had when he first joined the FBI. Thrilled to be accepted, he had excelled in the training courses and felt sure within months he would be on the trail of master criminals. So far all he had done was enter data. He might as well have been working for a bank. To alleviate the boredom of his job, he liked to log on in the morning and check the bulletin board. Surfing the university network when he was at school had been fascinating. Sure the FBI equivalent would be thrilling, he was disillusioned after the first few weeks by the news of upcoming basketball practice, where to buy a bargain PC and how to get cheap movies, which seemed to dominate the scene.

Arriving early, enjoying the quiet early morning

building, he greeted the security guard and made his way to his cubicle. It was good to get in early, that way he could read the bulletin board without his co-workers knowing what he was up to. Not that there was anything illegal about it, but he had a suspicion they would think he was juvenile, and Ed yearned to be accepted into the ranks of the granite-faced agents. He already wore dark gray suits, with a loose jacket carefully selected to hide a gun and a bullet-proof vest, something he had yet to wear. His early morning face glowed with health, and an impeccable close shave emphasized a well-defined jaw. Carefully hanging up his jacket on a hook on the partition wall, he sat down and logged on. The usual messages about date and time rolled up on the screen, and then one that caused Ed to sit up straight in his chair and stare at the screen.

"Hi there, Mr. FBI man, I've got some very interesting news for you about numbers. If you would like to get it, just reply to Friend. You don't need an address. I'll pick it up. Bye for now. Have a nice day. Ten days and counting."

Ed looked around warily, sure someone was having him on. He half expected to see someone leaning over the partition laughing their heads off. But the office was quiet. No one else was in. Puzzled, he continued to look at the message for a full five minutes, having to hit a key every once in a while to stop the screen fading, then he logged off. They weren't going to make a fool of him. Someone passing the cubicle during the week must have seen him logging on to the bulletin board and decided to have fun with him.

But the next morning when he came in, five minutes earlier than usual, it was there again, only this time it said, "Nine days and counting." Ed sat pondering over it for a long time. Should he reply? Hearing footsteps coming along the hallway, he logged off quickly and brought up the database to start the day's work.

On the third morning, totally engrossed, he didn't hear his supervisor come into the cubicle and stand behind him looking over his shoulder. When Howard Spencer spoke, Ed nearly jumped out of his skin. "What are you up to, Ed?" Ed turned a painful red, the blush reaching round to the back of his prominent ears as he turned to face his supervisor.

"I've just been looking at the bulletin board," he said miserably. "I thought I'd take a quick look before I got started. I'm not due to start until eight," he added in a rush.

"Is that all," Howard droned in his soft Southern accent, taking a sip out of the white Styrofoam cup in his hand. He was an odd-looking man with a small head, covered in thinning faded blond hair, and a body that grew wider as it moved from his narrow shoulders to his overlarge hips. To the casual observer he looked like a slightly overripe pear. But he was a kind man, stuck in a dead end job in an unglamorous data-gathering role, and he took an avid interest in the new people assigned to his department. He stood idly watching the screen, more to relieve Ed's embarrassment than out of real interest.

"What's this?" he exclaimed, more sharply than intended. Something about the message on the screen didn't look right.

"I don't know," Ed said hesitantly, "I think someone is putting me on. It's been on the screen for three mornings now."

"What's this eight days and counting bit? Has that always been the same?"

"No," Ed said dispiritedly, "it was ten days the first time I saw it."

Howard put down his coffee cup on the tidy workstation.

"Move over. Let's have a go at replying and see what happens." He was beginning to feel uneasy, but he had no intention of sharing his feelings with this green kid.

"Hello friend. Yes, we'd like to hear from you." Howard moved the mouse over to the send key and sat back, his eyes glued to the screen. Ed, watching fascinated, began to feel a bit better, and his blush faded. Maybe he wasn't such an idiot after all.

Behind them the office began to fill, and several people looked curiously at the two glued to the terminal, but intent on a cup of coffee they did not stop. The man in the next cubicle came in, hung up his jacket, yawned hugely, then leaned over the partition to talk to his neighbor about last night's ball game.

After twenty minutes of silent vigil, Howard got to his feet. "Doesn't look like he's going to reply. It must have been a fluke." As he picked up his coffee cup, leaving a ring on the immaculate work station and headed for the hallway, he noticed Ed's dejected face, and added, "Why don't you try checking during the day? Maybe he's just away from his terminal or something."

Ed slipped back into his seat and started working on the pile of paper in the in-basket. Howard wandered back to his office deep in thought. Absentmindedly taking a sip of the now stone-cold coffee, he made a disgusted face and headed for the coffee pot. Returning to his office, steaming coffee in hand, he was accosted by a distraught office worker who insisted on talking to him immediately. Suppressing a sigh, he told the woman to come on in and close the door.

It was mid-afternoon before he remembered the message. Dropping by Ed's cubicle he learned there had been no reply even though the enthusiastic youngster had checked every half hour all day long, not even stopping for lunch. "Never mind," he said consolingly, "maybe we'll get another message tomorrow morning." On the way back to his office, he fervently hoped it wouldn't happen. Something about the message bothered him, but he couldn't figure out what it was. The suspicion was creeping up on him that a hacker had managed to break into their system, but he knew that was impossible. Franklin, his best friend, was head of the white collar crime division, and he said there was no way anyone could ever get into their system. When Howard had pointed out gently that government offices, banks and even Microsoft had been plagued by hackers, he shrugged it off. In his view, he had said, laying a friendly arm across Howard's shoulder, the FBI system was as secure as Fort Knox.

Howard went back to his office and started hunting through manuals and office communiqués, trying to find something that matched the calling card of the mysterious message sender. By the end of the day, tired and frustrated, he sat back in his chair and tried to think what to do next. There was no way he was going to talk to his colleagues about this. They already regarded him as a bit behind the times, and in spite of an engineering degree, an MBA and a doctorate in physics, Howard still felt unsure of himself. Carefully packing his briefcase and putting on his jacket, he decided to wait until the morning. If another message turned up, he would have to do something. If not, he was off the hook.

The next morning when he pulled in to the still-dark parking lot at six, another car pulled in beside him, and Ed Miller got out and put on his jacket which had been neatly hung up in the back. Ed looked startled to see his boss standing by his car waiting for him. “Morning, Ed, you’re bright and early.”

Ed grinned sheepishly, “Morning. I thought I’d get in early and check to see if there were any more messages.”

Howard smiled encouragingly at him. “Good thinking. To tell you the truth, I woke up early and couldn’t get back to sleep again so I thought I might as well come in and get a head start on the day.”

Together they walked across the deserted parking lot; a scattering of cars looked forlorn under the yellow light shed by the lamps that illuminated even the farthest corner of the lot. As they walked in through the front door, the warm air felt good after the dank chill of the early morning. They greeted the guard, a stiffly erect ex-Marine with his short bristly hair showing streaks of gray, and showed their IDs. Then they went up in the elevator and headed for Ed’s cubicle, their pace quickening as they neared their objective. Ed, surprised when Howard followed him into his cubicle, said, “Shall I go ahead and log on?”

“Yes, yes,” Howard said impatiently, and the young man sat down without hanging up his jacket and waited while the system purred its way through the opening sequence. When the bulletin board finally appeared, they both watched, fascinated, as the response appeared, “Good to hear from you. I was beginning to think you weren’t interested. There’s a major scam underway. I’m going to encode the details in case the guys with the black hats are watching. Bye now. Seven days and counting.”

Ed looked up, his face pink with excitement, “Shall I tell him to go ahead?”

“Of course,” Howard replied, trying to suppress the urge to give Ed a kick.

Ed clicked in, “Go ahead, friend, we are waiting,” and

then positioned the mouse on the send command with a flourish.

Once more they sat waiting patiently for almost an hour, but nothing happened. Howard, in desperate need of coffee, said, "Keep watching, Ed. I've a feeling you may be on to something important. I need to get to my office now—there's a meeting coming up, but you let me know as soon as you receive anything. Doesn't matter where I am. If I'm in a meeting, interrupt. I don't think this is something we can ignore."

Three hours later an excited Ed rushed past Howard's personal assistant and burst into his office. "There's a reply," he exploded.

Howard pushed back his chair and walked rapidly down the hall, his leather shoes clicking on the tiles, walking even faster than the red-faced Ed who surged along in his wake. He sat down at Ed's workstation and read the message. It was all in some strange code he had never seen before. "I'm going to transfer this to my office and have a go at cracking it. It shouldn't be too difficult," he said confidently. "Why don't you have a go, too? I'm sure you're into those logic games." He quickly transferred the message to his own workstation, then as he headed back to his office, he added, "Forget your other work, this is more important."

Ed set to work, a determined frown on his face. Coffee breaks and lunch could wait. Howard strode confidently back to his office. If there was one thing he was good at, it was solving puzzles. Both his sons, now in their high school years, were computer buffs and spent hours playing games. He got a kick out of beating them at some of them, although he had to admit they were much better than he was most of the time.

At six p.m. a frustrated Howard poked his head in Ed's cubicle, "Any luck?"

Ed, looking completely worn out, said, "No, I can't work it out. I haven't gotten anywhere. I've tried all sorts of complicated patterns on it, but nothing works." He rubbed his hand across his tired eyes.

Howard smiled ruefully, "Neither have I." Putting his hand on the younger man's shoulders, he added, "Tell you what though. I know someone who can crack it for us, and he's coming over to my house for dinner tonight. I'll get him to take a look."

Franklin was an FBI field agent specializing in white-collar crime, and Howard intended to corner him sometime during the evening and lay the problem on him. Franklin never talked too much about his job, but Howard knew from scuttlebutt at the office, that he had a big reputation. He was a tall, distinguished-looking man with hair graying at the temples and a year-around tan that made him look like some East Coast banker. Howard, still uneasy about the message, felt sure Franklin would know what to do. He, himself, was still not entirely sure that it wasn't an elaborate hoax set up to make him look like a fool. Everyone would have a good old laugh at his expense if he fell for it. Not Franklin though; he was too much of a friend.

By the time he got home, Eva was already dressed for the evening in a simple black dress that made her look great. She might be getting a few wrinkles, but she still had a trim figure and great legs. He kissed her lightly and rushed upstairs to take a quick shower and change into casual clothes.

The evening went well, the conversation ranging from the government's health and education programs, to a great book Eva had just read, Shana's latest case, which was proving to be a particularly sticky one, and whether they should all join the new health center that had just opened up. It wasn't until they were leaving that Howard managed to corner Franklin on his own, and tell him about the strange message that Ed had received. Franklin was a good six inches taller than Howard and towered over him in the tiled entryway. Howard downplayed what he had seen, still not quite sure that he wouldn't look like a fool, but as he spoke, Franklin bent over, making sure that he heard every word. As he listened, his shoulders tensed, the relaxed attitude of the evening dissolving. "What did you say it looked like, Howie? Run that by me again."

Something about the way Franklin said it made Howard straighten up a little and say it far more positively than he had the first time. When he finished, Franklin moved away and kissed Eva lightly on the cheek. "Thanks for a lovely evening. It was a fantastic meal." Then putting his hand on Shana's elbow he said, "Come on, darling, let's head for home. Howard's just come up with something I need to take care of before I turn in."

There were still a few people working when they reached the office even though it was after eleven p.m. Howard sat down, logged on and showed the message to Franklin. Franklin watching over his shoulder, went very still. "When did you first see this?" he asked sharply.

"I didn't. One of the new guys showed me yesterday. We didn't get a reply until today. Well, not anything with any substance."

"What's this seven days and counting? Has that always been the same?"

"No, that started out at ten apparently, but Ed thought it was a hoax originally and ignored it for a couple of days."

"Don't you realize how serious this is?" Franklin asked, his eyes steely. "We've got a hacker in our network. Even if it's a joke, it isn't a bit funny. We need to track this down in a hurry." He gestured for Howard to move over and Howard quickly vacated the chair, letting Franklin take his place. "What did the first message say?"

Howard, standing awkwardly beside the workstation, his shoulders drooping, carefully repeated everything they had seen and their attempts to break the code. For ten minutes, Franklin played with the message without any luck, then he swung round in the chair, making Howard take a quick step backward to avoid being knocked over. "Look, Howard, I'm going to transfer this to my system, and restrict access to the bulletin board for the next few days. Tell that young hotshot of yours to keep his lip firmly buttoned. I don't want word of this getting out. And I'm serious about this. Don't even talk to Eva, and make it clear to your employee that his career will come to a rapid end if he talks." He spent another few minutes working at the terminal, then logged off and headed for the door. Howard hurried after him, trying to keep up.

Franklin drove quickly through the empty streets, his windscreen wipers slapping spasmodically against the light rain. Howard sat silent beside him. When they reached his house, Franklin pulled over and dropped him off, the engine still running. "Night, Howie, I'll give you a call." And almost before Howard had time to get out and close the door, he was gone.

When Franklin reached his office, he immediately called his superior, and filled him in on the situation. His manager's initial reaction was annoyance at being awakened, but when he heard what Franklin had to say, the annoyance faded to be replaced by incredulity. "Nobody can crack our system," he exploded, while Franklin waited for the storm to pass.

"Sorry, it looks suspiciously as if they have."

"Well, for God's sake, man, get on to it right away and clean it up. Don't get anyone else involved. See if you can crack the code first—grab Chris or someone to give you a hand. But I don't want you putting it on the supercomputer. Once it's there everyone knows about it, and the less people that know the better. This just cannot have happened."

"Good," Franklin said quietly, his voice deadly serious. "That's what I hoped you would say. It will be a disaster if this gets out. I don't see it as too much of a problem. I'm sure we'll have it worked out by morning, but I just thought I'd better put you in the picture." There was no doubt in Franklin's mind that he could decode any message sent by an amateur. And everyone outside the Bureau was an amateur in Franklin's eyes.

His next call was to Chris, a long-time trusted colleague. "Chris, sorry to disturb you this late, but I thought you might be still up."

"Yep, watching the late, late movie. What's up?" the voice was affable.

"Could you come in right away? There's a bit of problem, and I need you to give me a hand."

"Okay, be right there. It's a lousy movie anyway."

Thirty minutes later a lanky man, with dark hair cropped close to disguise a receding hairline, loped into Franklin's office. He had a sallow complexion, a long thin face and small dark eyes that peered out from under huge bushy eyebrows. The vigorous growth above his eyes seemed to have leeched all the strength out of his thinning hair. "What you got Frank, something interesting?"

Without saying anything, Franklin vacated his workstation chair and motioned to the other man to sit down. Chris plopped unceremoniously into the chair, banging his knee on the edge of the desk and cursing softly. He sat fascinated as the message scrolled up. "I don't believe it. Someone's hacked into our net." Then swiveling the chair round to face Franklin and narrowly missing another crack on the knee, he asked, "Is this the only one you've received?"

"No, back up and you'll see it all started a few days ago."

Chris turned back to the screen, watched silently for a few moments and then said, "Have you had a go at decoding this yet?"

"Yes, I've been at it while I was waiting for you, but no luck so far. Howard had a go at it too, and he didn't get anywhere."

"So let's go run it through the computer. It'll have this code cracked in no time."

"No can do. We've got to keep this under wraps, and if we take it down to the computer room it will be around the building in no time. They run the busiest gossip center in the office, and let's face it, if word gets out about this, we'll be a laughing stock."

Chris's face broke into a wide grin, "You're right there. Okay, let me move it on to my terminal and I'll have a go. It doesn't look too difficult."

Six hours later, Franklin, looking tired and disheveled with a dark shadow on his jaw, came into Chris's office. "Any luck?"

"Not yet. Let's go get a Coke and think about this for a bit." He led the way down the hall and inserted coins in the Coke machine. When the cans fell with a solid clunk, he picked them up and handed one to Franklin. Popping the top of his and taking a substantial gulp, he said, "I think the problem so far is that we've all been taking this far too seriously. I bet it's some kid playing a game, who just happened to end up on our screens by a fluke."

"But he said, 'Hello, Mr. FBI man,' remember," Franklin said icily, still holding his unopened can. "I think that's a pretty clear indication he achieved his objective. It wasn't just a random message. It's someone trying to tell us something."

"Nope, I still don't think it's that complicated. It's probably some very simple key. He's just having fun knowing all you experts will suspect some complex code devised by a mastermind. After all," he said, grinning wickedly, "nobody but a super mastermind could break into our network. Tell you what. Why don't we ask him for a clue? He's obviously enjoying playing games, so let's stop trying to show how smart we are, and play him at his own game. All this seven days and counting bit; he's very clever, but it's all a bit juvenile. Let's tell him how clever he is, say we haven't managed to crack his code. That should get some action."

"We can't do that." Franklin was outraged. "We'll lose the confidence of all the government departments if they think we can be outsmarted."

"Somehow, I don't think he's going to tell anyone about what he's done. I think this is a Deep Throat Internet style. He wants to give us information without letting us know where it's coming from. After all, breaking into our system is a federal crime."

"You may be right," Franklin said slowly, rubbing his jaw, "he did sign it 'friend' so it could be that he wants to tell us something serious, but is afraid if he just puts it up on the net the wrong people might see it." He grinned and put his arm across Chris's shoulder. "Okay, you're on, let's try being humble. It's against my religion but just this once I'll go with your gut feel. You've been right before. Once, I think it was back in 1991."

They both headed for Franklin's office and keyed in. "Okay, friend. We'd like to get your message, but are having trouble with your code. Can you give us a clue?"

"Is that humble enough for you Chris? I don't know about you, but I'm going to nip home and get a change of shirt. He won't respond for a while if he runs true to form."

Six-thirty the next morning saw them both in Franklin's office once more waiting impatiently for the system to come up. When the message, "Good to hear from you. Why don't you take a trip to Auckland, New Zealand? Buy return tickets; it works better that way," came through, Chris sat back and laughed. "I told you this guy was a games player. Now all we've got to do is figure out what that means. You any good at crosswords?"

For the rest of the morning they brainstormed extracting a six-digit number from the message. Again without success. "It's got to be something simple-minded," Chris insisted after they had tried the number of miles, then nautical miles to New Zealand, the name of the New Zealand Prime Minister converted to numbers, the number of sheep in the country, the number of stars on the flag and a dozen or so other hair-brained ideas.

"I know, let's try the airlines. Which ones fly there?"

"There's Air New Zealand, Qantas, British Airways, Singapore Airlines, Cathay Pacific and United," Chris said in one quick breath. "I think. What does that buy us?"

"Let's try converting their names to numbers and using that." They worked away for another hour using the converted number as a code. Again no success.

"Wait a minute," Chris said, "think simple-minded. We need a six-digit number to crack the code. What about the flight numbers."

"Yes, but flight numbers are only one, two or three numbers." Franklin picked up the phone and called a secretary. "Get me the flight numbers of all the flights going to New Zealand. ASAP." He listened. "Why do you need the dates I'm traveling?" Another pause. "No, I'm not traveling anywhere. I just want the flight numbers." He put down the phone in disgust. "Jesus H. Christ, where do they find these bimbos? Don't have a scrap of common sense."

Half an hour later they were busy trying flight numbers: Qantas, Air Canada, Singapore, Air New Zealand didn't work, but when they hit United they were home. UA 842 Los Angeles to Auckland, and UA 841 Auckland to Los Angeles. With the key 842841 the code gave up its secrets. "I'll be damned," Franklin said as the message began to unfold. "You were right, Chris, it was so goddamn simple it was ridiculous. I bet he knew we'd expect it to be complex. Whoever that guy is, he's having a hell of a laugh at our expense."

Chris, intent on the message, said, "I don't know. I think he's very clever. Look what he's telling us."

Franklin sat, frozen in his chair, watching fascinated, as a complex tale of a major system with a module developed in New Zealand being shipped to Finsat in California unfolded. Inside the module was a section of the software set up to milk financial transactions. And, the message added, the system is big, very big. It's set up to handle millions of transactions. "If this guy knows what he's talking about, this must be one hell of a scam. We've got to talk to him ASAP. Have you got a trace on him yet?"

"No, not so far, the messages keep originating from all over the shop. Two were from Seattle, one was from San Jose, another from New York and the other from London. Yet he says it took place in New Zealand. God knows where he is. I tell you he's one smart cookie. I'd like to meet him." Chris's eyes were shining with admiration.

Franklin's feelings were mixed: elated that they had finally found the key, eager to clean up what sounded like a major scam, but angry that some nobody could make fools of them all. He was very glad he had sworn everyone to silence. He knew he could trust Chris and Howard to keep quiet, and young Ed was so thrilled to be recognized for his work that, sworn to secrecy, he'd never tell a soul. His face took on that abstracted look Chris knew so well as he wandered away from the terminal along the hall to the water cooler. When he returned, he called Howard into his office and said, "This is how we're going to handle it. I'll get a flight out to the Coast tonight and start looking into this Finsat company; see what it is they're about to ship. I'm assuming the ten days and counting was the time to shipment date, or system completion or something. That would make it the twelfth. Then I'll get the white collar guys to move in if it looks likely."

Chris said, "I don't know about you two, but I'm fucking sure he's on to something, and he wants us to put a stop to it big time."

"Yes," Franklin answered quietly, "I agree. What I want you two to do is to make sure there are no leaks. If anyone gets wind of it, just say it was a big hoax, someone rattling Ed's chain, and he was smart enough to report it just in case it was real. You should give him a bonus, Howard, for handling a hoax so well."

"So we're just going to sit on it?" Chris asked. "And not go after this guy?"

"I haven't made my mind up about that yet. Let's first of all find out if his information is correct." He stood up dismissively.

Chris got up and stood awhile without moving. Stroking his chin, he looked reflectively at Franklin, amusement flickering in his eyes. "If you've got any sense, Franklin, old buddy, you'd go after him and put him on the payroll." Chuckling softly, he took off for his cubicle.

CHAPTER 31

"He did what?" Sally said, sitting bolt upright and spilling champagne on her tailored shorts.

"Do you mind," Kelly said, "that's Pelorus 96 you're tossing all over the place. Not some cheap French junk."

They were sitting on the deck in the late afternoon, the sun casting a golden glow over the ocean and highlighting the drama of the headland. As the sun moved slowly down the sky, it picked out individual rocks and trees, illuminating them as if they were on some extravagant stage set. Then it moved on, and the rocks and trees slipped back into the anonymity of the blue-green bush.

Between the two women, a small wooden collapsible table held a frosted bottle and a plate of hors d'oeuvres. "I must say good old Steve had great taste in wine. I'm sure wherever he is up there," Sally said, raising the slim flute to the sky, "he must be happy that I'm appreciating it. How come you have only one husband and when he dies he leaves you a cellar full of beautiful wine? All my three ex's have ever left behind is a couple of bottles of Cooks, and that was by mistake."

"Well, next time you get married, old dear, have a prenuptial agreement drawn up that specifies the sort of cellar you expect him to lay down, and the fact that it's yours when you separate."

Sally surveyed a shapely foot which was toasting nicely in the sun. "I don't think I'll bother to get married again. Too much trouble. Anyway, as usual you are changing the subject. You were just about to tell me what that crazy Mike did."

Kelly held her glass up to admire the fine bubbles rising to the top, took a delicate sip and said complacently, "He decided to tip off the FBI so they could catch the crooks who infiltrated our software."

"And how pray did he do that? Drop them a line saying excuse me but some flaky software's being exported from New Zealand."

"No, you idiot, he's not that stupid. We don't want them to know where the information is coming from." She paused, then said, even more complacently, if that was possible, "He tipped them off on the Internet."

Sally turned in her chair to look incredulously at Kelly. "Oh, so it's on the Internet. No problem. Such a wonderfully anonymous way to send a message. How about the fact that the message shows the address?"

"We had to take that risk. It was critical we got their attention in a hurry before these crooks get away with it. If we'd gone to the police or tried to contact the FBI directly, they would either have ignored us, or spent weeks interrogating us."

"So what did you do?" Sally's eyes were alive with interest.

"It was Mike's idea. He came up with the notion of hacking into the FBI's system—that would get their attention in a hurry, and they'd know we weren't a couple of dingbats trying to make a name for ourselves."

Sally put down her glass and walked over to the rail, turning her back on the scene. Leaning back nonchalantly, dressed in a halter top and shorts that showed off her long slender legs, against a stunning background of sea, sky and a dramatic headland, she looked like an advertisement for casual living. "Kelly," she said slowly, "this is the FBI you two are messing with. F as in Federal, and that makes breaking into their system a federal crime. If you commit a federal crime, you'll be paraded into court in chains. Haven't you seen these people on TV shackled around their ankles and wrists when they come into court? I can just see you and poor old Mike. As top heavy as he is, he'd fall flat on his face, which right there doesn't impress the jury. Then there's you. They dress you in those ghastly orange jumpsuits. You'd look terrible."

"You do have a tendency to go over the top, as I believe I've pointed out a couple of times before." They both stopped talking to watch a boat skimming towards shore, its wake carving a white trail across the mirror-like sea. "Anyway, there's no problem. Mike has lots of friends scattered all over the shop. One of the great advantages of being a Kiwi these days is that some proportion of your friends are always off on an OE or on job contracts overseas. He got in touch with them, vaguely sketched out our problem and they all forwarded his message, scrambling the address as they did it. The FBI must have traces on addresses in Seattle, New York, London and several other places by now."

Sally turned and looked at the sea for a while, admiring a gannet sailing over the shallow water near the shore on elegant wings. When it finally made its dive, hurtling bullet-like into waist high water, she said absently, "I wonder how many gannets break their necks doing that?" then wandered back to her seat and sank gracefully into the padded deck chair. "So the system has been shipped to the States already?"

"No, not quite yet, but it was all ready to go when I left. They were just doing a couple more tests, then it was off. Anyway, my bit is all over so I decided to come home," Kelly said, topping up their glasses. Champagne had a way of disappearing quickly when you weren't paying attention.

"It was quite something the way that team came through. We were only about four weeks late even after the David problem."

"That's a miracle for software, isn't it? You kept saying how good they were, but I figured it was your usual enthusiasm getting the better of you." She picked up a sesame cracker spread with smoked hapuka, and nibbled delicately.

"They are first rate, but the most impressive thing was the way that John stepped right into David's shoes and pulled it off."

"But he's the mole, isn't he?"

"Yes," Kelly said, a little too hotly, "but he did complete the whole thing on time, which meant that Colin's gang succeeded. They'll be paid now for the part they shipped. It should be a fair old whack too. Colin's rapt; it means he has a successful company on his hands now."

Sally wiped her fingers on a paper napkin that had been firmly anchored under a table mat. "Of course, no one knows there's any flaky software involved, and if everything goes according to plan, no one will ever know. There'll just be some Swiss bank balances growing exponentially."

"That's right. You have to hand it to them. Mike is absolutely convinced that the links from John's module to the rest of the Auckland system are completely pukka. Identical to the specifications. John did a hell of a job."

Sally looked at her friend sympathetically. "He was quite a guy, wasn't he?" Kelly said nothing, simply sitting looking out to sea for several minutes. Finally, to break the silence, Sally added, "I suppose he's gone back now."

"No, he'll go back when it's all complete, which shouldn't be too long now. Then he'll be all set for the next project, and ten to one there will be another gullible woman involved."

"Don't be so hard on yourself. You didn't give any secrets away, and you're only guessing he was assigned to keep an eye on you. You don't know that for sure. Obviously he was here to gum up the software, but I don't think you were planned for." She paused a moment, and took another sip of champagne. "My take on him was that he was genuinely smitten with you. And geez, he was gorgeous—soft brown eyes and kitten hips. I was seriously considering taking over as tour guide when I first saw him, thought he needed the guidance of an older woman, but when I saw the way you were looking at him, I decided to back off. I'd hate to break up a beautiful friendship. Well, at least until Steve's cellar is empty."

Kelly ran her hand through her hair. "You must admit I was pretty stupid though. He was about ten years younger than me."

"So what's wrong with that? If a man ten years older than you made a pass, you wouldn't think anything of it. Come on, woman, it's equal opportunity time." Sally drained her glass and got to her feet. "Enough of this idle chit-chat. The kids will be back in about half an hour, so I'd better get some food on the table." She moved to the patio door, but stood with her hand on the door handle and looked back. "It just struck me. If the FBI takes Mike's message seriously, they're going to start asking questions at Finsat. Don't you think it might occur to the bad guys that someone in New Zealand tipped off the feds? It couldn't be anyone else. And who's the someone who's been running around asking questions, taking trips to the U.K., no less. If you consider how quickly they knocked poor old Andrew James off just because he was a link to them, I should say you are a much more likely candidate. I think you'd better start checking the bay for limousines carrying men in dark glasses."

* * * * *

It wasn't until she was drying the champagne glasses that Sally's words sank in. Kelly hadn't thought about it before, but it would be a while before the FBI did anything, if they were like all the other government agencies she knew, and the crooks might get wind of what was happening and come down to New Zealand to plug any possible leaks. They were well-organized and had obviously been in business a while. They probably survived by making sure there were no leads back to them after a crime was committed. She went through to the study and hunted through her address book until she found Mike's home number.

The phone rang eight times before he answered. "Sorry, Kelly," he gasped when he finally picked it up. "I was doing some gardening, and of course I forgot to bring the portable with me. What's up?"

"Are you planning on taking a vacation now the project's finished?"

Mike's voice was puzzled, "Why, want to come with us? You're welcome. We're off to the Gold Coast, but we aren't planning to leave for a couple of weeks. Too many things to do around the house first. Poor Cathy, I don't do anything to help when I'm on a crash project, so I'd better start pulling my weight now."

"No," she laughed, "thanks for the invite, but the reason I called was it just occurred to me that the Mob, or whoever they are, might come looking for us. The FBI will start asking questions, which means they'll realize someone's worked out what's going on." She waited a moment, letting the words sink in. "You remember I told you what happened to Andrew James, and he'd been working for them for years apparently. The minute they thought there might be a link between them and a crime, he had to be eliminated."

"Bloody hell, I never thought of that." Mike's voice was shocked. "I was imagining the feds nipping right round there and putting them away, but of course, it'll take time, you're right."

"Yeah, so I think you need to take Cathy and Gavin and get out of town right away. You can't put them in danger. Just pack up and go visit her folks or something. Anywhere as far away from Auckland as you can get. Fast."

"You're right. I'm going to round them both up and then get the hell out of here. I don't mind taking on people over the Internet, but I'm not up for the real stuff." Kelly breathed a sigh of relief; for some reason she had thought Mike might want to stay and put up a fight. "What are you going to do?" he asked. "Where are you going?"

"I don't think I have a problem. They're not going to trace me all the way up here, and anyway it's such a tiny place, any stranger snooping around would be watched. Our neighborhood watch is hot stuff."

"I guess you're right, but if I were you I'd take off anyway. No point in being stupid."

"Okay, Mike, I'll think about it. You get going now and take care. Look after Cathy and Gavin." She realized suddenly she would never forgive herself if anything happened to the two-year-old. Holy terror he might be, but she couldn't help liking him.

Colin came into the conference room, tossed his notebook on the table, pulled at his straggly mustache and looked around at the team. As usual, they were sprawled in the uncomfortable chairs, notepads in front of them, hugging cups of coffee or cans of Coke. Lindsay was yawning hugely, Robyn was tidying up a set of papers, Angus was sitting with his eyes closed sipping coffee, John was talking to Carol who fidgeted with her hair. Only Mike was missing. The overhead projector sat cold and neglected, and the pull-down screen was rolled up. Only the whiteboards showed signs of activity with a mish-mash of flow charts inexpertly erased.

"Good to see you all so lively at this hour," Colin said, eyes twinkling. Most of them looked up and grinned. The atmosphere was relaxed, totally unlike previous meetings. The system had been shipped, and this was a final wrap-up session. "Well, it looks like we made it, gang. It seems as if our system has been integrated without any glitches. Finsat is impressed, as well they might be. It'll be going for field testing now, and their guys will be able to take care of any minor problems that come up. Worst case, some of us may have to nip over and do some work."

"I'd hate to think they found any problems with my stuff, but an all-expenses-paid trip to California wouldn't be too hard to take," Lindsay said, pushing his wire-rimmed glasses back onto the bridge of his nose. "Wish I'd thought about this sooner. I could have popped a couple of bugs in."

"So what have we got going next?" Angus asked, dark eyes narrowed.

"That's what I'm here to tell you about," Colin said, beaming from ear to ear. "While all you morons have been wrapping up this project, I've been out beating the bushes, and I've landed us a dilly of a contract. Amazing the difference these days, now that I can name-drop Finsat. They take us seriously right off the bat."

"So what is it?" Carol asked, leaning forward in her chair, her long hair falling round her face.

"It's an interesting piece of software Goldings are farming out. Right up our street. It's another American company, by the way, so we're hot stuff over there." He turned round, picked up a cloth lying beneath the whiteboard and wiped the board clean. "Basically," he said, "it looks something like this." And he began to talk excitedly about their next product.

An hour later, Angus leaned back wearily in his chair. "That sounds fine, Colin. I'm glad to know I don't have to go out and apply for a community card for a while. But isn't it time we took a break? These chairs were not made for lightly padded arses like mine."

There was a murmur of agreement around the table. "Okay, off you all go to play. Remember, whatever you're doing, you drop it the minute you hear from Finsat, that's top priority." He picked up his folder and made for the door. "Just one more thing though; eleven-thirty we're all going out for pizza and beer; to hell with the afternoon's work. My shout."

"Now those are words that gladden a Scotsman's heart." Angus too made for the door, and then stopped before leaving. "John, what are you going to be doing, are you going to stay with us and become a dinkum Kiwi?"

John smiled his slow smile, "I'd love to, but I have to get back to the States. The contract house I work for has another job for me. They know I'll have to work with Finsat if anything comes up during testing, but apart from that they want me back on the payroll."

"But you left them, didn't you, when you came to us?" Carol said.

"No, not exactly. I came down here for a three-week vacation originally. Then when I took this job and tried resigning, they persuaded me to take a leave of absence for a few months. If I changed my mind about staying here, then my job was still open."

"So, don't you want to stay?" Lindsay asked, surprised.

"It's great here. I've enjoyed working with you guys, but my folks are back home and they aren't getting any younger. Then too," he chuckled softly, "my Uncle Tony is a director of the contract house. Nothing like a little spot of nepotism to help my career along."

"You bloody old fraud," Angus laughed, "don't blame you at all. Wish I had a rich Uncle Tony someplace. My relatives all live on the wrong side of Glasgow." They started milling out of the room bumping into each other in the narrow doorway.

"When's Mike getting back, Colin?" Carol asked.

"He's not due back for another week yet, but he keeps in touch all the time. He took his laptop along so that he could work on the software if he needed to."

At eleven-thirty a.m. on the dot, they all gathered again, looking around for Colin. He emerged from his cubicle about five minutes later, pocketing his cell phone and saying, "Sorry, got caught by the phone just as I was leaving. Are we all ready?"

"Is the Pope Polish?" Angus said. "Lead the way, noble leader."

John, who had been talking animatedly to Carol while they were waiting, said suddenly, "Oh damn, I just remembered something. Go ahead. I'll catch you up."

"Okay," Colin said, "I'm starving, I don't know about you lot. Do you know the way there?"

"Yes, sure, it's only just along the road and round the corner at the top, isn't it?"

"Yeah, that's it, see you there," Colin called as they all headed for the elevator. John heard their babble of voices recede down the hall, then finally stop as the elevator doors closed. He turned quickly and made for his office.

Ten minutes later, they were in the restaurant arguing about what to order. Colin grinned to himself as the usual fight between the vegetarians and the carnivores grew more vocal than usual. It wasn't until the first pizza had arrived and they all started to dig in hungrily that Carol leaned back, her pizza untouched, and said, "What happened to John? Do you think he got lost?"

"No," Angus said, "he knows his way. Maybe he's calling his girlfriend in the States and didn't want us to hear. Relax, lassie, and eat up your pizza; you look as if you could do with some meat on your bones."

As the level of the jugs of beer went down, the conversation flowed and there were frequent gales of laughter as Robyn, normally so quiet in the office, grew pink and animated, telling funny stories about life on the family's Waikato farm. Carol, still uneasy, looked towards the door from time to time expecting to see John arrive. Angus, noticing, said, "Stop worrying. John's a big boy, and maybe there was something he had to do. After all, it is lunchtime. He probably popped along to the travel agents to find out about flights home and you know the age they take to answer the simplest question. He'll be along when he's ready." He passed the pizza over. "Try a piece of this pepperoni one. It's good."

They all contentedly munched and drank, and finally, about three-thirty p.m., drifted back to the office and scattered to their separate cubicles. Gradually everyone settled down, and there was the whir of terminals warming up.

A shriek from Carol's office caused them all to look up startled. Lindsay was the first to get there. "What's the matter?" He was sure something terrible must have happened.

"My screen's been wiped. None of my files are here." She was sitting looking helplessly at her screen. "I can't believe it. What on earth have I done?" She pushed her long hair away from her face with an agitated hand.

"Whew, is that all? I thought you'd been shot or something. Try hitting a few keys; you've just wiped it out by mistake. Happens all the time. And you have been drinking."

"I haven't," she said, furiously, "I only drank Fanta, and I'm not that stupid. I tell you, all my work's gone. I can't bring anything up." Lindsay stood irresolute until she swiveled round in her chair. "Go and log on. See if it's just me. Maybe there was a system failure." She followed him along the hall, then noticed Robyn sitting looking at a blank screen. She moved to the next cubicle. Angus was hitting keys, trying switches, but his screen too was blank.

Twenty minutes later, Colin, feeling sick, said to Angus, "All the screens are dead. Somehow the system's been wiped."

"That's impossible," Carol said. "No one was here, and there hasn't been a power failure. I checked with the office next door, they haven't had any problems at all."

Angus stood stock still, his heavy brows pulled together in a frown. "There was one person who was still here when we left."

"John, you mean," Carol said incredulously. "Surely you don't think he had anything to do with it. That's ridiculous."

"Something's happened, and where is John? He didn't turn up for lunch, and he isn't here. Did he leave a note for you, Colin?"

Colin walked quickly back to his office and checked his desk. "No, there's nothing here." He chewed furiously on the end of his mustache. "I wonder where he is?"

Angus, his face rigid, said, "Let's go and take a look in his cubicle. Maybe there's a note there." He led the way along the hall, quickly checked the top of the workstation, then sat down in the chair and started going through the drawers.

"Hang on a bit, mate, you can't go rummaging in John's drawers. He might have something personal in there."

Angus, ignoring Colin, continued his search. Then he walked over and checked the bookshelves. "I tell you what," he said straightening up, "the bugger's shot through. He's gone. All his drawers are empty and look at the shelves. Only our manuals there, none of his stuff."

Carol, who had been standing, worrying a long strand of hair while Angus searched, said, "This doesn't make any sense at all. You really think he's gone, without saying a word."

"That's what it looks like, lassie. He's taken all his stuff. He didn't turn up for lunch. I'd say it's pretty clear he's done a runner."

"But why would he do that? He hasn't taken anything. You said yourself, he left all our stuff behind."

Colin, his face pale, answered, "It looks as if he wiped the whole system out and then took off. We're all stuffed; we've no copy of our own system anymore."

"It still makes no sense at all," Carol persisted. "The system was shipped. It's at Finsat. We made our money." She went over and sat on the edge of the workstation, running her hand along the desk. "He was such a nice guy. There's no way he would screw things up for us."

"It beats me why he did it, lassie, but it has to be him. And he won't be the last nice guy to do something weird. When you've been in this business as long as I have, you won't be so surprised."

Colin shook his head in disbelief, "You're right, Angus. It has to be him. There's no other explanation. He must have flipped, but I can't believe it. He's always been so cool and contained. The pressure never seemed to get to him."

"Maybe he bottled it all up inside, and it was only when the pressure was finally off that it hit him." Carol was grasping at straws.

"God knows what made him do it, but it's done and he's gone," Angus said. "We've no product left, but cheer up, at least the original is now in Finsat's hands. Imagine what it would have been like if he had flipped before the system was shipped."

Carol, looking close to tears, walked quickly out of the office. Colin's face was bleak. "What worries me is what he is going to do next."

Chapter 32

For the next few weeks life settled down into a familiar comfortable pattern. With a fat check due from Finsat, Kelly saw no reason to rush into another major contract and instead contented herself with a couple of small, local consulting jobs. This gave her the opportunity to devote time to the thirty-acre property and large, old renovated house. Just keeping the garden under control ate up a lot of time, then there were gutters to clear, culverts to check, spraying the driveway, and the other myriad jobs she couldn't do herself but had to organize—like servicing the pump, trimming trees and fertilizing the paddocks. Yet again she thought it would make sense to sell the property. It was way too much for one person. But every time she decided to do it, she looked out the window at the view and was totally captivated again. There was no way she could let it go.

She seldom gave a thought to Finsat or the FBI. Somehow she knew that when it was all finally over the FBI would either come gunning for Mike, or if they wanted to keep it quiet, as Mike suspected they would, let the whole thing drop. Maybe if the fraud was discovered, it would make the inside pages of the *San Jose Mercury News*. She'd asked one of her friends in California to let her know if there was any news of Finsat, using the pretext that she had bought a bunch of their shares, and would bail out if there was any bad news. On the other hand, maybe they would never know. Deep down she no longer cared. David's death had been avenged, and they had done everything they could to stop the international criminals. Now it was in the lap of the gods.

On a sparkling Friday morning, looking out of the window and seeing the tide was in, which meant there would only be soft sand to run on, she decided to go for a run along the road. Putting on shorts, T-shirt, running shoes and a peaked hat, she shut the dog in and then set off down the driveway and on the long slog up the hill out of the bay. It was a steep climb, and her muscles, still stiff from sleeping, groaned with the effort, but gradually they loosened and she began to feel the first trickle of perspiration down her back. The road snaked upwards through the bush, the tall tea tree enclosing the early stretches, but gradually it opened up into a mixture of toi toi, ferns, smaller tea trees and a stand of rimu. Here and there ugly patches of dying gorse, sprayed by the road works gang, marred the scene. The road was rough metal and the verges a heavy straggle of grass and weeds. In the early stretches, running on the verge was impossible, so she ran in the road, confident that the morning traffic would be practically zero, and the few cars that passed would be people from the bay going out shopping who would slow down and wave as they went by. It was quiet on the bush-fringed road. Two quail scurried out of her path, and a fat hen pheasant dived into the bush as she approached. A possum lying in the middle of the road where some car had hit it in the night was already attracting a large quota of flies, and she stepped up her pace to get quickly by, holding her breath as she went.

When she reached the top of the hill, tired and short of breath, she slowed down for a few minutes, enjoying the wonderful panorama spread out before her. The bush gave way to orderly paddocks, brilliant green in the morning sun, spreading away to a line of hills blue-green in the distance. Sheep heavy with wool munched contentedly on the grass while their tiny offspring snuggled down in clumps of grass, or made experimental dashes on wobbly legs. In another paddock pedigreed Angus steers stopped grazing to watch her go by. Striding out once again now that she was on the flat, she was soon eating up kilometers, passing a couple of farmhouses but little else on the small country road.

Whenever she heard a car coming, she moved close to the grassy verge, but the rest of the time she strode along in the middle of the road enjoying the sense of freedom. Alone out there with green paddocks stretching away as far as the eye could see, she felt like queen of all she surveyed. It certainly beat plodding around suburban streets.

The sound of a car coming faster than usual caused her to step right off the road and run in the grass. It was difficult going, but she suspected from the car's speed it was an out-of-towner traveling too fast for the windy road. If they rounded a bend and saw her too late, they'd have trouble controlling the car. She vividly remembered the time she had been running along this same stretch when a car trailing a boat saw her at the last minute and swerved sharply away from her, almost overturning the trailer. Unfortunately, it was an aluminum boat and as it swung perilously away, something inside the boat came loose and crashed with a loud clang against the side. The driver managed to get car and trailer under control after an elongated slewing session, which hovered too close to the steep roadside bank. Then it continued on its way apparently none the worse for wear. However, the loud crash had spooked three stud Santa Gertrudis bulls in the adjacent paddock. Terrified by the noise, they took off across the field at a fast clip, but then they stopped, turned and in unison pawed the ground and looked up, ready to charge. The offending car was long gone, and the only thing on the road was Kelly. They all looked in her direction. She froze, terror-stricken. Even a hundred yards away, they looked very large, their hides glistening in the morning sun, their huge shoulders bunched, ready for action. By sheer good luck, she realized she had done the right thing. Standing stock still, they couldn't see her. The only problem was, the minute she moved, they would probably come barreling straight at her. She stood, hardly daring to breathe, for a very long ten minutes, wishing fervently that a car would come by. Finally, when they started to graze, she walked very slowly out of their line of vision.

When she told Richard about it, he had laughed his head off. Bulls were his business and he roamed around among them as if they were chickens. "You're in no danger from them," he'd said, "cars are far more dangerous on that road. Of course," he'd added, "if they had decided to charge, they'd have gone straight through the fence. It takes more than a solid fence to stop a bull when it's mad." After that she made very sure she never caused any car to swerve on her account.

The car was approaching fast and she glanced back over her shoulder. She was relieved to see the driver looking straight at her, which meant he had seen her, and would be able to slow down in time. However, instead of slowing down and moving over, he increased his speed. It wasn't until the last minute she realized he was heading straight for her. She tried moving even farther off the road, but there was only a narrow verge between her and a steep drop to the paddock. At the last minute, knowing with horrible certainty that he was going to hit her, she dived straight down the bank. But she was too late; the wing of the car caught her and she hurtled down the bank and hit something with a resounding thud. Everything went black.

Chapter 33

Gusts of hot damp air were blowing on her face. She couldn't imagine where she was. Slowly she opened her eyes and looked straight into the face of a Hereford steer. He was regarding her with soft brown eyes, his shiny wet nose only inches from her face. With consciousness came pain. Something was digging into her shoulder, and the pain was excruciating. She tried moving her head, very gently, and saw she was lying at the bottom of the bank up against a large fence post. Very carefully she tried moving her feet. They seemed to be okay. Next she tried moving her arms. The right one functioned okay, but for some reason the left one didn't seem to want to move. She realized that in spite of the sun blazing down on her she was freezing cold. With her right hand she gently explored her body, feeling for damage. When she touched her leg, which wasn't painful, she was surprised to feel something wet and sticky. The rest of her seemed to be in good shape, although there was something very wrong with her left shoulder, which was throbbing with the worst pain she had ever experienced. She knew she had to move. Down there at the bottom of the bank she was totally hidden from view. Even if a passing motorist glanced in her direction the tall grass verge would hide her. Carefully, painfully, she tried to roll over so that she could get up on to her knees. She knew with whatever she had done to her shoulder there was no hope of pulling herself up. Just the thought of putting any pressure on it made it hurt even more. If only she wasn't so cold, she knew she'd have more energy. She rolled over very carefully, but suddenly her legs, which hadn't bothered her up until now started to hurt. She stopped moving. She'd lie still for a while and maybe she'd be fit enough to move in a minute or two. But in spite of the pain and the cold, there was an overwhelming desire to sleep. She closed her eyes.

"Bloody hell, Kelly. What happened to you?" A very loud voice brought her to once more, and startled the steers who had gathered to watch. They pounded off across the paddock.

She looked up this time into the wide, friendly face of Todd, a farm worker who lived on the bay, and seeing his horrified expression thought maybe she was in a worse mess than she thought. He was a big man with a broad, florid face, light blue eyes and wild curly hair desperately in need of a cut. Very gently he checked her body, talking quietly to her all the time, telling her she was going to be okay. She saw him tear off his T-shirt, rip it in two and wrap it round her legs.

"You've lost a lot of blood, but that should hold it for the minute. Look, lie perfectly still while I go up the bank and use my mobile. I'll call the hospital and tell them we're on the way. They'll have a nice comfy bed and some pain pills for you as soon as we arrive." He was gone for a few minutes, then she heard him crashing down the bank again. "It's faster this way," he said, leaning over her. "It'll be well over half an hour before the ambulance can get here, and I don't think you can afford to lose too much more blood. I've got some pressure on the cuts with my T-shirt, but it's not going to hold."

Carefully he picked her up in strong arms and carried her up the bank. As he moved her, the pain shot through her shoulder like a knife. She willed herself not to yell out, knowing he was trying very hard not to hurt her. He strapped her into the passenger seat, checked her leg, and frowning, leaped into the driver's seat and pulled away in a flurry of dust. The trip to the hospital was all a blur. The only thing Kelly was conscious of was Todd's voice, talking incessantly, trying to keep her awake.

"I was working down on Samson's paddock putting in some fence posts when I saw some maniac drive past on the road going like a bat out of hell. God knows what speed the fucker was doing, but it was twice what makes any sense on this road. Didn't think anything more of it, but when I finished the job and decided to nip into town for some extra stuff I needed from ITM, I saw these skid marks. I was fully expecting to see his car at the bottom of the bank, so I pulled over and hopped out. The skid didn't go over the top so somehow he must have pulled out of it. Didn't deserve to, stupid jerk." He paused a moment and looked across at her, "Come on, Kelly, pay attention now, don't drop off to sleep on me. So I was just going to get back in the flat bed when I noticed the steers bunched up looking over the fence. Seemed weird. I thought maybe the noise of the car skidding had attracted them, but that didn't make any sense, so I got out to investigate. Took a bit of a look down the bottom of the bank." He stopped talking and she could hear the indicator going. He must have reached the main road. Thank God for that, the road would be a bit straighter now and maybe the jolting to her shoulder would lessen.

"Last thing I expected to see was you," he added.

After that, his voice faded away and nothing seemed real anymore, even her shoulder didn't seem to be hurting so much. She must have passed out for a while because the next thing she knew, competent hands were lifting her out of the car and onto a stretcher, and a nurse was saying insistently,

"Kelly, can you hear me? Kelly, you're going to be okay." She wished they'd keep quiet. All she wanted to do was sleep.

The next few hours were a blur. A cool, clean hospital bed. A gentle nurse cleaning her wounds. A merciful doctor giving her something that made the pain die and everything that happened after that totally unreal. Someone poking things in her and shouting they needed blood now. Something being done to her shoulder. Then on a stretcher again and the whoop-whoop of helicopter blades. The sweeping sensation of liftoff which matched her pain killer induced floating feeling. Then another hospital bed, more doctors. Finally, they let her sleep.

"Welcome back, Kelly." She opened her eyes to see Richard standing awkwardly at the foot of her bed, a large bunch of flowers dangling from his hand. He looked strangely out of place in the small, sunlit hospital room. Tall, lean and suntanned, he belonged on windswept paddocks, not here in this antiseptic environment of hushed voices and broken bodies. But she had never been more happy to see him. Until now it had been nothing but crisp white uniforms, softly spoken doctors and nurses and overcooked meals.

She realized she must have dozed off after lunch. Whatever they were using to dull the pain was making her act like an eighty-year-old. She was propped up in bed, her shoulder and arm strapped up, and her leg stiff with bandages, but apart from that she was feeling comfortable and rested. Probably when she started moving around it was going to be a different story, but right now it was fine. "Hi, Richard, good to see you. You didn't have to come all the way down to Whangarei; I'm pretty sure I'll be up and around and off home tomorrow." She looked around the small room with its pastel walls and tiny window, and thought longingly of her own bed with the sound of the sea to lull her to sleep.

Moving closer to Kelly, he handed her the flowers, then realizing she couldn't do anything with them, hesitated, confused. "They're beautiful, Richard, thanks. Why don't you put them over there on the side table? The nurse will put them in water for me."

Gratefully, he placed the flowers on the table, then sat down, his tall frame too large for the economy-sized bedside chair. "You gave us all one hell of a scare, you know. The amount of blood you lost made it touch and go for a while. I've been worried out of my socks, but they wouldn't let me in to see you before this. Only next of kin allowed." There was mild reproach in his voice.

"That crazy driver came straight at me, there was nothing I could do but dive over the bank. Didn't have time to worry about the barbed wire fence at the bottom." She shuddered, remembering the horror of the moment as the car bore down on her.

"Thank God Todd came along when he did. You'd have bled to death from that tear in your leg if you'd been there much longer. No one could see you down at the bottom of the bank; you could have been there for days." His handsome face looked stern. "I've been telling you for ages you're nuts to go running on that road."

She smiled at him, "Be much safer in the paddock with the bulls, eh?"

"Well, yeah," his face broke into a wide grin. "Anyway, they told me at the front desk you can go home tomorrow. So would you like me to drive you? Apart from the fact that you don't have a car down here, you'd have a bit of a job with that shoulder and a gammy leg."

"That would be great, but that means you staying over, doesn't it?"

"No sweat. I've a couple of mates out at Tutukaka I can bunk with, then come over and pick you up." He looked around at the trolleys rolling by and distraught relatives hurrying along the corridor clutching books and flowers. "I should think you'll be glad to get out of here, won't you? Hospitals give me the heebie-jeebies."

"It'll be good to get home, but they've been terrific, and let's face it, this is about the first day I've cared about my surroundings. I was just grateful for a bed for the first few days, and all I did was sleep."

He looked around again, trying to think of something to say. On the way down, he'd thought of a million things he wanted to tell her. Now seeing her lying there, pale and vulnerable, none of it seemed important, so instead he said, "Sally and Christopher are outside waiting to see you, so I'd better not stop long."

Kelly leaned over awkwardly and touched his arm, "Don't go yet, Richard. Tell me what's been happening on the bay while I've been gone." She found she was surprisingly glad to see him, and somehow his quiet strength provided a calm reassurance after the shattering events of the last two weeks.

"Oh the usual stuff. Couple of brush fires, and Teresa caught a whopping big kingie yesterday." He moved a little, trying to get comfortable on the inadequate chair, and launched into a chronology of all the minor events on the bay over the last few days, sensing that anything that happened outside the confines of the hospital would be welcome news. Then noticing that she was starting to tire, he said, "I'd better go now, or poor little Christopher will never forgive me. Sally neither for that matter, since she's trying to keep him quiet in the waiting room." He got up, leaned over and kissed her on the forehead.

A few minutes later Christopher rushed in, almost

tripping over a huge teddy bear dressed in an old fashioned dress, complete with pinafore, mop cap and small wire-rimmed glasses. His little face beamed as he proudly gave her the bear. "I was going to bring flowers, but Mum said you'd have to leave those behind. You can bring Mrs. Ted home with you." Noticing her bandaged arm for the first time, his eyes widened. "Wow, does that hurt?"

"No, not too much anymore. It won't be too long before I can play cricket with you again." She propped the bear clumsily on the pillow beside her. "Thank you, she's gorgeous."

As Christopher went to climb up on the bed beside Kelly, Sally grabbed him. "No, not today, Chris, Kelly's got a bad leg too, so I think you'd better sit on that chair and read this book I brought for you while I talk to Kelly." Sally had followed Christopher into the room and had been standing back while Christopher made his presentation.

Kelly, seeing Christopher's crestfallen face said, "If you sit on that chair Christopher, you can see all the doctors and nurses go by. You'll be able to tell the girls all about it when you go home. I bet Chantelle hasn't been to this hospital." Smiling broadly at the thought of being one up on his two older sisters, he hopped up on the chair, accepted the book from Sally and kept an eagle eye on the hallway.

"How's Riggles doing? Is he missing me?"

"Of course. Sits and pines all day until the food arrives, then chomps it all up. The kids love having him, and he's glued to Annette most of the time. Seems to sense she needs him. It's wonderful; she hasn't stamped off to her room and sulked once since he's been with us."

Sally sat down carefully on the end of the bed, well away from Kelly's legs. "So how are you doing? Met any handsome interns yet?"

"No, they've all been recruited by the soap operas; I've

been left with middle-aged men and women doctors."

"Tough. So when are they going to toss you out?"

"Tomorrow if everything checks out. I'm feeling pretty good now, although doing everything one-handed is going to be a bit of a challenge for a while."

"So what happened? All I've heard so far is that some driver clipped you as he was going by, and you landed down at the bottom of the bank." She paused a moment, her face serious. "Thank God Todd came by when he did and bothered to look down the bank. He was telling me about it. Apparently, if he hadn't seen that character speeding and noticed the skid marks, he never would have known you were there. You were damn lucky."

Kelly, easing her shoulder that was beginning to ache again, didn't feel too lucky. "It wasn't an accident. I was well off the road and he had plenty of room to get by even at the speed he was traveling. He saw me too. Just drove straight at me."

Sally glanced in Christopher's direction, saw he was totally absorbed in something that was going on in the hallway and said quietly, "You think it was deliberate?"

"Yes, it had to have been some sort of wacko who gets his jollies running joggers off the road. He saw me in plenty of time to slow down." She'd heard of people like that who picked on joggers and cyclists. For some odd reason they seemed to think roads were the exclusive domain of cars. "He wasn't to know I'd go flying down the bank and end up in a mess of barbed wire."

"Are you sure about that? It sounds to me as if he was following you and waited for a nice quiet stretch with a big bank. I know I told you to look out for people in dark glasses and stretch limousines, but I hadn't thought about how easy it would be to run you down when you're on our road. How many cars pass you when you do your 10K run?"

"Most days about three. On the weekend quite a few, but during the week sometimes nobody comes by. That's what makes it so great running on the road. You have the whole world to yourself. Sometimes the steers join in and run along beside me on their side of the fence, but mostly they just look at me like I'm nuts." She grinned suddenly. "I've never been so close to one as I was when I went over the bank. When I came to, there was this huge face looking at me."

Sally said, "So on a deserted road you were a very easy target for a hit man who had done his homework. Let's face it, it was sheer luck that Todd noticed his car. Logically you should have lain there and quietly bled to death."

Kelly, pale already, went even paler. "Bloody hell, Sally." She glanced quickly in Christopher's direction, mentally kicking herself for swearing in front of him, but he had slipped quietly off the chair and was watching something going on in the hallway, totally disinterested in what he knew from experience would be a boring, grown-up conversation. "I've just been lying here pretty much zonked out on drugs. I hadn't really thought about it, but you're right, it probably wasn't some random wacko. That California outfit is more efficient than I gave them credit for. I was worried about Mike and his family, but it didn't occur to me they'd trace me all the way out in the boonies."

"But John knew where you lived, didn't he? And he knew you went running along the road regularly. I bet you even told him how far you went. Leastways, you're always bragging about it to me so I'm sure you couldn't have resisted telling him. All the hit man had to do was check the road and find the most likely spot, then wait until you went running."

Kelly's stomach lurched, and she could taste the Jell-O

she'd had for lunch. "For God's sake, Sally, surely John wouldn't have set me up?"

Sally said hastily, "Of course he wouldn't have, you idiot, but it would have been very easy for someone to get the information out of him. There was no question he was smitten with you, so he'd have enjoyed talking about you." She watched Kelly carefully, hoping she was getting through to her, but she had the feeling her friend was not being fooled. Outside the room there was a shuffling sound as a patient flanked by two relatives went slowly by. "No, it will be someone the organization employed who did it. Let's face it, they bring in specialists for everything. Think what a smooth operation it was where David was concerned. It didn't occur to anyone except you that David's death was anything but an accident." She sighed heavily, "I told you to be careful, but listening to your Auntie Sally has never been your strong suit."

"You did, and you're right as usual." Her voice was contrite and sounded small and shaky even to her own ears. Blinking back tears, and cursing the day she'd met John, she took a deep breath and continued, sounding more like herself. "I tell you what, I will hang on your every word from here on in, and I'm definitely giving up this private eye stuff. It's way too painful. I think I'll take up embroidery or something for my excitement in future. I'll join the local sewing circle."

Sally raised an eyebrow. "Sounds far too exciting. Anyway, my girl, you are going to come and stay with me for a while. Fending for yourself with a gammy leg and an arm out of action is going to be pretty well impossible for the first few days. So I'll get Richard to bring you straight to my house."

"I don't want to come and stay with you; I'll be fine."

"You will not. Not for a couple of days anyway, and we'll talk about it again then. You will be immobile and forced to listen to Christopher and read stories to him all day, so it won't be a picnic. Be a wonderful break for me though."

"But it will make it so crowded. Why don't I just go home, and you can bring me a bowl of chicken soup?"

"No, I want you somewhere where you're surrounded by people for a few days. You're way too isolated in your house. The person who hit you on the road may find out that you're still alive, and come and have another go. At my house there are neighbors with large dogs, and John only two doors away." John was an ex-Provincial rugby player built like a barn door. "I don't think anyone will try anything."

Kelly, still feeling fragile and more shaken up by the accident than she was willing to admit, thought about the nights with only the sound of the sea and the bush for company. "Okay, thanks, you're on, but only for a couple of days. After that I'll disappear somewhere for a while, or at least until the FBI wraps this thing up."

Sally looked at her, her eyes warm with concern, but simply said, "Good, I'll get Richard to make the delivery. Come on, Chris, it's time we hit the trail, Auntie Kelly's getting tired."

"Oh, do we have to go already?" he whined.

"Yes, right now, so give Kelly a kiss and tell her you'll see her tomorrow."

"Are we coming all the way down here again tomorrow?" His face beamed at the thought.

"No, but Kelly's going to stay with us for a few days."

"Brilliant!" He rushed over to the bed and standing on tiptoe planted a wet kiss on Kelly's cheek. "See you tomorrow, Auntie Kelly. I've got a great new game you can play with me, so you won't be bored lying in bed."

Sally grinned over the top of his head and then they left. Within a few minutes, Kelly was asleep again.

Chapter 34

Franklin and Howard were sitting in the family room enjoying a quiet bourbon while they waited for Shana and Eva to get their coats. They were all off to try the new restaurant that had just opened downtown. Howard had heard it was good, but a bit pricey. However, since he was paying this time and they hadn't seen Franklin for a while, he figured it warranted a bit of a celebration. As a gale of laughter erupted in the kitchen, he raised an eyebrow in Franklin's direction. "Care for another one? I've a feeling it may be a while before those two get ready."

Franklin grinned, softening his superior East Coast banker looks, and making him look far more what he was, a thoroughly nice guy. "Yes, let's. I knew we shouldn't have stopped for a cocktail before we took off. One John Collins and those two can talk and giggle for hours. What time did you say those reservations were for?"

"Relax, we've plenty of time." Handing Franklin his drink, he settled down in an armchair. "So how did it go out on the Coast this last trip? I haven't managed to catch you since you got back."

"No, sorry about that, Howard, it's been murder. The work's been stacking up while I've been running around on this Finsat bust. Have to hand it to the guys out there. They didn't just take the info we had and run with it, kept me in the loop the whole time."

"It was one hell of a coup finding out the CEO was bent. I would have expected him to do a complete cover-up and throw a few of his execs to the wolves, not just cave in like that." He crossed one leg over the other and admired his highly polished shoe, then continued, "I knew the computer guys would be able to uncover the scam, whatever it was, once they had the clues courtesy of Deep Throat." A glint of mischief settled on his friendly face, "Or should we call him the Deep Down Under Throat?"

"Your guy did a great job picking up on that message in the first place, and he hasn't said a word. Think he'll go places." He cocked his head slightly, his graying hair catching the light from the ornate standard lamp behind his chair. "No, that CEO was a complete wimp. Starting out puffing and huffing like some major captain of industry, but the minute we hit him with a bunch of facts and a few hard questions, he caved in." He told him how Hank, the lead agent on the case, reeled off facts and figures, then asked questions in his quiet, Harvard tones, never letting up. It had taken a while, but Craig Bennett was no match for a seasoned agent. "To tell you the truth, I think he was glad to get it all off his chest. He seemed more relieved than worried about a term in jail. I think those guys in the Mob must have had him scared to death half the time."

"I don't think I'd fancy being under their thumb. So how many of them did you get? Could you track them down?" Howard, resigned to a life of processing data, could never hear enough about the exciting life of the field agents, and Franklin seldom talked about his work.

"We did pretty well. Nabbed a bent exec, and two software types."

Howard looked disappointed. "Is that all? What about the Mob or whoever they were?"

"We looked real hard, but there were just no links. They're damn good. Main thing is we stopped the scam going down. It must have cost them a bundle to set it up, and they aren't going to make a dime out of it, so they're hurting."

The sound of footsteps coming down the stairs meant the girls must be about ready to go. Howard could hear his wife calling to his son, trying to make her voice heard over the loud music that seeped through his bedroom door, the bass notes pounding throughout the house. "I guess stopping them in their tracks was the main thing. Pity you couldn't get to the top guy though."

"We'd need more information at the start of the project to do that. That's when we could get them, it's all too late once the thing is in motion. They're past masters at covering their tracks." He downed the last of his bourbon and set the glass carefully on the coaster. "However, thanks to Deep Throat we know how they get into projects. It's a great setup. They have a legitimate software house doing contracts for major companies. It's got an impeccable record, by the way, because they only hire the best. Pay them substantial salaries too, so they aren't prone to stray. Thanks to Deep Throat we knew it was that little company in New Zealand that produced the squirrelly module that was going to do all the damage."

"You don't mean some little outfit down there was all set to rip off the U.S. public?" Howard was outraged. He'd always had a soft spot for that funny little country a million miles from everywhere. He figured he and Eva would take a trip down there some time. Take a couple of weeks and take in Australia as well.

"No, no way. We put them under the microscope, without them suspecting a thing." He smiled reflectively. "It wasn't difficult. Hank set up a dummy company, and then went to this outfit in Auckland and asked them to quote on a major software project. Of course, as Hank explained to them, it was a government contract, so we had to vet all their software engineers. The project manager fell over himself giving Hank all the personal information he needed. It's so much easier when you're dealing with honest people; they trust you. Never suspect that a well-dressed American would be an FBI agent posing as a businessman. And they are clean as a whistle." He paused a moment, then said slowly, "There was one strange thing we discovered though. The last guy they hired was an American. He was recruited in a hurry when one of their software engineers was killed in a climbing accident. He worked on the key piece of the project. The bit that was set to do all the damage."

"So you talked to him?"

"No, we did a trace on him and found that he had been working for this hotshot software house called Quantum before he took a vacation in New Zealand. It all seemed a bit too pat that he just happened to be right on the spot with all the perfect credentials when this engineer took a nosedive down a cliff. There he was on full salary from Quantum, and he just happens to walk into an agency in Wellington asking for a job. We're pretty sure that this software house is a front and they infiltrate companies through their contract guys."

"How the hell did you find that out?"

"Hank's gang on the Coast did a massive check, and there'd been a few strange things going on previously, but nothing we could get a handle on."

Howard sat silent for a moment, letting Franklin's words sink in, then said, "Just a moment though. The module he worked on must have gone through all sorts of tests when it was integrated with the system in California. Why didn't someone discover something was wrong then?"

"That was the clever bit. All the external specs matched. Whatever this guy, John Celini's his name by the way, did to the module was completely invisible externally. We only found out what he was up to when we pulled it apart and analyzed it bit by bit. After all, we knew we were looking for a scam. The people running tests at Finsat would have only been making sure it handled transactions correctly."

"Yes, but wait a minute. What about when it was field tested? There's no way anyone would release a major financial system without trying it out on real people in the outside world." He exhaled sharply. "When I think of the trouble we've had with our systems sometimes. They're perfect in-house, pass all the tests, and then some idiot in a field office does something stupid and the whole thing comes crashing down."

"Pity that real people use these great systems, isn't it?" Franklin said wryly. "That's when we got suspicious about this John Celini. After all the field testing was over, he was called in to fix some problem with his module. It developed some minor bug during field testing, so he put in a fix, they tested in-house and it was shipped."

"So that's when he must have put in something that triggered the siphoning system," Howard said triumphantly.

"Right. During field testing no skimming took place. After field testing it was all set up to siphon off millions in infinitesimal amounts. No one would have known. And the only thing that happened between field testing and shipment was one tiny fix put in by John Celini. Bingo, we know how they do it."

"He must be a very smart guy."

"Yes, and he's working under instructions from some even smarter ones. They even had him wipe the system in New Zealand before he left so no one there could spend time analyzing his module."

"Why would anyone do that?"

"Chances are no one would, but you know when you have several nerds working together—and I gather this team was a collection of hotshots—they can be pretty competitive. One of them might have got curious. Both John Celini and his predecessor on the module, the guy who got killed, were exceptionally smart. One of the other engineers might have decided to do an analysis of the module just out of curiosity, and if they had, they would have discovered the module matched the external specifications, but was a whole lot different internally."

"So that would have started them asking questions."

"Exactly. That's the last thing Quantum wanted." Franklin took another slow sip of bourbon and looked across at Howard. "What's even more interesting is they made very sure the project team wouldn't have time to get curious about John Celini and his module. They hired them to get started on another major project right away. They'd done their homework and knew they were young, keen and very new in the business. All they had to do was give them a nice lucrative project with a tight deadline, and that would be all they'd think about for the next few months. The Finsat project would be forgotten."

"Wow, they're an impressive outfit. But anyway you did get that John Celini, didn't you?"

"No, we've left him alone. We're just going to sit back and keep him under surveillance. If it works the way we expect it to, he'll be on another project soon, and this time it will be the beginning of the scam. We should be able to get them all this time."

Kelly was just about to leave the house and go on a shopping trip to Kerikeri when the phone rang. Shoving the chilly bin on the back seat beside the dog, she ran back to the house, hurried through the front door and dashed down the hall to the study. She clipped the study door as she went by, causing a pain to shoot through her shoulder. After several months it was completely healed, but the slightest jolt was always a sharp reminder of the dull pain that had persisted so long after the accident. Only when she was toweling off after a swim or a shower did she notice the long scar on her leg which the doctors assured her would eventually fade.

"Hi ya, Kelly." She was surprised to hear Joe's slow drawl. She hadn't heard from him since he left Finsat several months earlier.

"Joe, good to hear from you. Where are you?" she asked, expecting to hear that he was back in Texas. As usual the phone connection sounded as if he was just next door.

"Some place called Whangaroa Harbor, they tell me. We sailed in last night. That's somewhere near you, isn't it?"

"Yes, only about forty minutes away. That's fantastic. What on earth are you doing there?"

"Sandy and I decided to take a little trip around the world. To tell you the truth she was sick of me running off to the Himalayas every chance I got, so she suggested a round-the-world trip by sea. I loved the idea. I could just see myself out there hauling in the sails on one of those wonderful old teak-decked schooners with all the mahogany and brass fittings."

"Brilliant. This I have to see. I love those restored classics." Kelly had a yen for one ever since the America's Cup when some magnificent classic yachts had congregated in the Viaduct Basin.

"Sorry, all I said was that's how I saw myself. Sandy had a different idea—I think she had the QE II in mind when she suggested it. Said there was no way she was going to be hauling on ropes for several months. Reckoned it would ruin her nails. So we comprised. Bought ourselves a motor cruiser. Have to admit I'm enjoying it. Nothing like being skipper out there on the ocean."

"So how long have you been cruising?"

"Months now. Chugged over to Hawaii, then made our way down through the islands. Goddamn beautiful, some of them."

"Well, that's it then. I'll drive over and pick you up, and you can spend a few days on dry land. And in case Sandy gets withdrawal symptoms, tell her my house is right on the ocean."

Kelly put down the phone and did a quick run around the house, picking things up. All in all though it was in pretty good shape. Ever since her accident she'd been a lot tidier. After all, as her mother used to say when she was little, "Must wear clean underwear, you never know when you might be in an accident." She now knew the wisdom of it; she'd hate everyone to find out what a slob she was when she was on the way to the grave.

Over the next few days they spent a lot of time discussing the scam at Finsat and its aftermath. One evening as they sat out on the deck enjoying their after-dinner coffee, Joe started talking about the possibility of some major criminal organization being involved in the scam. As he warmed to his subject and talked about how ruthless they must be to have killed David just to get their engineer on the project, Sandy, who was watching Kelly closely, put her hand on his arm. "Stop it, Joe. Don't be such an idiot."

Startled, he said quickly, "Of course, I'm sorry. You must have been scared out of your socks after they tried to kill you."

Kelly, who had gone a little pale as he spoke, said, "No, that's okay Joe, it has been months now and if they were going to do anything about it, it would have happened ages ago."

"Yes, but you're so isolated here," Sandy insisted. "You must still be worried."

"Well, I was to start with," she confessed, "so I took off for a while and visited some friends down in South Island. Then when I got back, Richard seemed to find an awful lot of things that needed doing around the property. All of them seemed to be in very close proximity to the house, and they seemed to necessitate carrying a shotgun in the back of the pickup." She grinned widely. "Something he never does normally. Then there were his two favorite dogs along for the ride. Somehow I think I was pretty well protected."

Joe looked at her closely. "But you are still a bit worried aren't you?"

"I suppose so, yes," she admitted grudgingly.

He moved over to the sofa where she was sitting and put his arm round her. "Honey, you have nothing to worry about. The FBI are happy. They stopped the scam going down, so it's all over as far as they are concerned. The only reason the Mob wanted you out of the way was because you were stirring things up and that might get the FBI interested. You're not dealing with a bunch of Al Capone-like gangsters. These are businessmen. They made a major investment in order to pull in millions. The investment failed. They'll just cut their losses and move on. They have nothing to gain by wasting time worrying about what happened."

"You're right. It's all over. And anyway I have Rigoletto—Riggles to you—to guard me."

Riggles, who was now a large dog, looked at her soulfully and the end of his tail moved slowly to and fro at the sound of his name. "You're right. No one looking at him would think he was an old softie," Sandy said stroking his ears. "Incidentally, why did you give such a magnificent looking dog a ridiculous name like Rigoletto?"

"My last dog's name was Tosca so it seemed logical at the time." As they both laughed, Kelly thought this was an opportune moment to ask the question she had been dying to ask ever since Joe called. "How come you left Finsat, Joe? I thought you really liked it there. You were cleared, for goodness sake." Then before Joe could answer, she said, "It would have been okay once it all blew over, wouldn't it? With a company that size, they'd have weeded out the problem and then shorn it up. They'd have had to keep it quiet, or it would have shaken the market's confidence if the whole story came out."

"Yes, I could have stayed, but to tell you the truth the whole thing made me feel sick. Just thinking how I'd been a part of the whole dirty scam without being smart enough to smell a rat, kept me awake for nights."

"And being a suspect yourself wasn't too swift, was it Joe?" Sandy said sympathetically.

"No, you're right, it was terrible." He put his empty glass down on the coffee table and got up, restlessly walking over to the window and looking out into the darkness. "So, anyway, I thought, screw it, I'm out of here. I had enough stock options to bring in a pile of money, so we didn't need the money anymore. So I decided to retire while I'm still young and handsome and have fun. And we have had fun, haven't we, hon?"

"It's been fantastic. I've been thinking of sending a thank-you note to the Mob, but I'm not sure what the protocol is."

Several weeks later Kelly was sitting on the deck flipping through the mail. It was the usual exciting stuff: phone bill, power bill, an appeal from the Cancer Society, a notice from the library about an overdue book (she really was going to have to do something about getting books back on time), a letter from a friend in California who still persisted in writing letters in spite of the convenience of email. Then she noticed the postcard. It was from the South of France, a beautiful bay on the Mediterranean with white villas clustered on the hillside. Who on earth did she know in France? No one. Who was going there on vacation? No one she could think of, the only candidates being Mark and Sandy, but they never, ever sent postcards. Thought it was far too gauche. Having exhausted the possibilities, she decided to turn it over and read what she knew would be a short, inane message from someone, saying, "Lovely place. Food is great, weather's marvelous. Went to some Cathedral or other. It was spectacular. Love."

Instead, written in John's immaculate hand with a wide-nibbed fountain pen was the short message. "Kelly, I have a job here for six months. I miss you. Please come and join me. Life's no fun without you. John."

She stared at the card. Then a slow smile spread across her face. He hadn't been pursuing her as part of the job; she wasn't such an idiot after all. She sat fantasizing about a year in Provence. Well, not exactly Provence, and not a year, but close enough. Beneath her a hawk sailed low over the bush seeking its prey.

A minute later she sat bolt upright in her chair as a chilling thought struck her. Maybe he was still working for Uncle Tony, and just maybe Uncle Tony suggested he invite her to Europe so they could tie up the last loose end. Someone in New Zealand had to have tipped off the FBI, and she would be the prime candidate.

She stared at the card for another ten minutes, scarcely

moving. Finally, she scrunched it up and tossed it to the dog. In a few short minutes it would be a pile of soggy cardboard, the ink and address long gone. She walked over to the rail and looked out at the sparkling ocean. Then the realization hit her, and with it came a great sense of relief. It didn't matter whether he genuinely wanted her there, or whether he was still working under instructions. She really didn't care.

About the Author

ILENE BIRKWOOD, who was born in England, worked in the computer industry in California's Silicon Valley in a variety of management positions. She now lives in New Zealand on a beachside property in the sub-tropical north with her husband and a bull mastiff called Diva.